The Sleeper

Unhallowed Ground

Veil of Darkness

Also by Gillian White

RICH DECEIVER
THE PLAGUE STONE
THE CROW BIDDY
NASTY HABITS
MOTHERTIME
GRANDFATHER'S FOOTSTEPS
DOG BOY
THE BEGGAR BRIDE
CHAIN REACTION
THE SLEEPER
UNHALLOWED GROUND
THE WITCH'S CRADLE

VEIL OF DARKNESS

Gillian White

CORGI BOOKS

VEIL OF DARKNESS
A CORGI BOOK : 0 552 14564 5

Originally published in Great Britain by Bantam Press,
a division of Transworld Publishers

PRINTING HISTORY
Bantam Press edition published 1999
Corgi edition published 2000

1 3 5 7 9 10 8 6 4 2

Set in 11/12pt Times by
Hewer Text Ltd, Edinburgh

Corgi Books are published by Transworld Publishers,
61–63 Uxbridge Road, London W5 5SA,
a division of The Random House Group Ltd,
in Australia by Random House Australia (Pty) Ltd,
20 Alfred Street, Milsons Point, NSW 2061, Australia,
in New Zealand by Random House New Zealand Ltd,
18 Poland Road, Glenfield, Auckland 10, New Zealand
and in South Africa by Random House (Pty) Ltd,
Endulini, 5a Jubilee Road, Parktown 2193, South Africa.

Reproduced, printed and bound in Great Britain by
Cox & Wyman Ltd, Reading, Berks.

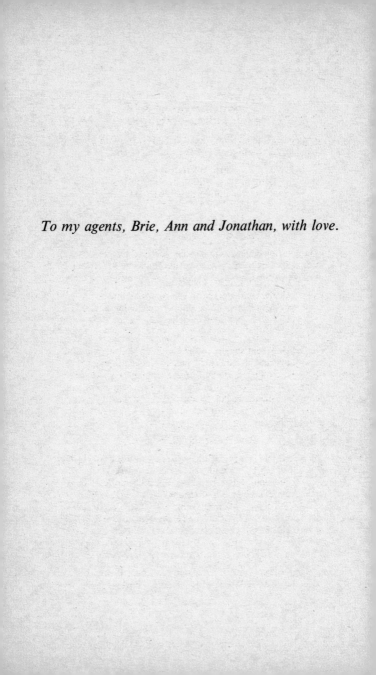

To my agents, Brie, Ann and Jonathan, with love.

VEIL OF
DARKNESS

One

'Jesus,' whined the man in the fable, looking back over the sands of his life. 'Why is it that when times were hard your footsteps disappeared from my side? Why did you always desert me just when I needed you most?'

And Jesus gave His chilling reply. He probably had it rehearsed for years, just waiting for this God-given question. 'My son, when life was hard there was one set of footprints because during those times I carried you.'

Game set and match to The Lord.

But where the hell is He now?

Poor Kirsty.

She can't spare a glance at this pious text that hangs above her mantelpiece, given startlingly prime position in her council-house lounge, produced like a rabbit from a hat out of her mother-in-law's straw holdall one particularly hellish Christmas. Nobody ever carried her, let alone Jesus, but then maybe she hadn't asked loudly enough. She'd stopped saying prayers after kindergarten. There's a crack through the frame from top to bottom, mended untidily with

11

Sellotape. There are cracks through so many aspects of her house and her life; black, sheer crevasses. Quick! Quick! No time for thinking. She can't spare a glance, she hasn't got time, she's got to be out of here in ten minutes, ten short minutes to escape from the house where she has endured eight years of marriage that feel like a long, slow lifetime. As if she's been ill. Bedridden. Seeing through a glass darkly. Recovering from some disabling disease. At last able to raise her head, now to eat, now to speak, now to read, now to see her situation for the first time through unblinkered eyes.

On crutches.

The kids have already gone – no, no, don't think of them now, don't weaken, don't deal in self-pity – there was no alternative but to separate, but the crippling thing is that they are too little at six and seven to understand, and she didn't dare warn them early in case they gave the game away. There was no time to explain that Mummy would come back and get them when everything was settled and safe. It was only this morning when he'd gone to work that Kirsty had got them up and dressed, then gently explained for the first time that there would be no school today. Instead, Aunty Tessa was here with her car and she was going to take them and their cardboard boxes to Maddy's.

She and the kids could have stayed together if she had agreed to go to the hostel, but she didn't want that. This way, at least, they'd have some sort of future. But the pain of parting had been agonizing.

She'd imagined the worst part would be breakfast this morning. She'd feared she might be sick with the strain, might crack or cry or give herself away with her eyes, but strangely enough she was as calm and cool as she'd ever been, her excitement acting as an anaesthetic, helping her to cope with the unnerving process of getting him out of the house without the surly grunts and curses that accompanied most of her violent mornings. Ah yes, this was her dream, that one day she would be woken by birds, not the beast in bed beside her at some dread hour between midnight and dawn.

He had kissed her goodbye and missed her recoil. Luck was on her side for a change. He had gone off to work as he always did, a thick-set man with heavy, dark eyebrows, a hard-working family man, nothing to single him out as sick.

He likes his socks to be ironed and folded.
Half a teaspoon of mustard on each slice of ham.
Half a teaspoon precisely.

Kirsty casts a quick glance at the clock on the wall – Marks & Spencer; she'd bought it herself when they were first married, thinking it tasteful. Tasteful – hah! What a laugh to think she was once bothered about rot like that. She stuffs his Adidas sports bag with her wash things, her small purse of make-up, her underwear, three pairs of shoes and two surviving paperbacks which he hasn't torn up. Her books, oh yes, her wonderful, wonderful books. They had kept Kirsty alive and sane and, seeing this, sensing rebellion, sniffing a rival, these books drove Trevor to the height of violence. Second only to her children, her books, mostly Mills and Boons, easy, quick reads like that, had tested Kirsty's bravery to the full. She could stay happy while she was

13

reading, so she hid them round the house, risking a beating each time she did so, each time he went on the rampage and found one. Sometimes, as a punishment, he made her read out loud on her knees while he mocked the dialogue and interrupted with crude remarks, or shot out his fist and sent her sprawling. The rest of her stuff is in the case they bought that time they all went to Weston. She shivers at the thought of that holiday. The only holiday they'd ever had. She had come back on her own in the end, on the train with the kids. No tickets, just a kindly conductor.

No, the most dangerous time in her menaced life hadn't been today's breakfast, but six months ago, when she'd first begun to scrabble her way out of the coma of fear, peeping and frightened. When she'd first begun to see Trevor Hoskins through the eyes of the world, with the help of the Samaritans, and then the centre to which they'd referred her. Hah. She'd been too scared to speak at first from the call box on Massey Street, for fear he might be lurking, or that he'd *know*, in the way he had of knowing whenever she failed, transgressed, was disloyal, dirty, lazy. Just as God is all knowing so Trev's spirit seemed to be everywhere. She thought of him as the Holy Ghost, which she'd never quite understood: ethereal, grey and able to change shape like porridge or some extraterrestial creature.

His favourite programme is *The Price is Right*. He curses the contestants. They watch the telly while they eat. He will not tolerate interruptions.

*   *   *

14

The Samaritans.

Thank God they didn't insist on her name, but perhaps, they suggested, she would give one anyway, any name so they might talk more naturally, her and the gentle-voiced stranger. Sad and quavery she gave the name Valerie because she believed that if she'd been called Valerie her life would have been very different. Valerie seemed such a strong name, not the name of a snivelling victim, or someone whose name might be casually altered to bitch, slag, whore, cunt, depending on somebody else's whim, or someone who'd been named after a mother who died at her birth.

Mummy. Mum. Mama. Mam. As a child she had tried out all the versions to see what they sounded like. Mother. Another victim – of sorts.

She'd been late for work that first day she'd phoned the Samaritans and he had wanted to know why there was £2.45 deducted from her wages. Resentful and secretive, she had lied and told him she'd missed the bus, but she couldn't do that every week and hope to get away with it.

So she'd started phoning during her lunch hour, with a hunger that was almost a sickness. She was unable to speak that first time, but pretty soon the rage and the bitter hatred flowed out, forged and hammered within her by every blow he had ever struck. It was the very personal rage of a victim, compounded by years of helpless humiliation, of broken ribs, of smashed fingers, of blue-black eyes, bruised breasts, arms in plaster and circles like purple chokers round her throat.

The girls teased her for having a lover. Called him

her bit of dong on the side. 'Ding dong bell,' they sang as she tried to push her money in.

She was terrified Trev might suss it out, or see through her; his piercing eyes catching her resentment. That he'd drag out her brain and sift through it like he sometimes did with the rubbish bin, leaving the stinking remnants strewn over the kitchen floor. Waste. And she would have been waste if she'd waited any longer. But even then, even then, as she was beginning her slow recovery, she'd had the morbid desire of the victim to fall on her knees and confess to the tyrant, to throw herself on his mercy, to give him a stick to strike her with to ease the guilt for her awful daring.

The phone at home was out of the question since the statements had started being itemized. He went through them with a fine-tooth comb and blamed her for any unexplained numbers, even when it was him.

That was the start of living the lie. That was the hardest part. Her books had been her only escape.

She has forgotten why she loved him.

For years she kept thinking he might change.

He reads the sports pages in the *Sun*. He does Spot the Ball in the *People*. When they show the lottery winners on telly Trev spits on the floor.

Pretty once, with brilliant dark-brown eyes before sorrow filled them, Kirsty stands at the open front door, a small figure in blue jeans and a navy parka with her keys in her hand about to lock something out of her life. Her house, so silent. Almost peaceful. No sign here of alarm or terror, all neatly

16

polished away, but flashes of memory trigger the pain. Number 24 Barkers Terrace always looks empty anyway by the time she has picked up everything and cleared it all away as he likes it, a house so empty and depressed surely no-one could feel at ease in it. How lovely to live in a happy house with a loving partner to come home to. A messy, comfy, colourful house, filled with the smell of home-made cakes and with jars of wild flowers with bugs on them, heaps of books, children's art on the walls and a red Aga at the heart. But her surfaces shine like small lakes of tears and she feels an overwhelming urge to leave something disgusting on the carpet, a used tampax or a turd, dreadful behaviour which her books never mention. Minimalist, they would call him, those arty types who consider it a question of taste. Spotless kitchen – not even a cloth on the draining board is allowed. No plates left drying in the rack to offend his desire for cleanliness. No knick-knacks on the shelves. No cushions on the sofa. No coffee table. No pictures, just a framed mirror over the fireplace and his mother's dreadful text. But Trev's obsession is paranoia, that is what Kirsty has been told and has begun, slowly, to understand.

Nobody seemed very surprised. Nor were they shocked by her story. It was all too common. 'He's mentally ill,' they explained. 'He needs help.' And, 'You must be determined and brave.'

Once she goes through that door she will never have to clean here again. Never have to whisper to her children or hide them when she sees a handle slowly turning. Never have to pretend to sleep. Never have to lie awake at nights waiting for the

17

pain to begin, or to cook fearing her worthless offerings will end up on the kitchen walls. Never again will he terrorize her, abuse her or humiliate her. Fear is a tool box and a smell of putty.

In photographs he is always smiling.

He likes her to stroke his feet with her hair, to pull it slowly between his toes. When she thinks he's asleep he wakes up. Hah. He was only pretending . . .

There is terror and an impulse to run. She must get out. She must break free. Is it possible she can take time and change it just by taking control of her life? She will not think of her children's bewildered faces: Jake's so resigned and defiant when she left him, trying not to linger over the goodbye; Gemma's awash with tears yet refusing to cling or beg. Children made old before their time, both sinewy and nervous. Their unhappiness breaks her heart. She hurries down the garden path, every footstep dogged by fear, casting her eyes this way and that, lugging her case, trying to look casual. When she looks back for the last time it's like lifting her eyes to his and staring out his smouldering hostility. Typically, it is raining. The litter in the gutters goes faster than she does, but summer is well on its way, thank God, for summer is so much kinder than winter. Shaven-haired youths, done with their loitering, head for free community-hall coffee. Bedraggled women with pushchairs and shopping make for the cover of the vandalized bus stop, each driven by some learnt momentum, nothing to do with their own.

Suppose he comes home unexpectedly?
Suppose the gaffer lets him off early?
If he should catch her now . . . ?

Her life is an agony of apprehension, with acts of contrition for every fault.

Just the thought of him returning home and finding nobody there is enough to make her cringe. Such disobedience. Such vile deviation. Such uncharacteristic deception. Trevor's complexion, if compared to a cake, Kirsty would call underdone. It would have to be tested with a skewer. He would probably need another ten minutes. She imagines his currant-eyed, flabbergasted stare as he pulls himself up abruptly in his crumpled blue Gas Board overalls and senses that she's gone. She sees his heavy legs placed apart and his thick hands on his hips as he calls suspiciously up the stairs and is met by continuing, heavy silence.

He has a habit of cracking his knuckles, of pulling his finger joints till they click. He likes to eat sausages raw, taking them straight from the fridge and sucking the meat from the skins. She is always amazed this has never killed him.

She imagines him all fired up, snarling quietly, 'Where have you been all this time?'

She hears his sarcastic laugh. His small eyes flame with rage, as black and soulless as a cruising shark's, as menacing as a pit bull on the prowl.

Then comes the slam of his fist on the table.

'Goddamn it, you bitch.' As his wrath turns to savagery and she tries to mash the potatoes as though nothing is wrong for the children's sake, but with her nerves on edge, she wonders if she'll have time to take them upstairs before it begins in earnest.

If it hadn't been for the kids she might have become inured to it all, numb to the fear, immune to the pain, worthless, deserving nothing. Thank God, thank God for two children who love her.

And did Trev really love God? He went to confession often enough. So many times she had wished he would die or that she might be brave enough to kill him. She reminded herself that he was dying, that every day he grew nearer to death, and this gave her some crumbs of comfort. What would she put on his gravestone? 'Here lies Trevor Hoskins, loving husband of Kirsty and much missed father of Jake and Gemma'? Or 'Rot in Hell, you bastard'? She imagined the smell of decaying flesh to be similar to the stink of putty.

She wished he would die or win the lottery, either one wouldn't matter. But she feared that his numbers wouldn't come up because, oddly, she has noticed that lottery winners have a certain look, as if they were born knowing some secret, a look which Trev doesn't have. If he'd won the lottery he would have left her, of that she has no doubt. He would have lived in the fast lane and killed himself with cars or women or booze.

He drinks Southern Comfort and lemonade.

He won't eat crisps, only pork scratchings. Perhaps that is why Kirsty loathes even the smell of pork and can only think of pigs in fear in the slaughter house.

He decided to buy his council house and his temper grew worse with the strain of it all, especially in the recession.

The rain comes down with full force as Kirsty catches the second bus that will take her to Lime Street Station, and there she will have to wait an hour for the train to Cornwall. While she waits she might have a coffee, frittering away her time and her money, something she hasn't done in years, and buy a magazine, or even a couple of brand-new books to keep her company during the journey. The centre provided the funds she needed; she will pay them back as soon as she can. She will no longer have to account for every penny she spends, or beg for money for the children's clothes. Once she came home with the wrong brand of mustard and ended up with it all over her face, stinging her eyes, choking her. Nerve gas. Now she will have to learn to make choices. But the thought that he might catch her up, guess at her plans, unearth some clue by using a devilish form of interpersonal communication, pad stealthily onto the station platform and lay a patient, malicious hand on her shoulder, this thought she must dismiss. She cannot live her life with a fugitive's instincts in every fibre of her being. Her eyes water with the strain of staring out into the dim evening, ludicrously seeking him out from the flocks of umbrella-slick strangers, while willing the bus to move faster, the traffic to ease, her head to stop aching.

Trevor will not lie down and take it. No way will he accept defeat. No doubt he will be forming some plan even now. No doubt he will make up some hackneyed tale of a runaway wife with a mental condition who's a danger to herself and her children, so plausible that they will believe him and activate some search before she has time to leave the city. 'You're hysterical,' he would often mock her. 'You're off your bleeding head.' As if he despised her sanity just as much as her happiness. Thank God the children aren't with her. At least the children are safe, and if everything works out well they will soon be together.

She had often had wild thoughts of running away, but common sense always came to her rescue. If she was going to go then she had to go properly, she had to make sensible plans or he would find her.

Hence the idea of Cornwall. The centre helped her to find a job. She used to sneak there while the kids were at school, taking time off work for the dentist. She almost lost her job through doing that. Her supervisor, Mrs Graham, said she would dock her wages, the dentist was not for working hours. But the girls in the food department rebelled and she told Mrs Graham it was root-canal work and she had to have several appointments. The Burleston Hotel, a Victorian pile with its own private cove, owned by a Colonel Vincent Parker, offered summer work and a self-contained cottage next winter. They held their local interviews in a suite at the Adelphi Hotel. Kirsty, self-confidence nil, never thought she would get picked, but she did. Kerry at the centre tried her best to persuade them to let Kirsty have the cottage at once, without going into her personal details, but the Burleston Hotel said it was let and would not be free till the winter. It was an offer too good to miss. A battered woman she might be, but Kirsty abhorred the thought of a hostel.

He rolls his own fags. His first two fingers are stained yellow. He keeps his tobacco in a genuine old Bisto tin that he reckons is worth some money.

He won't use tissues. Trevor demands crisp white handkerchiefs, which he insists she boil on top of the stove in the same way his mother does.

He makes her dial if he wants to phone.

The top of his egg must be sliced by a knife so that no bits of shell are broken.

In the meantime the kids will stay with Maddy, a friend and sympathizer from the centre, who sometimes helps out as a stop-gap measure for women with temporary problems. The best thing about Maddy is that she's unlikely to be traced: she is not a battered wife. Madeleine Kelly is a middle-aged woman of independent means who lives in a cottage in Caldy, the posh side of the river. Kirsty met her just once at the centre, and once was all it had taken for her to feel reassured. If only she'd had a mother like Maddy, a large, round Mrs Apple with a body all soft and folded, who could have come straight from a nursery rhyme. She searched her face most carefully. There was gaiety and relaxation about her, and her laugh was wholesome and catching. She has fostered difficult kids all her life and lives in a homely muddle under thatch, her garden has a stream running through it and she keeps three gentle old dogs. She would be overjoyed to have Jake and Gemma until the end of September and wouldn't hear of accepting any money.

They will not attend school through the summer, but Maddy will teach them herself, give them love, toffee apples, cake mix and cuddles. Kirsty is not to worry. Maddy is merely a phone call away; she will write at least twice a week, and at the first sign of the slightest trouble she will let Kirsty know. Trevor will not pose a problem. No leads will take him to Maddy. But four months is so long.

'Four months can be a very long time in the life of a child, Lord knows,' Maddy agreed, nodding so her two chins met. 'But not in my home,' she purred. 'Not with my old dogs, bless 'em. Not with my ducks and my chickens. You go on, my poor Kirsty. I know it's hard, but you're doing the right thing. Their four months with me will be one long, happy holiday. Now don't your kids deserve that much after all they've been through?'

And Kirsty, only dimly aware that there was a world like this with such people in it, burst into tears.

He wears the spiky crucifix he was given at his First Holy Communion. Sometimes the silver chain causes a rash on the back of his neck.

Kirsty had expected to feel triumphant by now, so what is this sense of anticlimax? The suitcase rumbles around in the bus. She steadies it with a sweating hand which she wipes on her rain-soaked jacket. Is that his walk? She presses her face against the glass when, with sudden terror, she thinks she sees him hurrying along because of the rain. No, no, it can't have been him. By now he will be at home in the dry, ringing his mother to ask if she's there. Hah. Why would she go there? She had gone there once in the early days, hoping for sanctuary, sympathy, advice and understanding. After all, Edna had given birth to eight children; she should have some answers worth hearing. Had she known that her son was an animal? Was his condition genetic? Kirsty would have liked to ask Edna something about her own married life. She didn't get the chance. She had struggled to Edna's with a broken arm and a push chair and a child with mumps. Some hope of help from a woman with 'I beheld Satan like lightning fall from Heaven,' embroidered on a plaque on the wall. Beside her small coal fire, in a house that smelled of Sundays and sprouts, Edna raised her head and closed her eyes tight. 'There is nothing more pleasing to God than suffering bravely borne,' she had said in a voice divinely inspired. Then she rang for the ambulance. The following Christmas she gave Kirsty the text that assured her Jesus would carry her.

Kirsty didn't want the doctor to know. He must have suspected something, of course, with all those hospital visits – accident prone, she laughed it off. She dreaded the kids being on some register, social workers nosing about and the threat of having them taken away. She was a bad and ineffective mother because she allowed herself to be abused, and Jake and Gemma saw the violence. They felt the violence, they ate, drank and slept the violence, although Trev never touched them – not yet – although there were threats. She kept them out of the house as long as she could at weekends – in the park, by the river. On weekdays they went to bed early.

And there was nobody else to help her. When

Kirsty first craved tea and sympathy she found this fact quite astonishing. How had this happened, her gradual and almost unnoticed alienation from the world? Since her marriage and the children she'd had little time to keep up with friends, and Trev was so disapproving, so rude to the few that were left, that it was easier not to bother. In some appalling and inexplicable way there was a comfortable justification in bowing down and submitting to him. After all, he loved her. He never meant to hurt her, to wrong her. He said he hated his own blind fury. Slowly but surely the Christmas-card list grew shorter and petered out, save for Trev's scattered relations. Kirsty has no family to speak of – just a brother somewhere in Australia, and he hasn't written in years, not since he married. She doesn't even know Ralph's address any more. They were both brought up by their father, who died the year after her marriage. The girls at the store have their own dramas and Kirsty has never mixed much with them, Trev's demands being so heavy, his jealousy and distrust so shaming. Because of the loss of her friends, Kirsty realized with a sudden and vast kind of loneliness, she hasn't laughed properly in years.

And all in the name of love.

'Nothing's ever fun with you,' Trevor said, 'miserable slut. Forever whining.'

'Laugh, laugh,' he would goad her, 'laugh for God's sake. Stop your bloody lamenting.'

But sometimes she wondered if he was gay, in spite of his loud masculinity, or whether he hated women, because of the things he did to her, and with such ugly ferocity.

*   *   *

Kirsty sits on the station concourse, nervously sipping an overstewed coffee, her eyes glued to the noticeboard, her ears straining to catch the announcements. She will board her train the minute it's in. The ticket in her hand is something to treasure, a jewel that took eight years to possess and which is more priceless than a Pharaoh's gold.

Two

There is still a long way to go. Heart pounding, half shambling, Kirsty eventually finds her booked seat and collapses into it, closing her eyes. Then, in panic, she covers her face with her book in case Trev might be raging up and down the platform, peering into the carriages through hooded, angry eyes. There are two spotty guys across the table and a girl with wild black hair sitting next to her; she took this in before she collapsed but not much else about them. Maybe they are going to the Burleston – a block booking, who knows? And that large girl across the aisle; she looks nervous and untravelled. As the train pulls out of Lime Street Station, Kirsty very slowly brings her eyes out of hiding, raises them shyly from her book, over the top of the smell of damp clothes.

She gives such a sigh of relief when the platform slips past without sight or sound of a rampaging Trevor that she fears everyone must have heard, including the girl across the way. Kirsty gives her a sideways glance. Poor thing. Kirsty might be nervous, but if so she's not alone. The timid-looking girl sitting opposite is far from happy with her surroundings and her distress reaches Kirsty across the airwaves like the tinny sounds of somebody's Walkman. Kirsty's focus dwindles uncomfortably to the three tipsy sailors who share the girl's table.

Yo ho ho and a bottle of rum.

A non-smoking carriage, of course, Kirsty muses, summing up the girl. This girl, identified by the labels on her luggage left in the recess next to the door, would not appreciate smoke attaching itself to that cheap new suit. Is that the first suit she has ever had? The first time she has ever left home? Indeed, the first long journey she has ever made without her family, except with the Guides to the Lake District when she was about twelve years old?

It looks pretty much like it.

There is such a fresh-faced innocence about her.

Kirsty deals in fantasy, a subject on which she has expertise. And her fantasy was later confirmed when Avril told her she had bought the suit with her mother's help and encouragement. 'Of course it's a business suit,' said her mother, insisting on going round George Henry Lees instead of Dorothy Perkins, which she suggested, quite correctly, would probably not stock her daughter's size. 'All suits are business suits. You wouldn't wear something as stiff as this for mucking about at home.'

Kirsty's favourite preoccupation is summing up other people. Pity she didn't work harder on Trev in the months before she married him.

Avril told Kirsty later how the conversation had gone. 'But there are other aspects of life, you know, Mother. It's not just home and work, home and work, with the odd outing to Safeways. Well, not for other people it's not.'

'Start', said her mother, 'as you mean to go on. If you look businesslike that's how they will treat you: with respect, politely. If you look like a ne'er-do-well – long, uncombed hair and mismatched accessories – then you can't complain if they treat you that way.'

But surely a suit from Dorothy Perkins wouldn't have ne'er-do-well stamped all over it? And it might be a tad more fashionable than the one they had finally come home with, the one which was itching her then, and constricting her arm and shoulder movements.

'Trust me, dear,' said Avril's mother. 'I said you would get the job, and you did. Fast and accurate, that's what you are, and you must remember that.'

The haircut that made Avril 'businesslike' is a short, sensible bob which accentuates her wide face with its flat, overlarge features. 'Strange', Avril told Kirsty afterwards, 'how the word business conjures up bowel movements, or something that is other people's and makes you seem nosy for asking. The sort of word Mother uses, and just as nasty; words spoken carefully and correctly, like vagina, napkin, testicles, motor car, time of the month and spermatozoa. When some people say them they make them sound shocking.'

There are certainly pluses to be gained from growing up without such a mother. Without any mother at all, thought Kirsty.

The diary, just visible over the top of the plump girl's bag, is headed Business Studies. 'My toes curl up when I have to say that's the subject I did,' said Avril when Kirsty got to know her. 'Not psychology or media studies; they were out of the question, courses that sounded like stars in the night, unattainable, there, shining, distant, tempting and beautiful at the far horizons of my world.'

Kirsty would love to have gone to college.

For a flickering moment she envied Avril, she envied her her dominant mother and Avril's complacent aura of safety.

'Even the students on our course looked suitably boring compared to the others in the tech art and design departments, drama, music, languages, or science and technology,' Avril told her wistfully. 'But Mother was right, as usual. I would stick out like a sore thumb doing any of those exciting subjects. I was too fat. I had no style. It was worse when Dad called me his little beauty.' But if anyone had bothered to look harder they might have realized that her dad was right: Avril could be improved upon, even though she is fat. Her face has a sweetness about it, her skin is flawless, her wide blue eyes are compelling to look at and 'merry' in an old-fashioned way, and if she'd had a decent hairdresser instead of Shirley at Carla's Parlour, if her hair had been allowed to grow longer so that it curled around her neck and gave her a bit of height on top, she might not have been beautiful in the popularly accepted sense, but she would have looked interesting, striking. Because of the world's perception of her, poor Avril is shy, boring and ultra-introverted, and she knows it. 'I mean, when I heard the news that the drama students sitting cross-legged in a circle at the very beginning of term were made to introduce themselves in a ringing, operatic fashion I nearly puked with horror.'

While those, like Avril, doing business studies

31

were given a file and a shared computer and sat in rigid, silent lines. Far more suitable. Far safer. And their tutors, thank God, were all women.

But Kirsty doesn't know Avril yet. She dreams on in her imagination, her head resting back on the seat, lost in the safety of let's pretend.

'Homely' is the word for the girl who sits opposite. And it's true, Avril does love her home: the comfortable bedroom at the top of the house with which she is so familiar; the dear old kitchen with its Formica tops which haven't changed since the house was built; the tiled beige fireplace into which is inserted that most efficient electric false flame with the wooden surrounds and its small brass ornaments. 'I Remember, I Remember', was her favourite poem at school. With that much-loved poem she won a certificate in elocution. Her family is tiny and super-nuclear. The word stifling comes to mind, and when Kirsty found out she felt envious again. They do family things like play Trivial Pursuit, go out for a Chinese on a Friday night and visit Granny on Sundays.

And now the poor child is leaving all this behind and taking off on her first great adventure. Kirsty tries hard not to stare as the girl tries to blink away tears, wiping them with a handkerchief corner as if there's something stuck there that she is trying, discreetly, to remove.

Avril's mother would despise her companions.

Her seat was booked by the Burleston beforehand; if not, Avril, increasingly uncomfortable, would have moved elsewhere by now. Although there are spaces and she would prefer a smaller, two-seater arrangement where she could park her bag on the neighbouring seat and thus discourage insensitive passengers, she lacks the courage to do so, and Kirsty sympathized with that when she told her. 'I felt nervous enough, worried enough, at leaving my luggage beside the door. What if someone made off with it? All my worldly goods in two Marks & Spencer tartan cases.'

Avril has her own sandwiches and a large flask of sweet tea. 'You don't want to pay those wicked buffet prices,' her mother had said, arranging the tuna. But her three companions care nothing for prices. Their whole journey so far has consisted of visits to the loo and the buffet, only to return with even more cans of extra-strong lager. 'I was dead scared of unwrapping those sandwiches, even though my tummy was rumbling. I knew what they'd make of that fierce smell of fish. What if those sailors thought it was me? What if they thought the smell came from my knickers?'

Kirsty knows what she means. The sailors are taking the piss. You can tell this by the rolling of an eye, the dig of an elbow, the wink of a lid, and Avril knows what is happening. She is used to looking for clues like this from way back in her early playground days. They have a particular way of speaking, defiantly vulgar, as if to include her. 'I kept my eyes fixed hard on my book but I couldn't take in one word,' she told Kirsty. 'I just hoped they would get out at Plymouth before they got too pissed and started behaving embarrassingly, showing me up, mocking me openly.'

Kirsty, who makes up people as a hobby, guesses this girl has never had a boyfriend.

It's possible that she believes nobody else goes

through life as wistful and utterly solitary as she. How wrong she is. How wrong.

'Yep, I was beginning to think that no man would ever want me or undress me or feel me or bring me flowers. I knew I would never get married. At times I thought I might be gay just because that would be easier.' She described the homely girls like her doing business studies, who went round in black tights, pleated skirts and anoraks. 'And I've read every book about nuns there is. I mean, what a happy release that would be.' Given time and faith she would worship God in the same sort of exquisite, tingling, distant way she had worshipped some boy in the fourth year. A habit might slim her down. She had fantasized, under covers of course, of throwing herself down on a cold, slate floor in the shape of a crucifix and confessing her sins to a cruel, black-clad inquisitor. Only in these shameful dreams she was naked, and afterwards everyone 'had her' as she lay back spread over the altar. Oh dear, oh dear, more satanic than Christian. And what would Mother say?

Avril plucks up courage and glances around. There would probably be other 'girls' like her on the train, Mother had said, all going to the Burleston Hotel to begin the new season. Mother especially approved of the idea of Avril 'living in'. A good way to 'grow into independence', and Mother has the housekeeper's assurance that she will keep an eye on young Avril. At the interviews for the various posts, Avril was surprised by the scope. There were chambermaid jobs, vacancies for waitresses, porters and office staff, like herself, one children's nanny, two lifeguards, porters, chefs, washers up and cleaners.

Why did they need to look in Liverpool? Weren't the locals more handy?

'There's probably no local population to speak of,' said Mother. 'The place is in the middle of nowhere, and the Cornish are notoriously lazy. It's the pace of life. It's a different world.'

But the Burleston was open all year round. Couldn't they keep their staff?

She had asked this at the interview – well, obviously not in those words. Mother rehearsed her, 'Will there be any possibility of a full-time job with you if you find my work satisfactory?'

The answer, given by a tarty recruitment-agency official with one-inch-long red fingernails, was simple. Raised expectations. 'In this day and age not many people, I'm afraid, Miss Stott, are willing to shut themselves away from the world for longer than one season.' The blond-headed woman with the blotchy lashes gave Avril a small, tight smile and tapped one nail on the folder before her. 'I must emphasize again, Miss Stott, that the Burleston caters for a certain, select class of guest. Those who are looking for peace and quiet, right away from the hurly-burly. Thus Colonel Parker's policy is not to offer any kind of glamorous nightlife, or organize events or outings, or encourage guests who are young or unmarried or groups of the same sex. Families are the hotel's bread and butter, young families during the summer and older clientele in the winter, you understand. Many go to the Burleston to use the exclusive nine-hole golf course and they sometimes arrange small competitions, I believe, if the guests so desire.'

So there she had it. It was just too boring. Mother's careful research had paid off.

A sigh runs down the length of her spine, all the way from Avril's shoulders. Well, at least she won't feel left out if there's nowhere to be invited. The nearest village is three miles away. The nearest pub is eight. And there's no bus service.

Who are Avril's fellow workers likely to be? The group of four across the aisle? Who else, like her, would be willing to forgo all social and sexual contact for the five long months of summer? Students? Avril peers across. That little group isn't speaking, but why is that woman staring? Avril catches Kirsty's eyes and she looks down guiltily. Irish or Italian migrant workers? How can she possibly tell? There can't be many young girls like herself – nineteen years old in the first flush of youth, with all their juices flowing.

Ugh! That's another of Mother's expressions that makes poor Avril want to vomit.

It has always been Mother's greatest wish that Avril should partake in 'the leaving of Liverpool'. Mother, because of the books she reads, has a romanticized and clichéd rags-to-riches view of the city that has kept her husband in his humble place since he first went to work twenty-three years ago at Burt and Sturgess, the gentleman's outfitters in the city centre. Straining after gentility, Mother has spent her married life longing to 'cross the Mersey' to the land of milk and honey, the Wirral, that exclusive, glorious mecca that lies on the other side. And if Graham, her wilful son, had had the wit to do as he'd been told – procured a few certificates and trained to be somebody – he wouldn't have got in with the wrong crowd, fallen foul of the law and ended up doing a stretch at Her Majesty's pleasure.

His name is not spoken in Mother's house.

And it is only because of Mother's dire view of life in the north of England in general that she has released her only daughter, albeit in a strictured way, to go off and make her fortune with a brand-new wardrobe in two Marks & Spencer suitcases instead of a red-and-white spotted handkerchief on a stick.

Outside the window now all is meadow and hedgerow and wood. The telegraph wires switchback from pole to pole. Avril thinks she can smell the sea.

All the nice girls love a sailor . . .

In a minute they will offer her a drink. With a dread premonition she knows it, she is touched with a foretaste of well-known pain, and they will offer it so expansively that the whole carriage will hear. There is no way she can emphasize her modesty by crossing her legs and looking stiff because of the short and fashionable suit skirt that she had foolishly insisted upon. She had practised bending over in the full-length mirror at home and discovered that the slightest angle could well give a glimpse of her underwear. Too late, too late to take the wretched suit back and change it for the version with the boot-length skirt. Avril should have known better. The young and nubile can get away with skirts that hardly cover their crotches, they can leap onto motorbikes, slide into cars, mount steps and dance leaning backwards without appearing obscene. Not so poor Avril with her plump and generous thighs.

'Come on, sexy, chill out.' The can is handed across with a belch.

Avril reddens. 'I don't drink actually.'

'Ha. Get that. I don't drink actually.' He mimics her bleating voice to perfection and leers, encouraging the others to join in. See, his look says, see, it's easy. She's a cinch. Come on, for a laugh.

She wants to beg them to leave her alone, them and their depravity. She wants to explain how they're hurting her. But, of course, you can't do that, so Avril smiles, trying to bring them on to her side in the only way she knows how. This friendly method had occasionally worked when used against bullies at school.

She can feel his knee touching her knee, her naked knee because of her skirt. She knows that her large breasts are overly defined in that tight brown body she insisted on wearing in spite of Mother's advice. If only she could do up her suit jacket.

'Whaccha bleedin' problem, love?' It's a crackling, drunken sarcasm. His face is shiny and innocent. Putrid, he makes her feel sick.

The smile is stuck to Avril's face as she murmurs. 'I'm sorry? I wasn't aware that I had a problem.' Oh God, she sounds like a prig, her voice like a hum in the back of her throat.

But discretion is the better part of valour.

The man pretends to look surprised. 'Ey up? So why doncha want to drink with us? Too fuckin' uppity, yeah?' And he nudges his grinning companion.

The passengers sitting within hearing distance, uneasy now, afraid of unseemly involvement, concentrate squeamishly on their books, and one man opens his lap-top computer and starts a desperate tapping. The young woman who has been staring

38

turns quickly away and stares out through the window. All of them settling, safe as they can, to watch the ensuing humiliation.

What shall we do with the drunken sailor . . .

Silent up until now, the beery sailor sitting in the window seat next to Avril puts one arm around her headrest so it's not quite touching her but almost. Out of the corner of her eye she can see sweat beads on his brow and there's dried froth on his upper lip where he hasn't licked it clean. Ugh! Revolting. Every sinew in her body urges her to get up and move, to stand in the corridor, if necessary, for the rest of the journey rather than submit to this. But how can Avril do this now without asking for more trouble? Is this partly her fault, because she looks like a tart? She had slapped some make-up on in the toilet after the train left the station, after she'd waved goodbye to Mother. Just a dab. A natural beige with a blusher and lipstick of matching pink from the Body Shop. She was sure she hadn't overdone it. Oh, dear God, let them stop. Please, please, make them stop, and her heart beats uncontrollably.

'Tell you what,' grunts the ringleader, leaning across the table with unfocused eyes, eyes that are opaque and dull, neither hostile nor unkind, but so close that his sour breath touches her and she sees bits of ham roll on his teeth. 'Tell you what, gel, why don't you and me get to know each other while we're stuck here bored as two fuckin' farts . . .' and she feels him stretching out his leg so it's firmly stuck between her legs.

'Good, innit? Eh?'

Everyone can perceive her shame. Avril goes

rigid, like a small animal caught in a trap, the kind of animal that might pull off its leg in order to break free. 'Shit,' slurs her antagonist, as he knocks over his can with his sleeve and the lager dregs drip over the edge of the table on her side.

Should Kirsty help? She knows that she should. But she is so frightened of men. This is awful. *Just awful.*

Out of the blue.

'Why don't you just sod off, you sad, pathetic dickheads!' Startled, Avril and Kirsty look up as the girl in jeans beside the window scrapes her belongings into a bag which displays a Burleston sticker, climbs over Kirsty's knee, half on, half off the table, and stands aggressively in the aisle, hands on hips.

Whooping with derision, the sailor withdraws his knee, happy to concentrate instead on this new source of torment, a much more fiery and worthwhile subject. Next to the aisle, he staggers up, but before he can gain his balance the newcomer pushes him hard on the chest and he falls back drunkenly, gaping.

'Come on, pet,' says the confident beauty to Avril, 'get your things and come and sit somewhere away from these animals. I need a bloody fag anyway.'

'But m–my cases . . .' stutters Avril, struggling to her feet, tugging at her skirt.

'Sod your cases, they'll be OK.'

And because her saviour is disappearing Avril is forced to rush to catch up, still holding tears at bay, clutching her handbag, her book and a carrier bag containing a heavy thermos. She can hear lewd cheering coming from the defeated sailors behind her as she clumps fatly down the corridor, following the long-haired girl with the droopy bag and the earrings.

And Kirsty, assuming she is the natural choice for alternative, handy victim, picks up her bags and follows. But her left leg has gone numb with the tension and she has to hang on to every other seat.

Three

On their stumbling way to carriage B, neither Avril
Stott nor her saviour Bernadette Kavanagh notice
the drab-looking woman who gets up to follow
them down the train. She could be an imprint on
the seat of someone who sat there journeys ago.
Avril is too nervous, too traumatized by her recent
ordeal to see anything but her own flaming cheeks,
while Bernadette yearns only for a fag. When will
this wretched journey end?

This is fine for Kirsty. Kirsty would rather not be
noticed. She is a watcher from safe places. But after
she has taken a seat, a spare seat opposite the others
in the yellowy, acrid atmosphere of the smoker's
carriage, she stares at the rescuer with a mixture of
envy and guilt.

'I'm Avril.'

'I'm Bernadette.'

Avril sees Bernadette's sticker. 'You're going to
the Burleston, like me.'

They do not shake hands like men would.

And Kirsty, pulsing softly and secretly, does not
reveal herself.

*   *   *

Avril is besotted.

Bernadette is a beautiful gypsy, a pure, untrammelled thing, wandering free, knowing nothing of cares or woes. Messy, but lovely in the uncaring, pure cotton-and-silk kind of way that shouts out style and confidence, quite the opposite to Avril's mother's ideas of neat-and-tidy jersey and man-made mixtures which always smell as if they've already been worn by women not quite in control of their hygiene. Rather similar to charity shops, as soon as you go through the door of Avril's mother's favourite boutiques you get that flour-and-water-pastey whiff of the unwashed elderly.

Bernadette isn't slightly bothered about her new companions, but concentrates instead on the quiz she is doing in her shiny magazine. With the pen top in her mouth, sometimes replaced by her smouldering fag, she demands of the rescued Avril, 'What would you do if you saw your best friend's bloke smooching somebody else? (a) tell her, (b) have a stern word with him, (c) beat up the other chick with your handbag, or (d) feel secretly pleased and do nothing?'

'I would tell her,' answers Avril, pleased to be asked, 'of course.'

'She wouldn't thank you for it.' Bernadette's green, cat's eyes narrow over a trail of smoke before going back, engrossed, to her work.

Avril, partly because of her sweet nature and partly because of her upbringing, feels it's rude to keep silent, particularly when she owes so much. 'Is this your first hotel job?' She is well aware of her boring question and Kirsty winces on her behalf.

'Yep,' says Bernadette, trying hard to be sociable, but far too unhappy to succeed. 'Never heard of the place before. Just took it as a desperate measure to stop myself going insane.'

'It's my first time, too,' says Avril, making it sound like sex.

'Got to make some money somehow,' says Bernadette shrugging.

At Plymouth they watch Avril's three sailors lurch loudly along the platform, being side-stepped by fellow passengers with disgust all over their faces. 'Thank goodness they've gone,' says Avril, keen, once again, to break the silence which she thinks of as uncomfortable and a failure on her part to be interesting.

'They don't mean any harm really,' says Bernadette in the Irish accent that makes her voice as alluring as the rest of her. It's so unfair. Bernadette's got everything while Avril . . . 'They're just rat-arsed, that's all.'

'I dare say you're right,' says Avril.

Misreading Bernadette's attempts at sisterly reassurance, Avril's inadequacy surfaces again. Bernadette considers her inadequate, unable to deal with a trio of sailors who were only having some laddish fun. Avril would go deeper into herself at this, except that she can't because of her stiff and uncomfortable jacket.

After being warned by a muffled male voice that the buffet is now closing, they rattle on to Penzance, Bernadette, half waking, half sleeping, curled up in the corner with her richly embroidered material holdall and half its contents – tatty old make-up and screwed-up tissues – spewed out over the table.

Kirsty, wide awake, keeps silent and watches.

Ah. Poor Bernadette.

Bernadette doesn't care any more. She just doesn't care. She can't try any harder. Nothing she does seems to be working. She unburdens herself on Avril, describing her dire situation, safe in the knowledge that her audience is captive, half by speed and half by good manners. Smoke swirls wildly over her crazy confidences. 'They warned me that if I didn't pull myself out of this depression soon, leave Merseyside for good and get myself some sort of future, I would end up a druggie stuck in some squat, and all because of Dominic Coates.'

'How awful, how awful. Poor you,' says Avril, seeing that her heroine is distraught.

There is no opportunity to invent Bernadette. So Kirsty listens instead. This isn't difficult. The whole carriage could hear if it wanted.

'Slime bag,' says Bernadette.

'He must be,' says the obedient Avril.

'Bullshitter,' says Bernie more savagely.

She leans forward earnestly, as if Avril has some handy balm she might apply if convinced of the need. She is a demented patient begging her doctor for Prozac. Bernadette had a good job working as a waitress at the Old Orleans. HE had come in with a crowd of students. HE had chatted her up. She was used to that, she never had trouble finding fellas, but, God help her, after his third or fourth visit she had begun to see him as 'different'. Hah! Laugh? She could cry. They were engaged within a month.

45

Kirsty sighs knowingly. OK. Bernadette might see the girl opposite with the huge diddies and sum her up as a poor little eejit, but when it comes down to the hard facts of life, Bernadette, with all her blarney, turns out to be as fragile as everyone else.

Bernadette paints dramatic pictures of how she came to her present plight. Her audience listens, transfixed, as her voice drones on piteously, seeking some kind of instant relief, as if sharing the pain might lessen it.

Dominic Coates was rich, well-spoken and bright.

Bernadette Kavanagh was poor, an Irish navvy's daughter and a money-grabbing slut.

That's what his toffee-nosed parents thought anyway. Jesus, one day she'll show them, for she has never known such pain. She loved being seen around with him and his crowd. How she would enjoy making good in *A Woman of Substance* style, run some multi-national concern, live in New York and return to their house and moon at all of them. She would cultivate that snooty look she had seen on Dominic's daddy's face until she got it off pat, as if something nasty was under his long, hairy-nostrilled, aristocratic nose. And his mammy, with that scoff behind her lips. In her dreams Bernadette drives to their house in a top-of-the-range Porsche convertible. She snaps up their businesses furtively, one by one, without them knowing who is responsible, until she squeezes them out with nothing.

Avril, out of her depth and embarrassed, tries hard to sympathize while finding this candour crude and shameful. Kirsty, hiding behind her Mills and Boon, carefully stays separate.

'Am I mad?' Bernadette asks Avril.

'No, of course not,' and Avril gives a tactful smile.

Bernadette admits she's ashamed of her thoughts. Sweet Jesus, will you listen to her now. She is surely a soul in torment. She wants to maim him, really hurt him, she loves him so much. She adored him. She would have been happy to be his Timberland Filofax, something he valued, was dependent upon and took round with him wherever he went. But while she still harbours these furious thoughts she is just as vulnerable as she's ever been. It's uncanny how love is so easily replaced by hatred. Both are burning strong. Bernadette must strive for the point when she stops thinking about him completely, the point of detachment when the name Dominic means no more than Daz or Mother's Pride.

'Ah well. Here we are at Penzance.' She scoops her belongings back into her bag, as though picking up all the pain and stuffing it back inside her.

The tired little party for the Burleston Hotel gather at the station exit, eight of them in all off this one train. They smile nervously at one another and check their various bags are in sight, and then along comes a smart minibus with the name of the hotel printed tastefully on the side. Avril squeezes in beside Bernadette; they have shared a carriage for the last three hours, Bernadette has opened her heart, and Avril, who has never made many, believes they are now firm friends.

'So what's your name?' she politely asks Kirsty, recognizing for the first time the woman who stared at her on the train. She seems amazed to find her

47

here, to discover they both had the same destination, as if it's some secret they share. Hey, it's not so amazing. The flotsam and jetsam of life.

Bernadette has sunk into silence, trying to discourage her companion's chatter and Kirsty can sympathize with this. It must be a shock for Bernadette, who had bared her soul in carriage B, to discover that her sweet-faced confessor is now demanding something in return. Mates. When they have nothing in common. Avril is desperately seeking a friend, like you do, so you don't have to go in alone, while Bernadette is not here for small talk: she's here to stop herself losing her mind and she doesn't want anyone clinging or thinking they can rely on her. If Avril thinks Bernadette kind, she is wrong; she is not kind, has no time to be kind, no time to soften towards anyone else or be considerate of their feelings. She has let too many people down to allow herself to do it again.

The two spotty boys must be would-be-waiters, although they don't look old enough and are certainly incapable of carrying a blazing tureen with style. Perhaps they are doomed to the kitchens. The two young teenage girls in the party are probably part of the chambermaid crew – changing sheets and sprucing up bathrooms, picking strangers' pubic hairs out of plug holes and off toilet seats. At least Bernadette got a job as a barmaid because of her past experience. She would loathe to clean up after the privileged, especially after what she'd been through. Dominic's folks considered her scum. She can well imagine that snooty family hotelling it and shitting on anyone more lowly than themselves.

The lanes are growing alarmingly narrow and so twisty Kirsty feels sick. There is nothing to see because it is dark, almost eleven o'clock, and the hotel has promised a cold snack will be served on arrival.

How do the others see her? A character from a tragedy, or a farce? Or probably just a dull-looking woman who looks as if she could do with a snack or something to revive her. She catches herself in the driving mirror. Her eyes are like two smouldering wounds, she has clearly been wet and dried off again, she has such a huddled, high-shouldered look and she badly needs her bed, poor thing. That is what they must be thinking.

But Bernadette is too tired to think. Bed, as usual, is intensely inviting. Bed is the only place she can throw off all sham and conjure up Dominic again and her short time with him – dream, wish, regret, weep, yearn and touch herself with the reverence he had used when he'd touched her.

That first time she realized that he had free time and was not seeing her.

Then the agonizing rumour that he was quite brazenly seeing somebody else.

The unbearable knowledge that he would be saying the same things, doing the same things, laughing at the same things as he had done with her. Making love to the same sweet summer fragrances, their lovers' kisses resting on the same still air.

But he loved me. *He loved me!*

Ah, Holy Mary Mother of Jesus.

Her anguish had only been bearable because it

was too much to suffer at once. She learned by heart these last lines from 'The Betrayal':

Under the mountains there is peace abiding,
Darkness shall be pavilion for my hiding,
Tears shall blot out the sin of broken faith,
The lips that falsely kissed, shall kiss but Death.

Mad with distress, suicide leapt to mind; it seemed such a natural thing to do and brought with it such a feeling of peace. The awful discord would be resolved, a jumbled-up kaleidoscope would be given the right turn and the harmonious pattern it made would bring serenity and calm. The thought of her wanting to die would bring Dominic back, for sure, never mind that it was a mortal sin even to make the attempt. She didn't consider it blackmail. To her great surprise she had a feeling that she wouldn't mind if it really worked; if she died then some great burden not yet shouldered would never have to be borne.

Now the long sweep of the drive.

What is this place?

The same question is on everyone's face as the little group alight from the minibus.

There are woodlands on either side – oaks, birches and dark firs filled with silence. The air is heavy with the resinous scent of pines after rain, woodsmoke and the crushed perfume of bracken. There are a few desultory shrubs and dark-brown flower beds. There is loneliness here, intense and hidden, like the massive high, grey cliff of a wall, towered and castellated like a fortress, that rises into a starless sky, up, up and up.

The Burleston Hotel. Following the ancient driver, a big, sad hulk of a man, obviously some retarded retainer with stains all down his corduroys, they pass through a door at the back of the building, traipse along a dark passage and then into a large, dull room with windows along one wall, looking out on to a drab yard. The walls are painted with a dark-green dado up to a height of about four feet, with a lighter green above. It is like an old-fashioned, dusty schoolroom cluttered with stale furniture; a table-tennis table in the centre is laid out with rolls, cold meat and cheese.

'I hope I'm with you,' Avril sidles up to say. 'If we have to share rooms, that is.'

'Merciful God. What? *Share rooms?*' This appalling thought hasn't crossed Bernadette's mind. 'I haven't had to share since we lived in the cottage in County Clare when there were three of us to the bed. By the time we arrived in Liverpool there was only me and Frances left so we each had a bedroom to ourselves.'

Bernadette knew very well that the affair was cooling, it started that autumn weekend when Dominic's parents came up from Surrey to visit and stayed at the Grosvenor in Chester. 'You'll have to come and meet them,' he said. She didn't have a ring then, although they were unofficially engaged. Dominic said he would ask his father for some extra funds from his trust so he could buy her something decent. To be truthful she would have been just as happy with something shiny from Top Shop but she knew how Dominic loathed bad taste.

Her heart was leaping and scuttling. The hotel was a dazzling palace with murmurs of perfume and cigars, all chandeliers and carpets and velvet, pristine tablecloths, silver cutlery, glamorous women and prosperous men. The sherry she had to start with gave her a warm, happy glow. 'Just be natural,' Dominic told her. That was the only caution she got. Dominic's father, who was in cardboard boxes but a top barrister in his own fantasy, was tall, heavy-bodied with unlaughing eyes and a firm-set mouth which turned down at the corners. His mother was an aged Barbie doll, like an American president's wife, shrill-voiced and brittle all over, and around her neck she wore green diamonds. Throughout the meal they were perfectly charming and Bernadette thought she was doing so well, but a trial had begun and she hadn't the nous to realize she was the defendant. Her nervousness quite disappeared as she drank more and more of the wine that flowed and, in response to Mr Coates's soft, friendly questions, she was soon telling them funny stories, so clever, so witty. She was so flattered by their interest. She failed to see it as a cross-examination, or to notice Dominic staring, saying nothing. It wasn't until the morning after that she'd realized her audience had not been laughing and had judged her as jumped-up Irish scum.

'On the station the last word Mammy said was, "Eat. The Lord won't forgive you a second time for He is a terrible, stern judge."' Mammy looked fraught and old these days, much older than she ought to, and that was mainly Bernadette's fault for putting her through such purgatory – her own daughter, a cursed soul lying in St Mary's hospital, damned by God and despised by the nurses because they had better things to do with their time than pander to a silly, love-sick girl who curled and uncurled so miserably in her bed, all because of some fella. Better to be afflicted by the most appalling disease than to commit a mortal sin and be shut in a fiery tomb for all eternity. 'I am living', said Mammy with hurt indignation, 'in a cloud of shame, thanks to you.'

So Bernadette had been found, of course, just as she'd intended to be. After all, she had left her 'note' on the kitchen table where they'd be bound to find it when they came home from work. It had said merely 'forgive me'. She hadn't been able to write more.

Still half asleep, she then found herself mechanically chanting responses to the sad-eyed priest who sat beside her hospital bed murmuring quietly. The bright light hurt her eyes; she had taken the pills in soft candlelight, a whole pack of the anti-depressants Mammy kept beside her bed. With his manner subdued and his voice low, Father Murphy muttered, 'Well, here's a pretty kettle of fish.'

'Am I in hell, Father?' she asked, terror-stricken.

He looked round the hectic, soulless ward. 'Dear child,' he said, 'thanks be to God there's a wide turning circle, for we meet at the very gateway.' And he slipped her a packet of Superkings.

There followed a winter of heartbreak.

Something had to be done or the shrunken Bernadette would pine away to nothing. Dominic must have heard by now, but the months went by with no response and her wounds continued to suppurate.

It was Bernadette's friend Maggie who saw the advert for the job at the Burleston, sent for the forms and accompanied her to the Adelphi for an interview.

And so now here she is . . .

'Now then, ladies and gentlemen, if I could have your attention please.'

'It's Mrs Danvers,' whispers Avril, giggling and nudging Bernadette in the ribs.

'Who in God's name is Mrs Danvers?'

'*Rebecca*! Surely you know *Rebecca*? The book?'

'I don't read books,' says Bernadette, eying the tall, reptilian woman with the paper in her hand, who manifested herself like plasma from one of the corners of the room. She must be 100 years old if a day.

'You've all met Colonel Parker, the owner of this hotel, so no introductions are needed there,' and all eyes flicker to the minibus driver who sits in a chipped Parker Knoll chair with a cup of tea in his palsied hand making catarrhal sounds. 'But I am Moira Stokes, the hotel housekeeper, so I am the one you'll be dealing with in your everyday work. There is no time now for a preparatory meeting, it being almost midnight, so I will read out your room numbers, then you can all get a good night's sleep. We will meet again tomorrow at eight o'clock here in the staff recreation room.'

With that a list of names is read out, followed by the relevant numbers. 'You will have no trouble finding your rooms,' barks Mrs Moira Stokes, the tortoise, buttoned up to the neck in grey. 'They are up the back stairs straight ahead of you, right to the top of the house, first corridor on the right.'

'So I'm to be with you.' Kirsty approaches Bernadette and Avril, to whom by now she feels she's almost related. 'Room one-four-three. Three of us to one room. Let's hope it's a big one. I never imagined it would be like this.'

'Nor did I,' says Bernadette, listlessly picking up her bags and cursing her interfering friend Maggie whose idea had brought her to this. 'But Mother of Jesus, it can only get better.' And she realizes, with some astonishment, that these are the first positive words she has uttered since she attempted to take her life. 'Listen to me now,' she says. Perhaps God is working His infinite mercy as only He knows how.

Four

The good ol' boy in the Taverners Arms on Victoria Street rasps his bristled chin with his hand and shoves it determinedly across the table towards his buddy and soulmate, Greg.

'She's a silly cow, Trev, she'll be back,' slurs Greg. 'She knows which side her bread is buttered.'

'You're telling me she'll be back,' burps Trevor Hoskins, one mauve muscle in his forehead beating with anger and booze, 'and by Christ she'll know all about it when she is.'

Kirsty craves her children – she weeps and she mourns and she yearns for her children – and with a lesser longing Kirsty craves books. Once again, when life turns dark, books would bring some light, but in this dead end of a place the nearest bookshop is in Truro and Truro is eight miles away. She has read her two new Mills and Boons, re-read them and lent them to Avril. She has read Bernie's magazines and been shocked by their bizarre proclamations: 'I sliced off my husband's balls', 'I slept with a male gorilla'. She doesn't believe a word of it and is amazed that Bernie does.

'You believe what you want to believe,' says Bernie tellingly. 'Or I do, anyway.'

'Only because you are such a good worker, Kirsty,' declares Mrs Stokes reluctantly one day, 'and only because of that am I going to allow you to go to the quiet room in the main hotel and choose some books from the shelves. I can see you have a literary bent, like myself. But be sure not to leave an untidy gap. Rearrange the shelves nicely afterwards.'

'Brown-noser,' says Bernie.

But the problem that now besets Kirsty is the cottage she was promised. The Burleston Hotel advised her that it was let through the summer, and so it is, by two unemployed layabouts who call themselves students, and the reason it is let to them is that the place is too much of a shambles to be let to anyone else. With its broken asbestos roof and its mouldy lean-to bathroom, the square breeze-block bungalow is nigh on derelict.

'It was a smart place once,' Flagherty, the gardener, remembered with one soily finger poked alarmingly high up his nose. She found him among the rhododendrons, radiant pastels of blues and purples stretching all the way down to the cove and making pathways with their sandy roots. He rolled his rheumy eyes up to the overcast sky. 'They used to let them to folks from the hotel on a self-catering basis, but that was way back in the Sixties when people were into bluebells and innocence and little stick fires. They used to come down here and go round barefoot, blowing recorders and playing let's pretend we're poor. They had blue and white jugs and crockery. Since then', he removed his finger and spent one long interested minute studying the sticky result of his search, 'they haven't touched it. It's gone to the dogs, as they say.'

She knocked on the door and got no reply, observed by Flagherty from over his spade.

'They're in there all right, the varmints. 'Tisn't decent, if you ask me, sleepin' all hours. Walk right in, maid, and rouse the blighters.'

So she did.

It's bad enough being consigned to a room little better than those at the battered wives' hostel, sharing her privacy with two others, delegated one chest of drawers and a quarter of one large, ugly mahogany wardrobe. It's bad enough that the beds and mattresses are obviously part of a cheap consignment from some closed-down hospital, ungiving and springless with their black iron frames. Avril, who knows these things, says the whole staff quarters are like something out of a workhouse. 'You might be uneducated, but you must have read *Oliver Twist*.'

'No,' said Bernie proudly.

The bedside tables have seen years of service, probably in the main hotel when Formica was first fashionable. It is hard enough to stomach the stained iron bath with its formidable geyser which knows no moderation, which boils the water or freezes it, let alone the chipped wooden lavatory seat that serves eight other members of staff, but to discover that her promised cottage is little more than a broken-down pigsty means an end to her hopes.

But Kirsty has gambled everything on this – a safe home for herself and the children, far away so that Trev can't reach them. And where will they go to school? And what friends will they have?

'You could do something with it,' wheezed the woollen-haired yob who eventually rose naked from his squalid bed in response to several tentative prods. 'Lick o'paint here and there.'

'I doubt that,' said Kirsty despondently.

'Yeah, you could.' He dragged a blanket round his stark, crucifixion-type loins and his shaking hands lit up a rollie. 'Hey, lady. It's not all bad. You've got an open fire.'

It looked like jackdaws had been nesting in it.

'You've got a cooker.'

Varnished with gobs of old fat, most of the enamel had peeled away leaving burnt black patches behind.

'And a fridge, by that bit of floor that's collapsed.' The damp had rotted through the linoleum revealing a loathsome carpet of fungi. 'Watch it,' he said, 'it's dodgy just there.'

'You're quite private,' said the tenant eventually, sensing her growing gloom. 'You can close your door and be real quiet here, and the bins are just round the corner. There's some good stuff gets chucked in those bins if you bother to look. Mostly salad.'

The one hope that remains is the caravan park a mile down the road where some of the mobile homes are let out all year round. It might just be

59

possible to make a home there – well, what alternative has she got – perhaps they run a school bus if there are other children around. She won't give up hope until she sees it and makes enquiries, but they won't be able to guarantee anything until the season is over.

The staff recreation facilities, referred to pompously by Mrs Stokes, consist of the large room they found when they first arrived, chairs in various states of distress, the table-tennis table with its cracked or missing balls, one black-and-white TV and a radiogram in a walnut cabinet. In the tiny kitchen adjoining it is a kettle, damp hotel sachets of coffee, tea and sugar, a tin teaspoon, a jar of dried milk and a bin streaked russet by teabags. The heavy iron radiators are strictly turned off on 1 April every year, come rain or shine, and piles of dead matches litter the floor around two inadequate gas convectors.

Not that there's time for recreation. The hotel is full, in spite of a damp and overcast June, and everyone is baffled to hear that because of its excellent reputation guests book one year in advance to be sure of a vacancy. Kirsty, in her lowly position, is up and dressed in her black-and-white uniform by seven thirty prompt, when a hasty breakfast is served in the kitchens. Then it's on to one of the three broad landings with her partner and a trolley loaded with clean sheets and towels, fresh soap, tissues, bin liners, shampoo, shower gel and cleaning equipment.

No sooner does one room empty for breakfast than they're in there like a couple of whippets, and the rush goes on until twelve, by which time she feels as though she's working in a sauna. It's heavy, sweaty work and although she has been hardened by stacking shelves at the superstore, this makes that job seem like a luxury cruise.

The hotel bedrooms, Wedgwood and white, sport king-sized beds in every room, four-posters in the suites, satellite TV, balconies, bidets, fridges, fresh fruit in bowls, trouser presses and bathrobes provided, no expense spared. All the luxurious fabrics match and the decor is straight out of *Ideal Home*.

Thirty minutes for lunch and it's off to the downstairs bathrooms, predominantly marble, sanitary crypts. If their luck is in they can get a sit-down, ease off their shoes and catch their breaths. When the guests' lunch is over they make for the bar. Then there's the dirty laundry; it has to be sorted and labelled and the incoming laundry stacked in the linen room (tablecloths to the dining room), silver to polish, bath mats to fold, incoming and outgoing guest lists to check . . . and so it goes on endlessly until tea time when they officially finish. But every evening during dinner they visit the bedrooms to tidy up and turn down the sheets, and theirs is a six-day week.

But, no longer menaced by fear, to Kirsty this feels like a warm room in winter with a glowing fire to welcome her home. It takes time to acclimatize to the missing threats and shocks to the system – going to bed is a blissful pleasure, as is waking and knowing she's not going to see him. She is no longer forced to tiptoe round forever metamorphosing herself so as not to annoy Trevor.

Sometimes she jumps when someone goes by and then smiles to herself when it's not him. Difficult guests don't bother her. She is used to smiling and being humble. She often wonders what steps he is taking to discover her whereabouts, and Jake's and Gemma's. His hold over Kirsty is still uncanny; although his physical presence has gone he is psychologically still her keeper. He will go to the school, she is sure of that, but the authorities can tell him nothing simply because they don't know anything. All she told them on the last day she delivered the children was that they were going on holiday. He knows nothing about the centre, but he'd get short shrift from there if he did. Kirsty left work without giving the required one week's notice . . . she rang up and said she was sick.

Whenever she thinks of him she goes cold.

But she has friends, real friends at last.

Close as chums in a Blyton novel, thrown together by bizarre circumstance – people in cold climates huddle together for warmth and safety – Kirsty, Bernie and Avril are confidantes and sympathizers. They have already laughed till they cried three times, a release Kirsty thought she'd lost long ago. But she doesn't get to see them enough because of Avril's office hours, and Bernie stays up until after midnight working in the bar. It is heartening how much they have in common when you know how different they are – Avril and Bernie being ten years younger – Avril all soft, jelly and custard; Bernie a fiery, reheated curry.

'Hell hath no fury like a woman scorned.' Avril frowns on Bernie's self-pity.

'How would you know?' quips Bernie.

Sometimes, like children in the dark, they talk so long into the night that Kirsty drops off in the middle of a sentence. Her only moans are of Bernie's sluttish habits – she stubs out her fags on the bottom of her shoes and drops her old pants around like litter – and Avril's adenoidal snores are as rasping as blasts from a liner's funnel.

'Give and take,' says Avril happily. 'We are family now. We must make concessions.'

'You're not my family,' moans Bernie. 'Prig.'

On her second day at the Burleston Kirsty had poured over a letter from Maddy and two precious home-made cards from the kids. 'All is going beautifully smoothly. I've taken some snaps which I'll send next time. Jake plays "Peggy Sue" on the guitar and Gemma is breeding newts for her farm. If those two children aren't in their element then I will eat my hat.'

Kirsty had smiled and hugged the cards close, trying to breathe their soapy smell, but the messy bits of glitter and sticker and the raving mass of colours had said more than words to comfort her.

This evening, after a hectic Saturday and one week after she started, Kirsty takes up Mrs Stokes's offer and heads for the quiet hotel lounge in search of the promised books. This is a room of antiques and pictures, made fluffy with tasselled cushions. Two elderly ladies reading by the fire sense she is staff and pointedly ignore her. She can smell the books before she reaches them, decaying paper, damp and neglect; dusted occasionally but rarely removed, they are in grave danger of welding together. Far more popular, it seems, is the vast array of periodicals set out on the coffee table, a far cry from those at the doctor's surgery because every one is up to date, thick, shiny and fashionable. Below the books are stacks of board games, playing cards and jigsaws for use on rainy afternoons, but these days how many kids would be entertained by such simple pastimes?

Most of the kiddies staying here have gone out to the many all-weather attractions, chauffeured in one of the Audis, BMWs, Daimlers or Range Rovers parked round the front entrance, giant wet lizards under the palms. Unfazed by the weather these hearty, healthy, high-spirited kids go riding, sailing, climbing or walking, never a moment's boredom. Bleep bleep bleep go their Gameboys in the evenings, and while their parents linger over dinner they shriek around in the indoor pool.

There are no lightweight paperbacks here, certainly no Mills and Boons among the colonel's collection. These are jumble-sale offerings, books you buy by the box-load. Kirsty loses herself for a while reading the introductions – so many travel books and manly adventures: *King Solomon's Mines* and *Moby Dick*, *White Fang* and *Huckleberry Finn*. She is searching for something more romantic, something written, perhaps, by a woman. Were there no silly women in the colonel's day? Ah, yes, here is a copy of Mrs Beeton, two by Emily Brontë, one Daphne du Maurier and several Reader's Digest compilations. Not nearly silly enough for her.

'Can I help you, my dear?'

One of the white-haired old ladies turns a cross, thin face towards Kirsty. 'Was there anything?'

'I'm so sorry, I didn't mean to disturb you.'

'Well, we can't help but be disturbed with you poking and prodding away in the background. What a nuisance. What is it you are looking for anyway?'

'I'm looking for something to read.'

'Well surely it doesn't take long to find something to read. There's hundreds of books on those shelves and all very worthy I'm sure. But this is supposed to be a quiet room . . . '

'Yes, I know and I'm sorry.'

The old lady tuts and looks away, her gnarled old hand reaching grumpily for the silver teapot. 'Oh, before you go, you could fill up my cup, if you would be so kind.'

'Certainly, madam.'

Hardly aware of what books she picks up, Kirsty hurries to obey.

'It's so difficult when your bones get old,' says the old lady unpleasantly, lifting a sugar cube with the tongs. And a dismissive, 'Thank you, dear,' as Kirsty hastily leaves the room.

She leaves the fat orange book called *Magdalene* until last. During the next couple of evenings she forces herself to get through the others, although the first one loses her completely, clearly a clever literary work, and the second is all about the Boer War: blood, dead horses and heroes.

'I'm going to Truro on Monday, I'll get you some Mills and Boons from the library,' says Avril. 'Anything to stop you moaning.' Kirsty has put *Magdalene* aside, fearing the worst; it's a waste of time. 'I can't think why they don't sell books in the hotel foyer,' says Avril. 'You'd think they'd sell out in this weather.'

'What about you, Bernie?'

'You could get me the latest *TV Quick* and a *Take A Break*, they'll do.'

Bernie, a bird-brained beautiful butterfly, has skipped through life without reading a paper or listening to the news. 'Now what would I want to do that for?' She laughs it off. She can name the present prime minister and she knows where Liverpool is on the map, but she runs out of ideas when she reaches the leader of the opposition. Ask her who Bach is and she hasn't a clue. 'Was it your school?' Kirsty muses. 'Will my kids end up daft as you? Or is it because you're so self-obsessed?'

'Obsession keeps me thin,' says Bernie, casting an unkind glance at Avril.

'I'd rather be fat than in your sort of love,' Avril sneers. 'Uncanny and unnatural, that's what you are.'

Bernie does every quiz she can find just to read questions about herself, delve into herself, test and judge herself by the pitiful answers on page fortynine. She devours all horoscopes as though she's starving for news of her future. And it isn't that she's stupid, far from it, it is just a complete lack of interest.

But although Kirsty knows she is limited with her easy reading and low expectations, how she wishes, now, that she had made more of her education. If she'd had a decent career she'd have had the confidence and the means to leave Trevor years ago. If she had bothered with exams she wouldn't be making the beds of strangers, with no prospect of a home for her kids. Even the poor, defeated Avril has managed to get an office job and is *au fait* with computers, despite lacking good looks and normal communication skills. Poor Avril is as dated as the Queen, overprotected, childlike, still stuck in the Fifties when children walked towards rainbows with their Clarks sandals properly fitted.

Oh my God.

This book is so utterly compelling she cannot believe what she's reading.

Never has she . . .

'*And the petty roundabout a woman must ride in order to reach her goal . . .*'

This is . . .

There are no . . .

Profane and shameless stuff from a nun posing in a state of grace. This woman is a set of wings, she is a suit of armour, with the black habit she dons and discards as her nefarious behaviour demands.

'*God deliberately created some of us to be evil. It is not for us to question why. It is up to us to worship, and on bended knee to give thanks for what we are.*'

Her first reaction is shock and confusion, before being drawn in by appalled fascination. She has to read on, breathless, excited. Some of this is outrageous, vile, she cannot believe it is here, in print, and that she could be so absorbed by such evil.

One hour passes. This is no good. Kirsty has to get up in the morning; if she reads any more she'll be exhausted, but she can't carry on reading in bed, cosy with the light on, without disturbing Avril and Bernie. Nor can she put this book down. So she creeps to the recreation room in her nightdress and her parka and curls up on a battered chaise longue; she can't put *Magdalene* down.

For these are no ordinary words.

This is not writing, this is witchcraft.

Everything in the world is forgotten as if it never existed.

'*I started my writing wearing gloves in a quiet corner of my room, covering each page with a hand as I went in case someone came up on me and learned the abominable secrets of my soul . . . like stone gargoyles on churches they were, be-winged devils straight out of hell . . .*'

Tense and taut through the weird experience, one moment Kirsty is laughing out loud, the next she is breaking her heart as she unconsciously curls up tighter, pulling her feet up under her and wrapping her arms round her knees, a variation of the foetal position because she feels in need of protection.

'*He who killed me with his smile had to die. I hated him for his treacherous tenderness. I loved him with the terrible burden of my own desire . . .*'

There is chaos in her brain as flash flash flash goes the book, connecting with Kirsty's most inner fears, speaking thoughts only she understands, riveting with its terrors, blood-curdling with its dangers. From blackmailer to martyr, one moment loving, the next depraved; the author terrifies, comforts and laughs like a close but alarming friend. No no no, yes yes yes, why why why, *be careful!* The book turns Kirsty lost and cold, as if she has wakened alone in a dark, strange room. '*Evil is not without purpose. I am a subterranean monster thrusting its head and mouth out of the earth in search of prey. Killing him is so sweetly easy . . .*' Occasionally Kirsty looks up, blinks and shakes her head like an owl, exhausted by emotional bombardment, but tenderness, humour and pity twist like wild roses through this blitzed landscape. Kirsty flies through the night on wings of exultation and courage, with a bigness in her head that is awesome.

Who is this person?

Kirsty is forced to pause, to wrench herself from the plot to find out.

Ellen Kirkwood.

Never heard of her.

This edition, in pristine condition save for the musty smell, was printed in 1913. The publishers, Bryant, list no other titles under the author's name. There is no biography, no photo, no clues.

The underlying story is simple, a tale of a woman and her awesome revenge, a black-veiled woman, a bride of Christ.

'*My entire being is filled by an awareness of him, trembling uncertainly between existence and annihilation . . .*'

If the force of this books grips Kirsty so violently then what about everyone else? The most incredible part is that a novel written all those years ago can strike the perfect chord today. It would only have to be slightly altered . . .

By the time Kirsty has finished, daylight is flooding through the streaky windows.

And all that makes the ending endurable is the knowledge that Kirsty can start at page one and read the whole lot over again.

Five

This could be disheartening. No decent person would choose to be introduced to this scrawny little blackguard, but Graham Stott, black sheep, ungrateful son and Avril's brother, has to be taken on board in order to be fully cognizant of Avril's lack of self-worth.

Life is so unfair. Graham's waist measures thirty and he tops the scales at ten stone exactly while poor old Avril . . .

Graham Stott prepares for parole after a three-year stint for burglary. It would have been longer, grievous bodily harm if the old biddy sleeping upstairs in the house had suddenly woken up, and the screw Mike Tarbuck despairs of a system that lets maniacs lose on the street when everyone knows they are worse than animals.

But Graham is homeless, poor lad.

Where on earth will he go?

With disbelief and raucous hilarity Avril and Bernie listened to Kirsty's outrageous plan.

'This is deeply immoral. You can't re-write a book and make out it's your own. It must be illegal for a start. What if you're caught? What if you're sued?'

Bernie took a more positive view. 'You're skint, she's skint, and they wouldn't send her down for that.'

'But what about your kids?' frowned Avril. 'They'd have a spiv for a mum.'

Kirsty was shocked by their response. This felt so right, it had to be done. The decision was taken, it was already out of her hands. It was more of an urge than a rational thought, a potent mixture of bliss and anger. 'You don't have to join me,' she said. 'But there'll be money in it, and a laugh.'

This sounded too crude for Kirsty.

'Count me in for the dosh,' said Bernie.

'What help could you be?' Avril scoffed. 'You're a moron, barely literate.'

'I'm the only one round here who's lived, and you need me for my experience of life.'

'You've both got to read it,' said Kirsty. Maybe her own reaction to *Magdalene* had been over the top, maybe the others would hate it. 'I'm going to bring it up to date, I know I can do that, no problem. Avril can read it while she's typing it up and if Bernie reads it when it's finished we'll know whether or not it's something special.'

'Well, it looks dead boring to me,' said Bernie, eying the mass of small print, weighing the book in a drooping right hand.

But Avril is grateful for a chance to do something really useful. When they'd first arrived she'd thought Kirsty didn't like her, that she saw her as fat and boring, and at first she'd been hurt by Bernie's teasing, but now she'd got this relationship going and had the chance to contribute something solid. 'I'll nick an audio machine from the office and you can try that out. It would be quicker, and then I can type it up in my lunch hours.'

Kirsty's gratitude was warming and pleasing, as was the way she sympathized with Avril's on-going homesickness.

'People find it hard to like me,' she once confided to Kirsty. 'That's why you two are so special. Strangers seem to try and avoid me, but I try so hard to be warm and polite.'

' "Smile and the world smiles with you" is a wicked lie,' said Kirsty. 'Smile and they think something's seriously up.'

Avril irritates. She is always offering her services, sharing her snacks and smiling. Prepared to put herself out for other people's convenience, she would make an excellent vicar's wife. But Avril is an invader of personal space in the way that cats rub strangers' legs. Yet she's sensitive to the point of obsession. There's no way she can handle the young pretender who runs the office, man-about-town, son-in-law of the dithering minibus driver, Colonel Parker, no matter how desperately she tries to please. She finds his military directness unnerving and Avril is greatly relieved that she works in the outer office and is not his personal assistant. That dubious privilege rests with Meryl Pudsey, a bag of nerves and no wonder.

Mr Derek, as they must call him, although this makes him sound like a hairdresser, is conceited, rude and impatient. He is a Mills and Boon hero come unhappily to life, the kind of man you think you might marry before you meet him in the flesh: strong, demanding and good-looking, with the square jaw of the craggy. On the first day, Avril fell foul of him because she was flustered when he came for the post. Naturally she was flustered, she had never sorted post before, and as her fingers grew larger and fatter and finally lost all control, she could sense his rage burgeoning inside him like a bloodied alien about to burst out from under that stiff, striped waistcoat and starched white shirt.

How different from comfortable Daddy in his cardigans with their leather buttons, shiny and tempting as new conkers.

'Just leave it,' he'd barked with exasperation, eyes whisking hither and thither. 'Go and sit down, who- ever you are. Leave it, damn you! Can't you see you're making things worse with your clumsy fussing?'

As tears threatened Avril's baby-blue eyes, as she chewed her dolly-pink lips, the thought of Mother came floating to mind, Mother in her fireside chair reading the *Daily Mail*, light from the standard lamp pooling her beiges in a pink glow of safety. But the game Miss Pudsey came to her rescue. 'It's just his way,' she said through a slightly twitching mouth that belied her calm. 'Take no notice of Mr Derek. His bark is worse than his bite.'

'He's a prick,' said Kirsty.

'He's a wanker,' said Bernie.

How Avril dreads the moment when her personal extension will buzz and Mr Derek will call her in with his now familiar, 'If you please.'

'Will there be bullies all through my life? Will they pick me out like beady-eyed seagulls pouncing on hot dogs?'

'There's a huge notice on your back that shouts out "hurt me". We must find out why and change it,' said Bernie.

At the summons of Mr Derek, Avril gathers her notebook and enters his office with a watery knock. She mustn't wait for any 'come in', that would only madden him further. All those beautiful clothes so carefully chosen by Mother are a total waste of time. Whatever she wears she feels fat and foolish the moment she flops over his threshold.

Fast and accurate mean little to her now.

Perhaps it would have been kinder to the students if Avril's business studies course had employed the odd cantankerous male tutor.

Wherever the six feet four manager goes he uses a stiff-backed rush, so his legs move faster than the rest of his body, as if he's riding a penny farthing.

But Avril will not be defeated. Spurred on by her recent social success Avril tries to befriend Rhoda, one of the few locals employed by the Burleston. But Rhoda with the rook's nest hair is careless and lazy, taking advantage of Avril's soft nature whenever she gets the chance, slipping extra work her way, taking an overlong mid-morning break, skipping off early and using the phone for personal calls whenever Miss Pudsey is out. She nicks pens, too, and smokes her menthol cigarettes in the ground-floor guests' bathrooms. When she throws the stubs down the loo, no matter how often you pull the chain shreds of tobacco come bobbing back up and someone is bound to report it.

And what if they think it's Avril?

*   *   *

'It is a tendency with you', said Mother on the phone, 'to rush things, dear. You can't expect everything to come up roses after only one week.'

'I don't expect roses, Mother, but I do expect civility and fairness. Is that too much to ask?' said Avril, with a choke in her voice. 'Well, is it?'

'No, dear, of course not. But you must bear in mind that Mr Derek is the boss and he shoulders many heavy burdens. It's not for him to go home and shed the problems of the day by turning on the TV over a bowl of cornflakes like your father. Oh no, a man like that is permanently on the go, tussling with important business problems. Backbiting, Avril, is no answer. Look what happened to the Conservative Party.'

But I'm efficient and fast, Avril wanted to wail, but I just don't get given a chance. It's not easy . . . there's hardly any straightforward typing. Instead she said, 'Some of the guests can be very demanding.'

'Naturally,' said Mother in her best customer-complaints voice. 'And wouldn't you be demanding if you were paying those kinds of prices?' as if she was buying vests from British Home Stores. 'You must remember, Avril, that you are a small cog in a vast machine, an essential cog, but a small one, dear, and it's up to you to put your heart into what you are doing so the machine can run smoothly.'

It is to the desk that the guests come if they have complaints or face complications. Because Rhoda sits with her back to the foyer, she pretends she can't see them and Avril is left to face the music.

'I asked for my tea at eight thirty . . .'

'Can you arrange these connections on Friday week for me and my husband . . . ?'

'No, I never used the telephone, that item should not be on my bill . . .'

'So why don't you give cash back?'

'That's all very well, but where is Nanny? I made it quite clear to her that I would pick Jonathan up here in the foyer after lunch.'

'I had a golf lesson booked with the pro and the man had the cheek to forget.'

And so on and so forth.

The cruellest offenders are the Miss Lewises, Peg and Vi, who have been coming to the Burleston for an early summer holiday since their parents used to bring them when they were just knee-high. These two Devon-violet old ladies expect, demand even, superstar attention, and are poisonous if they fail to get it.

They called her a dozy lump yesterday, and although Avril is used to being tormented because of her build – at school they called her Jumbo, quite an affectionate term, although Avril didn't see it that way – she believed that when she started work and entered the sensible world of adults she would leave such stigmatizing behind.

'You want to get off that big bottom of yours more often,' carped Peg Lewis, gathering up her rook-black cardigan and shaking it aggressively when Avril was slow to produce the key.

'I'm sorry.' Avril gaped, undefended and unwilling to absorb such an insult.

'They take anyone these days,' quipped the equally venomous sister, Vi, as they both tottered off towards the lift muttering under their breaths.

There was no-one to complain to. Mr Derek was out of the question and Meryl Pudsey didn't have the clout.

She longed for the understanding arms of Kirsty or Bernie.

When six thirty arrives Avril feels drained. This mixing with people is what finishes her. Any amount of shorthand, typing, menu-drafting, columns, indentations, noticeboard information, photo-copies – four, ten or fifty – she could knock all this off with her eyes closed, no problem. It's when it comes to people. She often grabs a quick, cold supper and goes straight to bed dreading tomorrow.

'You don't know you're born,' she moans at Bernie. 'No wonder I have mean, horrid thoughts, sometimes you make me so jealous that I feel sick and then hate myself for my wickedness. The whole thing's a vicious circle. Why is life so damned unfair? Every day you fend off men who ask you out clubbing or dancing. Why do men always go for the obvious?'

Bernie drags at her twisted fag. She picks tobacco off a shapely lip. 'I've got the gift of the gab and a face that might have launched ships, I suppose that makes men like me, but never the sort I really want. Why is it never the people I want?'

Kirsty remembers an article she read saying beautiful children have the advantage of being subconsciously preferred by teachers: beautiful children or just kids with attractive names. Examiners give higher marks to students with names like Victoria or Anastasia, while those with names like

Avril or June get stuck at the bottom of the list. No wonder Avril is jealous. Bernie could throw on an old sack, shake her shaggy head and look good, whereas Avril sleeps with rollers in and takes ages to adjust her tights and make sure she's got no panty line showing.

And Kirsty isn't the only one who is ultra-perceptive. 'I knew you were on the run when I saw you on the train,' says Bernie, in one of the few conversations when she forgets and stops talking about herself.

'And I thought you were hiding,' says Avril, flopped on her bed in her dressing gown, resting after a hellish day.

Bernie leans towards the fly-blown mirror on the chest of drawers in their threadbare room and pulls down one cheek before expertly drawing a black line under her eye.

'Hiding from the law.' One of Avril's favourite pursuits is watching *Crimewatch* on telly and hoping that she might recognize someone, posing herself that heinous problem: would she snitch on a neighbour? Would she even turn in her dad if she suspected him of some terrible crime such as rape or murder? She has sensibly decided she would talk to him first, and give him the choice between going for treatment or facing the full panoply of the law. But what if it was a child he had hurt?

'No. From a man. It's always a man.' Bernie attacks her other eye. Perhaps Bernie will show Avril how to apply eyeliner properly.

So Bernie had guessed.

'It's probably all in this book of yours,' says Bernie, filling the room with the pear-drop aroma

79

of cheaply perfumed lacquer. 'That's probably why you're obsessed by it, you identify with the story.'

Bernie reckons her Irish blood links her to writers and artists. She brags that she went round with them at Dublin University, she drank with them in candlelit cellar bars, she smoked with them in attic digs, she sat with them beside rivers and made music with guitars and harmonicas. Dominic Coates was an artist, she says, an artist at making love. And then the wretched Bernie cries, but even when she cries she looks charming, unlike Avril, bug-eyed and raw-cheeked.

'One day I'm going to get even, if it's the last thing I do.'

Eventually even Avril shared her sad love life with her friends.

At first Avril lied and told them she went out with Guy Fleming, a boy she'd had a crush on when she was in the fourth year at school. 'We were thinking about getting married, of course,' Avril ad libbed, 'but then I thought eighteen was far too young, that we should both see something of the world before we took a decision like that.'

'So you came down here?' said Bernie. 'Jaysus and all the saints, will you look at us.'

'Well, just to get experience. After this season's over I might try and get a job on a cruise ship.'

'Oh yeah? We're all the victims of men in one way or the other,' said Bernie, dragging on the tight black dress she wears to the bar in the evenings. 'Aren't we? We've all been forced into coming here to escape from something we're afraid of.'

'Well I certainly haven't,' Avril retorted defensively, so relieved that she wasn't having to get dressed again and go off to work.

How could Bernie be so shamelessly frank about her humiliation? How could she feel comfortable advertising to the world the way she was spurned, betrayed, made a fool of by a man she worshipped? If that ever happened to Avril she would keep her lips sealed, just as she never told a soul about the note she left in Guy Fleming's bicycle bag, the note declaring her love and her availability. She left it there just before the end-of-summer-term disco, suspecting that, once again, she would be the only girl in the class there without a boy. Perhaps if Guy Fleming, dark, tanned and athletic, realized she was prepared to open her legs for him, he would make an exception just this once for the sake of an easy lay.

Well, Mother made it perfectly clear that sex was the main thing boys were after, and that after they'd used you they despised you, thinking you cheap and tarty. Avril would happily be despised for the sake of having a partner at the end-of-term disco.

Her note read, 'Dear Guy. I think you are the most attractive boy in the school. Sometimes I watch you at break time and wish I was with you. I would do anything for you, *and I mean anything*. If you want to see how true this is, meet me at the end-of-term disco. Love from Avril Stott.'

That night she hardly slept for excitement and tantalizing hope. 'You're in an odd mood, Avril,' said Mother, eagle-eyed. Avril felt a huge sense of fondness, not just for Mother, but for her whole family, even the hapless Graham. She had such energy she changed her own sheets, tidied her room and even her drawers.

Shame on him.

They were gathered round the school gates when she arrived the next day, Guy Fleming and his crowd, all smirking and messing about. Dear God, she had never in her worst dreams imagined that Guy would stoop so low as to show her letter to all his friends, surely he understood that her words came straight from the heart, and that to do this was to crucify her.

Her hope and happiness melted away and lay like boulders in her stomach.

'Hey, Aaaavril,' they shouted in silly voices, 'what d'you mean by *anything*? Come on, fatty, show us what you mean by *anything*.'

'How about the art room in break?'

'Give you ten p for a feel of yer muff.'

'For a wank.'

'Show us yer titties, jumbo.'

Then one of them held out a condom and snapped it in front of her eyes.

Shaking all over she walked on.

It wasn't long before the whole class knew.

Guy Fleming pinned the note on the board.

She spent the evening of the disco at home watching telly with Mother and Father. She got in the bath that night, eyes red with weeping and wrapped in a dull hopelessness that floated around her with the scummy water. She scrubbed her offending parts with a nail brush until they bled, parts she had been willing to sacrifice, but parts so unworthy that they didn't even tempt Guy Fleming to be seen with her at the end-of-term disco.

When finally Avril shared this secret, when she felt she trusted her friends, when she confessed in the dark, in whispers, one night, the three of them laughed till they wept, and Avril's laugh was the worst of all. She was eventually forced to get out of bed and creep down the dark corridor to the loo, giggling and hiccuping all the way. It was a most wonderful cleansing.

But Bernadette has no such inhibitions.

'Bernadette Kavanagh, you have no pride, and that is your trouble,' said Avril.

But look, life for poor, homesick Avril is taking on a new meaning. The following day, in her lunch break, she starts to input Kirsty's novel, copying the first few pages from the author's own hopeless typing, but continuing at a much faster rate once Kirsty starts using the tapes. She has never been so totally absorbed by anything she has read in her life . . .

'No, you go off, I'll cover for you,' Avril tells the shirking Rhoda, heart beating, pulses racing.

'Are you sure?' Rhoda pauses, peers nosily over her shoulder. 'What are you doing anyway?'

Avril doesn't want to share this new, overwhelming experience. 'Oh nothing important. Just catching up with some stuff . . .'

Such passion. Such drama. Suddenly she is exhilarated, expectant and alive, almost thrusting.

This author can read Avril's thoughts. Even ones she never knew she had.

She is enraged when guests come flapping round with their foolish orders. 'Sod off, you buggers,' she wants to shout, totally out of character. It is only when Mr Derek returns that Avril reluctantly exits the disk and changes it. She will stay on this evening to finish the tape, and she hopes that Kirsty will have more, a good, long, juicy chunk for her to read tomorrow, because while she is gripped by this novel everything else in her comfortless world fades into pale insignificance.

Six

The adored one.

Bernie's *raison d'être*.

Another character we would rather not meet.

Son and heir to a fortune made from the manufacture of cardboard boxes, young, dark and handsome Dominic Coates looks down at the naked woman in his bed whose name he cannot remember. *Shit.* How will he get out of this one? Why do women cling so? They imagine their open legs are church doors, their fannies the rings they desire on their fingers, their grunts and screams of passion the responses they intend to make at the altar. One big mistake last year that almost resulted in disaster and the parents, hung up on ideas of self-discipline, have sent him to Cornwall for the summer . . . as a lifeguard in St Ives . . . *I ask you.*

'We have got some serious complaints to make regarding the falling standards in this hotel.'

Mr Derek sighs with professional acceptance as he holds open the door of his office to admit the Miss Lewises – *again.* Why the hell do these two old bitches keep coming here if they're so bloody pissed off with it? And why stay a month? It's not as though they enjoy themselves or make use of the facilities: they rarely use the bar or the fridge in their rooms, they never dine à la carte, they pick the same back room every year, the cheapest in the hotel because of its proximity to the lift shaft, and they never tip anyone, ever.

There have been disturbing reports from the staff that they pee in the sink in their room. Mr Derek would rather not know how that rumour came to be.

'Do come and sit down, ladies.'

'If it's not one thing it's another,' starts Peg Lewis, warming up to her favourite subject: the hopelessness of the staff.

'It is the thin end of the wedge,' her sister, Vi, joins in with shaky, arthritic enthusiasm.

Mr Derek wrings his hands. 'You know how difficult it is these days to find people with the right sort of attitude. We at the Burleston try our best to ensure . . .'

'Don't try that smarmy political clap-trap on us,' snaps Miss Peg testily. 'What's the time, dear?' she asks her sister.

'Nearly nine,' replies Miss Vi.

Miss Peg does some quick addition in her head. 'Well, in that case, if it's nearly nine we have been sitting in the quiet lounge for over an hour and a half waiting for our after-dinner tea. We told the girl we would be in the lounge. We are always in the lounge after dinner.'

'Perhaps if you had reminded her earlier and not sat waiting for quite so long . . .'

Miss Peg smiles triumphantly, the lines on her face stretching tautly like bundles of elastic bands. 'So it's our fault.' She turns to her sister. 'What did I tell you, Vi? Mr Derek, how many times would you suggest that we order our after-dinner tea? *Two, three, four or more?*'

Mr Derek brings a tired hand over a wearied brow. 'I am sorry. It is quite clear that somebody forgot—'

'And that is not all,' goes on Miss Peg. 'Last week we were in the quiet lounge when a member of your cleaning staff came in quite brazenly and started sorting through the books on the shelves in there. Now, I am no snob, Mr Derek, but when you pay huge sums for exclusivity from the masses, you do expect to find it.'

'I will speak to the person concerned,' says Mr Derek sorrowfully. 'I can assure you that this will not happen again . . .'

'Because if every Tom, Dick and Harry came and removed books at whim, the guests' choice of reading would be reduced severely. What if Vi or I had been in need of some holiday reading? Not that either of us would dream of coming away without our own books; there is something so distasteful about the feel of books leant to all and sundry. Vi and I stopped visiting the local library long ago, as we found so many books torn and stained.'

'Don't forget that other girl, Peg. The fat one with the attitude problem.'

'Ah yes, I was coming to that, Vi dear. There is somebody new in your reception. A slow, bumbling girl who looks as if she'd be more at home in a cow shed, to be perfectly honest. She has no charm or poise, Mr Derek. Half the time she looks vacant. And the other day, when I chided her for her dilatory attitude, she just stood there gaping like a fish with a hook in its mouth. It is not a good advertisement for your hotel to have a girl like that at the front desk. First impressions are important, and yet she is the first thing you see when you enter the Burleston.'

'I think I know who you mean.'

'I am quite sure you do.'

'Miss Stott is a willing worker if a little inexperienced.'

'She is certainly willing. She is still there now in the back office, typing away, trying to catch up, no doubt.'

'But your immediate problem is with one of the bar staff?'

'Yes,' nods Miss Vi, her stringy chicken neck expanding like an accordion. 'That is where we ordered our tea. And all I can say is it wasn't Charlie. Now Charlie is an excellent barman. No, it's that Irish person with the absurdly tight dress. She never looks as if she is listening . . . miles away . . . dreaming of some chap, no doubt.'

'If you would be so good as to return to the lounge I will bring you your tea myself, ladies.'

'And do we get no compensation for this lackadaisical treatment?'

'The tea is already in with the meal,' he hastens to remind them.

'Then perhaps a couple of schooners of sweet

sherry? Not too much to ask, surely, when my sister and I have been treated with such lamentable negligence?'

'Of course, with my compliments and apologies,' says Mr Derek, bowing a defeated head as he gets up to open the door.

Cowbags.

'I passed the order down to the kitchen and then forgot all about it,' Bernadette apologizes in her husky voice. 'We're very busy tonight, Mr Derek. It's the kitchen's fault for not bringing it up. If they'd brought it up I would have served it.'

'Pour me a double Scotch please, dear, and I'll have it when I come back.'

Thus Mr Derek disappears humbly with a silver tray and a pot of tea and two fluted glasses of sickly sweet Bristol Cream.

Just how near to the verge of madness is Bernadette Kavanagh creeping? Why are her smouldering green eyes fixed on the door of the bar even now, hoping against hope that the next person through it will be Dominic Coates? She clenches her fists and drives her nails into her hands, fighting against the great hope, but it goes on rising, attacking her throat with an emptiness and anticipation that forms one great, tragic delight. There is not enough going on around here to take her mind off her lost beloved, not even when they are busy, not even when the orders roll in and she's flirting with some other customer and adding up prices, wiping glasses and working the till at the same time.

Talking to her friends doesn't help. Talking about him fuels the passion.

God help her.

'You really should be over it by now,' Kirsty told her unhelpfully last night. 'After all, it's been a year. Perhaps you need counselling.'

'What I need is something massive, a war, an earthquake, a hurricane, something so huge that it sits on my head and blots him out completely.'

'Drama queen,' laughed Kirsty, for once failing to pay proper attention, head down behind that scratched swing mirror narrating her dratted novel. The constant sound of her voice is soothing, as if someone is quietly praying, and it reminds Bernie of how Mammy was after she lost her last.

'I should have been an actress,' agreed Bernie, 'somewhere to put my passion. I was good at it at school. I love being somebody else.'

'You should try another relationship.' Kirsty is trying to cheer her up, but even talking about Dominic seems to bring him closer. 'Give it a chance. It's not as if you lack choices.'

'It would be different if I was rich,' said Bernie, rolling a thin cigarette. 'If I was rich I'd have so many options. I could travel, couldn't I just, I could buy a powerful sports car, I could go to posh London clubs and dance the night away.' She looked around her sadly, taking in the mean little room with its curling wallpaper and patchy rainbow carpet. 'Go wild. Let my hair down. But if I'd been rich he'd never have left me.'

This is her garden of Gethsemane.

Perhaps she should have a little fling with the

dandy, superior Mr Derek; he obviously fancies her, and the difference between his attitude to her and to the unfortunate Avril is so obvious it's embarrassing.

From the bar she can hear him venting his spleen on her shy friend in the office.

'And what the hell do you think you are doing working at this late hour? The office should be closed by now. The night porter is already on duty. Anyone would think you were keen when all I get are moans and groans about your lazy attitude.'

'I'm sorry Mr Derek . . .

'Well pack it up, whatever you're damn well doing, and when you next see the Miss Lewises it might help if you apologized, and for God's sake, girl,' he sighs, 'smarten yourself up and jump to it in future.'

Poor Avril. She means to please. She's right, life is very unfair.

Mr Derek returns to the bar and downs his Scotch in three desperate gulps.

'Another one, sir?' Bernie asks him.

'Oh go on then. Why not?'

Men are nice to Bernie and she knows the effect she has on them. Mr Derek has no intention of tearing the kind of strip off her that he tore off the inoffensive Avril. Poor man. Married to sweet Sophie, only child of Colonel Parker by his third wife, Dulcie. Sweet Sophie, her senile father's darling, is not a well woman; she requires constant pampering, and is forever reminding Derek that if he hadn't married her he would have ended up the manager of some tatty little dive in Newquay. No wonder Mr Derek, who loves to lord it as managing owner of a five-star hotel, takes out his many frustrations on those weaker than himself.

'Damn, damn, damn. I might as well deal with it while I'm here.'

Mr Derek picks up the phone and dials six.

'Mrs Stokes? Ah, you are there. I have had a complaint from the Miss Lewises about members of staff visiting the main hotel in the evening to borrow books from the quiet lounge.'

There is a pause while he listens impatiently.

'Well, if you did give permission kindly refrain from doing so in future. And have a word with the young lady in question.' He puts down the phone, '*My God,*' he says in a strangled voice, 'that daft old crone, as if I didn't have enough on my plate.'

Trawling for sympathy.

Bernie looks him over. Perhaps she ought to give him the eye. Although in his mid-forties he has taken care of himself, no paunch, smooth-shaven, clear eyes, if vaguely haunted. But she knows his type, she knows how he would perform in bed: automatically, with the striped-pyjama mentality of an English gent, still firmly believing the results of surveys he reads surreptitiously in women's magazines. What sort of women fill in these surveys? Only men still believe that women are turned on by smoothies posturing, lads with firm arses, that women enjoy arousing their partners by boring and relentless rubbing, swallowing handfuls of sperm, sucking a wrinkled penis dry to the rhythm of a Strauss waltz.

They know nothing of frenzied African drums. They miss the sultry tragedy of 'Private Dancer'. They don't know what can be done with a feather.

92

'I suppose it's straight to bed for you when you've finished this duty,' enquires Mr Derek with a randy gleam in his eye.

'Usually, yes,' says Bernie, casually serving another customer.

'All work and no play . . .' suggests Mr Derek transparently, one elbow resting on the bar, one finger running round the rim of his glass.

'It's all work at the Burleston, for sure, there's little doubt about that.'

Mr Derek slowly works himself up. His finger moves faster round his glass till it rings. 'And anyway, what's someone with your looks doing in a hotel bar? You could be a model. An actress. I bet you've got a good singing voice, too.'

Bernie draws her tongue round her lips. Her Irish eyes are smiling. What a fool he is making of himself. 'You're right. Ah yes. How different life could have been.'

'If . . . ?' prompts Mr Derek hopefully.

'If I'd stayed away from men,' says Bernie.

'*That woman.*' Kirsty feels like weeping. 'You'd think we were back in the dark ages. She gave me permission to look for a book and now she marches in here and suggests that I went into that damned quiet lounge like a Millwall fan on the rampage.'

It is rare for Kirsty to be awake when Bernie comes off duty. It is even rarer for Kirsty to express any strong feeling, like anger.

'For the love of Jesus, take no notice.' Bernie is thoroughly ashamed. How had she considered Mr Derek?

'And now I've got to replace the books and never darken the quiet lounge again.'

'So what? Sod them. You can keep *Magdalene* back. They'll never know it's missing.'

Avril, too, is nursing her grievances, hugging her knees in her spartan bed.

'I heard him bullying you,' Bernie commiserates. 'He went too far, sad little bastard. But think on it, a few more months and all this will be over.'

'But I don't think I can stand a few more months,' Avril wails. 'If it wasn't for you two I'd have gone home already.'

'How about you?' Bernie asks Kirsty.

'I've got to stay because of the kids. If I can get on the caravan site I'll have a job and a home.'

'I can think of better places. There's nothing here, it's shit.'

'Have faith. Five chapters go off tomorrow with Kirsty's synopsis. That's what they said they wanted in the yearbook in the library.'

'But we can't depend on that.' Bernie leaves her fag to smoke in her bedside ashtray while she undresses. 'Think how many people write books that never get off the ground.'

'Wait till you read it, Bernie. This is amazing, awesome,' says Avril, recovering from her dressing down, sniffing only occasionally now, while correcting the last few pages before handing them back to Kirsty.

'I already told you, I won't like it, I'm not used to books.' Bernie scrubs off the last of her make-up with some filthy bits of brown cotton wool. 'They're too much of an effort. They're boring. And anyway, how will you get it finished now Avril can't work in the evenings? And then what if they do accept it, you won't get much for one old book unless you're the right sort of glamorous person.'

'Oh yes? And you are, I suppose?' mocks Avril.

'I am. Or I could be. Just give me the chance.' Hah. What would the Coates family say if Bernadette Kavanagh turned into a famous author? Almost better than being an actress because it looks as if you've got brains. 'All those first nights. Think of the clothes you'd have to have. Film contracts. Telly appearances. Round-the-world publicity tours. I read about it once in *Take a Break*. There was this girl who'd never been near the States and she made it all up from brochures . . .'

'Hardly that,' says Kirsty, 'but we could get a couple of grand.'

'We could get more,' says Avril, seemingly cheered after Mr Derek's vicious attack. 'It's a thousand times better than anything I've ever read.'

'Who are we sending it to?' asks Bernie. 'How did you decide?'

'I chose the agent who seemed the most friendly and there's a list of authors under their names. I went for the one with the longest list.'

'What if we don't hear anything back?'

'We'll try another; there's hundreds,' says Avril.

'So what will we honestly get out of this?' Bernie tugs at the sheets and blankets provided by the Burleston, who have refused to up-date with duvets. To Avril's dismay she relights the stub of her old cigarette. 'Apart from the thrill of doing it?'

'Someone like you wouldn't understand, but I have enjoyed typing it up, and I'm glad to help Kirsty out.'

'Jesus, Avril, get real, you sound like a nun – sanctimonious prat. God meant us to have some joy, didn't he? It can't all be burdens?'

'You are selfish and wicked and full of uncharitable thoughts,' says Avril. 'Money's not the only motive.'

'But it's all so sad,' Bernie explodes. 'Look at us now. Here we are, young and fit and fancy-free, working like nerds in this armpit all summer and making up crazy dreams. Rats in cages. While somewhere out there there's a whole world waiting; mountains are beckoning, lagoons are calling, exotic, hot lands of camels and spices tease us with every poster we see. Any one of these super-rich cretins who come to the Burleston every year could be languishing on a cruise liner now somewhere off the Maldives for little more than the exorbitant sum they have to pay for a double room here.'

'Yeah. Dickheads.'

Since the weather has calmed, since the air has turned warm and caressing, the dickheads clamber to the cove each morning with their beach bags and their children. Down in the cove there is waterskiing, snorkelling, surfing and sailing, and the Jack Tar beach bar, run by the Burleston, is doing a steady trade. But although the setting is charming, with its winding pathways of rhododendrons, the clean white sand, the fringe of fir trees and the unexpectedly clear water, although dolphins can sometimes be spied with a pair of expensive binoculars, who the hell would choose Cornwall if you had the whole of the world to explore?

'Not I,' says Bernie, 'not I,' as she slides into sleep, curled up around Boots' own rose talcum powder and troubled dreams full of passionate hunger.

Seven

High in her cubicle office in Gatsby House, Mayfair, powerfully dressed literary agent Candice Love leans back in her swivel chair. Her designer spectacles slide down her nose as she drags over the slush pile – unsolicited manuscripts that arrive like daily bread and which, when stale, fall to any unfortunate with a spare moment to peruse the first page of each before slapping it back in its stamped addressed envelope along with the standard rejection letter.

Some of the authors' covering letters are so damn illiterate there is no point in starting.

Everyone has a book in them somewhere, and everyone seems to have picked this point in time in Candice's busy, busy life to give their one book the fling it deserves.

Candice, an ambitious young woman, has rarely read further than page one. Few she saw ever merited it. Most of what she sees is crap, but it's precious crap, she knows that, and it pays to be careful in this business. One never knows when one might pick up a gem. She slithers one leg across the other, confident in her power-dress purple with its snazzy little jacket; her bangles jangle as she pokes back her specs with one well-manicured fingernail and settles down for a no-doubt wasted half hour before lunch.

While Candice Love tries her hardest to concentrate, the stocky Trevor Hoskins is using his Gas Board van for more personal business than ever before.

He will get caught if he's not careful.

How that miserable cow ever plucked up the courage to get up and leave him is beyond understanding. She hasn't disobeyed him in years; he can't remember when she last raised her voice and he's certain that she has been influenced by some of those lezzy women's lib bitches you see in curtains and crew-cuts. How they got their hands on Kirsty is a puzzle he is determined to solve.

But why does Trevor want her back if he despises her to the extent of putting her in hospital and turning her into a quivering wreck?

That is not the point. The point, as he informs his mate Greg, is that Kirsty is his wife goddammit; she owes him for eight years of support, eight years of working eight to six up other people's pipes and under their floorboards. OK, she did her bit for £2.42 an hour at the nearby superstore, but it was him, Trevor Hoskins, who fed her and the bleeding kids, gave them a roof over their heads and saw to it that her worst excesses were kept under control.

Let's face it, Kirsty was hopeless with money, soft on the kids, a poor cook, a lazy housewife, miserable in bed, and forever sticking her nose in those books that gave her uppity ideas.

*   *   *

'But my wife had no right to take my kiddies from school without my permission.'

'I am sorry, Mr Hoskins,' says Mrs Barnes the junior-school head when finally he gets to see her after sitting around in a miniature chair. 'We had no idea the situation was a delicate one. Your wife merely informed us that she was taking Gemma and Jake on holiday, and as the children broke up that week anyway, we considered their education would not suffer markedly. We have always dealt with your wife in the past, Mr Hoskins, and we saw no reason why this time would be any different.'

Trevor listens impatiently. Shit. They've got answers for every bleeding thing these jumped-up farts. Just because he is wearing overalls. 'But did she say where they were going?'

Mrs Barnes thinks for a while. 'No, no she didn't mention her destination, I'm afraid. The children might have talked to their friends. We could ask them if you . . .'

'Don't bother.' Kirsty wouldn't be so careless.

'I am sure she will be in touch soon.'

His look stops Mrs Barnes in her tracks. 'And when this is over I'm going to demand a bleeding inquiry into this, make no mistake. I'm not one of your retards, I know my rights and I know bloody well that what you did is negligent.' Trevor gets up and storms towards the door with a backwards, 'My wife is off her bleeding chump, in case you didn't know, Mrs I-know-it-all Barnes, and what d'you think the law is going to make of that?'

In fact the law are no more helpful. Trevor gives them his name and address, describes the children, gives their ages, but when he is asked for his doctor's name his patience snaps. 'What the bleeding hell d'you want with him?'

'If your wife is mentally ill we need to know more about her condition and only her doctor can tell us that.'

'She never went to the bleeding doctor.'

The policeman's hand pauses a while over the form on the desk. 'So your wife never had treatment for this condition of hers?'

'She wouldn't go for sodding treatment, would she, she was too daft to know she was mad.'

The policeman's voice is polite and considerate. It is hard to know which way his mind is going. 'And you never insisted, for the sake of the children?'

'You didn't know Kirsty,' Trevor says darkly, running an angry hand over his close-cropped, fuzzy, action-man hair. 'What I had to put up with no bugger knows. And my bleeding kids are in danger.'

'I will discuss this with my superior,' says the gormless copper, 'make some further enquiries and let you know what we decide.'

Now the very same morning as Candice Love snails her way through the slush pile, the selfsame morning as Trevor Hoskins visits his local cop shop, Kirsty, on her second day off, sets out to visit the caravan site, Happy Stay. There is no transport so she walks.

Kirsty is not used to the country, to the narrow lanes without pavements, the badly positioned signposts that look like pictures out of Dick Whittington, the delicious smells of wild flowers occasionally interrupted by little puffs of death from the hedgerows where some small creature, seeping and putrid, is hidden away in the thorns.

She has never been deceitful before, save in defence against Trevor, so this exercise with *Magdalene* has come as a great surprise. But the determination and strength to use another author's book had swamped her so utterly and with such mighty, obsessive force that there was none of the usual weighing up of problems, absolutely no conscience probings or concerns about being caught.

It was like being hit by a stone on the temple.

So what if she is exposed as a fraud?

As Bernie says, if they prosecute her she has no money, no home, nothing to give up save her children and surely this is the kind of crime that doesn't merit time behind bars? The author, Ellen Kirkwood, is probably long dead, and the book itself must be years out of print. She is doing no harm to anyone, if anything she is awakening people, because if *Magdalene* brings to others a fraction of the shocked understanding it gave her and Avril, where is the wrong in that?

And anyway, no-one will know.

Not that Kirsty honestly believes the enterprise will get very far in spite of Avril's enthusiasm. She doesn't tend to have that sort of luck, and her Mills and Boon experience does little for her understanding of all things literary. Kirsty's education may have been mediocre, but she is far from stupid. She knows all this very well. Publishing a book never crossed her mind until her hypnotism by *Magdalene*. Since then the book has changed her life, the rewriting process is so intense and intriguing it has turned into a sacred mission.

'*Magdalene was, of course, very much interested*' had to turn into 'Magdalene listened hard'.

'*He expressed the greatest satisfaction*' was simply changed to, 'He was thrilled'.

'*But though not a motive to action, the thoughts in which this dream is shrined bid fair to make action sweet*' was translated to say, 'It seemed like a good idea'.

It was that sort of thing, simplifying the wordy style into ordinary everyday language. Most of the text, luckily, was able to stand as it was.

But as the days roll by and Kirsty hears nothing, she and Avril – who has bravely ignored Mr Derek's unkindness and works until nine o'clock every night – are nearing the end; they finished the last batch on page 704.

'It's a blockbuster,' said Avril, trying, once again, to count the words without the aid of a calculator. 'The longest book I've ever read was *Roots* and I had to hide it because Mother disapproved – I put a Maeve Binchy cover on it – and it must be as long as that.'

The Happy Stay caravan park is one enormous grey campus of concrete with square patches of dry grass in between. It stretches way back from the cliff top to adjoin the coast road half a mile back, from one promontory to the other. You can tell which vans are permanent homes because they have picket fences and flower beds, but all have names, some yearning names like Seawinds, Osprey and The Nook, and some romantic like Joyvern and Glendoris.

'I'll show you the sort of thing,' offers Mrs

Gilcrest, the owner, closing down the shop with a stained yellow placard in order to take Kirsty to one of the larger 'bungalow homes'. 'This one's empty, but only until tonight. We don't normally let from Sundays but they agreed to pay for the extra day and that's up to them.'

'I have two children,' Kirsty explains immediately.

'No problem. There's several kiddies live here.'

'How about school?'

'There's a bus,' says Mrs Gilcrest, puffing, keys round her waist like a gaoler. 'The council have to run it by law because the school's five miles away and they reckon kiddies can't walk that far. It was quite different in my day, of course.'

The wind gets up as they near the cliff top and windbreaks have been erected round some of the little green squares. Behind these squares sunbathers shiver in the draughts coming from under the vast caravans; those who prefer to remain near home rather than take the torturous track down to the beach with all their belongings.

'Here we are, four-oh-nine.' Mrs Gilcrest climbs the three small steps and unlocks the dented cream door.

'It's much bigger than I thought,' says Kirsty, imagining how the children would cope in such a confined space in the winter. They would play out a lot, she supposes, something they rarely did when they lived at 24 Barkers Terrace because Trevor couldn't stand it. The noise of the neighbouring kids drove him barmy and, as the small gardens were open-plan, to confine them to their own was impossible.

It is almost too far-fetched to hope for, but if, by some miracle, *Magdalene* is accepted, she might just make enough money to be able to buy an old banger that would make living here bearable. The poor wages paid by the Burleston mean she will qualify for family credit, but if life becomes too hard she'll just go on the dole until she can find a job that pays better.

'There's more than fifty bungalows permanently occupied,' Mrs Gilcrest explains in between pointing out the charms of the well-designed, practical caravan. 'But it can feel lonely here in the winter. And the weather does tend to be wet most of the time.'

I can tolerate this, thinks Kirsty. I can tolerate anything so long as I'm not constantly on edge, trying to please and failing, steeling myself for the next blow, the next humiliation, the next shock.

So long as I've got *Magdalene*.

'This is all very nice. It's fine.'

'I will give you first option then,' says Mrs Gilcrest, swinging her keys in a businesslike manner, 'but I hope you understand that these homes are at a premium round here, being as cheap as they are. And I'll need a month's rent in full before you get the keys.'

Back in the bustling capital city, stuck like a battery hen high up in her air-conditioned cubicle at the offices of Coburn and Watts, Candice Love's coffee cup pauses at her lips. What's this?

She re-reads page one of the well-presented manuscript and moves on to page two quickly. This author has been lucky, her padded envelope, which arrived last week, has made its way to the top of the pile because of a slip of fate, or, more correctly, a slip made by Linda, Candice's secretary, when she was heaving the pile from the main office to Candice's room and one high heel gave way, badly twisting her ankle.

Damn. And she's got a date for lunch. An author she doesn't much care for has come up to London for a free spaghetti and an opportunity to nag Candice about the miserable offer for her latest effort.

Damn. And yet she's got to read on. This one is looking astonishingly promising and she certainly doesn't want anyone else picking up the manuscript while she's gone. There is only one thing for it. She will have to take it with her and read it this afternoon.

All through lunch with her distressed author it's murder for Candice to concentrate and she finds herself touching her briefcase as if to reassure herself that her 'find' is still close.

'The thing is,' she says abstractedly over the checked cloth, 'there is less and less of a market these days for your kind of historical romance.'

'It might have been helpful if you'd warned me of that before I started on another,' grumbles her author over the stench of Parmesan cheese.

'All advances are down these days,' Candice continues, not hungry and picking at old candle-wax, 'it's not just you. Nearly all my authors have been forced to accept considerably less than they did before.'

'But they promised me my next book would be the one that made me!'

Candice shakes her well-groomed head. Why oh why do authors continue to believe in publishers' hype? Are they too blinded by their own importance, too mentally frail, to accept that publishers rarely say what they mean?

'"This is your year," they keep telling me; they say it on every Christmas card.'

'Well, I know and I'm sorry,' comforts Candice. What is she expected to say? Perhaps she should make no bones about it, maybe she should come straight out with the truth, that it had taken all Candice's skills to persuade a reluctant editor to accept her client's book at all.

Dammit, the woman insists on a pudding, and cappuccino afterwards – three cups. She has finished her morning's shopping and is obviously filling in time until her train is due in this afternoon.

At last Candice can wave goodbye to her grumbling author, who goes off promising that her next book will be fast and lusty. 'If it's sex they want, then they'll get it, I'll shock 'em all,' mutters the elderly woman with the powdered face and the newly replaced hip. Candice hopes it will take some time. She's not looking forward to reading it.

Candice is a fast reader. Back in the office and it doesn't take her long to reach the end of a chapter. Bloody hell! Good God, if the rest of the stuff is anything like this she has something huge on her hands. Staggering. Phenomenal. Something bigger than she, and possibly her boss, Rory Coburn, have ever handled before. Could she possibly be mistaken? Should she ask for a second opinion before taking action? She could go to her boss right now, but she is tempted to act on her own initiative. She will never be forgiven, of course, but that won't matter if *Magdalene* is as big as Candice thinks it is likely to be.

She reads the introductory letter again. It gives little away. She reads the short synopsis. It's good. What an amazing first this would be . . .

On impulse she dials the number on the letter head and waits for a worrying length of time. Finally the phone is picked up.

'Yes?' Spoken crossly.

'Is that Kirsty Hoskins?'

'No, this is Mrs Moira Stokes.'

'Well, Mz Stokes, would it be possible for me to speak to Kirsty Hoskins, please?'

'No, it certainly would not. It is not my job to go chasing round after all and sundry. This is a large building, and if you must make telephone calls to the staff it would be more considerate if you would arrange to ring at a mutually agreed time in future.'

Candice Love is not used to this kind of rude reaction. Her business might well be cut-throat, but no matter how nasty the meaning, the words are always coated in saccharine.

'Um, Mz Stokes, I can see that I have disturbed you—'

'Yes, you have.'

'Only this is an important matter. I am phoning from London—'

'Well that doesn't impress me one jot.'

'And it really is essential that I speak with Kirsty Hoskins.'

'Is it a matter of life and death? Has there been some tragedy in the family?'

'Well, no, of course not.' And Candice is tempted to add, Don't be an arsehole. But she tries to persuade the woman instead: 'Please take a note of my name and address.'

'If I must,' says Mrs Stokes, pausing to do so. 'But in future please ring at a more convenient time.'

And then, to Candice's enormous surprise, the phone goes dead in her hand.

Damn.

Damn.

Damn.

Eight

Five years older than Avril, so that his sister hardly knew him, Graham Stott heaves his army and navy rucksack over his bomber-jacketed shoulder, gobs twice on the pavement and leaves the prison gates behind him.

Graham Timothy Stott is a thoroughly bad apple and a nasty piece of work, although social workers consoled Mrs Stott by agreeing with her, superficially, that she could not have been a better mother and that the lad had been given everything he had ever wanted.

'I never worked,' sobbed Avril's mother in her cosy, germ-free lounge – apart from Fluffy the cat's chair – with scarlet tissue paper stuffed in the fireplace because it was summer. 'Everyone else in the terrace did, of course,' she sniffed, 'and that has been the problem. Kids with no-one at home messing about in the street after school. Of course Graham was tempted out there; how could we keep him indoors after he reached the age of eight?'

'It has been very hard for you, I know, Mrs Stott,' was the typical professional response.

Mrs Stott removed one of Fluffy's hairs from an

otherwise immaculate pair of nylon navy slacks. 'And now you come here doing reports, asking us all sorts of personal questions, as if we are somehow to blame. Poor Richard,' she wept for her humble, hard-working husband, 'he always did his best. Never a day off work. He tried his hardest with Graham; he was always in the shed with him playing with tools and wood. Sometimes he even took him fishing. But where is the gratitude now, I ask you?'

'It has been very hard for you, I know, Mrs Stott.'

Fluffy farted and filled the room with the rancid smell of fish-in-the-bowel. The poor, almost hairless creature had been ill for the last five years and yet she lives on defiantly. 'And, if we're not careful, Avril here is going to go the same way as Graham. They say it's in the genes, but there's nothing wrong with Richard's genes; there was never the slightest whiff of scandal in the Stott side of the family, and as for my own parents, they are being made ill by all the worry.'

'It has been very hard for you, I know, Mrs Stott.'

'You can see his bedroom if you like, although, of course, it's been given a thorough clean-out since he went away. I found all sorts of vile magazines and photographs.' Avril's mother shook her head and wrinkled her lips like the edge of a pasty. 'I can honestly say I never knew such horrible things existed.'

'It has been very hard for you, I know, Mrs Stott.'

Mrs Stott picked up Fluffy, laid her on her knee and stroked her, to the social worker's abhorrence. 'And no, we won't have him back. I know that might sound hard, as if we've abandoned our son to

111

his plight, but you'll never know what Richard and I have been through over the last few years, what with police coming round at all hours, terrible people calling for Graham, the bad behaviour, the swearing – such a bad influence on Avril. He used his father and I like a couple of old doormats. No, we've given this matter a great deal of thought and we will not have Graham back. Let the authorities find him somewhere. I don't even want to know where he is and that's flat.'

With a surprising small show of violence, Mrs Stott got up and threw Fluffy out in the garden.

Graham Stott hops off the bus outside 2 Maple Terrace, Huyton. Soon he will have wheels of his own, no more travelling about with losers. Here it is, home sweet home, no change, even the symmetrical rows of brown and orange chrysanths are probably in the exact same order with the exact same slugs inside. Dad, he knows, will be at work and Mum will be doing whatever she does during her long and tedious housewifely day. There are always signs of work lying round in a pointed, angry fashion: a duster hung over a banister, clothes in a basket on top of a washing machine that is never still, wet dishcloths hanging on hooks by the door, peas to be shelled on the kitchen table, neat piles of bedding left on the landing.

The doorbell peals the Westminster chimes.

'Whatcha, Ma.'

'*What on earth are you doing here?*'

'They told you I was getting out, didn't they?'

'No, they did not, thank goodness.'

'Aren't you going to invite me in?'

112

Mrs Stott casts anxious glances up and down the terrace before retreating backwards into her neat little hallway followed by her skinny son. He looks as if a train has hit him. He looks worse than he ever did, with the pallid, acned skin of a heavy potato-eater and those filthy, skin-tight jeans. His boots look like something worn by the Nazis.

'You're not stopping here, Graham.'

'I see Fluffy's still going strong.'

'I said, you're not stopping here, Graham, *so don't think you are.*'

'Any chance of a cup of tea?'

'Make it yourself. And then just go. I don't want your father coming home, seeing you here and being upset again.'

Graham mooches around in the kitchen as he waits for the kettle to boil, picking up bits and pieces as if to connect himself with the house in which he grew up. She doesn't ask, How are you, son? Or, How did they treat you in there? She shows no interest at all in the child who has been away for three years.

'How's Avril?'

'I don't think that's any of your business.'

'She must be what, eighteen now? Still living at home, I guess?'

'Avril has her own life now, and a very successful one, I might add.'

'Unlike me.'

'You said it, not me.'

Mrs Stott sits stiffly at her kitchen table playing nervously with the salt.

'I thought I might kip down here for a while . . .'

'You haven't heard one word I've said.'

'You're not going to kick me out?'

'Graham,' says his mother firmly. 'If you stay here one minute longer after you have finished that tea I shall ring up your parole officer and tell him you are causing a nuisance.'

Graham gives a quick, appraising look. 'You would, too. You hard bitch.'

'You drove me to it.'

Ten minutes later Graham leaves the house in Huyton with Avril's address printed on his mind. It was on an envelope on the sideboard in his mother's handwriting, and although, at the moment, he has no plans to visit his long-lost sister – let's face it, they never got on, that drip with her fluffy-toy collection – you can't miss a trick when you're likely to be down and out for the foreseeable future.

Something very serious has happened.

The staff at the Burleston, gathered to order in the recreation room, can tell this because of the weaselly expression on Mrs Stokes's face. She stands before them grimly, with her arms down by her sides, hard fists clenched at the ends of her cardigan sleeves.

'I am sorry to have to say this, but the Miss Lewises have reported that an expensive item of jewellery has gone missing from their dressing-table drawer.'

There is silence and then a shuffling from the audience gathered before her.

'Now then,' Mrs Stokes goes on, 'Mr Derek is reluctant to report this matter to the police for very obvious reasons. The last thing any of us want is for the reputation of the hotel to be besmirched in the slightest way. Therefore he has decided, with the kind permission of the Miss Lewises, to wait for twenty-four hours before reluctantly taking the appropriate action. If anyone here knows anything about this distressing matter, could they please, first, come to me, or simply leave the bracelet in my office which, as you all know, is always open.'

'Why us?' asks one of the Burleston waiters, incensed by the injustice. 'Why the hell do they immediately assume that if there's something nicked it's one of us?'

'Typical, the sods.'

'More likely the slapheads have gone and lost it.'

'They've got one hell of a nerve to stand there and accuse us lot.'

'We should tell them that this is right out of order,' says another outraged employee.

'We ought to make them call in the law. After all, who gives a toss about this doss-hole's reputation.'

Avril, in her corner, goes red. She feels her cheeks puff up around her and there's nothing she can do to fend off these guilty feelings. Of course she knows nothing about the bracelet – she never visits the guests' bedrooms – but she is keeper of the keys and it is entirely possible that Avril slyly picked her time before going up to a room which she knew to be empty and stole the bracelet as simply as that.

This guilty reaction has dogged poor Avril since early childhood, when her mother would try to catch her out, probably concerned that Avril might follow in her brother's wicked footsteps.

She blames the whole thing on Graham, and

Kirsty and Bernie agree that her brother has been her undoing.

For instance:

'Have you made your bed yet, Avril?'

And if Avril said yes her mother would fly to check on her daughter's truthfulness.

'Did you brush your teeth this morning?'

She would check the wetness of the toothbrush.

'Have you posted those letters I gave you?'

She would rush to Avril's blazer pocket.

On the few occasions when Avril was found to be lying, as all sane children do in order to get out of trouble, she was severely punished with a hard smack on the leg, or an evening shut in her bedroom, no supper, or having her favourite toy confiscated in a kind of religious ceremony with her mother as lord high cardinal and herself as grievous sinner. And various other unpleasant consequences.

By the time she went to school Avril was not only secretive but had guilt in gold-leaf lettering printed upon her soul. And because she was plump and gormless and looked so obviously guilty, she was the one singled out and questioned, and hence she discovered confession to be the simplest way out. If she put her hand up and took the blame the awful tension that made her breathless would be over all the sooner. Compared to her mother's punishments, the school's were reliably tame – lines or detention, nothing to fear. But by owning up to so much she created her own vicious circle. School reports were worryingly bad and provoked Mrs Stott to chastise again. Although her school work was always pleasing: 'Avril tries hard.'

'Do you know anything about this, Avril?' asks

Moira Stokes, on spying a perfect victim, puce and quivering in a corner. 'I must say I would be most surprised.'

'No,' says Avril firmly, determined never again to volunteer for self-sacrifice. She has grown up since those days. She has friends. She has a job. She no longer misses her mother. 'Of course I don't know anything about it. Why are you asking me anyway?'

'Because you look so upset.'

Avril is not at school now. Nor is she a child in her mother's house. She is an independent young lady with a job and a future, fast and accurate. And what is more, she has just played an essential part in producing an almost perfect manuscript for Kirsty's wonderful book, something she can be duly proud of. If Magdalene had been hounded in this kind of way, she would have put her inquisitors firmly in their place and she would have sliced their balls off.

'Right,' says the beady-eyed Moira Stokes, twenty-four hours later. 'On your heads be it. Unfortunately nobody has, as yet, come forward with any information regarding the Miss Lewises' bracelet, and so Mr Derek would like to see you one by one in his office before he informs the local police.'

'Shame!' shouts out Jimmy Smithers from the kitchens.

'No way,' adds Jacky Butcher.

'Get stuffed.'

'What's your problem? Call the cops. Nobody here gives a damn.'

Moira Stokes looks shocked and her pointed chin turns up at the end like the striking tail of a scorpion. 'Are you saying you refuse to help Mr Derek to deal with this matter sensitively?'

'Too right.'

'It's a bloody nerve.'

'Why don't you search their room?'

All heads turn towards meek Avril, who has never spoken in public before, and now she looks racked, crucified, as if the bracelet in question is deep in her own pocket.

'We are not about to start questioning the good faith of our guests,' snaps Mrs Stokes, taken aback.

But everyone else supports Avril.

'It's not the good faith, it's the sodding senility.'

'They're nasty-minded hags,' says Bernie.

'Nothing but trouble. Same every year.'

'They're stinking bitches, both of them,' says Avril, swallowing. Something has control of her mouth . . . she has never used such words before, but the release she feels is exhilarating.

'I have no further option than to inform Mr Derek', says Mrs Stokes, drawing herself up in tight disgust, the same way she tightens her pelvic muscles, 'that you all refuse, point-blank, to assist him in this distressing matter. I know what his response will be. Mr Derek will now have no option but to go to the police with all the unpleasantness that will involve.'

'You were ace in there, Avril.'

'Well, you'd think they'd have searched the room before they came blaming us.'

A bubble of pleasure bursts inside her. Avril is thrilled by her little rebellion. Contrary to her normal melancholy she feels good and strong, and when the letter arrives the next day, typed and addressed to Kirsty Hoskins, she knows immediately who it's from. The only other letters Kirsty gets are the bulky ones addressed in large, untidy writing, which always include notes from her children.

Avril sorts out the mail, separating that of the staff to take to the recreation room where there's a box for the purpose. She can hardly contain her excitement. Could it be possible that their novel will interest someone from London? An agent?

'*It is from them,*' cries Kirsty, excitement replacing the strain on her face as she unfolds the precious document.

'Read it out,' gasps Avril, breathing heavily over her shoulder.

'*Dear Kirsty, (may I?)*'

'It must be good news if she wants to use first name terms.'

'*I read the first five chapters of your novel with great pleasure and I am certain we can find somewhere for it.*'

'I don't believe it!' Avril screams fatly as Kirsty looks up in surprise.

'*Have you completed any more chapters? If so, perhaps I could see them, or, even better, would it be possible for us to meet next time you are in London . . . ?*' Hah! That's a laugh.' Kirsty pauses. 'When would I be in London? Anyone would think I visited regularly. What for, d'you think. The theatre, a shopping spree, important meetings, or just passing through to the airport?'

'Go on with it,' Avril urges.

'*I did try to telephone you on Monday afternoon but was unable to get through . . .*'

'Typical,' says Avril. 'That must have been Mrs Danvers.'

'. . . *so I wondered if you could phone or fax me; we should meet as soon as possible. All best wishes, Candice Love.*'

'Wow!' says Avril. 'Ring now!'

'Hang on.' Kirsty's reluctance is a surprise. 'Let me think about this.'

'What is there to think about? They like our book!'

'But my name has to keep out of this.'

'What do you mean?'

Kirsty pales and lowers her voice. 'Trevor, of course! I'm a fool. Why did I use my own name?'

'What you need is a *nom de plume.*'

Kirsty shakes her head and looks suddenly small and defeated. 'I can't go to London anyway, I don't have that sort of money.' These seem like excuses.

'We'd find the money,' Avril enthuses.

'What the hell's the matter with me? I could never have a book published under my name.' How could she make such an obvious blunder? 'Somehow Trevor would hear about it, he'd trace me, track me down . . . and anyway, Avril, what's happened to you? Where are your strict moral values now? You seem quite happy to get started on this sordid deception.'

'Sod the moral values,' says Avril, quite unlike herself. And then her face lights up with hope. 'Bernie would do it,' she cries, pop-eyed.

Kirsty frowns and stares at Avril. Avril has a mad glint in her eye . . . a ferocious glint . . . a worrying glint. 'Bernie could do what?'

'Bernie could pretend to be you. Go up to London. Use her name. Bernie would kill to do something like that.'

'But it's all too late,' says Kirsty, suddenly needing Avril's new energy. 'I've already sent the manuscript up under my own name. They're going to think it's peculiar if we start using another.'

Avril will not give up. 'Say you made up the name Kirsty Hoskins.'

'But why would I say that?'

'All sorts of reasons. You were shy, in case they turned you down. You didn't want anyone to know what you'd done, or you thought Kirsty Hoskins sounded more like a proper author.'

'We could get round it, I suppose,' Kirsty slowly agrees.

'We can't stop now, we have to go on,' says Avril, whose heart and soul are sunk deep in the project. Never has she felt so determined. Stupid, uncanny really, and hard to explain how urgent this feels.

'Well, we could ask Bernie what she thinks and get her to ring up. And Bernadette Kavanagh sounds more professional to me.'

So Avril breathes a sigh of relief. Never before has she taken part in a venture so abandoned and daring.

The following morning a formal memo is issued to the staff. Mrs Stokes pins it up discreetly on the recreation room noticeboard and retires with haste before she is seen. It reads:

The Miss Lewises, who recently mislaid a piece of jewellery in their possession, are happy to say

121

that the item has now been found. The manage-
ment apologizes for any inconvenience caused
by this matter. Derek Pugh.

Nine

The night life in St Ives, although not a patch on Liverpool, gives Dominic Coates the release he desires after spending day after day lolling vacantly on the veranda outside the lifeguard's hut surrounded by sultry beauties. A pretty boy, with the looks of a girl, he has never suffered from pimples.

With his long, curly hair, enormous brown eyes fringed with long, dark lashes, and his suntanned chest with its couple of whiskers, he feels like the macho hero he is as he struts along in his flip-flops and shorts, staring importantly at the silver water. How Canute would have loved his power. Occasionally, to impress and to reinforce his own self-worth, he shouts into a megaphone warning the brain-dead on lilos to come in closer to shore, or admonishes those who insist on swimming outside the two red flags.

But the most threatening aspect of his sweep of the beach are the lusty lads, like himself, who leap and sway and wobble and thrust themselves about on their surfboards, mostly locals whose favourite patch has now been invaded by sunburned grockles with flaming thighs. No wonder they are aggressive when you think that they endure their sport through the most majestic of winter storms, when the mighty waves curl and rise as high as the roofs, and the furious spray foams and screams into crests of blinding whiteness . . .

Compared to these heroes Dominic's surfing efforts are feeble, so he has to compensate in other ways to prove his manly credibility. Luckily he has an impressive crawl, the result of holidaying regularly in the deep blue seas of the Caribbean. The life-saving certificates he gained at his public school are impressive, while his ability to pull birds is awesome.

His peers, impressed, watch his methods covertly while outwardly taking the piss.

The sea is so calm today that the surfers are resting and each isolated swimmer spreads a halo of rings around him. All is well with the world. Dominic can afford to relax. Bodies on the sand move restlessly, arms wave, faces turn, shining surfaces flash back at the sun, and flags and towels and windbreaks slump without a breeze. All is massed and pulsing life, flickering and astir. Dominic's concentration wavers.

To Bernadette he gives not a thought. OK, she was a great lay for a while, and OK, he admits, he did lead her on to think they might get hooked one day. She assumed it, he didn't deny it, and who is to blame for that? A looker, a real head-turner wherever they went. It's fun to mix with those from the other side of the tracks now and then, but she was a clinger and Irish, highly strung and dangerous. God, she tried to top herself after they'd finished

and they said it was because of him. Shit. Some of
the tricks women play.

'I shouldn't drink on duty.'

'It's only one can of wine,' says this classy bird
from Yorkshire, rich and husky, here with her
family and bored out of her mind. 'It's beautifully
cold. What's up, can't take it?'

'Don't tempt me.' He grabs her by her bare
shoulders and bites the nape of her neck, daring
her to taunt him again. He has already downed two
lagers.

She gazes at him full in the eyes, but he won't
respond, he makes her work for it. Leaning back on
one casual elbow he rips the strip from the can and
puts the chilled metal to his lips, watched by his
small throng of groupies.

Beads of sweat form on his forehead as the sun
beats down mercilessly – if only he could cool off
with a dip, but while he's on duty that is out of the
question. He must maintain his watch, but the sun is
so hot that a haze has formed between him and the
edge of the water, a haze through which a blend of
sounds echoes: the shrill laughter of women, the
happy screams of children, the mock-terrified
shrieks of swimmers, and behind all these the whispering sea.

Dominic glances once again at his expensive
waterproof watch. Three more hours to go, bloody
hell, he only got four hours' sleep last night.

The girl from Yorkshire is giggling now as she
traces a sandy line down his leg, between the soft,
downy hairs.

He needs something spicy to keep him awake.

'Get us a cheeseburger, sweetheart.'

'You'll get BSE with all the crap you eat. You don't know what they put in those things.'

'I'll get you one, Dom,' says a large-breasted rival of the Yorkshire grockle. 'Sauce and mustard?'

Dominic Coates is not quite sure what first turns his blood to ice as adrenalin surges through his body. It is like a silence on the edge of sound, a tiny, unidentified pocket of alarm with a heartbeat all of its own, and it comes to him like something primeval, like whales or dolphins communicating. He is up before he hears the first frantic screams.

'*It's a child in the water!*'

'*Help, get help.*'

He is like Cupid with wings on his heels, but the shifting soft sand holds him back. His eyes seem congested with bright red blood. His breathing thunders in his head as if he's reaching the end of some marathon. Dear God, let it not be too late.

Terrorized and impossibly white, her eyes gone black with fear, a woman stands at the edge of the water pointing out into the distance. 'She's out there, Melanie, she's only three . . .' and her teeth chatter with cold and fear.

Three or four disorientated adults group helplessly round her, gaping stupidly into the void of disbelief.

'*Help me, God help me.* My husband's already gone out, but he's not a strong swimmer.'

Dominic's desperate eyes scan the water, and there, at an impossible distance, almost beyond the fringe of the bay, he spies something floating.

He runs at full pelt through the knee-high water until he can throw himself into his crawl. As his strong, young body picks up the rhythm he curses

126

the booze that restricts his pace. He turns his head for breath now and then, gasping, gasping, trying to glimpse how far he has come and how far there is still to go.

Dear God help me.

Pace yourself. *Pace yourself.*

He imagines himself in the pool at school, swimming for a medal in the relay, swimming for the cup. Now he is swimming for life itself. He had always believed this would be fun, a challenge, a test of his strength and courage.

What crap.

The sudden blow to his head almost stuns him. Bewildered and blind he gasps for breath and struggles to undo the heavy arms that clutch at his body like suckers and threaten to drag him under. '*What the fuck?*' Such desperate strength, a madman gone wild beyond reason. The terrified words play back to him, 'My husband's already gone out . . .'

'It's OK, Dom, I've got him.'

Dominic can breathe again. Thank God, it's Justin, a young local lad, a surfer.

'I've got him,' screams Justin, 'help me kick him off, get his neck.'

With all the force at his disposal Dominic chops at the throat of the man with the beaten eyes and the mouth full of screams. If he wants his child saved he must loosen his grip.

Now it's just him and a hostile sea totally indifferent to the interests of men. And somewhere a child. And incredible silence. His body blunders on, but his spirit moves in an infinite waste where he sees no reassuring horizons. If he fails in this he can't live with himself, knowing he should not have drunk alcohol, knowing full well what it does to the stamina.

Her hands shake, her body jerks.

Bernie gapes at the morning paper, *at the front page of the local paper*, at the near-naked figure of Dominic Coates emerging from the sea with a child in his arms. Has she reached the stage of hallucination, has her madness gripped her with such intensity that she sees him when he's not there?

She must get her thoughts in order. Her wounds burn afresh with this memory.

'What is it? Bernie! Hey! *Are you ill?* Speak to me,' shouts Kirsty. 'You look terrible. You look like a corpse.'

Bernie hands over the paper. 'Holy Jesus. That's him, Dominic Coates, the fella I was with.'

'What's he done? Let's see what it says.'

'He has rescued a three-year-old girl who they all thought was dead. He brought her back to life on the sand in front of a crowd of people. He's a hero. Hang on, let me read.'

They read on together. 'They're getting at the mother, the kid was out of sight for half an hour before she even missed her. What's the matter with these sad people?'

'The father died. How dreadful.'

'He should never have tried if he couldn't swim.'

'They brought his body in half an hour later.'

'God. Just imagine.'

But this life-and-death drama means little to Bernie, far more important than this is the fact that Dominic is working in Cornwall as a lifeguard for the summer. So he followed her after all, and yes, it would have been simple to discover her whereabouts, just a matter of chatting to friends. He must be biding his time, he'll get in touch when the time is right. He is probably nervous about her reaction after the suicide bid. Secretly Bernie has always believed that Dominic still cares. You can't love someone as strongly as she does without any reciprocal feelings, *surely that's just not possible?* After all, when you look at things calmly, it was his parents who caused the split and influenced Dominic with their snooty beliefs, who threatened to cut him off, who must have made him as desolate as she.

Yes, yes! It makes sense. All is not lost. Life, intolerable yesterday, is now filled with relief and joy. Hope, which springs eternal, walks once again at her side with hot, sandy feet.

It is a reborn Bernie, gagging with hope, who dials the agency's number from the communal phone outside the recreation room.

'I ought to have read it,' she whispers to Kirsty. 'Hell, if I wrote it, I ought to have read it.'

'Shut up,' hisses Avril, plump legs crossed with excitement.

After a short but nerve-racking pause Bernie is speaking to Candice Love.

'There was a mess up,' says Bernie. 'Your phone call got lost in the system. That's my fault really, I used a false name, the name of a friend. I'm sorry, I thought it sounded better. I was just too freaked out to use my own.'

She raised enquiring eyebrows. Had she said that

convincingly? They had rehearsed this excuse, at length, together.

'Your real name is perfect,' says Candice, thinking what cranks some authors are but, when all's said and done, this one's rather special with a right to be eccentric. The agent is taking one hell of a risk by keeping this marvellous find to herself and not sharing it with her boss, RC.

'The main question is, Bernadette, when can you and I meet?'

Money is the problem. Bernie, Kirsty and Avril have worked this out and the only way they could club together to buy a return from Cornwall to London is if they got hold of an Apex ticket, which means buying six weeks in advance. Otherwise they would be faced with an eighty-quid bill, not possible.

'Funds are rather low at the moment,' says Bernie cautiously. They will beg, steal or borrow if necessary, but honesty has to be worth a try.

'Fine,' says Candice happily. 'You tell me when you can come and I'll send you the ticket.'

Bernie's next day off is on Friday, the most expensive day of the week, but this means nothing to Candice. 'I'll order the tickets today and get them sent directly to you. Now, let me explain where to come.'

She asks how much of the novel is ready. When she hears it is finished she immediately demands that Bernie should bring it with her. 'Although I can't promise anything yet,' she says with professional cunning, 'but if the rest of the book is as good as the first five chapters I think we can be sure of some interest.'

'But how long will it all take?' Bernie asks, over-excited.

Candice decides it is best to be truthful, assessing, correctly, that this writer knows nothing. 'I'm afraid these things do take time.'

'This year, next year?'

'Not until next year, I'm afraid, at the very earliest.'

'How much would we be talking about?'

'Stop it,' spits Kirsty with a nudge and a glare, while Avril closes her eyes in shame.

Candice gives her professional laugh while her eyelids bat like cash machines. 'I can't tell you that either, not at this early stage, but the first impression I get gives me hope. It all depends on the rest of your novel, of course, and the state of the market at the time.'

'So we just have to wait and see?'

'It's a slow and painful process, but you must have found that when writing *Magdalene*. It probably took you a long time.' Candice is holding her breath, for this information could be all important – best if an author can knock out one a year.

'About six weeks,' is the pleasing reply.

When the hair-raising phone call is over, Bernie fetches a bottle from the bar and they go upstairs to their sparse attic room and drink a toast to *Magdalene*.

They raise their glasses and see one another happy and glowing through Sicilian red. They are friends. They have come together. They have a goal in common. 'Share and share alike,' says Kirsty magnanimously. 'Whatever we get we split three ways.'

'It was your idea, you did the work, you should get more,' says Avril unsteadily, unused to alcohol.

'What d'you think I should wear?' asks Bernie, too het up to fret about such details. 'What sort of person should I be? We don't want them to think I'm pig-ignorant.'

'But you are pig-ignorant,' worries Kirsty. 'And the less you say the better.'

'Then I'll dazzle them with my personality.'

'The only reason you don't sound stupid', says Avril, 'is because you've been around,' and she searches for the right words, 'life. Well, men, sex, that's what I mean.'

'What? *You think I'm a whore?* You're right, I've had more men than you've had hot dinners.'

'And if you really did write a book it would be in a black cover on the top shelf of the motorway services.'

But there is a serious point here. Bernie is not your stereotype author. To start with she is a slag, or was (innocently promiscuous is how she sees it); secondly she is only nineteen and never took English at GCSE. With her IQ in such doubt, all the school would put her down for was RE, Drama and Art.

'But there's one thing I do have,' she says to cheer her downcast conspirators, 'and that's a rich imagination. That was written once in my report. If I get the chance I'll work on that.'

'Just be yourself,' says Kirsty. 'Don't show off or try to be clever, you couldn't keep it up anyway. Let's hope your looks will pull you through.'

*　　*　　*

The dress rehearsal arrives unexpectedly when Bernie is doing her shift that evening.

'Off to London then?' asks the odious Mr Derek with a nod and a wink, still hoping he might be in with a chance. 'Off to the big smoke. Must be something important.'

'I've written a novel,' says Bernie, still on top of the world and bursting with confidence now that she knows her lost lover is back in the picture.

Mr Derek's smile is contemptuous. 'Oh yeah, and I'm the Queen Mother.'

'Hey? Now why would you think like that?' asks Bernie, peeved. 'Why wouldn't I write a novel?'

'You're not serious,' says Mr Derek, irritating beyond endurance with that superior, amused expression.

'Fine, if you don't believe me,' says Bernie, stiffening, 'but what's more I've found an agent who thinks she might be able to sell it.' And won't Dominic be surprised and impressed when he discovers his little colleen has more about her than he imagined? Won't his mammy and daddy feel bad when they hear they snubbed a famous author? This is the gloss on the gingerbread. Because famous is what Bernadette Kavanagh has always been determined to be. She now has the platform she's always desired. Thousands never get the chance, and all she has to do is throw herself off.

'Well, what d'you think?' asks Kirsty, finding Bernie immersed in the manuscript, her mess of magazines abandoned on the floor, covered with ash and snagged pairs of tights. She has been reading for an hour now, a unique situation for Bernie, whose normal concentration span is five minutes.

Bernie looks up, shocked, and still half immersed in the story.

'I can't put it down.'

'There, we told you, it's gripping.'

'But there's much more to it than that.'

'Of course there is. That's the whole point.'

'This Magdalene,' starts Bernie doubtfully, and her face takes on a clouded look, 'there's something abnormal . . .'

'She's a winner,' Kirsty enthuses. 'She's unscrupulous. We could all be as strong as that if we tried. It's just that we've all been conditioned to accept our limitations.'

'I hope we'd never be like her.' Bernie looks down at the thick wad of paper, and then back to Kirsty, bewildered. 'She's evil. It's scary. It makes me go cold when I'm reading, *can't you feel it?*'

'That's because of the strength of my writing,' says Kirsty with a triumphant smile.

'No.' Bernie shakes her head once again, dark curls tumbling around her face. 'No, it's not that. There's a word Mammy sometimes uses for things she can't understand, like heathens and werewolves and paedophiles. She calls them accursed,' murmurs Bernie, starting to shake uncontrollably, 'and there's something about your Magdalene that is definitely accursed.'

Ten

While Trevor Hoskins might look like a man, talk like a man, walk like a man, as the days turn into weeks and his wife and kids remain out of reach, inside he feels like a cougar. Sniffing. Stalking. Snarling.

He has visited all the obvious places, spied on the neighbours, opened her post. Driven by pride and raging vengeance he has bagged and burned her remaining clothes, torn up the photograph albums, binned her goddamned trinkets and savaged the hidden books he found.

All this left him exhausted.

But the woman is thick as a bloody plank. There's bound to be clues left somewhere around.

'She used the phone, didn't she, Margot, she used the payphone at lunch times. I always thought that was odd.'

Other than busybody Margot Banks, most of her workmates were discreet.

'And she never said who she was ringing?'

Margot Banks shook her head and took another fag from his packet.

135

'Some of them thought it was some bloke. They used to rag her something awful about it.'

Trevor went cold all over. How would Kirsty get a bloke with her miserable face and tired expression? She made it clear sex with him was disgusting. No, no, Trevor cannot tolerate the thought of another man. 'But you never thought it was a bloke?'

'Nah.' Margot took a deep drag and blew it out into a shaft of sunshine. 'Not Kirsty. She was far too shy, no confidence. She wouldn't say boo to a goose.'

'But you never saw her with anyone? Out here? In the carpark after work?'

'Hang on a minute, there was a time, a couple of times now I think of it, when she was picked up by some woman in a car. I never gave it a second thought, well, you don't, do you?'

Trevor, tired of Margot's big rouged face and the thrill she got out of his discomfort, said, 'So there was nothing else?'

'She had lots of dental appointments. I always wondered how the hell she could afford it. Craig and I never go any more, well, not unless we're in agony.'

So, she was up to no good behind his back in spite of his careful checking. Women are all the same. Wouldn't you sodding well know it? He checked the dentist, of course, but the receptionist said they hadn't heard from Mrs Stott for some time and wasn't he, Trevor, due for a check-up? Unknowingly he came quite warm when he rang the Samaritans, for that was the kind of pathetic, whingeing thing he suspected Kirsty would do – moan about

136

him for hours on end, not knowing when she was well off. OK, he lost his temper at times, but she drove him to it with her constant moaning. And he hadn't touched the kiddies, had he?

'She's disappeared and I'm concerned about her,' he said, cursing to himself on the other end of the phone. The tossers.

'I'm afraid we operate in total confidence and never reveal our clients' names to anyone,' said the snooty voice.

'But I'm her husband and she's taken my kids.'

'We would be very happy to talk to you, Mr Hoskins, if you felt we could be of some help. My name is Angela—'

'Piss off,' said Trevor as he slammed the phone down.

Kirsty has no friends that he knows of, no relatives save a brother she hasn't been in touch with for years, and the kids' friends don't come home. She has never been into that school bit, car-boot sales, swimming-pool duty, hobnobbing with other parents, off to sports days and PTA meetings. There was no chance for Kirsty to go out at nights; after a busy day's work it was Trevor who needed to go down the pub, and she had to babysit.

Perhaps she's in one of those hostels? Or convinced someone she's badly done to . . . everyone's at it these days. There's plenty around who will listen to women, but how about the men? Who has Trev got to listen to him? And he almost weeps at the unfairness of it, he is so sorry for himself.

Well, look. He comes home from work to an empty house, no food on the table, nothing but old

137

ham that's gone green round the edges in the fridge. He's having to live on fish and chips or takeaway curries. He watches the telly on his own – there's not much sodding fun in that. Mostly he dozes off in his chair and wakes up cold and shivery, only to have to make his own cocoa and plod up the stairs like a sad bastard, where he lies recumbent and open-eyed, cracking his knuckles.

Twice he has been late to work 'cos there's no-one around to get him up and he is too tired to hear the bleeding alarm. And far from being admired and respected, he knows they are talking about him now, gossiping like old fishwives. 'She's upped and left him', 'sodded off', 'not much of a man if he can't keep his own wife' . . .

Sometimes he gets so bleeding angry at home alone with the silence that he kicks at the sofa like a child in a rage, sinks more Southern Comfort than he can handle, so his breathing goes strange and he wonders if he's unconscious, and shouts to himself with the telly up so the neighbours won't hear his thunderous outrage.

A man right at the end of his tether. The only thing that brings him peace is the thought of what he will do when he finds her.

'I'm not worried,' says Maddy in her letter, 'because it's only a cold which is lingering, but I think I ought to register the children with my own doctor, just to be on the safe side, in case they should catch the normal childhood bugs and need medical treatment. So if you give me the name and address of your doctor I'll organize it. We ought to have done it before, of course, but there's so much in your head in the heat of these moments.'

One hasty phone call to Maddy and a happy chat with Jake and Gemma reassures Kirsty that all is well.

She has returned the books she borrowed from the hotel quiet lounge, all apart from *Magdalene*, of course, which she took to the boiler room and burned. In great trepidation she stood and watched the pages curl, the cover slowly disintegrate. She watched through the little glass door until the book turned to ashes in the fiery furnace.

What is going to be tricky, if all should go well, if *Magdalene* finds a publisher, is the prospect of a second book. Browsing through the quiet lounge of the Burleston Hotel, the chance of picking up another choice gem must be nil. If only Ellen Kirkwood had been more prolific, but then, if she'd written more, her work would probably be better known.

As it is, all three women are praying that nobody is going to remember a novel they read in 1913. That no friends or relatives kept a copy carefully dusted and preserved in pride of place on their bookshelves. That no ancient reviewer associates their book with something he might have dug up in the cuttings department of his library. Perhaps they should have changed the title – she rolls her eyes despairingly – but everything has happened so quickly.

Everyone in the hotel is talking about Bernie's book. Bernie, a natural exhibitionist, makes sure everyone knows and Kirsty dreads that the colonel himself might be roused from his vegetative state to declare *Magdalene* as one of his favourites. After all, the book was in Colonel Parker's collection, although the other titles do suggest they were probably bought as part of a job lot.

Mrs Stokes is all condemning. She has watched Bernie flirting shamelessly with all and sundry, but is unaware this is learned behaviour and that no-one shapes up to Dominic. 'If that girl manages to get a book published then pigs will start to fly,' she says indignantly through pursed lips. 'Silly fool. Trying to show off. More likely the trollop has gone off to London to see some man.'

'She's jealous,' says Avril knowingly, understanding how the old woman feels. Although she has to admire Bernie's nerve. Avril would not have the guts to assume the title of author and go off alone to face the music.

But Kirsty's peers are greatly impressed. 'Bernie has kissed the blarney stone,' says Lorna Hodge, who does the top landing, folding the edge of a new toilet roll into a neat triangle. 'And she's got the looks to carry it off.'

'She might be only nineteen,' Marie with the varicose veins agrees, 'but these days lasses younger than that know a damn sight more than their own mothers.'

'That boyfriend of hers let her down badly.'

'Oh, didn't you know? He's turned up again like a bad penny. A local hero, no less, bit of a lad from all you hear.'

Kirsty spends the big day, Friday, in alternate states of fear and excitement, her hands clammy, her heart racing, waiting for Bernie's return from London.

Bernie is childishly indiscreet. If only she was more circumspect. How long will it take before she forgets and lets the truth slip out? Kirsty would have no alternative but to put a stop to *Magdalene* if her name ever came up, although a couple of thousand pounds among three is a sum not to be sneezed at, the chance of a car for her and the kids, some decent second-hand winter clothes, a few homely touches to that stark mobile home which would make all the difference.

She has underestimated Trevor before and she is not about to do so again.

Bernie comes home smiling broadly.

'I felt so special, I've never felt that special before.'

And they all understand what she means.

But everything sounds too good to be true. Is this another example of Bernie getting carried away, letting fantasy get the better of her, or can the glowing reports of her lunch with Candice Love be anywhere near the truth?

She certainly sounds convincing enough, and she went to London looking stunning in a nymphlike full-length summer dress, blue with white daisies.

Innocence personified.

'The train was late. I was hysterical. We had lunch at a bistro called Le Fromage Frais. She was really kind, but frightening, you know. Nothing normal like any of us. I could smoke, and when I ran out she asked the waiter and he brought me a packet of Gauloise.'

Come on, come on, stop waffling. Kirsty's urge is to shake her, but she doubts that would calm Bernie down. Quite dazed with happiness, her green eyes shine with anticipation, but anticipation of what?

'Shut up! For God's sake shut up!' shouts Kirsty. '*Did she believe you?*'

Bernie gives a coy half-smile. 'Of course she believed me,' she coos in her most coppery voice. 'What is this? The inquisition? Why does nobody think that someone like me could write a book? I do come from Ireland you know, land of musicians and bards.'

'But did she ask you about the plot?'

'She asked what happened in the end.'

Kirsty sweats on the answer. 'And did you remember?'

'Of course I remembered.' Bernie turns lofty. 'I'd only just read it, hadn't I, and I had nothing else to read on the train, so I got halfway through it again.' The crucifix round Bernie's neck is nothing like the one Trevor wore, that sharp, cruel reminder of suffering, with Christ's skinny legs pinned down by nails. Bernie's is more like a chunky medallion, with soft aquamarine for eyes. You can almost forget what it signifies; the man on the cross could be her lover.

'So, did she ask you about your background? How you came to start writing? That sort of stuff?'

Bernie's green eyes dance. 'May God forgive me, I said I'd been writing since I was eight. To my eternal punishment I said I'd always wanted to be a writer. I told her *Magdalene* was my first attempt at a full-length novel and that it only took me six weeks. She seemed to like that.' Then Bernie remembers, with a wink that only adds charm to her impish beauty, 'And she did seem quite chuffed by

142

the fact that I was so young and looked pretty. She ranted on about publicity and the fact that most of her authors look like elephants' arseholes.'

'How long is it going to take her to read the rest of the book? Did she say?' asks a hiccuping Avril, halfway through her second Mars bar of the evening.

'That doesn't seem to matter. She's been in touch with some editors already; she's going to get the first five chapters off to them tomorrow. You should have seen her wicked leather jacket. I had to sign some letter saying that I agreed for them to be my agents. It must be quite a simple letter, I managed to understand it.'

Bernie digs deep in her bag and hands the crumpled letter over. Out of the bag spill hundreds of Candice's cards. 'I took a handful.' Bernie shrugs. 'I thought I might as well. They were free.'

'*And what about you?* What did you tell her?'

Kirsty and Avril wait impatiently while Bernie sticks a rollie together with the curled-up pink edge of her tongue. 'She was fazed when I told her I worked in a bar. And then I went on about other places I've worked in Liverpool, even the strip club where me and my mate lasted for four days and got the push, and that Daddy is with Costain and Mammy works for Littlewood's Pools. She seemed to like this better than if I'd come from some classy home, or been to university, or had posh connections.'

'You didn't mention my name at all, are you sure, *not even by accident*?' And Kirsty is struck by the realization that she feels no scruples at all. All she cares about is pulling this off, and the others seem equally determined. Where have Avril's reservations gone?

'Jaysus. What d'you take me for?' Bernie is scornful. 'An eejit?'

'So, what now?' asks Avril, calmed and reassured as she awkwardly fixes her rollers. For every hair she wraps round the spool there's three others stuck out at right angles.

'We wait till Candice hears from those editors. And I suppose we wait until she's read the rest of the book.'

'But how is she going to get back to us if she can't get through on the phone?'

'I gave her the hotel fax number. So it's up to Avril to deal with that.'

'No problem,' says Avril.

'She's going to fax us if she wants us to ring her.'

'That should work OK.'

'She understands how we live down here. I told her about the vampire Stokes and slimy Derek Pugh. She said they could star in my next book.'

'She's already talking about another?'

'She seemed to think that would just come.'

'Damn,' says Kirsty.

'Writer's block,' says Avril, fixing her pink hairnet. 'And let's face it, surely some authors only write one. You can't expect ideas to spew over like the contents of the magic porridge pot.'

Kirsty and Bernie ignore her. Avril often surprises them with nostalgic childish references.

There is a new girl at the doctor's surgery. She has been here on work experience before; they were impressed so they took her on. But before she reaches receptionist standard she must learn to be rude to intractable patients, sharp like a robot on the phone and quick with the doctor's coffee. Until she reaches these dizzy heights she must deal with the everyday forms, drug-company blurb and enquiries that litter the mat every morning.

For instance, here is a request from a surgery on the Wirral for the medical cards of two of Doctor Worthington's patients. Well, we don't hold the medical cards, the medical cards are held by the patient, but busy, secretarially over-stressed Gloria, having tried the mother to no avail, uses her initiative and rings the original home number to see if, by any chance, the cards are still there.

Mr Hoskins sounds confused on the phone, slow, as if he's only just up. Yes, he thinks that he probably has them and will drop them in this afternoon, but is the surgery certain that his wife does not have them with her?

People can be so disorganized. Honestly, you just wouldn't believe . . .

They miss their appointments, stub out their fags in the porch geraniums, forget to reorder their drugs, vomit on the floor of the toilets, tear bits out of magazines and sit for hours for emergency appointments when they've got a splinter in their finger or a small head cold.

It is shocking to know what diseases and infections some of the snootiest patients pick up, brazen as hell. And so many folk are depressed and suicidal, in total despair, on Prozac. Until she worked here she never realized how lucky she'd been with her body.

This is all rather confusing. 'I think somebody

has already been in touch with your wife down in Cornwall, at the hotel where she works. She was sure the medical cards were not with her.'

'No worries, love, OK,' says the affable Mr Trevor Hoskins, 'I'll bring them in this afternoon.' His breathing sounds more laboured than it should be, a forty-a-day smoker no doubt. He will soon regret his habit, gasping his last, drowning in emphysema.

Eleven

Bad egg, Graham Stott, prowls the streets of China
Town for the most likely victim he can find.

Since his release from gaol three weeks ago life
has not gone well for poor Graham. He was well
miffed when his mum chucked him out with no
more thought than she'd give a bad carrot. You'd
have thought she'd give him a few days' grace. After
all, he is her first-born, and there was a time when
she seemed to love him. A short time after this bad
trip, Graham, bitter and hard-done-by, dusted himself down, grabbed a wash in a gents' public bog,
scraped the top layer of stubble from his chin and
hitched his hungry way to the centre of the city,
where he called on his father, Richard, at Burt and
Sturgess, the gentleman's outfitters where he has
worked since the day after his marriage.

'Hi, Dad.'

Even as a small child it had always hurt Graham
to visit his father here. Burt and Sturgess has
stooped his father, lined him and virtually effaced
him, as he spent his working life ingratiatingly
serving the gentlemen of the city with their bowler
hats, pinstriped suits and chill-proof under-

garments. Among rows of brown drawers, behind oaken counters, Dick Stott lives out his life with a tape measure around his neck, which is more constricting than leg-irons.

And why the hell does he do it? Why has he laid down his life like the generation before him? There will be no medals for him, no little white cross in the corner of some foreign field.

Has he laid it down for that mean little house with the stiff woman in it, for children ungrateful and angry, for a five-year-old car and a caravan, for a video recorder and a microwave? For sex on Saturday and a joint on Sunday? For a garden full of chrysanthemums and a crazy-paving path with weeds persistently growing through it?

What of travel? What of adventure? What of love and lust, wine and music and dancing? How come Graham has missed out as well, as if, from egg to embryo, he has lacked the gene to lead him to the secret.

Since his opt-out from school in the fourth grade, when Graham had the wit to see that he would never be one of the chosen who drive fast sports cars and pull the birds with their high-flying lives in the glass skyscrapers of the world's great cities, Graham's concrete future flanked him with its multi-storey car parks, garish arcades and underpasses where he went with his mates for a quick shag, a beer or a smoke. Here yesterday's youth threw cans, graffitied the walls, exchanged their dreams and watched them spiral away on the ring roads around suburbia's smog.

'Graham?' exclaimed his father, looking furtively round. It would not do for Mr Sturgess to see such an uncouth yob in the shop.

'I went home,' said Graham, lolling against the polished counter, worn smooth by years of sliding tweeds. There was a chance that mother might not have mentioned his visit. 'And that was a waste of time.'

'I could have told you that. I'll be off in an hour,' said his father underhandedly, 'why don't we meet in the Kardomah?'

Oh yeah, the Kardomah. Don't say that stuffy old dump was still going? With a pang of pain Graham remembered that his father and mother considered it appropriate to fraternize reputable eating places. No dark, smoky wine bars for them. No public bars in red-carpeted pubs, perched on stools in the daytime like losers. No burger bars, no pizza huts, no pancake parlours, no spud-u-likes, nothing remotely suggestive of anything more titillating than the nine o'clock news or the weather forecast.

'I need cash,' demanded Graham, seated in a booth where the plush velvet hangings enveloped him in the smell of ground coffee.

'But I don't have any cash,' said his dad.

'Just a few quid to see me through.'

'I would if I could, son, believe me.'

'Can't you go to a hole in the wall?'

'You know your mother. She won't touch that sort of thing with a barge pole.'

'I'd pay you back,' Graham lied.

'I know you would, son. I know you would.'

'Only I've nowhere to kip tonight.'

His father's sad eyes moved off him. 'There must be places.'

'Hostels? Hostels for the homeless? Old tramps and piss heads?'

149

'Cheap hotels. They must have given you some money, son. Surely they wouldn't have thrown you out without a penny to your name?'

'I don't suppose there's any point in you talking to Mum? Changing her mind? Just for a couple of days?'

Richard Stott sagged in his chair and his cheap work suit sagged around him. 'She has taken enough, Graham. Her nerves are shot. Try to understand. She is not a well woman herself, and she's got young Avril to consider. What you must do is look for a job, a steady job with prospects.'

It is like a tribal initiation, savage cuts made by old men on the young. I suffered, so if you want your own hut, your own spear and a wife, you must follow in my footsteps. But once Graham believed his dad was a king, with his tools, his balsa-wood models and his paintbrush. 'Oh yeah? A job? Like yours, Dad?'

Balls. He should have kept his mouth shut. What was the point, after all? What triumph was gained from watching his father lamely search for excuses? Richard knew what he was, he understood about sacrifice; he, presumably, had been young once, with all the passions, hopes and dreams . . . but it all boils down to a Bluebird caravan and shepherd's pie when he gets home.

The old woman limps towards him, but Graham is invisible in the night, squatted down in some lawyer's basement, teeth bared, senses charged.

He hopes she has been to bingo – the old Odeon has long since been converted to a mass of gobbling money machines that straddle the carpets in armour of chrome and silver. Through the foyer where he went as a child, popcorn in one hand, Coke in the other, it is now a vast open space done up tastelessly in reds and gilts, like the soulless debating chamber of some Eastern-bloc country.

Her handbag is heavy, it weighs her down. It's more like a hold-all; she probably takes her valuables with her, her specs and her medication, her tissues and snaps of the grandchildren. He waits in the shadows of the basement steps, wound up like a clockwork toy whose spring is about to snap, but quietly patient. Since his meeting with his father, Graham has spent too many nights in basements like this, on cold, ungiving pavements, disturbed by the community-mad, the derelicts and the dope heads.

When the old biddy draws alongside, Graham steps up quietly behind her. The Stanley knife glistens in his hand. He holds it against her throat, inadvertently shocked by her birdlike frame, so lightweight and fragile under the coat, and the elderly smell of face powder.

She squawks but offers no other resistance. In two swift movements he snatches her bag and shoves her against the wall in order to give his flight impetus; she is merely the punch bag he can bounce off. All he wants is her dosh, her winnings, *some hope*. All he wants is some time to find the right people, men who don't care where he's been, what he's done, men who might consider him useful in the dark underworld of the city.

With a tight-lipped grimace Mrs Stott thrusts the evening paper aside with its grisly front-page picture of the local pensioner who has been in a coma for the last seven days. Probably a happy release now she's gone. Mugged for £1.39. The poor old biddy would never have slept easy in her own bed at night if she had lived. These animals roaming the streets of every city in the land ought to be put down like dogs – no nonsense.

'I wasn't going to mention this, Avril,' says Mrs Stott to her daughter, during one of the prearranged telephone calls they have twice a week, to Avril's increasing dismay, 'but I've had a visit.' She draws in her breath dramatically. 'From Graham.'

'Then why did you mention it, Mother?' Avril knows very well why Mother has brought up the subject, she is only surprised how she has kept this disturbing news to herself for so long. Mother wants sympathy and condolence and reassurance from Avril that it was not her lack of parenting skills that drove young Graham off the rails.

'There is no need to take that attitude, Avril. I can't imagine what's going on down there, but every time I speak to you you seem more distant, harder somehow, not like my Avril at all.'

'And I wish you wouldn't ring Mrs Stokes up behind my back,' Avril decides to add while she's at it. 'Apart from being unnecessary, not to mention shaming if any of the other members of staff found out, it's time you stopped checking up on me.'

Mrs Stott's voice takes on a manipulative wobble. '*But, Avril, I do these things because I care.* I wouldn't be a proper mother if I didn't care.'

'So what happened with Graham?' Avril would rather switch to this subject, repetitive though it might be, than paddle around in the slush of her mother's emotional turmoil.

'He looked just the same.' That hard edge is back in her voice. 'Prison hasn't changed him. Came here thinking he could just move back in and start using his father and I again. Huh! He must think we're daft, and his language is still as bad – cursing and swearing in my own kitchen.'

'So you sent him on his way, did you, Mother?'

'Don't take that bored tone with me, Avril. *What has got into you lately?* You of all people know how much I suffered over all those years with your brother in the house and his dishonest, coarse, aggressive ways.'

'Well, I'm sure you did the best thing by turning him away.'

'As you know, I'm a bag of nerves as a result of those dreadful times, I sleep badly, my blood pressure's up and Dr Hunt says I must take things easy. But there's your father to look after, poor Fluffy and this house, and then, on top of all that, Graham comes along as cocky as you please. They should have warned me. The shock could have killed me. I mean, there he was on my doorstep like the proverbial bad penny.'

Now, since *Magdalene*, Avril can put words to her pain, lyrics to her childhood song. And, what is more, she can share it with friends who understand and support her.

Graham, Graham, Graham. When she was younger, before his name was banned from use in her mother's house, Graham was the standard by which Avril was judged. 'Don't be like Graham, Avril. Please, do something with this untidy room.'

153

'If Graham won't help me I know Avril will.'

'Just because Graham will only eat chips, doesn't mean that you should copy him.'

'Never take money from my purse without asking' – as if Avril would dream of doing that – 'If you need anything, Avril, just say.'

She did say. But she didn't get it.

And Graham getting away with murder, Graham bringing his friends to the house and teasing fat Avril until she cried and hid herself away when she heard them coming through the front door. Graham hiding in the cupboard in the bathroom while she was on the loo. Graham springing out on her, Graham nicking her savings by smashing that lovely pink china pig, Graham's little blackmailing scams, Graham twisting her arm in a Chinese burn till she screamed.

And so on and so forth . . .

Poor Avril grew up terrified of Graham. Why couldn't they make him behave? Just because he was a boy? If she'd ever behaved like him her punishments would have been grim. And why wasn't he taken away and locked up? Why did the police bring him home over and over and over again, more secure and triumphant in his wickedness than ever?

Avril must be polite and biddable.

'Look, our Avril's a lovely girl, nothing at all like Graham.'

And Avril, in her white socks and shorts, would stand there fatly, smiling.

Was there something in Mother's psyche that welcomed Graham's rebellious streak, something connected with a sense of vengeance towards her weak-natured husband?

154

'Goodness knows where your brother is now,' Mother continues painfully. 'He even had the nerve to pay your father a visit at work, cadging money off him, as usual.'

'Poor Father.'

'Poor Father? Poor me more like. It's always me who has picked up the pieces, tried to smooth the troubled waters. If I'd left anything to your father, goodness knows where we would be now. I dread to think. I really do.'

'Well, let's hope that was Graham's last visit. At last, perhaps, he will leave you alone.'

'I doubt we've heard the last of him,' says Mrs Stott darkly.

Avril's small amount of self-esteem has been given a mighty boost just lately by the sudden attentions of Ed Board, the Burleston golf professional. Her unusually cryptic response to her mother might partly be due to this turn of fortune. Add the punch of her two close friends, mix these with the force of *Magdalene* and it makes a pretty heady concoction.

Ed Board, thirty-eight, with red hair, a paunch and a stiff moustache that she tries to ignore, began his courtship by inviting Avril for a free lesson on the practice ground. 'You look like a golfer in the making,' he told her, slapping her soundly on the back.

'He fancies you,' said Bernie immediately when Avril shared this odd experience.

'But he's thirty-eight.'

'So? There's nothing wrong with thirty-eight.'

'But I don't know if I like him.'

'*Get on,*' laughed Bernie. 'Give it a chance.'

155

So, in the still, warm peace of the following evening, Avril set out with the blessings of her friends. She made her way over the springy turf and puffed through the bramble and long grasses. On Kirsty's advice she wore a long skirt and a loose, baggy T-shirt. Her shoes were solid and sensible.

'Hi there!' called Ed Board sportily; head down, he was chipping away from a transparent tube full of balls.

'I don't know a thing about golf,' said Avril. 'But I'm willing to learn.'

Before Avril knew it he was behind her, so close she could feel the shape of his paunch, busily positioning her arms. Unaware that she, herself, is an invader of space, she worried that he might be deliberately rubbing himself against her. Was he taking advantage? Bernie would know, so why didn't she? 'Head down,' he ordered, 'now swing!'

Avril swung, missed and giggled.

'Don't worry, that's bound to happen,' said Ed gamely. 'Here we go, try again.'

She was not disturbed by his proximity, in fact she was quite enjoying it, so perhaps that was a clue to his motives. Avril did not feel uneasy in the way the police had warned them as children – if you feel uneasy about it, follow your instincts, they are usually right. So Avril did not dissuade Ed Board, and gradually she made progress until she was hitting one ball in three.

How could anyone in their right mind take a game like this seriously, let alone teach it?

'Jolly good!' said Ed, encouragingly, now wrapping and unwrapping her hands round the club head until she was holding it correctly. Avril's guilty feelings made her compare the rubbery head of the club to the staff of an erect penis. Was Ed having similar dirty thoughts? Was he getting a kick out of this? Just as she was beginning to think she was allowing him far too much feely-leeway, he suggested a drink at the bar. 'It's a lovely evening still. We could sit outside. I could murder a beer, I don't know about you.'

'Well, perhaps not a beer,' said Avril, relieved. 'But I wouldn't turn down a tomato juice.'

'With a tickle of vodka, no doubt?' And Ed nudged her rather uncouthly. He meant no harm, he was just one of those 'touching' people, probably because of his job.

The sun was setting over the sea by the time they reached the hotel bar and took up positions on the patio overlooking the bay. The fairy lights made chains of bright spangles. The white wrought-iron tables set with flowers added scents to the summer magic. A piano was playing behind them – something from *South Pacific*, thought Avril – 'Younger Than Springtime'.

'I'm enjoying this,' said Ed, nodding and humming along to the tune with a line of foam on his moustache.

'So am I,' said Avril.

'We must do this again.'

'That would be nice,' she told him, and he took her left hand and pressed it.

'You really must understand, Miss Stott, that to receive personal faxes on the hotel machines and in office hours could well be construed as petty pilfering from the company.'

'Nonsense,' says the new, vital Avril, turning a flaming puce face towards Mr Derek's contemptuous one. 'I fully intend to pay for these two sheets of fax paper, and I'm prepared to work one minute overtime for nothing to make sure you are not in any way affected.'

'The point is', says a nonplussed Mr Derek, taking one squeaky step backwards, 'that some important message might have been coming through.'

'Don't be silly,' Avril follows up, sounding far too much like Mother for comfort, 'anyone finding the number engaged will simply try later.'

'I do not like your attitude, young lady.'

'And you have always been rude to me; right from the beginning your treatment of me has been very unkind.' Avril is shaking like a blancmange. Behind her back the stubby fingers of one hand are clutched tightly in the other, but she is determined to see this through. 'And unfair.'

Instant dismissal?

She will now be sacked for insolence and have to slope back home in a cloud of shame. She will unpack in her little bedroom again, 'The little window where the sun came peeping in at morn', lie her pyjama case on her bed and have to be down for breakfast at eight. Mother will boil her egg for four minutes, just as she likes it. She will catch up with all the soaps, of which Mother is a reluctant addict, until these simplistic programmes become more exciting than real life itself; the stars her friends, their highs Avril's highs, their lows her lows. Eventually Mother will find her an appropriate job, nearer to home this time because, in her eyes, Avril will have been tainted by her first taste of freedom. The first sign of the family disease will be diagnosed and treated.

'Well, please don't let this happen again,' Mr Derek is saying, regarding her with curious new eyes before disappearing into his office.

'G–g–gosh!' exclaims Miss Pudsey with open-mouthed admiration.

'Good on you,' says lazy Rhoda. 'You put that nerd in his place.'

But Avril is so shocked that she nearly forgets the offending fax, and when she does remember she discovers that her hands are still wet and trembling.

Twelve

'As I was going to St Ives . . .'

Besotted Belinda from Bath does not sound like a problem-page contributor for nothing. When blond-haired, blue-eyed Belinda scans the cards of congratulations sent to her heroic partner, she stops short when she reaches the one from Bernadette Gallagher.

'Who the hell is Bernadette Gallagher?'

'Some girl.'

'She sounds like more than that, Dom. She sounds like something dead serious.'

'It was ages ago, *don't go on.*'

'She's working down here, at the Burleston Hotel. Why would she come down here?'

'She probably followed me. She had the hots for me, if I remember rightly.'

'Well? Are you going to see her?'

Dominic rolls over in the large lumpy bed in a ground-floor room at the guest house that is his home until September. He strokes Belinda's forehead and bites his lips; there is a teasing gleam in his eye. 'I might do. What's it to you?'

Belinda pouts. 'I wish you wouldn't act like this,

Dom. I don't think you realize how much you hurt people. You and I are sharing something now that is very, very special and it's really sick to talk that way . . .'

'Shut up and turn over.'

Embroidered with flowers like a tapestry cottage, Dominic's little guest house – four fishermen's cottages knocked into one – is huddled in a cobbled street leading down to a paint-by-numbers harbour. Where have all the fishermen gone, a stranger might well ask. The mullioned windows let in the scents of wild wisteria and window boxes, fish, chips, burgers and garbage strung around every alley by viciously marauding seagulls.

Against these alluring backdrops the godlike Dominic has posed for photographs, given interviews and received all the accolades he so richly deserves. Even the mother of the rescued Melanie, while grieving over the death of her husband, can be comforted by remembering him as a valiant hero who died attempting to save their baby.

'It's a bugger,' said Justin Mellor, the surfer deep in his cups during one of the many glowing, long-lingering celebratory nights. Belinda leaned over to listen, the juke box was too loud for conversation in this pub. You had to shout to be heard. 'It's a bugger, the poor sod died well in his depth. If only he'd put his legs down.'

'Well, why did he die, then?' slurred Belinda, not too sober herself, 'if he was in his depth?'

'Could've been Dom's karate chop. Could've been cramp.' Justin belched and closed his eyes against his own hazy smoke. 'Could've been that the poor bastard's lungs were already filled up with water.'

Justin Mellor, whose one aim in life is attaining world fame as a surfboard champion, has since departed to Aussie land, there to take part in a competition, all costs covered by some private sponsorship.

Since then, Belinda once asked Dom casually, 'Did you take karate at school?'

'Yep. But I gave it up. I was just too good at it.' And he gave her a gentle high-kick to the ribs.

In the comforting dark of his whitewashed room, behind the drawn gingham curtains, when the moon-kissed sea whispers softly and the drunks have all gone home – at around about four in the morning – Dominic has been known to weep, held safely in Belinda's arms. 'Jesus Christ, if I hadn't been drinking I might have been able to save them both.'

'Don't, Dom,' comforts Belinda in her most motherly fashion. 'Don't do this to yourself. You saved another human being, a little girl, a baby, you have achieved more in your life than most people achieve in the whole of theirs. And the father was a fully grown man, and drowning; he could have killed you both. You had to leave him and go for the child, you know you did. Everyone knows you did.'

'I know that,' sniffs Dominic. 'But I'll never forget that poor man's face and the way I had to fend him off. I'd had two lagers, two cans of wine – that's the equivalent of half a bottle – and before

162

that, at lunchtime, I had a Tequila some Yank insisted on buying me.'

'But nobody knows this, Dom.'

'*I know,*' Dom weeps again, great, dry, sobbing gasps pass through him. 'Don't you sodding well understand, *I know.* And I can never forgive myself.'

'How could you behave in this way, Candice, you could have lost us the author; you could have lost the firm thousands, let alone the kudos of handling her.'

Candice Love jangles her bangles in a nervous show of contriteness. It is as near as she can get to an apology.

'You knew bloody well what might happen to this novel and you deliberately and deceitfully tried to deal with it yourself, leaving me completely in the dark.' Rory's velvet voice rises until it reaches rasping proportions. 'What if you'd fucked up? Who do you think you bloody well are? We're not in this for personal acclaim, in case you hadn't noticed. We're supposed to work as a team! Jesus Christ, Candice, you must have known you couldn't carry this through on your own. Once someone else had read this it was bound to cause a sensation.'

And then poor Candice, whipped like a dog, had to account for the third time for all her actions since reading page one of the manuscript of *Magdalene*.

At the high-powered offices of Coburn and Watts the morning has been spent frenziedly trying to repair any damage the lone Candice might have caused. Handled correctly, this author will make a fortune from book rights and advances alone.

Candice's painful downfall was caused by the immediate interest shown by the four publishers to whom she had sent copies of the début novel. The first two replied the following morning, one even arrived at the office by taxi and, unfortunately, met RC on the stairs only to discover he knew nothing about the book. The first action taken by Rory was to dish out extra copies to four more publishing houses and he knows damn well that the faxes and phones for the film rights will soon be buzzing. The North American rights should be huge.

The biggest film deal he has clinched for an author is a staggering $8 million record-breaker, and he reckons he can do the same here.

'So come on, Candice,' Rory grabs her when he has a spare second, Rory the dynamic hunk who Candice has lusted after for years without even a suggestion of returned eye contact, so that she is beginning to suspect the worst, 'tell us,' drawls this literary Adonis, 'what is this phenomenon like?'

Candice, with the stuffing knocked out of her, must somehow redeem herself in the eyes of her influential boss, otherwise she's out of the publishing world for good with no chance of getting him into her bed. 'She is nineteen, Irish and beautiful.' And I wish I was her, she might well have added, aware of Rory's fetish for authors.

'Has she any idea of the situation?'

'No, her expectations are limited. She's a barmaid in a hotel. The best job she has ever had was stripping in a Liverpool nightclub. I think she is surprised that her novel has attracted any attention at all.' Candice thinks back to the girl with the green, excited eyes. 'But she is ambitious. Loads of charisma and energy. I'd say she was the most perfect author that any publicity department could dream of.'

'Better and better,' says Rory, twiddling with the orchid in the button hole of his black velvet jacket.

'Married? Involved?'

'Not that I know of.'

'Not that you know of? *Christ!* Candice! This girl is one hot property; she's young and needs to be carefully handled. I would go down to Cornwall myself, but I need to be here to deal with the bids.'

'I could go.'

'You'll have to.' The faxes are whirring, the phones are bleeping and Rory's egg sandwich has gone dry on his desk. 'You can fly to Penzance in the morning. Kavanagh needs to be warned right off about media interest, fakes and scavengers.'

Back in the bar at the Burleston.

'And who the hell are you?'

'You don't know me, but my name is Belinda Phelps, Dominic's friend.' When Bernie stares blankly back the girl assumes she needs to remind her, 'You wrote to him. You sent him a card with a personal note?'

'*A private note.*'

'OK, OK.' The blonde bimbo looks round, her black leather miniskirt sliding with her as one. 'Can we go over there – sit in the corner?'

Bernie is not allowed to sit in the bar while on

165

duty, but Charlie seems to be coping well and this is an emergency. Belinda has the word 'urgent' in neon across her peeling forehead.

'This is all rather sensitive, you understand.'

'I haven't got very long,' says Bernie.

Belinda, her wide eyes paler than any recognizable blue, starts off in a conspiratorial manner, as if the two women are on the same side. 'Only Dom is going through a really hard time just now.'

'Yeah?' Bernie is trapped, brain whirling, she can see nothing clearly. She is forced to light up a fag. She can't sit here doing nothing with her hands and she has an aversion to olives.

'You might imagine he is in his element, what with all the publicity crap, but underneath he's going through hell because he believes he ought to have been able to save them both.'

If only Bernie could snap herself out of this semi-coma. She is already nervous about Candice Love's arrival in the morning. The fax said nothing more. And now, baffled, she still fails to see what this is leading up to. '*Save them both?*'

'The dad and the kid,' nods the blonde, blinking wildly. 'He was forced to fight the father off and it seems that this might have caused the man's death. Did Dom have a drink problem when you were with him?'

At this Bernie can't help snorting. 'Like hell. We all did. We were pissed as farts the whole time.'

'Aha,' says Belinda knowingly. 'So it started a long time ago.'

'Not so bloody long,' corrects Bernie. 'Last year to be exact.'

'Last year? *Are you sure?* Dom assures me it was ages ago.'

'Look,' says Bernie impatiently while inside her heart sickens and sinks, hurting so much it's like there's a chainsaw hacking its way down the centre. She wants to hide and be alone. '*What is this?* Why are you here? Did Dom send you? Does he want to see me?'

'*God, no,*' says Belinda, 'that is the last thing he needs right now. Dom and I are working hard to build up our relationship. Poor Dom, he's so insecure underneath, so emotionally vulnerable, a child at heart with such a thick defensive veneer . . .'

'Balls,' says Bernie too loudly, causing several Burleston guests to pause and look distastefully at her.

'*I'm sorry?*'

'I said balls.'

'But you must have noticed Dom's inability to form any lasting relationships, especially with women. His desire to hurt them. To love them and leave them. It's his mother, you see, he wants to punish her for sending him away at eight years old. Did you know that, Bernadette?' And Belinda leans forward confidentially in order to pass on these special secrets. Bernie wants to slap her face and knock it out of the way. But she does nothing. She just sits here taking it. 'Poor Dom was sent away to prep school when he was just eight years old. Before that there was a string of nannies. I can see from your expression that Dominic must have hurt you, too. He must have hurt you very, very badly, Bernadette.'

'I don't need this shit.'

'Bernadette. Please don't push me away like this.'

'You fuckin' eejit. I'll push you over this bloody table if you don't get out of here.'

'Now now, ladies,' says Charlie the barman, gliding over on feet like castors, his circular tray making do as a shield. 'This is not the time or the place to be fighting over young men.'

'Young men?' screams Bernie, losing her cool. 'Young bastards with their brains in their pricks.'

Poor Belinda looks mortified as she hurries out of the Burleston bar, red, palpitating, muttering and wondering whether it might have been wiser to leave matters alone. But she'd been so afraid that the questing Dominic might take it into his head to renew this old relationship, which had clearly been rather special, *on her side*, that much was obvious. Is it possible that Belinda might have construed matters wrongly in spite of her psychology A level? After all, she and Dom have only been a serious item for twelve days, five hours and . . . might she, too, be the victim of some lamentable infatuation?

Heartbreak hotel.

Total is the darkness of Bernadette's despair.

'But Bernie, he sounds like a right little jerk.'

'But I love him, Kirsty, I love him.'

'How can you possibly love a man who makes you so unhappy?'

'You don't understand,' Bernie weeps majestically on. 'How can you understand?'

'Ask a silly question,' says Kirsty, eyes staring back into memory.

Bernie is dragged from her deepest pain by the look of fear on Kirsty's face. 'You can't still think he's looking for you?'

'I know he is.' Kirsty goes quiet.

'But why can't you divorce him? Take out an injunction or something? Surely the law has some way of protecting women from bastards like him?'

'I never dared tell the police', Kirsty spreads helpless hands, 'when it was all going on. Listen, I was so scared of Trev at that time I believed he was hiding out in my head. And if I'd asked for help he might have kept away for a while, but sometime he would have been back, crazier than ever. He's always made out it's me who's cracked and I was frightened they would believe him and take the kids away. He said that's what he'd do if I left him.'

'But he won't find you here. He can't.' Poor Bernie's face is bruised from crying. Her eyes are so swollen and sore she can only just peer out.

'I don't think he will. Not really. And the kids are safe for the moment, thank God, as long as I can keep out of the limelight. It's not that Trev reads books, but news like that gets around, especially locally, and Trev has his mates; there's blokes at the pub he goes round with. He'd know if I had a book published.'

'So can't you divorce him from here? Where you're safe? There must be ways of doing it without him finding you.'

'I will. But wait till I get my kids back. Wait till I find a home for them. The moment I get on my feet I'm off to find out what I can do. But first I have to get my head together.'

'He's evil.' The sniffing Bernie is briefly inflamed, and relieved, by straightforward hatred. 'Sick. You need to get even with him just like I need to get even with that cocksucker, Dominic.'

'Look at you, Bernie, look in the mirror, see what you're doing to yourself. We mustn't give in, that's what's important now if we want to come out of this winning,' says Kirsty, squeezing her hand. 'Think what Magdalene would do if she saw us being so pathetic. God, she'd have taken those nerds apart and fed them to the ducks by now. Like the time she found that rapist and took out his eyes with the crochet hook she used for her hassocks.'

'Stop it, Kirsty! Stop it!'

Bernie shivers, terribly tired, and it's not the result of the crying this time. Trying to imagine Magdalene's revenge makes her blood run cold. If Trev is a monster, then what does that make Magdalene? The anti-heroine in Kirsty's book, the nun with her prayer book and her arsenal of weapons, is more innately evil than Anthony Hopkins in *Silence of the Lambs*, madder than Jack Nicholson in *The Shining* and more manipulative than Glenn Close in *Fatal Attraction*.

Bernie laughed at all those films, but she can't raise a smile for Magdalene.

The nun has the power to draw people to her.

Sometimes Bernie thinks she would rather not be part of this, as if, in some unexplained way, contamination might be possible. Perhaps she should make an act of contrition, lest her sin be proclaimed at God's tribunal in the valley of Jehoshaphat and she suffer the punishment of the damned.

As Mammy has so often threatened.

It's still a puzzle to understand how a character so grotesque can evoke such reader satisfaction, such understanding of where she comes from, demented black laughter, even, when joined by eye to Magdalene, this savage, satanic, sanctified sister.

Thirteen

Like a hound who has finally found the scent –
proved by the satisfied howl he emitted when the
girl at the surgery made her disclosure – Trevor
Hoskins can now make some progress. He spends
hours during his long, lonely evenings dialling
through the telephone book – a Cornish edition
of Yellow Pages that British Telecom sent him for
free, a service he hadn't known existed.

'Good evening,' he says authoritatively. 'I am
detective inspector Bates from Merseyside CID and
I'm looking for a white female with two children
believed to be working in a hotel in Cornwall. Her
name is Kirsty Hoskins, thirty years old, height five
feet five inches. She could be using a false name. She
has long brown hair worn up in a knot, a pale
complexion, large brown eyes, and her main dis-
tinguishing feature is the gap between her two front
teeth.'

He smiles when he puts the phone down and
crosses off the last name on the list. One down . . .
more to go. He can afford to take his time. He will
track her down eventually, as she must have known
that he would. If they ask what the law wants her

for he merely says, 'That's confidential, I am afraid,' in a voice that suggests something sleazy.

Trevor visits his solicitor and fills in the legal-aid forms. Now he is hot on Kirsty's trail he must plan his next actions with care. His solicitor is too young, in Trevor's opinion, to be dealing with cases other than driving offences – which Trevor considers a waste of time – and he seems concerned that, although Trevor is not suing for divorce, he wants custody of his children.

'I love my wife,' lies Trevor, in Gas Board time, the give-away van safe in the firm's private car park. 'She can't help her mental illness. And I doubt that she'll want to divorce me, either. We've been to hell and back, me and her. But we're fond of each other, Mr . . .'

'Gillespie.'

'Well . . . Mr Gillespie,' says Trevor, uncomfortable with the higher rank in spite of the tender years, 'she has lied to my own mother on occasion – broke her own arm once and swore I'd done it – and my mother will testify to this. Kirsty seems determined to show that during our eight-year marriage I constantly abused her.' Trevor pauses to roll his eyes, to smile with mock understanding. 'She was always cutting herself with bits of mirror, bruising her arms, biting bits of her own body. If I was smashing the hell out of her, don't you think she'd have left before now?'

'Unless she was too afraid,' says Mr Gillespie, meeting and holding Trevor's eyes. Is he a poof? Trevor worries.

'Kirsty was never afraid of me. My wife used to fantasize, you see. It was the bloody books she kept

173

on reading. She'd see herself as the heroine and start believing she was a fashion designer, or an airline pilot, or a sodding film director. Anything. Can you believe it? Whatever the latest book was about. But she couldn't have been bored. She worked full time,' and Trevor hots up, sensing audience disbelief, 'and none of her workmates ever heard her complain about me or her marriage. And I've already spoken to one or two.'

'What a good thing her heroines were always benign,' muses Mr Gillespie. 'How about the neighbours?' he asks next, his sleeves rolled neatly below his elbow in the fashion of namby pamby professionals who have never done a decent day's work.

'We never lived in our neighbours' pockets.' Trevor shifts in his chair, remembering the several occasions when nosy parker Mr Terry from next door came banging on the door to ask if everything was all right. 'But there were times when Kirsty's fits grew hellishly violent, sometimes I had to physically control her and it could be that people thought the worst.'

Mr Gillespie leans forward, tapping his teeth with his silver pen. Why isn't the bugger getting all this down? 'Why is it that during all this time you never asked for help with Kirsty's problem? You could have spoken to your doctor, the social services, the mental welfare department. How is it you never considered getting professional help? I mean, your children's health must have suffered a great deal as a result of your wife's mental state. You must have been very concerned, particularly over her violent outbursts.'

Trevor hangs a sorry head. 'If she'd had the kids

174

taken away Kirsty would have lost it completely.'
His eyes take on an unhappy shine and he swallows
hard to digest the lie. 'I put her first, Mr Gillespie,
and that is where I fell down. My overriding concern was always for my wife. And despite everything
the kids did love her.'

The solicitor crosses his legs and leans back,
something Trevor cannot do because his chair is
too upright. This puts him at some disadvantage.
'But now you've changed your mind? Now you're
prepared to take action?'

'Well yes, who wouldn't be? I can't have Kirsty
hauling my kids up and down the land on a whim. I
can't allow that. Without me to keep an eye on the
situation, God knows what will happen to them.'
Trevor shrugs his solid shoulders. 'Hell, I don't even
know if they are alive! And I tell you this, I've lost
my patience with this basket case; she's gone too far
this time and I'm bloody angry. Wait till I get my
hands on her!'

Mr Gillespie nods many times. 'Has she ever
shown any violence towards the children in the
past?'

Trevor's lies slip easily off a well-practised
tongue. 'Only awful rages. She locked them in their
rooms a few times, scared the poor little buggers
stiff. You should see her, Christ, she turns into a
raging witch, so bloody strong, and it's getting
worse. I think it might run in the family; her dad
was a very odd bloke. She was brought up by her
dad, you see, because her mother died when she was
born.'

'And you went to the police, you say?'

'They weren't interested,' says Trevor defiantly,

his brain disorganized by anger. 'It seems that unless there's a proven history of trouble they call it another marital scrap and they're not prepared to take any action.'

'Are you quite sure the police haven't investigated the whereabouts of your children?' Mr Gillespie goes carefully on. 'It could be they have made enquiries and discovered that all is well.'

'They would have told me.'

'Not necessarily.'

This young man is too damn flippant.

'Why the hell not?'

'Not if they thought things were best left.'

Trevor sits forward. His fists are tightly curled balls. 'What are you bloody well getting at?'

'Calm down, calm down, these are matters I will have to go into before we take this any further.'

'But you do think I have a case?'

'If what you've told me is true, certainly, you do. Her illness sounds, to me, like a form of schizophrenia. What we would have to apply for is a section order under the mental-health act, something that's harder to achieve than you might imagine. It involves the signatures of two psychiatrists.'

'I wouldn't waste my bleeding time coming here and making up all sorts of crap, of course it's true. But Kirsty's not going to break down in front of two of your shrinks; she acts as sane as you or I. On the surface no-one would ever believe . . .' With difficulty Trevor takes hold of himself, noting his lawyer's anxious eyes.

'Look here, Mr Derek,' says Candice Love, leaning forward confidentially. 'It isn't going to look too good, to be honest, if the media arrive to find your barmaid slumming it in some garret.'

Mr Derek looks mortified. He has agreed to lunch with Candice Love, this sophisticated woman from London, in the conservatory, a vast Victorian structure of iron and glass, filled with vines and trailing blossoms. They share a table for two in the window overlooking the bay through the fuzzy tips of fir trees.

'What do you suggest we do?' enquires the hotel manager over a frosted ice bucket of terribly dry white wine while Candice picks at her lobster.

'Bernadette tells me she has no intention of returning to Liverpool, which is a pity because that's where her family are and, although they don't sound too bright, at least with them she would have some protection.'

'Protection from what?' asks a well-intimidated Mr Derek.

'From exploitation, of course,' says Candice, dabbing her lips with a napkin. 'Your barmaid is about to become a very wealthy woman.'

'Then perhaps it might be best, for her sake, to keep her out of the public gaze.'

Candice's laugh is as brittle as the frost round the rim of the bucket. 'Can't be done, I'm afraid. Not if we want to do our best for her, which is, after all, what we are about.'

Mr Derek hesitates before suggesting, 'I suppose I could—'

'No, no, no, a big mistake. It wouldn't do for somebody in authority over her to take on a protective role. That could be construed as taking unfair advantage.'

'There's always Moira Stokes,' muses Mr Derek.

'Oh no, that would give the wrong image completely. No, are there any particular friends who are close to Bernadette, anyone slightly more worldly, for example?'

Now Mr Derek has dealt with many rich and famous guests during his time at the Burleston. New money, old money. Pop stars, aristocrats. But this is the first time he has come face to face with a vamp so totally confident that she picks her teeth openly with a lobster claw, pulls her knickers free from her crotch while pouring herself extra wine, snaps him to silence by batting a mauve eyelid and cuts him in half with a cutlass scorn produced by a slight twitch of the lips.

'There's always Kirsty Hoskins,' Mr Derek starts gingerly; 'she is slightly older than the others and strikes me as a woman with some common sense.'

'And who is Kirsty Hoskins?' The name rings a bell. Oh yes, that was the name on the letter, the name Bernadette first used, the person Candice asked for when she first telephoned the hotel. Miss Love produces a cigarette holder in exaggerated Hollywood style.

'One of our seasonal chambermaids. No, now I come to think of it, I believe Mrs Hoskins is employed on a full-time basis, keen to rent a cottage in the grounds for the winter season. Other than that, I'm afraid, there's only Avril Stott.'

'I had better have a word with both of them.'

Mr Derek automatically holds out a lighter towards Miss Love's swaying cigarette, ignoring the 'no smoking' sign hidden behind the side salad. He

178

clicks his fingers for an ashtray to be brought to their table.

'Which doesn't answer the question of what to do with your old barmaid.'

'Old barmaid?'

'Well, you surely don't imagine that Bernadette will continue to work in your bar? Not now!'

'I hadn't given it much thought, to be honest; this is all so sudden and unexpected. What would you suggest, Miss Love?'

'If you want your hotel to benefit from the surge of worldwide publicity about to explode around this little cove, I would suggest that you find Miss Kavanagh and her chosen companion a decent room pretty pronto.'

Mr Derek could counterattack with the fact that the Burleston is full most of the year and no longer needs to court publicity. In fact, many of the hotel's regulars would shy away from that sort of thing, privacy being paramount. And yet, and yet, you cannot ignore the worrying trends – business is not good for most of the Burleston's competitors; one day they might be glad of a famous author and her entourage. But instead he hears himself saying out of habit, 'I don't think we have any rooms that would be suitable.'

'Oh come, come, Mr Derek, I am not one of your average punters. A five-star hotel like this must keep at least one vacant double room. I got in without much trouble.'

'Only because of a last-minute cancellation.'

'I would advise her to leave, but she seems to want to stay here for some undisclosed reason,' says Candice, leaning back and stretching, flicking her ash aimlessly onto the marble floor. 'If you do have a room available it would look pretty bad in the interviews if Bernadette was denied it because she was a mere barmaid.'

'I see your point.'

'I thought you might. And remember, one day Bernadette Kavanagh might be well worth knowing. Now, how about a pudding?' And Candice Love disappears for one merciful moment behind an enormous, shiny white menu. Only her long scarlet nails are showing like streaks of blood on the edges.

'You know I don't want anything to do with this. I don't want any part of it,' says Kirsty quickly after hearing about the sudden upheaval.

'But I want you with me,' splutters Bernie, 'dammit, I need you. I wouldn't mind staying here, but Candice seems to think I should cash in on this opportunity. The Burleston are offering a free double room on the strength of what Candice has told them. Mr Derek, the slime ball, thinks I might be famous some day.'

'You know why I have to stay out of this.'

'Candice says some early press interest will help push the bids up.' Bernie shakes her head in astonishment, loosening her thick, silky hair. 'I still can't believe the kind of money she's talking. D'you realize that, if this is real, none of us will ever have to work again?'

'But we can't share Kirsty's money now,' worries the flustered Avril, meeker than ever, out of her depth and embarrassed that Bernie should suggest such a thing. 'Not in these circumstances.'

'I said we would split this three ways, and that's what we'll do,' says Kirsty, who cannot envisage £10,000 let alone a million. 'You're going to have to work for it, it's not coming for free. But I can't help you out any more. It's all down to you and Avril.'

'But how can we move out and leave you here? Look at it. It's disgusting.'

She never believed this would work so well. It is only with a great effort of will that Kirsty can go on with the plot. It seems to have blown up in her face; her little deceit has taken her over, her simple dream has become menacing. 'You can and you must,' she says with dull courage, now more fraught than ever for fear that her devious deed will be revealed. If this book is destined for fame, filmed and sold all over the world, surely someone, somewhere, will remember this early work by Ellen Kirkwood? She and the future of her kids will be destroyed by the scandal.

'But it's wrong, it's not fair, all the money will go straight to Bernie,' Avril bursts out, her face puckered anxiously.

'Oh. So don't you trust me?'

'Of course we trust you,' Kirsty reassures her, while Avril sighs and folds her hands in unhappy resignation. 'You will have to divide it three ways, that's all. That's if Candice Love isn't talking out of the back of her head, and I still can't believe—'

'No-one can,' says Bernie, pleased, unconsciously running her hands over her beautiful body. 'That's why we're getting all this attention, no-one as young and stupid as me has ever written a book like this. I'm going to Truro with Candice tomorrow to get some new gear for the interviews.'

Avril just cannot accept it. 'But it's Kirsty who

ought to be going. It's Kirsty who should be giving up work. She's going to be cleaning our room while we live like queens. Kirsty's only human, how long can she keep that up?'

'As long as it takes,' says Kirsty. 'I don't mind cleaning rooms.'

'Or being suspected when anything's missing, or watching an old black and white telly, sleeping on broken springs and eating reheated food.'

'It won't be for ever.'

'She's right,' says Bernie, 'and that's where women like you fall down, Avril. Too short-sighted. Too small-minded. You have to trust me, there's no alternative. If this works out Kirsty can buy Trevor off and get him out of her life.'

But now Kirsty is silent. There is another, bad side to this equation. If she had money she could travel, that's true; she could take the kids out of the country, even if Trevor did fight for custody and get it with his convincing lies. But the law is the law wherever you go and Kirsty would not want to live in some backwater of the world like Ronnie Biggs – all bungalows, bars and swimming pools – in some corrupt, lawless nation, for ever a fugitive from home.

She notices that her knuckles are white and hides them in her overall pockets.

No. She is under no illusions. If Trevor got wind of pound signs he would be relentless in his pursuit of her and his children. He would sell his soul for money. No matter how good and expensive her defence, somehow he would triumph over her, as he's always done, making her falter, stammer, forget, mistake what she means, crumble. If *Magdalene* had really been written by her maybe she would have the self-confidence boost to fight the dragon on her own terms. But Kirsty hasn't discovered her talent, she is merely a cheat and a liar, and these actions do nothing to build her self-worth, if anything they reduce it.

Kirsty's wounds are deep, deeper than anyone knows.

But she forces a smile as she listens to Bernie and Avril discussing their new station in life. They are off to the main hotel tonight on Candice Love's instructions. They are to dine with her this evening while they discuss 'essential strategies'.

There is a sharp knock on the door.

'Come in.'

Nobody has ever bothered to knock before.

Moira Stokes stands like a ghost in the doorway; she stands there stiffly in her high-necked dress, every button carefully fastened.

'I hope you have gathered your things together,' she addresses Bernadette with an acid politeness. 'As soon as you are ready we are to move you into the main hotel.'

Bernie nods while poor Avril blushes.

'And you', she says to Kirsty, 'will have this room to yourself.'

'That'll be nice for her,' says Bernie. 'She'll be able to get up to all sorts of tricks under the covers. All on her own.'

'Don't be silly,' says Mrs Stokes. 'You might be dazzled by all this excitement, but you ought to remember who you are.'

'I am a famous author.' Bernie laughs, getting up

183

and twirling round deliberately to annoy Mrs Stokes.

'Not yet, you're not,' snaps Mrs Stokes. 'You might yet find this is all a sham. You should remember the wise old adage, don't count your chickens before they hatch.'

'At least I've got some eggs,' says Bernie. 'Unlike you.'

Kirsty stands by her bed and says nothing, screwing and unscrewing the knobs of the bedstead. She thinks of the dingy bindings and the dusty smell of the old book.

'It seems that somehow you have missed out,' says Mrs Stokes unkindly.

'I don't mind,' says Kirsty quietly, her face blank and set. All she wanted was a couple of thousand to buy an old car and equip the caravan. 'I'm quite happy as I am.'

'If you expect me to believe that then I'll eat my hat,' says Mrs Stokes. 'Two's company, three's a crowd, and that's what has happened here. Perhaps', she says, 'your day will come,' as she goes out and quietly closes the door.

'Cow,' says Bernadette, considering her image in the cracked old mirror.

And Kirsty gives the bed knob such a twist that it comes right off in her hand.

Fourteen

Murder most dastardly.

An old lady of seventy-nine killed for £1.39 and the streets crawling with homicidal maniacs oozing up from the bowels of hell.

The hunt is robust and bloodthirsty, baying voices howling for justice echo from tabloid to poster to street corner and back, and Graham Stott, fugitive from justice, guilty of the most abominable of crimes, keeps his head well down like Brer Fox. He creeps through mean backstreets that resemble an eerie London Whitechapel, or ventures into the semi-green countryside and uses the stanchions of motorway bridges for cold and unfriendly cover.

So far nobody knows who the culprit could possibly be, but the police are out in full force to pacify a horrified public. Those out in community care, the senile, the odd bods, the drunks and the druggies, are all pulled in for questioning.

'She was a right card, was old Annie, gave us a song before she left, although she'd just lost twenty quid at the bingo. A dab hand on the harmonica long as she took her teeth out first.'

'She'd had a hard life, had Annie, lost her husband last year of the war. Had to struggle to bring up three kids . . .'

'We'll miss her terribly,' says an eldest son who hasn't seen Annie in years. It was just that her escalating drinking habits were so unsavoury in front of the children.

But Graham didn't mean to kill the old bat; if only he could take time back he could have ripped her bag off her gently. It's no good appealing for clemency this time – after his conviction for burglary the pundits made out that because the old woman upstairs had feigned sleep, she had been remarkably lucky. This unjustified connection with violence is so bloody unfair; just because he ran with a gang whose leaders were done for GBH – and that was way back when he was a kid – they have always assumed he would, one day, be dangerous. What do the shrinks know anyway? Graham can wrap them round his little finger, them and their transparent ink blots.

The papers are still full of his crime.

His brain is working, always working.

Sometimes he plays with the dream that the mugging never really happened.

Sometimes, dawdling at a shop window, he thinks he's being followed.

Sometimes he thinks people look at him strangely.

But God, what evidence had he left behind him? What would they do if they caught him? How long would he get? He would probably get sent to a high-security nick this time. Perhaps he would need

186

protection, one of those wankers on the special wing.

And come out with AIDS.

Now he has no mates left in Liverpool except for a few crazed potheads in squats who would give him away for less than a fiver. His fellow gaol inmates are scattered around, boozing away their days or injecting it in the kind of dives watched by the pigs, not the sort of hostelries best suited for Graham at this moment. And when it comes to a crime like murder – murder of an old woman – even the hard men don't want to know, there's no kudos in that; it's not like working for your dealers.

Graham lights a fag and strolls out of the shadowed doorway. He has to get right away from here, away from the streets that know him, but it feels like breaking into the open, into the vast unknown. London is too obvious, and anyway, Graham doesn't know London. Then there's the problem that if they pull him in in some strange city, they'll think he is on the run, assume he is guilty.

He seizes on one glimmer of comfort and walks with a feigned carelessness, a cigarette between his lips and one hand in his pocket.

Not if he does something perfectly natural, like going to visit his sister. I mean, here he is, jobless and homeless, what more reasonable reaction could there be than to leave the city where he has no prospects and try his luck down in Cornwall? Graham laughs silently. He must keep cool and get this in proportion. How inconsequential he really is; he looks just the same as every other guy in bomber jacket and frayed jeans. He might get a seasonal job, although they're already halfway through August, it might be worth a try. And nobody is going to think of looking for the China Town murderer in the frigging armpit of the world.

Graham is not the only member of the Stott family from Huyton to be heading for Cornwall on this sunny Saturday. The Bluebird caravan has been hosed down and connected to the green Ford Sierra, which is just back from its annual service. In the miniature fridge and the cupboards, groceries, fruit, cans and packs are stacked and neatly labelled. Well, Avril's mother is certainly not prepared to pay the kind of inflated prices they charge at caravan parks.

Both Stotts are exhausted after a night of heated discussion, Mrs Stott wanting to set out at dawn and Mr Stott saying it's unnecessary.

'But we always leave at dawn.'

'There's no need, now we haven't got the children.'

'Well, on your head be it then.' And she despises him for his lack of adventure.

The car's back seat is given over almost entirely to Fluffy the cat, and after the animal is settled in position the little vanilla pine tree that hangs over the windscreen is overpowered by the stench of feline flatulence. 'If you can read this you are too close.' The sticker on the back window, which Mr Stott still considers a hoot, will be obscured by the weaving caravan on the journey down today.

The packed lunch is kept in a cool box. The Stotts will park at the motorway services but will purchase nothing there. The prices are quite outrageous, and most of the food tastes like cardboard. In her white summer handbag Mrs Stott keeps a folded oval piece of transparent plastic and a pair of surgical gloves, which she uses when visiting public conveniences – she has read about the faecal horrors on public lavatory chains, not to mention the lethal content in wrapped, cut sandwiches.

'Avril will be pleased to see us,' says Mrs Stott on the motorway, sucking a barley sugar nervously. She feels good in her smart new slacks and a shimmery sweatshirt with a gold leopard embroidered upon it. The leopard's eyes shine redly in front of Mrs Stott's nipples. 'And I'm sure it's time we paid her a visit. I'm getting quite worried about Avril; she sounds so different on the phone.'

'She'll be pleased to see Fluffy,' says Mr Stott, in the slow lane.

'I think it's those friends she's got mixed up with. I don't like the sound of them.'

'So long as she's happy,' says Mr Stott, casual, today, in his holiday tracksuit and large, startlingly white trainers.

Mrs Stott feels her anger rising. She cracks the barley sugar hard between her teeth till it's crushed to smithereens in her mouth. 'That's just it, Richard. That says it all, doesn't it? That's always been your attitude and look where it got us with Graham.'

'Don't let's get into that now, dear.'

189

'And I hope that's not a traffic jam I see!'

'It won't last long, probably roadworks.'

'Roadworks in August, I ask you.' But if Richard had listened to her and left home at dawn they would be there by now ... without this awful queuing.

The Stotts have booked into Happy Stay, the caravan park near Burleston that caters for both the cruising and the larger static. As usual, Mr Stott sent off to the AA for a route, and Mrs Stott sits with this on her knee, even though the journey is quite straightforward and nobody needs to refer to it. With luck they will see Avril at least once every day and they hope to have a look round the hotel and perhaps take tea in the pavilion if the charges are not too exorbitant. The rest of the time they will visit gardens, a particular favourite of Avril's mother, a few country houses and craft shops. They will not eat out. They will take their own sandwiches every day and have a hot meal when they return.

'I hope they approve of Ed.'

'They will, Avril, stop worrying.'

'I wish they weren't coming here.'

'Well why didn't you stop them?'

'Because they booked two months ago and Mother and Father never change their plans.'

'They won't believe it when they see you here. When they know what's been happening.'

Bernie's right. Avril can hardly believe it herself. Here they are on a Saturday, sitting out on their balcony, while in the room behind them there is a wonderful, huge, split four-poster bed and a tiny dressing room surrounded by mirrors, in which there is a spare put-you-up. They bounced away on that first night on a mattress high and springy, in bedding which foamed with masses of lace, embroidered coverlets and white cotton.

'Poor Kirsty.'

'I know. Poor old Kirsty.'

For Avril the small press conference was one long nightmare – not so for Bernie, however. But that was fine because Avril was merely a hanger-on, not the star, not the young genius, the literary talent freshly discovered by those who know greatness when they see it.

'You just sit there, Avril, and try not to smile too broadly,' said Candice Love, 'nobody's going to ask you anything. You are Bernadette's right hand, her friend and confidante, her first and greatest fan, no-one will want to speak to you so there's no need to adopt that goofy expression.'

In fact, Candice Love did most of the talking, taking the literary press by storm by declaring the astonishing interest being shown, worldwide, for this young girl's first novel. 'And all the while here she was, a nobody, a little Irish barmaid from Liverpool, grateful for any employment she could get, working her heart out for peanuts . . .'

Here Mr Derek cleared his throat and shifted uncomfortably.

'. . . and now, suddenly, the world is at this author's feet, clamouring for the rights to her work, from Hollywood to Frankfurt, from New York to Hong Kong. Yes, this author makes Ruth Rendell and P. D. James look like beginners in the art of plotting; it places Margaret Drabble and Aldous Huxley back in some literary kindergarten and yet it appeals to all nations, all ages, is timeless, *is magnificent.*'

'This must have been a great shock for you, Bernie. Can you give us your reaction to all this?'

Bernie smiled charmingly and captivated them all. 'I am overwhelmed by it. To be honest, it hasn't really sunk in yet.'

'Is there another book in the offing?'

'You'll have to wait and see,' smiled Bernie.

'And what about your mum and dad? What do they think about all this?'

'Mum wet her knickers and said the Hail Mary and Dad nearly passed out. It's all this dosh that's knocked them flat – like winning the bloody lottery.'

Candice Love cleared her throat. 'Of course there will be advisers on hand to help the Kavanagh family handle this new direction in their lives.'

'She's got a past from all I hear,' called the one low-life tabloid reporter who had sneaked in among the respectable group. On holiday at the time, he thought he might as well come along in case he could sniff out something dodgy.

Candice smiled and her lipstick clicked. Ah, this is what she wanted. The oaf thinks he has dug something out and it won't hurt to interest the wider public. 'Bernadette is a bit of a rebel, as are most talented people. I doubt she could have written *Magdalene* if she hadn't seen life in the raw.'

'How raw?' asked the dickhead with a hopeful leer while the flash lights exploded around them.

192

'Pretty raw,' said Candice temptingly.

'Mammy's not going to like that,' said Bernie in a quiet aside.

'Just leave this to me, this is going even better than I planned,' Candice whispered back with a sparkle in her eye.

'How about your love life, Bernie?'

And Bernie, the star, the sensation of the morning, suddenly quailed from admitting to the world a fact that had never worried her in private, that her love life was non-existent, and gave a rich Irish laugh instead. 'He's gorgeous,' she told them all with pride. 'He's a local hero, a lifeguard; he's a university student.'

'What's his name, darling?'

Bernie knew she had gone too far, and Avril was nudging her hard to shut up. 'I can't tell you that,' said Bernie shyly. 'That's my secret.'

'What'll you do with all this money?'

'I haven't got it yet,' said Bernie.

This disrespectful member of the press overpowered the rest. 'I hear you're sharing it with your friend there. That's very unusual. She must be a really special friend. What does your boyfriend think about that?'

Oh no, no. Avril, sitting there quietly, had hoped to be kept well out of this, and Candice Love hoped so, too. But Bernie smiled at Avril, quite happy to involve her. 'Avril did most of the hard work, didn't you, Avril?'

Avril cringed, turned puce and stuttered. 'N–not really. I only t–t–typed it. I didn't do much really.'

'Have you two been friends for long?'

193

Candice Love sussed which way the questions were going. It wouldn't do Bernadette any harm to be thought of as bisexual, it would only add to the fascination and hidden depths of her new author, except that Candice knew this to be untrue and so it could make for future misunderstandings. She would have to nip it in the bud. 'They work together,' she answered for Avril. 'They have only known each other since June.'

Meal times are difficult. It's easier when Candice Love shares their table because her outrageous confidence carries them through, and they're so busy discussing the future that they take no notice of their fellow diners.

But at breakfast this morning Avril found the experience painful. Not that the waiters were rude or nasty, it wasn't anything like that, but they were taking the piss, and Bernie didn't seem to mind, but Avril's eyes were constantly searching the other guests for signs of amusement, and, to her shame, there were many.

The half-hidden smiles were the worst. The smiles followed by whispered remarks as, in Avril's imagination, they were watched for bad table manners, for being too showy, for lacking *savoir-faire*. They were clearly the talk of the moment, the Cinderellas who had made good, and naturally it was difficult for people used to giving the staff their orders to suddenly accept them as equals.

Avril ordered a kipper, thinking this might atone, but hardly anyone else had kippers, she could happily have chosen bacon and egg. When Bernie lit up she nearly died and Michael, the head waiter,

194

had to step over politely and ask her to refrain from smoking until she left the dining room.

Only the thought of Ed Board waiting for her outside gave Avril the courage to go through with it all. 'You were brilliant,' he told her after the interview, giving her bottom a painful slap.

In spite of a lifetime of Mother's contrary signals, Avril knows only too well that the Stotts are rather common. The same could be said for Bernie, of course, but being from Ireland, she can carry it.

Unlike Bernie who seems to have shed it completely, or never had it, Avril carries the burden of guilt when it comes to poor, neglected Kirsty. There is something so basically wrong with all this – that she and Bernie are living in luxury while Kirsty works her fingers to the bone and worries about her children. Where is this going to end? Kirsty plans to move to a mobile home at the Happy Stay when the season is over, but surely they will have money by then, real money, not the silly money enthused over by Candice Love and the press. Then she and Bernie will rejoin Kirsty so she no longer has to contemplate those cold months in spartan conditions at the bleak and windswept Happy Stay, which must be so soulless in winter.

Oh dear.

But there's something more worrying going on, something so subtle it's hard to pin point, but it keeps Avril awake at nights, even in the comfort of their wonderful bed. The three of them seem to be growing apart. Gone is the closeness there once was between them. Avril feels awkward in Kirsty's presence. When Kirsty comes in to clean the room they still laugh together, of course – they still have this mighty secret to share – and Avril makes sure she has cleared up beforehand so that Kirsty's workload is halved. But that bitch Bernie just lies on the bed, smoking, or preening herself in her new clothes, or ordering snacks and drinks from room service when they're not hungry. She won't even rinse the cups when she's finished.

No, the only time Avril can relax and be her true self is when she's on the golf course with Ed. When Ed first heard the amazing news about the book and the funny money he took her straight into his shop and made her equip herself properly.

'But I can't pay for this,' said Avril, staggered by the prices. 'I'm still poor as a church mouse.'

'Not for long,' said Ed. 'Don't worry. If you want to play golf seriously you must have your own clubs and it's essential to look the part.'

Oh Lord. Avril still isn't sure. Fashion sense is not her bent. She came out of the pro's shop with a manly beige skirt with a pleat, a padded waistcoat in hunting green and a pair of white studded shoes. It took hours to choose the right clubs. Ed put a peaked cap on her head and said it was his treat, but she feels it doesn't do her justice. She hasn't dared show Bernie yet. She hasn't even dared get them out of the wardrobe to try on in front of her mirror.

'You might find my family rather prissy,' Avril tries to warn Ed, afraid this friendship might be jeopardized, too. 'They are quite old-fashioned, conservative with a capital C, they never swear and they don't like jokes.'

'I don't care what they're like,' says the kindly, carrot-headed Ed, his stout moustache bristling protectively. 'It's you I care about, Avril, not them, and I'm not that bad, am I? Most people seem to like me.'

But most people aren't like Avril's mother.

Fifteen

'Let me get this quite straight.' And although Dominic Coates throws out a small embarrassed snort, nothing about this woman is funny. 'You had the nerve to get me here under false pretences and now you're telling me that if I don't go back to Bernadette you're going to go to the family of that little kid and tell them I caused the death of their father.'

'Well, didn't you?' asks Kirsty.

Dominic, who has only just recovered from the surprise of Bernie's success, now regards Kirsty steadily, wondering what she knows, and if she knows. How the hell does she know? He has never met this odd woman before, although she works in Bernie's hotel. Somehow Bernie must have found out, but who else could have let on but Belinda?

And Belinda has gone back to Bath in a huff. That beautiful relationship lasted less than three weeks and he has since regretted the morbid stuff he came out with when he felt he was safe in her arms. He was upset, unnerved, hyper during that megacrazy time.

Is his visitor high on something? He searches for

signs in her eyes, in the steadiness of her small hands. 'I'm not sure I know what you're getting at.'

She had called him at the guest house, a phone call right out of the blue having asked the council for his number, saying she had something of his that she'd promised to return. She refused to tell him what. His curiosity was naturally aroused and so he agreed to meet her at a café in St Ives. He arrived early and watched this woman be dropped off by a taxi. And now he twiddles the sugar tongs while waiting nervously for her answer.

She doesn't look like a blackmailer: T-shirt, jeans, sloppy espadrilles. If she was younger she'd be quite attractive, especially with that Jilly Cooper gap between her two front teeth. But her dark-brown eyes have a strangeness about them, as if they aren't seeing him, but looking right through him into the birdcage directly behind.

She sounds like a copper reading his notes out in court. Each word calculated to convict. 'I am getting at the fact that your alcohol intake was considerable on the afternoon you were called out to rescue that child. I am getting at the fact that, had you been on top form, you might well have rescued them both, and I might as well point out, while I'm at it, that the coroner might be interested to hear that a direct karate chop to the drowning man's throat may have been something to do with the cause of death. Not the unknown floating object they assumed must have hit him at the inquest.'

'Belinda must have told you this.' At this point, astonished, Dominic leans back, laughing coolly, his fingers tapping on the table. Shit. He can get out of this. This is all hearsay. A right load of crap.

'Belinda has one helluva vivid imagination. Anyway, for your information, the inquest is closed.'

The woman across the table just shrugs.

'Did Bernie put you up to this?'

'Bernie knows nothing about it,' says Kirsty, knowing full well she has won the fight. A weak man he might be, a flighty, cock-driven runt, but Dominic will make a useful spy and she needs someone close to keep watch on Bernie. Despite what she might say in public, Kirsty does not trust her Irish friend one inch.

'But what the hell are you doing this for?' he splutters. 'Bernie doesn't want me back, not when she's got all this fame going for her. Bernie was over me months ago.'

'That shows what an ignorant sod you are.'

This is unbelievable. Dominic looks round to assure himself he is not stuck in some booze-induced dream, but no, there are a few other customers in here, mostly having scones and cream, there's a high chair with a snivelling baby and an elderly couple holding hands. No, he couldn't be inventing them all. 'You're telling me Bernie's still interested?'

What a fool he is, what a fool.

They will give him a Morgan when he gets his degree and send him round the world for a while, backpacking with the proles and an American Express card.

He will marry well, in the end, an upper-class girl with a daddy who thinks the sun shines out of her arse. They will drive BMWs and Porsches and live in a house with a shingle drive and a turning circle round a rose bed.

Dominic must be punished. Of course Bernie

passed on to Kirsty all that Belinda had told her, supplied the right ammunition, or Kirsty would not have the weapons to bring this beach bum to justice, as Magdalene the nun would have done.

Kirsty is not happy this morning. The latest letter from Maddy upset her. 'The children keep asking for their daddy, but don't worry, I fended them off. It's often distressing but understandable the way traumatized children do this. In my experience this often means they are trying to work the past through their systems. No doubt they will stop asking soon. Otherwise all is well . . .'

She takes a sip of her tea and dunks a plain digestive, staring stonily at Dominic Coates.

'I've a good mind to get up and walk out of here.'

'Go on then,' says Kirsty, 'that's your business. But you know damn well what will happen. Mummy and Daddy must have been thrilled by your bit of fame, their precious son hitting the headlines. I bet you sent them the local papers. I bet they ordered the original prints from the local photographer, especially that one of you coming out of the sea like King bloody Neptune with the little mermaid in your arms.'

'What the hell has this got to do with them?' This can't get any worse, thinks Dominic. What has he got here, some serious head case? This is the kind of stuff you read about or watch in American TV dramas. She'll bring out a knife in a minute.

But Dominic can't help but imagine his father's disappointed face, just when he has started to believe that Dominic will make a man yet. And his mother will go back on the Valium and start booking into nursing homes.

'So what the hell do you expect me to do?' But still Dominic pretends amusement, summing her up, taking the piss.

'Ring Bernie up and suggest a meeting.'

'You know she'll probably turn me down.'

'She won't turn you down.' Kirsty leans closer. He can see every muscle is taut as if she is fending off some old anger. 'If Bernie agrees to meet you then do it dead right! Are you listening, you arsehole? You tell her you've missed her, all you want is to start again, you want to be around her, support her, to make all those wasted months up to her and to beg her forgiveness for the shit you gave her.'

'Bugger that.'

'OK,' says Kirsty with menacing sweetness.

'What d'you get out of this, are you some control freak or something? Getting some weird kick out of buggering up other people's lives?'

'Yep, I probably am.'

'You bet you are, lady. If Bernie found out you were doing this she'd die of humiliation. Nobody wants this sort of sick joke played on them behind their backs. And anyway,' Dominic pauses, 'it couldn't possibly work. You can't convince someone you love them, not when you don't give a damn.'

'I'm sure you can,' is Kirsty's response. 'If you try hard enough.'

'I go back to Liverpool in September. So we're only talking about three weeks.'

'Now that's something you'll have to put off.'

'Now you're really kidding me on. Miss out on my last year?'

'What will it matter whether you get a degree or

202

not? I'll bet you my next week's salary that you will end up in Daddy's firm anyway.'

'So this is all down to envy, is it?' Dominic leans back and smiles a superior smile. 'Jesus Christ, I should have known.'

But Kirsty snaps back with venom, 'D'you really believe it's that simple?'

'Why do you hate me?'

'I have no feelings for you. Certainly nothing as strong as hatred. If it's anything at all, it's distaste.'

'Quite a one for the compliments, aren't you?'

'Why the fuck don't you grow up and face up to what you are?'

Despite this brief show of strength, Kirsty, in her disturbed state, is beginning to relish the role of martyr, mooching about and sighing, sending out messages of 'unfair, unfair', lingering in Bernie's suite, being pandered to by the gullible Avril, who wants to make amends.

She might have ousted her terrible husband but Kirsty still needs to play the victim.

'Don't be taken in by it,' Bernie sneers at Avril, too excited to be bothered with such qualms of conscience, 'Kirsty knows that in the end everything will equal out. She agreed to this deal. This is only a blip; when we leave the Burleston Kirsty can come with us.'

But Avril is not convinced. The fat girl's hurt face streaks with indignant pink.

But Bernie, on the other hand, sincerely believes she is carrying them all. Without her genius they couldn't pull this off; it is Bernie's charisma and charm that has captivated the national press and given them the sensational headlines that so delight Candice Love. And although all this was Kirsty's idea, and they owe her some gratitude and consideration, Bernie just wishes the gullible Avril would show her the same sort of appreciation. Kirsty might well be suffering – she carries the suffering on her face like Bernie carries Boots' Sierra Sunset Blush – no wonder she drove her husband to violence. But Bernie is suffering, too – from stress. Every time she opens her mouth Bernie is afraid she'll cock up. It is she who has to look her best while Avril trails along behind looking like a damp old pillow, part of the background furniture. Avril, with her moans about unfairness and her disapproving glances, has done rather well out of this arrangement.

She is, after all, only the typist.

Bernie's mounting disloyal thoughts remain harmlessly in her head. If only she had someone else with whom she could swap ideas. Most of her old scouse mates would sympathize and take her side, have a giggle, a drink and a good old slagging-off session, fired by injustice. But she can't do that with boring Avril, who won't hear a bad word said about Kirsty, who takes life so bloody seriously, especially her farcical friendship with that old bore Ed Board. Ed is clearly some kind of pervert who likes a bit of rough with big women, and Avril is so naïve she couldn't see how his small eyes lit up when he heard about Avril's good fortune. But it's not up to Bernie to dampen her ardour, to pour scorn on the first relationship the moron has experienced in her whole life.

* * *

The phone call from Dominic comes through to the suite just as Bernie is preparing for dinner with Candice Love's preferred editor, a woman from the publishing house that paid the highest auction price for *Magdalene* – a record, goes the rumour, but the details have not yet been made public.

It's important that Bernie and this editor hit it off. They will have to work closely together, both now and in the future. So Bernie feels more nervous than normal.

Avril, as usual, picks up the phone. Always at hand. Ready to help. Sometimes Bernie fights the urge to kick her out of the way. Boring boring *boring*.

Avril gasps. 'Bernie, it's Dominic.'

Bernie whirls round blinking, eyeliner still in her hand.

'Dominic?'

Avril nods stupidly.

'I thought I'd give you a ring,' says Dominic. 'Congratulations! I read about your incredible book and everything that's happening and I wondered if you'd remember me now you're famous.'

'I don't believe this,' says Bernie, and still, after all that has happened, his voice affects the rhythm of her heart. She is conscious of nothing except his voice. Breathless with hope, ecstatic is the only word for her now.

'And I wondered if we could meet again.'

She would have said tonight, but remembers the meeting with the editor which could go on until late. She drops a heavy sigh. 'What's happened to you and Belinda?'

He doesn't answer immediately and Bernie stops

breathing. After the pause and her gasp he says, 'Oh, you know me, Bernie, I've always been selfish, but I've had a long time to think, to look at the way my life is going, and I can't go through another month searching for something I lost when you and I split up last year.'

This doesn't sound like the carefree Dominic Bernie once knew. She can't remember him ever going into himself and his feelings without some stupid punch line at the end.

'I've been very lonely, Dom,' she says.

'I don't expect you'll ever want to give me another chance?'

'I never found anyone else.'

'And I know you won't have lacked offers.'

Dominic sounds so serious. This change in him is astonishing. It's as if he has had a religious experience, like Paul on the road to Damascus. This couldn't be a joke, could it? There couldn't be people listening in, holding back their hysteria, ready to burst out laughing the moment he gives the signal? No, no, no, even Dom could never be so cruel, although . . . she doesn't know what to think any more.

'We could have dinner tonight,' he says. 'I know a place—'

'I can't,' are the most difficult words Bernie has ever spoken.

Dominic pauses, sounds almost relieved. 'I ought to have known, I'm a fool—'

'No, no, it's only because I'm meeting someone. Tomorrow . . . I could meet you tomorrow?'

'We've got so much to catch up on, you and me.'

This can't be because of the money, can it? Here

she is, suspecting Ed Board of coming on strong because of the dosh, and silly Avril being blind to the truth, but no, Dominic's family is rolling in it, Dominic doesn't need money. He is heir to a cardboard-box fortune. Why oh why can't Bernie stop thinking that nothing deeper than greed drives him back?

'Tomorrow night then, I'll come and get you. Is eight o'clock OK?'

'Fine,' says Bernie, closing her eyes on a miracle she had begun to despair of, 'I'll see you then.'

Oh, Dom, oh, Dom.

Avril has ordered supper in her room and invited Kirsty to join her. This is far more appropriate for Bernie than having Avril tagging along, although, this evening, after that magical phone call, Bernie feels a warm flow of love for everybody around her. But Avril is always so irritating, droning on about her own little problems, she'd bore any dinner guest stiff with talk of her family's arrival, or her little flirtation with gross old Ed. Especially a dinner guest as influential and sophisticated as this one promises to be. It's hard to imagine how anyone else could outdo Candice in the role of super-dominant, manipulative human being. Perhaps she herself will be like that one day.

'Do I look OK?'

And although she asks, she knows the answer, and what is the use of Avril's opinion?

Bernie sets off downstairs, beautiful and blessed. Some magical light shines off her, and it isn't because of the tight black taffeta or the sling-back shoes or the diamanté earrings Candice lent her. It is the light of love, the power of passion, the trembling turbulence of tumultuous obsession, as blinding and yet every bit as delicate as the thousands of prisms that twinkle in the great chandelier above her head.

It's an old lady in a scruffy brown wig.

The majestic Candice bears down on Bernie, pulling the crone behind her. 'This is Clementine, Bernie.' Candice makes her introductions before leading the way into the bar, the usual cloud of designer perfume lingering in the air behind her.

As Candice orders the drinks, Bernie stares hard at her new editor, who almost disappears in the lumps of the ancient leather chesterfield. Her small, narrow face, almost worn to the bone, is well-shaped, and her eyes are set deep in their sockets, from which they still peer, sharp and bright. She could have been a spy in the French resistance, Odette grown old, or the little sparrow singing sad love songs, there is such a mischievous look about her.

'Rum and coke for you, Bernie,' says Candice, not without a sniff, 'and a double brandy for Clementine.'

The papier mâché banana earrings worn by the editor look incongruous with the twinset and kilt, the knee-length socks and the ethnic sandals. This is obviously a woman, barely five feet high, who prefers to be comfortable, and not only that. This is obviously a woman, with wisps of grey hair showing under the brown, far more shrewd and knowing than Candice, with all her worldly assurance, and Bernie feels uncertain, as if she's already been sussed.

'What an exquisite child,' says Clementine Davaine, in a voice surprisingly deep and strong. 'I have been so looking forward to meeting the author of *Magdalene*, by far the best book I have read in years. Congratulations, my dear.' And Clementine Davaine holds out a gnarled old hand, the arthritic fingers set firmly in a pen-holding grip.

Sixteen

Hah! God lives. He ought to have known the Burleston Hotel would not have bothered with the Yellow Pages. Trev thinks they are possibly ex-directory when he receives the understated brochure, but on such expensive top-notch paper you can't help but guess at the quality of the place.

Trev was three-quarters of the way through his free Yellow Pages directory, but had certainly not given up hope when he came upon the article in *Country Life*. He was having his tea break at the time, installing a new central-heating system for a Mrs Strange of Birkenhead. A fine old house surrounded by new development, with a ten-foot fence to keep out the masses.

The article itself was boring: some food and wine convention held by those obnoxious snobs who have time for such crap. There they were in their evening clothes, clashing their long-stemmed glasses together and gazing glazenly into the camera. Now Trev doesn't have the memory of an elephant, but the name of the hotel bugged him, he didn't think he'd heard that name, and when he got home he checked up. He rang directory enquiries, fearing the worst, but the computer voice gave him the number slowly and clearly and Trev was quickly into his Inspector Bates persona.

Rhoda, on the other end of the phone, feeling hard done by because, since Avril's sudden rise in the world, Mr Derek has not yet supplied a replacement, nevertheless responded with interest when she heard it was the police.

'What d'you want Kirsty for?' she asked quickly.

'Oh, nothing important. Just checking up on a few things.'

Typical, the fuzz are so mysterious. Like squeezing water out of a stone. Rhoda wouldn't have known about Kirsty if she and Avril hadn't been friends; she would have had to look up the list of Burleston employees, and might well have denied they had such a person to save herself the trouble of searching for it. Well, there's so much extra work lately, the phones always going and faxes from London for that snooty Candice Love.

'Kirsty Hoskins is one of our chambermaids.'

'And could I have Mrs Hoskins's address?'

'Oh, she lives in. They mostly do, the seasonal ones.'

'So presumably her children are not with her?'

'I've never heard of any children.'

'Right, that's all I need to know, thank you. Naturally I would be grateful for your discretion on this matter, Miss . . .'

'Carp, as in the fish,' said Rhoda, a habit Mr Derek is trying to train her out of. 'Shall I send you our brochure?'

'Why not?' said Trevor, taking his final bow as the sleuth Inspector Bates.

No bugger is willing to help him, nobody will believe him, everyone takes the view that Kirsty must have had a reason to run. And, as if life isn't fraught enough, Trev's bid for legal aid has failed and he's been forced to cough up for that useless meeting with that weedy poof Gillespie. But Trevor has two weeks of his holidays left and, although it's 1 September on Tuesday and a busy month for holidays, he persuades his best mate, Greg, to swap. He was only going to his mother-in-law's and seemed quite keen to oblige.

If the kids aren't with Kirsty then where the hell are they? A caring mother, too caring thinks Trev, she would be highly unlikely to dump them just anywhere. Trev's anger grows. If only he'd acted before, or talked to someone other than his mother. He ought to have guessed she would bolt one day, but Trev is the type of macho man who believes that to discuss private problems is a symptom of weakness, and there is such a thing as disloyalty to the family.

He thinks of himself as the strong, silent type.

His is a nonchalant, carefree image. Wife and kiddies at home, central heating, double glazing, everything in his garden is rosy – although a quick look at Trev's garden would soon reveal some hidden truths: discarded clothes-pegs dropped about, cardboard boxes just tossed anywhere, rotting sunbeds not put away, patches of border dug but not finished, now sprouting dandelions amidst pale-green grasses – all signs of Kirsty's malaise in

Trev's sick mind. Trev sincerely believes that Kirsty is to blame; he has convinced himself that black is white in his pursuit of vengeance. 'Part of her problem was her cleanliness phobia,' he tells disbelieving friends, turning the truth on its head. 'The house had to be spotless, even if it meant tipping little messes – old pans of fat and the burned remains of casseroles – out of the kitchen door onto the abandoned beds.' All lies. 'And although she dumped bits of broken bike and pram in the garden, indoors the kids' toys were never in sight – under the beds they had to go, one toy out at a time was the rule. Bloody hell, sometimes I got home and thought I'd arrived in hospital, so strong was the damn disinfectant smell.

'The cow would shout at me, "Take your shoes off." Never, ever, "What sort of day have you had?" or ask about the traffic. And the meal was always banged down on the table, mustard, mustard, mustard with everything, and gravy poured all over it. I found her books hidden everywhere, three or four on the go at a time, as if the bitch felt guilty for reading and needed to hide her dirty deeds as though they were some kind of female secret.'

Trev couldn't care if she read or not so long as he had his *Sun* for the sport and the *Sunday People* for the competitions.

Kirsty was obsessive, he told them.

She insisted on ironing and folding his socks.

She hated talking over the telly.

She hid the bills until he had it out with her – when the telephone was cut off, and the electric, he came home once to find them sitting round in the dark, a cold tea, ham with mustard, ready for him on the table. And she's got such a fetish about her hair, she never allowed him to touch it. She tried to sell his Bisto tin once, knowing it was a favourite of his; she took it to a second-hand shop, along with his mum's coronation mug. When he finally got the truth out of her, when she admitted what she'd done, he was forced to take his pride in his hands and try to explain at the shop.

The slightest thing would set her off. OK, he admits it, he has hit her in the past; he had to, he had no alternative, it was the only way to bring her to her senses. She thought she was one of her bloody heroines, Amelia or Bethany, Bettina or Wanda – crazy names acted out in even crazier situations. She was lost in a haze of designer gowns or artists' studios or in the clinics of famous surgeons. Those damn Mills and Boons hypnotized her; chameleon-like, she became the heroine. At times like these she left him; he could wave his hand before her face and she didn't even flinch, she was gone into another, happier, more glamorous world than Trev could provide.

He told them that he'd tried his best to be patient, that the kiddies didn't know what was happening; he bathed them and put them to bed but it was their mummy they wanted.

But now, at least, he knows where she's gone and he's determined to confront her. This is the last time she will mess them all up – Trev, his mum, the kiddies – Trev's patience snapped long ago; that nutcase will agree to have treatment if he has to drag her there himself, and he goes off to hire a

Vauxhall Cavalier, reliable wheels for his south-bound journey.

'You should teach that cow a lesson,' says Greg in manly sympathy, as Trev hands over the van and drives off looking lonely.

'The High Priestess of the Plot' is how *Magdalene*'s agents refer to the author, and yes, Kirsty, like the nun, now has the power to make things happen. Look how meekly Dominic Coates is obeying her instructions – you see how little it takes to bring these bullies to their knees.

The hippies from the hotel 'cottage' come over to bid her goodbye and they hand Kirsty the single key to their derelict home. 'At least you won't have rent to pay,' encourages the one with the woollen hair. 'Mind the hole in the kitchen floor if there's kiddies around,' he says. 'There might have been a well underneath it, or something deep at any rate from the stench it sometimes gives off.'

Kirsty takes the key he offers without bothering to explain that she's found a more comfortable home. She wouldn't dream of living anywhere so unsavoury and dangerous with her kids. She will return the key to Mrs Stokes.

'You blooming well keep that key, maid,' says Flagherty the gardener, closing one papery lid over a watering eye. 'That might stop the blighters being tempted to let it out again and I'm sick and tired of the riffraff that's taken to coming down here. Seems I'm the only responsible one in this place any more.' He kicks a soily boot against his stationary spade. 'You could allus store things in him.'

215

She gets a curious pleasure from watching her literary tableau unfold from the wings, from handing over the power to Bernie and seeing Avril take her rightful place in the limelight. Trev once called her a masochist – hah! She laughed at him, where did he get that long word from? But Kirsty was forced to look it up and it sounded as if he might have been right. Depriving herself, hurting herself, lowering herself – all this is part of a need she has to find real contentment.

Kirsty likes to suffer. That's how the vicious circle turns.

The permanent penitent.

The scourging of the guilty soul.

Sometimes, with a splintering thrill that verges on the erotic, she imagines herself as a servant in the little attic room where she now sleeps alone, a servant back in the bad old days when they were forced to get up at five and not return to bed until late. She pretends she has no bed covers and lies in bed shivering, imagining the dinners and balls going on downstairs. She will skip a meal and purposefully go to bed hungry. Sometimes she scrubs her hands with a nailbrush till the fingernails bleed, as the skivvies' hands must have bled in the big houses of yesteryear. She sees Mrs Stokes as the wicked housekeeper who throws erring maids onto the street, where they have to sell their bodies to survive, or watch their illegitimate babies starve. Mrs Stokes is an easy target: unknowingly, yet expertly, she fulfils this role every day.

And all this dark, debasing stuff Kirsty shares with her heroine, Magdalene.

Magdalene is a masochist, too. That's why she became a nun. But Magdalene has risen above it.

The sensitive Avril is sympathetic to Kirsty's hurt expressions and sorrowful body language. Avril can't do enough to help, but Bernie is not so driven. So pleased with herself is Bernie that she doesn't give a thought to anyone else and now Dominic is back on the scene her selfish attitude is escalating.

Oh dear, dear.

And poor Kirsty has done so much for Bernie.

All her hard work is for Bernie's good. When she cleans another lavatory Kirsty dwells on ungrateful Bernie and all the miseries heaped upon her. When Bernie makes it to the top, she will probably turn on Kirsty as Trevor turned on her before.

Bernie will probably try to cheat her out of the money completely, just as Trev used to watch her with money, and take it away when he found it.

This is the luggage Kirsty carts with her. But Magdalene says it must stop.

Kirsty visits the Happy Stay to pay Mrs Gilcrest a month in advance. At last she has managed to save it up. She once asked Bernie if Candice Love would give her a small advance, but Bernie said no as if she was talking to a stranger. 'She doesn't give me money. She says the advance on the book won't be long. Sometimes Candice pays for the odd expenses, but it's Mr Derek who's footing this bill because he thinks I might be famous and he still wants to get his leg over.'

Avril and Ed give Kirsty a lift to the Happy Stay in Ed's old VW.

'I don't want to go,' moans Avril, over and over again. 'I really don't want to see them just now and I know Mother will be nasty to Ed.'

'*Avril,*' says Ed with admirable patience, and his red eyebrows flatten out across a broadly accepting forehead, 'I've already told you, it's no skin off my nose, whatever your Mother's attitude is it will make no difference to us.'

'She'll even be rude to you, Kirsty,' warns Avril, back to her old slouching ways, biting her nails, defeat in her eyes. 'Mother has never approved of my friends. She'll find something to criticize, and when she meets Bernie, God knows what she'll say.'

Is Ed after Avril's money as Bernie seems to think?

And does this matter if he makes Avril happy?

Her parents can't be as bad as she says. Avril has some chip on her shoulder, probably dating back to her childhood. Now that she is independent and so much more self-confident with Ed at her side, how can her mother possibly affect her?

'Oh,' says Avril's mother, emerging from the caravan with a pinny tied round her waist and a dishcloth in her hand. 'Oh, Avril, we thought you would be alone, didn't we, Richard?'

'This is my mother,' says Avril, cheeks aflame, holding Ed's arm tightly. 'And, Mother, this is my friend Ed.'

'Friend?' says her mother, her nose sharpening.

'Well, my boyfriend actually,' giggles Avril like a schoolgirl before the head teacher.

'You never wrote to me about him. You never mentioned him on the phone.'

'I wanted it to be a surprise.'

'Well, it certainly is a surprise.' Avril's mother makes a show of wiping a wet hand down her pinny before holding it out to Ed. 'Good evening, Ed. I really have to apologize, my cauliflower cheese won't stretch to a fourth.'

'I wouldn't dream of intruding—'

'I don't want any either,' says Avril quickly. 'We've all already eaten. And this is my friend Kirsty.'

'Quite a reception committee,' says Avril's mother dryly.

Driven to break the awkward silence, Avril carries on miserably, 'Kirsty is renting one of these caravans for the winter.'

'Oh, my dear, how ghastly for you,' says Avril's mother. 'Whatever happened? Are you homeless? Come and sit down in one of our deckchairs. They're quite comfortable really. Richard, Richard! I asked you to put the other one out . . . and would anyone like a drink? As you're here, I think we can stretch.'

Between the Stotts' caravan and its neighbour there is a gap of about twelve feet, and onto that space Avril's mother has already stamped her presence. A folding clothes rack, neat with tea towels, hand towels and clean yellow dusters, is parked beside a hedgehog foot scraper, two flowering pot plants and two extended sunloungers complete with fringed parasols.

'I wouldn't say no to a beer,' says Ed, quickly taking a seat before offering one to Avril.

'Oh no.' Mrs Stott's laugh is haughty. 'Nothing alcoholic, Edward, I'm afraid. Home-made lemonade, Avril's favourite, or Lilt, Richard's preferred tipple. And what do you do for living, might I ask?'

'He is the hotel golf professional, Mother.'

'Oh? That's nice. And how about you, Kirsty? Do you do anything interesting?'

'No, I'm just a chambermaid,' Kirsty admits.

'One of the Burleston skivvies,' jokes Ed, siding with Avril's mother and accepting her home-made lemonade.

'Oh, no, it's not like that—'

'I'm sure', crows Avril's mother, 'poor Kirsty doesn't need you to speak up for her, Avril.'

'Avril is easily influenced, I've noticed that,' says Ed, joking again.

'It's a jolly good thing you have noticed, Edward. That has always been one of Avril's weaknesses, hasn't it, Avril?'

'Oh, Mother, do stop it! You've only just arrived. Please leave me alone.'

'Your mother cares about you, Avril.'

'And there's no need for you to side with her, Ed.'

Now they are all sitting round awkwardly, three in deckchairs, including Ed, and Avril and Kirsty perched on the end of the two sunbeds.

'Avril,' and Ed reaches over proprietorially to take her hand, 'when are you going to tell your parents about Bernadette's book and all the excitement?'

Avril withdraws her hand. 'Actually, I did want to wait—'

'What's this? What's been going on, Avril? What haven't you told us?'

'Well, it's all quite extraordinary,' Ed butts in. 'I must say, Mrs Stott, this lemonade of yours is marvellous. Avril's little Irish friend has written a book, with the aid of Avril's office skills, and both of them have been leading quite the high life of late.'

There is no worse way Avril's mother could have been told about the success of her daughter, and Kirsty could slap Ed's face. If Avril's involvement with Ed continues, all she is doing is swapping one undermining influence for another.

'I've been doing my best to help her spend all this free time usefully by trying to introduce Avril to golf, but it's been a hard slog in between all the magazine articles, interviews and photographers. I am quite surprised, Mrs Stott, that you haven't already seen your daughter's picture in the *Guardian*.'

'Stop it, Ed,' cries the stricken Avril, sickened by Ed's disloyal behaviour.

'We don't take that sort of paper,' says Avril's mother sniffily, 'we prefer to stick with straightforward, sensible news. The *Daily Mail* is good enough for us, and we don't bother with music and the arts, do we, Richard?' Mrs Stott turns angrily on Avril. 'I hope Ed is not suggesting that you've given up your job, that good job I helped you to get, all those important qualifications you worked for?'

'Avril's young, Mrs Stott,' says the wretched Ed, to Kirsty's absolute fury, sitting, amused, on his deckchair with his chubby legs spread, resting his lemonade on his paunch, 'don't be too hard on her. When you're young it's easy to be tempted by ideas of quick fame and fortune, and some of the people surrounding Avril and her dramatic little friend Bernie are really not the sort I think you and your husband would approve of.'

'I have obviously come down here just in time,' says Avril's mother with steel in her voice. 'I had my misgivings, Richard knows that. Thank goodness you were here, Edward. And what sort of part have you been playing in this vulgar little fiasco?' She turns to face Kirsty.

'Kirsty has nothing to do with it,' cries Avril, puffing up, close to tears, 'and it's nothing like what Ed's just told you. Listen!' she almost shrieks, summing up the dregs of her courage, 'let me explain—'

'Oh, Avril, don't waste your time,' snaps Kirsty, mortified to see her friend brought down so unjustly and with the aid of the one person she has just learned to trust. 'You have no need to have anything more to do with these paganized people. Remember Magdalene! Would she have put up with this? Ed is a brown-nosing, big-headed idolater who only wants you for your money.'

'Who do you think you are, young lady?'

'Be silent, you unholy creature. Just remember this when you're old and alone and Avril is living it up on the other side of the world. The pen is mightier than the sword and if I had a pen in my hand now I would poke out your devilish eyes.'

How did she come to make such a speech? Where did those words come from? As Kirsty makes her way to reception to see Mrs Gilcrest she is overcome by the anger inside her, the fury that spilled out so fluently, the word power she experienced and the intoxicating sense of elation as she saw Mrs Stott's shocked face and the admiration in Avril's.

Magdalene?

Oh yes. The power is hers.

But where will it take her and what should she do with it?

Seventeen

Seas of trials and cups of sorrows.

Calamity and Slough of Despond.

The luckless Ed Board has passed over and Fluffy the cat has gone missing.

And this is a most inopportune place for Graham Stott, the murderer, to find himself in.

The Burleston is swarming with pigs and Graham, whose nerve-racking journey has tired him out, is unaware that the hotel pro has been found in the rough with his head staved in by his own four wood. So rightly paranoid is Graham that he thinks they are all waiting for him.

Since his last lift to the end of the A30 he has had to walk, or skulk, for eight miles before reaching his destination and, although Graham is not used to walking, to nick a car at this sensitive time would do fatal damage to his new image. Not that there are many cars around that the street-cred Graham would be seen dead in. Kicked out of his home by a cruel mother, Graham is a young boy looking for work, and visiting his sister for help. When he thought of it this way a blistering self-pity welled up in him, and once he had to wipe his eyes on the sleeve of his bomber jacket. He was hobbling now, his right foot was blistered and his hunger and thirst increased, but nobody cared. Nobody cared. Every time he saw headlights creep over the sky like a sunrise being wound on, Graham dove into the nearest hedgerow. The few cars passed slowly, as if their drivers were asleep. Every time he heard a dog bark he detoured round the threatening farmhouse. He soon grew used to the country sounds – the hoot of an owl, the low of a cow right next to the hedge, a bird, disturbed in its nest – but a vixen being pursued by a dog fox raised the hairs on the back of his neck. He thought it was a mad woman screaming and the sound stayed in his ears like eardrops, tickling and freezing them long after the sodding creatures had gone.

It was warm work on this hot summer's night and he still shook under the blow of the horror of the crime he had committed. At least here, in the dark night, he was safe from the multitude of eyes in the city, the awful publicity of the sunlight. The stars overhead presided over a frightening stillness, something Graham was quite unused to. The signposts he passed looked like gibbets. What a good thing people weren't hanged any more. Graham rubbed his neck, shivered all over, and lit another of his precious fags. He wished he was safe back in prison, they shouldn't have let him out. Were they after him even now? Had the forensic blokes come up with something that linked him inexorably to the crime?

His unhappy fingers felt the dark stubble on his chin and his hunted eyes stared round him. He was not inhuman. He had not meant to kill her, so why did everyone hate him? God knows the inside of his head. God must be on his side.

At daybreak he was well on his way, and sign-posts to Burleston Cove gave him hope. The sooner all this was behind him the better. Avril could give him the alibi he needed. Avril could tell them he had been with her. He had always managed to manip-ulate Avril and nothing had changed since then, had it? Poor, childish, timid little cow.

The road, no longer climbing, led into a broad driveway fringed with high rhododendrons. Mainly in darkness, save for the few odd glimmering lights, the building itself rose up to his left, and Graham took the sandy track to the beach where he planned to wait and get some kip until morning.

Little irritations become large annoyances.

Avril is not one for spiteful thoughts, but Bernie and Dominic are so selfish. In the hard put-you-up in the dressing room she wakes to the bleeping of the bedside phone and thumps and squeals from the four-poster bed that Bernie and Dominic have taken over.

She picks up the phone. 'Avril! Avril! Is that you?'

Oh no, not Mother. Not now.

For one blissful moment she had forgotten about the hideous row she and Mother had had last night; not just she and Mother, but she and Ed had finished up not speaking. Avril walked home with Kirsty. Ed, for whom Avril had such hopes, has turned out to be a disloyal cad and as elderly in his thinking as Mother.

So her heart takes a plunge as reality dawns. And

it plunges further when she hears the news. 'Fluffy has gone missing!'

'Oh no!' And the very worst thing of all is the surge of guilt, because in all the confusion of yesterday evening she never gave poor Fluffy a thought. She hadn't even asked after her; she had failed Fluffy by not even bothering to go into the caravan to search her out. Fluffy must have known that Avril was there, and perhaps she tried to struggle out of bed, mewing hopelessly.

'Your father let her out before we settled down to bed and Fluffy never came back. We haven't had a wink of sleep, searching round and calling for her, because this is alien territory for Fluffy and she's probably lost somewhere and frightened. She's already missed one lot of tablets.'

'I'll be over right away,' says Avril, climbing out of her rosebud pyjamas.

She would have to walk, of course, because nothing would induce her to ask the despicable Ed for a lift, and Candice Love, with her black Saab convertible she had driven down from London, doesn't get up until gone ten.

There's no point in disturbing Bernie to tell her where she's going. Avril has done her duty as supporter and companion, and now, more and more, she is left out of discussions and meetings and replaced by Dominic Coates. Mostly she feels like a spare part. Bernie is in her element and Dominic makes the perfect escort, suave as he is, at ease in the very best of company, protective and romantic. As Candice Love said yesterday, 'Dominic adds that particular *frisson* that was needed to make it a perfect partnership.'

Avril is surprised to be accosted by a man in the revolving doorway of the foyer. 'May I ask where you're going, miss?'

'Yes,' says Avril, ever eager to oblige, 'my cat is missing and I'm going to look for it.'

'Can I take your name, please?' And he produces a list and ticks her off.

'Does this mean you will be remaining in the Burleston hotel grounds this morning?'

'No,' says Avril, still too submissive to think of asking what this is about. She does notice that there are more people than normal hanging around the reception area at this early hour of the day, strangers, people not in holiday mode. When she looks outside she sees two police cars with uniformed policemen on walkie talkies. But she waits politely until she is told. 'I am going to the Happy Stay caravan park where my parents are staying.'

'Then I'm sorry, miss, I will have to ask you to change your plans and stay in the vicinity for the rest of today. A man has been found dead on the golf course and unfortunately it looks as if the death is not a natural one.'

'But what about poor Fluffy?' Avril is almost in tears, talk of death on the golf course is really the final straw. Who could it be? Some old, ailing guest having an early morning putt?

'I can't help you there I'm afraid, miss, I have my orders.'

'What do you mean by not natural? Has there been an accident?'

The brown-suited man lowers his eyebrows as if they are in mourning. 'It looks as if somebody else might be involved.'

'Who?'

The policeman smiles patiently. 'If you could make sure you stay around so we can ask you questions if we need to, we would be grateful, Miss Stott.'

'Avril, can I have a word,' says Mr Derek, gesticulating.

'*With me?*'

'Just for a moment. Step into my office, would you?'

So Avril, perplexed, steps inside.

'Sit down, Avril.' This is a very far cry from the first time she was summoned in here by Mr Derek's fearsome call, when she was made to sit in the hardbacked chair, trembling over her shorthand. Now she sits dizzily in a round, pink, silken effort with long, sturdy arms and tasselled cushions. She feels like the Queen on her throne. She looks at her former employer with questioning dolly-blue eyes.

'I thought I'd better tell you, Avril, I thought it might be kinder if the news came from me, but I know you and Ed Board were fairly friendly.' Here Mr Derek clears his throat and takes a reviving sip of water. 'So I realize it will be painful for you to know that the body they found at seven thirty this morning was that of Edward Board, our golf professional.'

She can hardly breathe. The shock is tremendous. That someone she knew so well is dead. 'Oh no . . .'

But there is more . . . 'and that his wife, Margaret Board, is already on her way.'

'*His wife?*'

Mr Derek nods sympathetically. 'I believe she is leaving the children with her mother.'

'But I never knew Ed had a wife, or children.'

Mr Derek carries on gently. 'Margaret Board lives in Tintagel. She preferred not to live in at the hotel; considered it too cut off for the children, I believe. Ed visited regularly, of course, and spent most of his free time there.'

'You said Ed's body has been found?' Helplessly shrugging, Avril can hardly take all this in. Ridiculously Avril tries her hardest not to feel like Ed's murderer. She couldn't possibly have killed Ed, could she? She certainly hates him enough. But she has an alibi, the police will know that. There is a limit to what anyone, even Avril, will own up to of her own free will.

'A vicious blow to the head, apparently. Of course the media will make a meal of it. It's all rather ghastly and certainly not the sort of hanky panky we want going on round here.' Mr Derek's refined nostrils flare. 'The police pathologist is with them now. They think Ed was searching for a lost ball.'

'But I was with him last night. When could he have been playing golf?'

'His body was still warm, they tell me,' says Mr Derek queasily, 'so we can only assume poor Ed went for an early morning practice session. He was always an early riser.'

Shamefully, Mother's favourite expression comes instantly to mind, 'The early bird catches the worm.' Well, Ed caught a damn sight more than worms. He probably had dew on his moustache, that ugly red scrubbing brush seemed to catch any available liquid, and Avril finds herself oddly unaffected by the thought of Ed's violent demise. She is far more concerned about Fluffy the cat.

Avril hurries back upstairs to tell Bernie and Dominic the news. Thank God they are no longer bonking, but Bernie is padding around drinking coffee in her new sea-grey negligee and Dominic looks like a male model, tucking into a princely breakfast of smoked salmon and scrambled egg.

The dramatic news hardly concerns them, they are so engrossed in each other. The fact that Ed was important to Avril seems to have slipped Bernie's mind, which is hurtful. Bernie has no knowledge of Avril's upsetting experience last night; as far as she knows Avril must be heartbroken.

'He was always a bit of a nerd,' she says unkindly, gliding towards the window to see if she can spot any drama, but you can't quite see the golf course from their room. 'He wanted you for your money, that's all. It's better that he's out of the way. Avril, you'll get over him.'

'But Ed could have been murdered! Dammit!' says Avril, infuriated by Bernie's cold condescension. 'A man is dead, there's a murderer on the loose!'

'Probably some tramp—'

'Since when have you seen a tramp around here?'

'Well, I don't know, Avril, do I?' sighs Bernie, the silken drape of her sleeves hanging like moon-struck moths' wings. 'As long as the publicity doesn't push us out of the limelight. Does Candice know yet?'

What is the point? 'I really haven't a clue. To be honest that thought never crossed my mind.'

'Perhaps I ought to give her a ring. She might

think we ought to get out of here. She's been talking about moving for days; she says London would be more convenient.' And then Bernie turns round quickly and glares hard at Avril. 'I hope you're not going to be involved in this mess,' she says coldly. 'Holy Mary Mother of God, you playing the victim, mourning your lover, playing up to the cameras, I can just see that.'

This is intolerable. 'Don't be so hateful!' Avril is tempted to slap Bernie's face. 'Ed is married! There was never anything serious between Ed and me. And why would I want to hog your limelight? We're on the same side, remember!'

And the true reason why Avril rushed upstairs to find her friend seems quite ludicrous now. Bernie just isn't interested. Bernie has left her and Kirsty behind. Bernie wouldn't give a damn, let alone hold out a comforting arm, over poor Fluffy the cat.

Just one hour later . . .

'Have you a brother, Miss Stott?'

What's this? Avril has to pause before she answers, she hasn't seen Graham in years. 'Well, yes . . .'

'And has he been living down here with you since the middle of last month?'

'Living with me?' What does this mean? Avril shakes her head. 'No, of course he hasn't been living with me.'

This frowning policeman, keen-featured, clean-shaven and well-tailored, and the younger man at his side are obviously trying to tell Avril something. But what? What?

The first man shakes his head and smiles sadly.

'And I have to ask you this, Avril. Soon after you arrived here, a couple of hotel guests, the Misses Peg and Vi Lewis, lost a rather important bracelet.'

Avril nods, feeling her hands begin to sweat. She recognizes interrogation when she sees it; it was a feature of her youth.

The man's eyes flash and his voice rises slightly. 'I believe you had access to the keys of the Miss Lewises' room at that time?'

'I worked on the reception desk. Yes, I did have access.' Access seems such a law-laden word.

'And when Mrs Stokes called a meeting of the staff, I believe it was you who advised the manageress to go and have a look in the Miss Lewises' room.'

Avril can hardly remember. 'Yes, well, that did seem quite an obvious thing to do. They were old, they did tend to get things muddled.'

'And lo and behold, when Mrs Stokes did go to look, she found the bracelet there in the dressing-table drawer.'

Avril gasps, panic-struck, as the awful truth hits her. 'You're saying I took it, aren't you?' The colour drains from her face.

'We are merely asking you, Avril. Mrs Stokes has mentioned that you looked very uneasy when she first mentioned the missing piece. And you had the wherewithal to replace the bracelet; you would see when the Miss Lewises went out.'

'This is unbelievable!' cries Avril.

'The Miss Lewises departed from the hotel insisting that they had not been mistaken. They are certain that bracelet went missing.'

'The Miss Lewises are vicious, small-minded

233

snobs who love to cause trouble and would never admit they were wrong,' says Avril indignantly, struggling now to keep her cool. This is all so unfair. 'And what has this got to do with my brother?'

The policeman crosses his legs and leans back in Mr Derek's swivel chair. 'You wouldn't have taken the bracelet with a view to passing it on to him, would you, by any chance, Avril?'

'I have never stolen anything in my entire life,' Avril declares, clenching her fists and banging them down on Mr Derek's office table. 'Just because my brother's a crook doesn't mean to say I'm like him.'

The tick tick tick of Mr Derek's onyx carriage clock is the only sane sound in the room.

'Just one more thing,' says the policeman, watching Avril narrowly. 'I believe you purchased some items recently from Mr Edward Board's shop?'

She can't cope with this. 'Well, yes, I did.'

'Have you, by any chance, got the receipts?' His is a strangely quiet politeness.

So disordered are Avril's thoughts that her brain goes bumping round like a waltzer. 'I haven't got any receipts because Ed told me I could take the items and pay him when I got my own money.'

'And where are these items now?' asks the smart detective with studied carelessness.

'They are in my wardrobe, in my room.'

'At the bottom of your wardrobe, Avril? Would you say they were hidden away at the bottom?'

Avril sinks back, defeated. Menace! Menace is everywhere. Some little imp still living inside her shouts, 'Admit it, Avril, admit it!' But no, no, she won't, she's not that hopeless fat girl any more. 'Stop bullying me like this! *Stop it! Stop it!* They are scrunched up in a bag at the bottom because I was too embarrassed to get them out and hang them up. I was afraid of what Bernie would say if she saw them because they make me look fatter than ever.'

'I see. I see. I quite understand,' says the detective slightly more pleasantly, as if there was never ill-feeling between them. 'Please don't be too upset. We have to ask these questions, I'm afraid, in an enquiry such as this. You see, the main problem is that we found your brother a little while earlier hiding out in the grounds, and he swore blind that he'd been living here with you.'

'But that's a lie.'

'Yes, it would seem so. But we had to scotch some of the stories we always hear in these sorts of investigations. Unfortunately all sorts of rumours get put about.'

'It's that evil woman, Stokes, isn't it? She told you about the bracelet. But what about the golfing gear, what made you check up on that?'

'Oh that's just a matter of going through the dockets in the shop,' says the first detective mildly. 'The figures didn't add up, so we had to check them out. From what we already have on that brother of yours, he's trouble, and you, unfortunately, were dragged into it. These things happen.'

'But what is Graham doing here?' pleads Avril, totally bewildered.

'That is precisely what we would like to know,' says the detective, showing her out. 'But in the meantime, to be on the safe side, we are taking that young man into custody.'

Eighteen

Life is not half as hellish as Dominic Coates, turn-coat, had imagined it might be. In fact, this kind of luxurious existence suits him to a T; he has even telephoned Mummy and Daddy to tell them about his old love's success. They, of course, knew already, being subscribers to the correct sorts of papers, and their new attitude to his Irish skivvy is an interesting change. No, his main worry is that Kirsty Hoskins, in her madness, will snitch on him on a whim, and Bernadette will kick him out on his arse.

Dominic does not see much of Kirsty, a woman very seriously disturbed, because she works long hours and still lives in the staff quarters. He has made several abortive attempts to quiz Bernadette about her sick friend, but his famous girlfriend will not be drawn.

'Oh she's just someone we shared a room with when we first arrived. Yes, she's odd, but she's been through shit, despises men probably, after all that grief. She's on the run from her husband; she's getting her kids back next week.'

Sometimes, when she thinks about Kirsty, Bernie

236

feels a new anger well up and it's almost as if she can't tolerate thoughts of her sad old friend any more. Sad – the word enrages her. 'But she's a loser, born a loser, happy to be a loser, miserable most of the time and complaining, like Avril.' Bernie hung her arms around him as she coldly dismissed her two best friends. How freeing it felt to be so censorious of them. They had been close. They had been a family, or coven. What was happening to make her so vicious? 'Don't you find it strange, Dom, how some people seem to be born to good luck?'

'They're not born to it,' says he, forgetting his own privileged birth; 'it's an attitude of mind. Now Kirsty would never have dreamed of attempting the kind of challenge you took when you sat down and wrote chapter one. Nor would Avril, they haven't got that thrusting germ of ambition in them. And they don't have the turn of phrase, or the stamina. Frankly, they're just boring little people.'

'But you'd love me even if I wasn't a writer, wouldn't you?' Bernie puts on her little girl act, curling up, teasing him like a monkey.

'You know I would.'

'But you left me . . .'

'We've been all through that. I was scared, Bernie, scared of commitment, scared of feelings I couldn't control.'

And that seems to satisfy his little Irish genius.

Candice Love had a long talk with Dominic when he first arrived on the scene. He was nervous, not sure what to expect. Hell, this whole scenario was based on deception, it couldn't get much more bizarre than it was.

'I don't want any cheating, heartbreak, or talk of personal space crap,' she said. 'If you're going to move in here you've got to understand exactly what we're dealing with.' Candice tapped her nails firmly on the table as she emphasized every word and Dominic could hardly bear to watch: he has a thing about nails bending like chalk squeaking down a blackboard. 'Bernadette is a genius. Now that might sound overdramatic, but you've only got to listen to Clementine Davaine, and she is the best in the business, frankly we are thrilled to get her. The press have seized on her image, partly because it's the back end of the silly season, we realize that, but we don't want anyone messing up now. And if Clementine says Bernadette is a wonder then nobody's going to argue with her.'

All this is quite hard for Dominic to grasp. 'When I went out with Bernie before she didn't show any signs of genius; we were pissed most of the time and she was just like any other girl working in a scouse restaurant. I never even saw her read a book – sometimes a magazine, but that was only for the quizzes.'

'No, well, it's not the kind of thing you can spot,' Candice Love went on with confidence. 'People don't have GENIUS emblazoned across their foreheads, and it's not something that is inherent. Perhaps Bernie's talent developed as a result of the unhappiness she went through after you left her: suicide bids, depression, obsession, the works. That could have done it.'

But Dominic thought of the few cards she wrote him, that abject letter after the split, and the way she hated Scrabble because she couldn't win – it wasn't fair, she used to say, just 'cos she'd missed out on an education.

'What we're all waiting for now is a second novel,' said Candice, her long fawn hair held back that morning by a brown chocolate-box bow that rested on her back. Dominic admired Candice's style, he admired her directness and was impressed, in spite of himself, by the way she name-dropped so effortlessly – authors, actors, film directors – that was the world she moved in and Dominic wouldn't mind that for himself. His future in cardboard boxes had never inspired him with much passion. How exhilarating it would be if he could move into the publishing world, and he could, with luck, on the back of starry-eyed Bernadette.

'A second novel. That's what they're clamouring for now,' Candice carried on, sipping her blue curaçao cocktail, having shoved the delicate paper umbrella straight in the ashtray. 'These days authors aren't worth their salt if they can't churn out at least one a year, although, in Bernadette's case, with *Magdalene* such a classic, there's not quite so much pressure.'

'Perhaps it's just a one-off,' said Dominic, still unconvinced.

'Maybe,' said Candice. 'But I hope not. And I don't want you causing Bernie any distress or distraction. She is charismatic, dynamic, with the looks of a superstar, and I hope you understand what I'm saying.'

God, Candice was bold and sexy.

This is beyond the pale.

It looks as if Avril's dreadful brother might be

involved in this grisly murder – that is the rumour flying round the hotel; it splutters and twists like a burning fuse – and Bernie hurries off to interrogate Kirsty in her dingy quarters. This really takes the biscuit; it's bad enough Avril hanging around moping, playing gooseberry, never contributing anything positive to this uncanny tabloid frenzy, but to have the sister of some scouse hood contaminating Bernie's impish, Irish image is to take the original talk of fairness a tad too far.

If only Bernie had really written this blooming book. If only she didn't need Kirsty or Avril.

'We just can't afford to have Avril around any more,' argues Bernie, sitting down abruptly on her vacant old bed which already smells of mothballs. 'She's an embarrassment, she doesn't fit in and it's time we ditched her.'

Kirsty, who can't help being shocked by Bernie's sudden disloyalty, had nevertheless anticipated it. She has watched the subtle change in her friend even before she arranged for Dom to move back. Something has touched her, tainted her beauty, and this hatred feels like a kind of possession. 'How can you say that? That's awful. I mean, what would happen to Avril if she had to move out? She hasn't got a job any more since she gave it up to support you.'

'You seem to be surviving OK.'

'Oh yeah.' Kirsty looks annoyingly miserable. 'But then I don't have any alternative.'

Someone has to be positive round here. Bernie musters her best lilting brogue in her attempts at persuasion. 'You must talk to Avril seriously and tell her this business might ruin the project, get shot of her before the tabloids link us up again and turn

240

everything murky. Praise God they ignored her from the beginning; she's not the most memorable woman I know.' Kirsty doesn't look comfortable with this. But Bernie's the one they're dependent on. 'While the press are obsessed with this poor little Irish peasant made good, Avril has faded right out of the picture, but imagine how the headlines would change if they made that connection now.'

Kirsty shakes her head sadly and this further infuriates Bernie. Sad, sad, sad. Everything about them is so bloody sad. 'Avril is pretty uptight right now . . .'

'I know. And I'm sorry for her. Jesus, everyone's always sorry for Avril. But, Kirsty, she mustn't ruin everything! Not now we've come so far.'

Kirsty blinks hard, pausing to think, but nothing she says can influence Bernie and there is some sense in her argument. 'Where would she live? We haven't got paid yet and we still don't know when that advance is coming.'

'I've thought about that. When you move into your caravan why can't you take Avril with you?'

'She might not want to come.'

'Of course she'd come. She's needy. She knows she has a future with us. She's found two friends, probably the first she's ever had, and she won't want to leave us and go back home with that mother-from-hell.' Somehow Kirsty must be convinced. 'And she might be a real help with your kids when you're working back here.'

This is disturbing stuff. It looks like Bernie is right, although so much spite runs through the logic. 'Have you spoken to Candice yet? Does she feel the same?'

Bernie would rather have skipped this bit, but now she might as well get it over. 'Candice wants us to leave this weekend,' she confesses, watching hard for Kirsty's reactions. 'To London, to her uncle's flat while he's away touring Australia. He plays the piano. She's arranged everything. We'll be there until *Magdalene* is published, probably till after Christmas. Dom has decided to skip his last year; he'd rather stay with me and help me through all this.'

The rat. 'So it's working?' interrupts Kirsty, lifting one curious eyebrow.

Bernie's green eyes shine with triumph. 'Yeah. Good, isn't it? He's so different, Kirsty, I can't believe it, he doesn't screw around any more, he doesn't get rat-arsed every night, he's not mean-minded like he used to be, he seems so much more grown up.'

This, at any rate, is good to hear. Dominic is behaving himself. 'But if Avril doesn't move to London with you how will you do the corrections?'

Bernie has thought of this, too. 'You can do the corrections, no problem, I'll have to keep ringing you up, that's all. But what with this Ed Board crap, and Avril's bloody brother, what's the point of her hanging around? You must see that I'm right.' How can she put this more forcibly? It must be as plain to Kirsty as the nose on Avril's flat, chubby face. Avril is a burden, she has outlived her usefulness and that's all there is to it.

And Kirsty is too blinkered to see it.

The police investigation builds up around the hotel and its excited guests; everyone is interviewed, everyone is revelling in it.

You pay for murder weekends like this.

The weapon has not yet been found. They know it was a number-four wood because of the measurements and the imprints on the wound, and because that was the only club missing from the professional's golf bag, and now there is a tent on the spot where Ed Board's body was found and a fluttering ribbon round it.

Most people go to have a look and pretend they just happen to be passing.

They say he was searching for his ball and someone came up on him from behind.

It's an unnerving feeling to be so near to where a murder has just been committed and Bernie finds herself staring at people – *was it you?* And although the preferred thinking is still that Graham Stott, the ne'er-do-well, must be the killer, it still comes as a thrilling shock when he is accused, not of Ed's demise after all, but that of a little old lady in Liverpool.

'The bastard must have done them both in.'

'Bring back hanging.'

'They had him behind bars once, so why did they let the sicko out?'

'Animal.'

'Throw him to the masses and let them deal with the scrote.'

He killed poor Annie for £1.39, but why, they muse, did he kill Ed?

'The poor sod must have disturbed him while he was looking for his ball. The bastard must have been skulking about in the bushes.'

No-one believes the police announcement: 'While we have charged Graham Stott with the murder of

Mrs Annie Brenner, we have no reason at this time to connect him with the recent death of Mr Edward Board of Tintagel.'

It would be of great assistance, announce the police, if they could locate the murder weapon, and so everyone at the Burleston joins the local force to stroll, head down, round the golf course, squinting down old rabbit holes.

It is an anguished Avril, eyes protruding with horror, who begs Bernie, 'I can't stay here, at the hotel, not with all this . . .' and she bursts into tears again.

She goes on in a voice not in control, but breaking and gulping alternately, 'Kirsty says I can go and stay in her caravan, it's empty now, and Mother and Father are near by and they need me. They're devastated of course, nothing seems to matter any more, not the book, not even poor Fluffy, but I hope you don't think I'm deserting you.' Still anxious to trouble no-one.

This couldn't have worked out better. Bernie struggles to hide her smiles. 'You go, Avril, we're fine without you, really, please don't worry about us, I just can't imagine the kind of hell you must be going through.'

'Kirsty says you're going this weekend . . .'

'Yes, Dom and me.' Bernie shivers in Avril's presence as if she carries some hidden infection. If only she would shut up and go. Bernie ought to feel guilty as hell for being unkind and short with Avril, impatient with Avril and thoughtless with Avril, whose eyes are so deeply shadowed, whose cheeks seem thinner and older, and all because she suddenly can't bear to have her near, may God forgive her.

'But as soon as—'

'I know.' Now Avril sniffs unpleasantly in an effort to pull herself together. 'As soon as the book gets published we can all be together again, be friends again, and by then the worst of this will be over.'

At the sight of Avril's tears, at the sight of Avril, defeated, bewildered and emptied, Bernie has to tighten her lips to stop herself from shouting at her, even from slapping her silly fat face. What is this sudden repulsion she feels towards a loyal friend? Instead she says, trying to be gentle, 'It's not your fault, Avril, this has nothing to do with you.'

'It's just odd, you know, coming from the same womb, being his sister, sharing a childhood, you know, someone who can take a life . . .'

'I know, Avril, I know,' says Bernie, tensing, coming to put her arms around her, and then it slowly dawns on Bernie that Kirsty had a good point – without Avril on hand, Avril, who has taken exams and who can write proper English, how in God's name is she going to deal with the incomprehensible changes and corrections Clementine Davaine was talking about?

The flat is in Arundle Mews.

Bernie's leave-taking of the Burleston required the empty kisses and promises that mean nothing at all. You would think Mr Derek was some close relative, you would think Mrs Stokes was a favourite granny, you would think the snooty residents were all part of some much-loved extended family the way they lined up to see their famous author off.

'Yes, I will send you a signed copy.'

'Yes, of course I'll keep in touch.'

'No, fame will never change me.'

And Dominic held her hand and opened the car door for her – the perfect escort – and her departure was a very different occasion to her arrival those few months ago, when all she had was her rucksack and her floppy embroidered bag with a few bits and pieces in it. Then she went to the back door and dined on stale bread and cheese. Now she has just breakfasted on grapefruit segments, porridge and a delicious kedgeree.

She waved from the car like the Queen Mother, but of Kirsty or Avril there was no sign.

Candice had left an hour ago, driving back in her Saab and calling on friends for lunch. Dominic and Bernie were to be chauffeured to the airport and a car was already organized to meet them at Heathrow and take them to the flat.

Life was suddenly oh so easy.

She looked forward to London. Bernie came to London once when Mammy and Daddy won tickets to the Palladium at Christmas time. She saw the pantomime *Cinderella* with people from the telly in it and almost cried with all the excitement and glamour. It was then Bernie decided she wanted to be an actress, too; she panted to be one, she trembled to be one, but they went home the next day to their terraced house next to the cleaners having spent the night in a Trust House Hotel, and she ran straight up to her bedroom, locked the door, closed the curtains over the grimy glass and cried for over an hour.

'Dom, tell me this is real.'

She walks through the door with quiet dignity, erect, head up and one hand holding Dominic's.

This is what she has always dreamed of. This is the sort of house she will buy once she gets her hands on some money and she and Dom are married.

The Mews flat is opulent and quiet. Thick Chinese rugs and jade lamps. Immense chairs with footstools. Elegant arrangements of flowers and impressive pictures dominated by a white grand piano. Good taste reigns supreme because nobody has to live in it for long. James Tate, Candice's uncle, spends most of his life on the road. The peering, short-sighted woman who opens the door and introduces herself as Joyce Parfait, informs them dinner will be at eight thirty – turbot à la creme with mushrooms, the kind of food Bernie detests – and that she lives in the garage conversion.

'Just press the bell if you need me.'

'What are we going to do all day, Dom?'

'Well, you'll be needing to work, presumably. And I won't be bored in London.'

Work? Is Bernie expected to work? Here she is in London with very little money, just the odd hand-out from Candice or Dominic and only the promise of big things to come. She can hardly have a ball, she knows that, but is she really doomed to shut herself away from now until Christmas in some make-believe office with a computer she can't work and with notes she can't understand? And while

Bernie is closeted away like this, what the hell will Dom be doing?

Living the life of Riley?

Cheating on her again?

'There's people I know in London,' he says, seemingly surprised that she should ask. 'Friends. Family friends. School friends. There are a few contacts I would like to make. I'll join a sports club, play some squash, visit old haunts . . .'

'But you never lived in London.'

'No, but that doesn't mean to say I'm a total stranger in the city.'

'Oh?'

'Don't sound so pissed off! You won't want me hanging around once you get down to it again. Don't worry, I promised Candice faithfully that I wouldn't distract you. We're all dependent on you now, Bernie.'

Damn, damn, damn.

'Down to it' means sneaking to the post box with Clementine's notes and odd pages of manuscript and telling Clementine she's working on it. 'Down to it' means ringing Kirsty in a panic – but, Jaysus, Kirsty's not on the phone! Why hadn't they thought of that? Perhaps they can arrange a mobile? She must ask Candice next time she sees her. God, God, it would have been so much simpler if Avril had been able to come. At least she could have shared the secret, they could have worked out the problems together and Avril could have made the simpler amendments to the script herself.

But Avril is contaminated and has become . . . repellent.

And Kirsty has turned against Bernie.

Bernie feels suddenly and worryingly alone, wrapped in helpless consternation and nothing but trip-wires strewn in her path.

Damn Graham Stott. Because this is his fault. If that double murderer hadn't turned up at the Burleston, Avril's presence wouldn't have posed such a threat to Bernie's naughty-but-nice little girl image, and maybe her intense dislike wouldn't have reached such giddy proportions.

Damn him to hell.

Nineteen

She must be losing her mind – like Bernie, too close
to *Magdalene*, too haunted by those dire revelations, battered by the experience. Twice, now,
Kirsty has mistakenly imagined she has seen Trevor
– the first time she thought he was skulking down by
the raspberry canes. She trembled while her heart
stopped beating; she came near to wetting herself;
she cried with relief when she saw it was just old
Flagherty and the reason she made that mistake was
because he was moving so slyly.

'Rabbit, the varmint, I sees 'e,' said he, brandish-
ing his spade as a weapon while he crept on between
the berries.

On the second occasion Kirsty was helping un-
load the laundry van. She was laden with cold crispy
sheets, lost in the glaring whiteness of them, pile
after pile, almost to the point of snow-blindness. At
once a dark image appeared, a shadow on her iris?
She dropped the load and stood, dumb with terror,
as a hare might, caught against the brilliance.
Painfully, as her eyes adjusted, she could make
out a cardboard cut-out man, a target for police
marksmen, bobbing behind the privet.

Her legs gave way. They would no longer hold her. The heat from the sun burned from inside her.

For this is how Trevor had sometimes appeared when he snuck up to the house after work, hoping to catch her curled up with a book.

'Maid,' it was Flagherty's voice again, pulling her out of her dream state as he passed the van with a full wheelbarrow and gave her a soily hand to grasp. 'Look, yous dropped the lot. Push 'em down underneath so Mrs Stokes doan' see 'e.'

And when Kirsty's terrified eyes went back to search the hedge there was nobody there.

Now Trevor Hoskins hasn't got where he is today by being dumb. Trevor is a man who likes to keep his nose to the ground, so when he reached the end of his journey, when he signalled right into the drive of the Burleston Hotel, and when he saw a line of policemen beating the overgrown hedges with sticks, he quickly righted his indicator and drove straight on.

OK, so something's up. Damn. He must be more circumspect; if the fuzz are alerted by a hysterical Kirsty – because she's bound to lose her head when he first shows his face – he will be wrong-footed, and most likely booted out of the place before he has time to convince anyone.

The next place Trevor came to along the winding coast road was a caravan park called Happy Stay and so he pulled in. He parked his hire car and went into the shop, where a pallid girl in a sundress was serving. Hell, all summer in Cornwall and no tan whatsoever. Whenever Trev gets the chance he rips off his top, and as a result his hands and arms are always tanned and healthy looking. As per usual, people are taking these bloody health warnings too far. Food, fireworks, drugs – when the kids were babies Kirsty refused to put them on their stomachs, and that's why they bawled their bloody heads off all the time, that's what Trev's mother used to say.

'They say there's been a murder there!' the girl replied breathlessly to Trevor's first question. 'They say it's the golf pro, hit on the head with a golf club yesterday morning and they still haven't found the weapon, or the killer. Mostly, down here, all we get is drownings or suicides off the Pengellis Rock.' Her limp ponytail whisked in excitement and moved an assortment of black flies from off the greasy counter.

'Is it OK to leave my car here and look round for a while before I book in? I guess you've got some spaces. I'll only want something small.'

'Yeah,' said the girl, tonguing her gum, 'that's OK, so long as you're back by six, we close dead on six.' Click, click, click, she went, her tongue sticking through stretched pink peppermint. She's probably in-bred. Trev believes that anyone brought up in the country is in-bred and thus a potential monster. Look at Fred West.

Trevor, casual in jeans, a T-shirt and trainers, padded his way along soulless roads of concrete, like an abandoned airfield with mobile homes and brambles crammed upon it, and soon found the cliff path where a few families were blackberrying. Oh yeah. Great holiday, thought Trev.

But Trev wouldn't know what a great holiday was. He and Kirsty and the kids only went once, to

252

Weston. They met this other couple in the caravan next door. Christ, she was a randy cow, and the bloke, what was his name? Gavin? Yeah, that was it, Gavin and Elaine. They had no kids, and they grew quite chatty when they sat drinking beer outside the van when it was warm in the evenings and the kids were in bed. He and Gavin sometimes left the wives and popped down to the pub. Kirsty moaned on as usual, trying to spoil everything. She didn't like Elaine because Elaine was cheap. God. Gavin must have been pretty pissed when he suggested that card game – he and Elaine got up to it all the time back in Harlow where they lived. What a laugh, said Gavin, telling Trev all about it.

'D'you think your Kirsty'd be up for it?'

'Strip poker?'

'Yeah.'

'Why not?' It was about bloody time Kirsty let her hair down and let him have some fun once in a while.

They went to Gavin's caravan and even then Kirsty complained about leaving the kids alone. 'There's fires in caravans . . .'

'Shut up! We're only next door for fuck's sake.'

They had a good laugh, drank like fishes, and then Gavin fetched the cards. Scruffy, they were, and gone all soft like cards do when they're played with a lot. There was lots of giggling from the girls and that wild Elaine was throwing her hair back and showing her boobs in that low dress. When it was Kirsty's turn she was happy to take off her cardigan, then her sandals. By then Elaine was in her underwear and still going strong. Trev couldn't keep his eyes off her; he could smell her wet excitement, what with the heat and the booze and the sex that fizzed in the air along with the paraffin fumes.

Kirsty gave him a wounded look, the kind of smile that's on the *Mona Lisa*, the kind of smile you want to wipe off because there's something so bloody smug about it. 'No, I don't want to go any further, Trev.'

'Come on now, honey,' he wheedled and Gavin clicked his tongue and winked.

'I think we should go back now.'

'Dammit,' Trev hadn't meant it to sound that savage, 'Christ, you bitch. Get your fucking skirt off before I come over there and rip it off you. D'you think you're so sodding special or something? Different from Elaine here? All coy is it, you cow! You're bleeding well not going to show me up and go all righteous on me. You'll do what I want or God help you later.'

So they played the game of poker. And the next night. And the next. But Kirsty fucked it up with her miserable face and her sighs and her lack of spontaneity. She wouldn't know a good time if it hit her in the face. And the morning after that she sneaked home with the kids on the train.

Trev breathed in deeply. So near yet so far. Aha – the stillness of sea and sky. The wash of the spray on the rocks below, and the gulls and the caves and the flaming bracken. Trev passed strange chimney stacks perched on the cliffs, broken-down ruins overgrown with ivy, and old tracks he could only just make out in the earth. Something to do with old mine workings, he thought, walking on, getting nearer now, sensing his quarry.

254

He had to catch her alone, that was the most important thing. He knew Kirsty was living in at the hotel, so all Trev had to do was discover the number of her room and wait there quietly until she came. Never again would Kirsty cross him. Never again would that batty cow snatch his kids and do a bloody runner making him look like a right tit.

Kirsty convinced herself she hadn't seen Trev, there was no way he could find her. But after those two false alarms Kirsty's nerves stayed raw all day. She knew there was something wrong and it wasn't just Ed's murder or Avril's devastation over her brother's unspeakable crime. No, this was something that gnawed at her subconscious like a childhood smell she couldn't identify, or the line of a song she had once heard but couldn't quite recall. She couldn't concentrate on her work, and it wasn't to do with Bernie's departure, although there were many disturbing aspects to that – at least she has control of that situation. A phone call to the spineless Dominic, a few threats to expose him for the sham he was had worked the first time and there's no reason to suspect her influence over him will diminish. She has him by the short and curlies.

Before reading that haunting book blackmail would never have crossed Kirsty's mind. She would never have found the nerve to corner the cad in that bland café. And it seemed to have given her visionary powers; how else would she have guessed how Bernie's easy nature would change, how she would become unbalanced by fame, revelling in her new-found role, how she would flaunt herself and her moment as if she was owed it.

And now Bernie foolishly believes that Dominic has changed.

Kirsty views her with contempt. How blind and ignorant she is to be so easily deceived.

Yes, Dominic is serving his purpose and Kirsty has Magdalene to thank for that.

But no, it was none of these things that caused Kirsty's unease that day. Maybe it was because of the children's imminent arrival, and the fear that something would go wrong to spoil it. So far she had coped so well, with the job, finding a home, pulling a fast one over the eyes of so many experts with her rewrite of *Magdalene*. Is she getting too confident? She is way out of her league and it's sod's law something will happen to bring her down to earth with a crash.

She saw him.

This time she was certain.

So. She was lost. It was all over. He had run her to earth like a terrified rabbit.

She was sure that she smelled him first.

So, her reality was distorted, she had been living on dreams again. And a hopeless sorrow filled her eyes.

She saw him sitting on one of the benches overlooking the tennis courts.

How? How could he have found me?

She saw him from the back, but she knew, oh yes, she knew it was Trevor.

Oh, God help me. God, tell me what to do.

But the next time she looked with her darting eyes he was gone.

'Yes,' says Kirsty to the copper, looking out the key to the cottage that was to have been her winter home. 'Yes, of course I'll let you in.'

She leads the way across the drive and through the trees to the ugly breeze-block bungalow, still shaking from her last sighting of Trevor and trying with a numb desperation to convince herself she had been mistaken.

'It's just here,' she tells the two searching policemen. 'It's a bit of a mess.'

Kirsty, still in her working uniform of white dress and black apron, inserts the key and follows them inside. The first man sniffs, 'Ugh! Smells like something's dead in here.'

Kirsty shivers. 'I think that's the damp.'

'And you say two students were in here?'

'They left a couple of weeks ago. I was supposed to move in, but as you can see . . .' She has no need to explain any further.

The students had not felt it necessary to clean up before they left. Empty tins lie scattered about. A bulging black bag, disgorging half its disgusting contents, straddles the floor like a vomiting drunk, and the fireplace is full of cigarette butts and old boxes of matches.

Upstairs is no better. The filthy mattresses have been stripped and every stain and mark is evident, the foam pillows are curled and yellowed. Fags have been stubbed out on the small mantelpieces, and coffee-cup rings vie with each other for space.

'Animals,' says the second copper, searching behind curtains streaked with rust. 'There's nothing here, or nowhere for a golf club—'

'Ugh! Cat shit!' groans the first one, picking up his heel. 'God, the local strays have found their way in.' And he picks up a piece of newspaper and wipes the offending mess off his boot.

'And they had the nerve to offer you this?'

'I don't think anyone knew the sort of state it was in,' says Kirsty, forcing herself to concentrate on something that seems so irrelevant if the figure she saw on that seat was real.

Downstairs and back in the kitchen she remembers to say, 'Keep away from that bit of floor, there, next to the fridge where the lino is cracked. One of the guys who lived here told me that bit was sinking.'

'There's bits of this place that are probably alive and heaving,' says the larger policeman, making eagerly for the door. 'God knows what's in the walls, multiplying. My God, the stench.'

'Thanks, anyway, Mrs Hoskins, we'll let you get back to your work.'

'What do you want me to do with the key? Will you want to come in here again?'

'No, best lock it up. There's nothing in there to interest us. Lock it up so kids don't get in, I doubt very much if it's safe. I mean, even the roof looks dodgy to me.'

But Kirsty, in shock, cannot go back to work. Indifferent to her surroundings, hardly thinking, only staring, she needs some time on her own to cope with this new intolerable horror. Could it be Trev? No, not possible. Is she really so close to losing her mind? Best if she stays here where no-one can see her or Mrs Stokes will start nagging on. Now, quite beyond tears, the muscles of her face taut, as if clamped by a hot rubber mask, her head aches so thuddingly it could be made of solid wood.

She has no idea how much time goes by until she dares to lift her face and sees him thick and huge in the doorway. She tries to cry out loud but fails, she can only moan as if in a nightmare.

'Hello, Kirsty.'

She continues to stare at him for a while, as if he is her own manifestation. 'You were watching. You saw me come in here.'

'Yep, I saw you helping the nice policemen.' He is shaking his head, slightly smiling, with pure malice in his eyes.

And she watches him, terrified. As much at his mercy as ever.

'I was curious to see where you were – naturally, as your husband. So what's this? I see you have the keys to this place.' Trev puts his car keys on the cooker to show that he intends to stay for as long as this is going to take. 'Was this the home you planned to move into with my children?'

'It's no good,' replies Kirsty quietly, 'as you can see.'

'I would have thought it would suit you perfectly, slut as you are,' and he takes two steps towards her and raises his right hand.

How can she get out of here? Cold sweat breaks out on her forehead and over her face and neck. Her eyes close and she sways forward. Trev catches her expertly only to shove her upright again. 'Stand up, you fucking bitch! This time there'll be no performances from you. This time you're coming out of here with me and we're going to find a nice doctor and tell him how sick you really are, how cracked in the head. Too ill to be in charge of my two kids.'

'But there's nothing wrong with me, Trev.' Kirsty's voice is pitiful and pleading.

'There's either something wrong with you or I am a cruel, battering husband.' He raises his eyebrows and lets his voice scrape along her bones. 'That's what you told the bastards, isn't it? That's what you went blabbing on about, and now, by God, you're going to convince them that you don't know what the hell you are saying, that you're so far gone in the fucking head that everything you told them's a lie!'

She watches him. With every word he speaks Kirsty finds it harder to breathe. So that is what he's planning to do, he has threatened this in the past – if he caught her reading one more book, if he caught her spending one more penny, if he saw one crumb on the draining board, if she forgot to spread his fucking mustard – he would get her locked up for the rest of her life so she'd never come out again.

And in his own psychotic way, Kirsty knows that Trev believes it. He really does consider her insane – so great and outrageous is his own self-denial.

And now, slowly, steadily and implacably, Trev is advancing towards her. She will take such a beating she'll be willing to say anything, do anything, by the time he has broken her body and crippled her esteem. This time he will grind her down, he will annihilate her completely with his insane, brutal rage, while her two small helpless children . . . and she screams in frantic fear and despair.

No standards.

No values.

No morality.

Just a tyrannous lust.

She backs her way round the kitchen, moving from sink to cooker to fridge, and all the while Trev holds her eyes like a tormenting cat with a terrified bird. Her fear turns into a heedless stampede and she's out of control running.

She sees him stagger, grip the fridge and call out some curse that rings in her ears. She hears a deep, cracking sound as the fridge tilts, as though there's an earthquake, and leaves a hole where it once was, a hole filled with Trev's frantic activity until, with his black eyes blazing with mockery, he disappears like a ghoul in a dream with a great crashing sound and a rushing landscape of dust and rubble.

Kirsty stands there gagging in air that is thick with chaos, afraid to trust to the new sound of silence. Mesmerized by what seems to have happened, she is incapable of movement. The waiting is the worst part. The waiting for Trev's head to reappear above the floor, leering, as he sometimes used to, over what he called his little jokes. The worst was the nail through the bandaged finger. She wants to drop to her knees, but daren't, although there are no bones left in her legs.

Then comes the horror of horrors, while she stands there rigid, transfixed, her face takes on a helpless, childlike stare. Trev's disembodied voice comes from deep down in the ground. Her mind gives a jerk – *a well* – had somebody told her of a well in the corner of this terrible kitchen, of a deep hole that led to nowhere, so damp that the whole house reeked?

A well? Her common sense comes to bear, but grindingly slowly, through the haze of her disembodied state. Not a well, surely, but a mine shaft. The coast line is littered with old mining works from the days when the tinners worked this land, mine workings centuries old, which extend way beneath

261

the seabed itself. They went fathoms deep in their desperation, those wild Cornishmen they had told her about, and she'd only half listened while she worked.

There is a restless, rushing excitement as feeling comes back into Kirsty's limbs. Here comes that sound again – a hollow, echoing sound from somewhere deep in that broken corner. A strong man, and fit for his age, is Trev gathering all his strength to climb out while she stands here waiting? And is she prepared to let this happen?

How far has her husband fallen?

She has to know this, she has to know.

With a primal ruthlessness that comes naturally now, Kirsty creeps, inch by awful inch, very aware that the floor where she's standing might be unstable, might give way at any moment and pitch her into some black hell. She reaches the part where the lino first cracked and kneels down slowly and listens, tears streaming down her cheeks and little sobs breaking from her spasmodically.

After a while, when the mourning is over, Kirsty Hopkins rocks back on her heels and starts to laugh uproariously.

Because the hilarious, the insane, the extraordinarily funny thing is that Trevor is still alive.

Twenty

'Stone walls do not a prison make,
Nor iron bars a cage;'
  But they make a bloody good job of trying.

After a brief, inglorious court appearance when
Graham Timothy Stott, dulled, defeated and
blunted, was put on oath to give his name and
plead not guilty, he was remanded in custody for
the murder of one Annie Brenner, aged seventy-nine
– why must they keep repeating her age, surely
killing someone who's old is kinder than killing a
kid? – and the questioning sessions continued by
detectives working on the Ed Board case.

There were hisses and boos when he came out of
court and he'd ducked his head to hide his face when
he climbed into the van. It had all been so indifferent
and formal he'd almost welcomed this sign of human-
ity, the first in the sterile proceedings. And then, ah
yes, there it was again as the gates closed behind them,
the familiar smell of disinfectant and piss, and a
draughtiness blew at him from the ruthlessly clean
walls and the shining metal of the landing rails.

*   *   *

263

'They haven't got a thing on me,' Graham swore to his brief.

Graham might be a Trevor-in-waiting but for his slighter build, his nasal voice and his vastly superior cunning. And Graham has no pride, unlike Trevor. Part of the jobless generation, he grew up pampered and overprotected while Trevor's dad made free with his belt and drove his mother to a glinty-eyed Christ.

'Well,' said his brief, an experienced man with a jaunty, confident manner, who knew damn well Graham was guilty, 'they do have a good deal of circumstantial evidence. Your cigarette ends for a start, they were found in an empty milk bottle on the basement steps adjacent to the crime, traces of material from your jacket lining were found caught in the rusty railings and, most telling of all, your fingerprints are all over Annie's bag.' The man sat back with his hands on his briefcase, case proven.

'OK,' wailed Graham, 'so I was in that basement; I had to sleep somewhere, didn't I? I'd been kicked out of home, no dosh, cold, hungry, and I've already told you I saw Annie being attacked; it was me who picked up her bag afterwards and went to give it back to her.'

'And, like any innocent bystander caught up in a violent crime, you hot-footed it to Cornwall and swore you'd already been here a month, living with your sister and doing odd jobs for the hotel?'

'I knew they'd try to pin it on me.' Graham started blabbing. 'What would you have done for Christ's sake? Just hung around till they picked you up? A piece of scum they can do what they like with. Yeah,' he gulped and his overlarge Adam's apple

264

did a leap from the base of his throat to his chin. 'Self-preservation, that's what it's about. Look after number one. No-one ever looked after me.'

But his mother used to look after him.

Graham's brief closed his weary eyes. 'Graham, please listen to me. If you come clean and plead guilty to manslaughter – we know you didn't mean to kill Mrs Brenner – then the murder charge will be dropped.'

'I never touched her,' moaned Graham, lighting a fag for comfort, and well he might – he wasn't going to get it elsewhere. None of his family had been in the court, nobody was around to speak up for him. 'Everyone has conspired against me. Even you, who's meant to be on my side.' And this time they would put him away for most of his youthful life. When he came out of gaol he would be an old man, thirty or forty most probably, and he thought of the things receding from him for ever – pubs, sex, clubs, cinemas, holidays abroad, marriage, kids – Jesus, Jesus. And here was this prick who was supposed to be defending him, who'd scarper off out of here in a minute, no doubt off to dinner or the theatre or to some sodding old boys' reunion.

Bloody hell, it was all so unfair.

He never had the right start in life.

And now look what's happening. He should be back in Liverpool by now, but the pigs are trying to pin this one on him, as if he's ever heard of Ed Board, let alone bumped him off.

Kirsty was in trouble yesterday – an unusual situation for Mrs Stokes to be tearing a strip off Kirsty because Kirsty is normally so reliable.

'I just needed to go off on my own,' Kirsty told Avril, and it looked as if she had been crying; she seemed so pale, so shaky. 'It's the thought of the kids coming down and all the responsibility of that . . . but here's me going on selfishly while you're in such a state.'

Avril's voice quivered. 'And there's been no sign of Fluffy.'

'I really meant Graham and your mother.'

'Oh yes, yes, I know. And the press have found their caravan.'

'Oh no. Why don't they go back home? What's the point of stopping down here?'

'Guilt. That's what it is. They feel they ought to stay here until this thing with Graham is finished. Punishing themselves, that's what it's about. Mother keeps saying, "But I'm still his mother, Richard, no matter what he's done." But she hates him, Kirsty! She hasn't got a good word for him. And, oh God, I wish they would go home. I wish I was still living in at the Burleston and not stuck here ten doors away from them. Kirsty, the hassle, I can't bear it.'

Preparing the caravan for Kirsty's children doesn't provide one hundredth of the kind of diversion Avril needs to relieve this hell. The mobile home is a spartan place, it would need re-designing to make it a home, but with colourful rugs and mats and lamps bought from a local car-boot sale the atmosphere can be slightly softened. But every moment Avril spends cleaning the place, stocking the larder and filling in the window gaps, is a selfish moment away from her mother, who needs her at a time like this.

*   *   *

266

'So you've decided not to visit him?' Avril's voice is accusing.

Mrs Stott pales visibly. 'In that place, Avril? You must be mad.'

'But he must be out of his mind right now.'

'He might well be out of his mind. But how about me? What do you think all this is doing to me, Avril? Your father took me to the local surgery this morning, but I didn't think much of the doctor, not a patch on dear Dr Hunt who knows me, but even so, he gave me some stronger tablets, seeing the situation I'm in.'

'But there's not much point in you staying down here if you're not going to visit Graham, is there?'

Mrs Stott views her daughter searchingly. 'What is the point of you staying down here, that is the question I would like to have answered? Never mind me. You've given up a perfectly good job without the usual notice, so that means references are out of the question. You've moved into that terrible caravan and intend to live there with that woman and her children. On what, Avril? I ask you, how do you intend to live?' Mother lets her eyelids flutter to signify instability. 'The dole, I suppose, if that char woman is anything to go by.'

'You're wrong, actually. Kirsty is still working.'

'You will live a hand-to-mouth existence in the wilds of Cornwall on the dole while putting your faith in a silly venture that everyone knows is a five-day wonder.'

'Mother, why don't you listen to me? This is not a five-day wonder! They say the UK publisher has offered a record advance and in the States they have just agreed to a sum that's more than they pay

Stephen King. Mother, they are signing these contracts at the moment.'

'*Who is signing?* Avril, talk sense. This is the kind
of nonsense you read about, but you know none of
it is true, it's merely a lot of trumped-up nonsense.
What has come over you to be taken in by all this,
when I brought you up so down-to-earth?'

'There is really no point in discussing this any
further.'

'Avril.' Mother swirls the teapot over her little
caravan sink and pours the dregs into a piece of
newspaper. No newfangled teabags for Mother. 'If
you are coming into this sort of fortune, what are
you doing slumming it down here with hardly a
penny to your name and hardly able to buy your
groceries? Now, madam, answer me that.'

'I need to be here at the moment, Mother, so that
Kirsty and I can liaise when the time comes for us to
play our parts in this venture. I have told you
before, this is a three-way thing.'

'Liaise? Oh yes? So you let that little minx Bernadette scamper off to London with her playboy
boyfriend.'

This is outrageous. 'You don't know her! You've
never even seen her!'

'I have seen her picture,' says Mother firmly,
scouring the bases of the taps with a toothbrush.
'And I don't need to know her to realize what game
that one is playing,' she says archly. 'The only thing
that infuriates me is that you refuse to come home.
And at a time like this, when families should be
sticking together.'

Mother, of course, is very aware of the stigma
attached to her and her caravan now that her son is

in the news for such a grotesque offence. Passers-by pretend not to look, but they cast their eyes across just the same, and Mother huffs and puffs and wishes she could beckon them over and assure them that she is every bit as disgusted, and just as uninvolved as they are.

But Mrs Stott is not given this chance. Nobody wants to know her. All they do is gossip about her. Even when she goes to the shop the limp girl at the counter drops her eyes, and Mother has been forced to stop complaining on account of her new inferior status.

Avril knows very well why Mother has chosen to stay in Cornwall. Terrible though this notoriety is, it would be much worse back at 2 Maple Terrace, Huyton, the patch where the dire deed was committed. The shame, oh the shame. Mother is in hiding. She has gone to ground. They could well get offensive material shoved through their letter-box, bricks through their windows and obscene phone calls, so vigorous will be the fury of the local population who have taken seventy-nine-year-old Annie Brenner to their infamously warm Merseyside hearts. At least here at the Happy Stay nobody knows Mother; her fellow campers are ships in the night and, after one haughty look from her, they drop their excited eyes and sail on.

'Stick and stones may break my bones but words will never hurt me,' says Mother.

And as Kirsty reminds Avril constantly in their close and intimate conversations, Graham has ruined her life, Graham is the cause of her low self-esteem and the reason for her comfort eating, the reason for ending up doing business studies.

'You wouldn't be fat if it wasn't for him and I don't know why you should feel slightly concerned.'

But Avril cannot abandon Graham, and not for any noble reasons. She is pulled mawkishly towards him, to her he has the ghoulish fascination of a fatal accident. Her victim is down and blooded. A perfect time for attack. The torturer is helpless – that person who gave her such grief in her childhood, who moulded her weakness and insecurities as simply as if she were Plasticine, Plasticine gone old and brown, still warm from a vicious little hand. That brute is now at her mercy, safe behind stone walls and iron bars. She is compelled by some overwhelming urge inside her to go and visit him, to triumph at last, to mock, to enjoy.

'That slob deserves all he gets, and the rest,' says Kirsty.

Damn Graham. *Damn him.*

Sitting in the bus on the way to the prison Avril casts her mind back, finding it hard to remember exactly what he looks like, she hasn't seen him for so many years. Her clearest memories are of the time when she was around ten years old and Graham was fifteen and well off the rails.

He was hiding under her bed one night when she went up to get undressed. She was naked before she heard him snorting in that particular way he had – with a sneer in the snort, and a mockery. She leapt back in embarrassed dismay, scrambling to find a nightie or anything with which to cover herself.

'You fat sow,' said Graham, wriggling out, as large as a man, not a schoolboy who might be

270

playing such classroom pranks. 'Come on, jumbo, let's have a look.'

'*Get out, Graham,*' Avril screamed, but he came at her and wrestled her nightdress from her hands and held her arms behind her back, all the time sneering and jeering at her new breasts, which were early, nobody else in the class had breasts or that suggestion of hair down there which Avril was trying her best to deny. Ugly, horrible, wiggles of hair which she dreaded the others might see when they were changing for swimming; they made enough fun of her as it was.

'*Get out, Graham,*' she screamed at the top of her voice, then pushed him with all her strength so that he fell back on the bed. She fled from the room out onto the landing and dashed into Graham's bedroom because that was the only door that was open.

'Mother! *Mother!*' shouted Graham, hanging down over the banisters while Avril, an Everton towel round her waist, tried to barricade his bedroom door. 'Get this tramp out of my room! This is the third time she's forced her way in there and I'm fed up with trying to tell her—'

'What on earth's going on now, Graham? Why can't you two manage to get on together for one second? We're in the middle of *Eastenders.*'

'I don't like to touch her, Mother, not when she's in this mood. I'm not going to lay myself wide open to her spiteful lies.'

'Mum, Mum,' cried Avril, cowering behind Graham's door.

'Oh for goodness' sake . . .' and then the sound of Mother's nimble tread as she came, annoyed, up the stairs.

'The last time she did this Nick was here.'

'Did what, Graham?' said Mother.

'Pushed her way in stark naked. I didn't know what to say. Tell her, Mother, for God's sake. She must be a bloody nympho.'

'Avril, Avril, what on earth is the meaning of this?'

Avril squeezed herself round the door, sobbing violently now that she was safe. But Mother grabbed her arm and held it in a vicelike grip. 'Avril, what are you doing in your brother's bedroom?'

Avril gulped, 'I ran in, I had to get away—'

'But why not the bathroom, Avril?'

Avril stared, wet-eyed, along the passage. The bathroom had seemed an impossible distance when she was running so blindly, while Graham's door was wide open.

Mother asked in horrified tones, 'Is what Graham's saying true?'

And on Mother's face was the same disgust and revulsion as Graham had shown at the sight of Avril's naked body.

'Graham was hiding under my bed,' Avril said tonelessly.

'Graham is fifteen years old, Avril, and not likely to be messing about playing such infantile games.'

'But he was . . .'

'That's right, Mother, believe Avril, you always do.' Graham shrugged nonchalantly.

'But why, Avril? *Why?*' Mother's voice was cold and unreasonable. 'And Graham says this isn't the first time! Why do you need to flaunt your body, and you a budding woman?'

Avril nearly puked with disgust she so hated that phrase. Budding – that's exactly what her horrid new breasts were doing, and woman, that is what she was turning into. A smelly, bloody, bulging vessel into which men would push their penises and through which babies would come with awful agony because of Eve.

A boiling sense of injustice gave Avril the courage to shout fiercely, 'You're filthy, both of you, with your filthy, filthy minds and your filthy, filthy words.'

Mother's slap left a hand print on the top of Avril's leg that lasted for four days.

And that was just one example of the way Graham used to get her in trouble. There were many, many more.

Kirsty is right. He does deserve all he gets, and the rest.

Avril's bus arrives at the prison and she gets out surreptitiously, not wanting to be identified as a visitor with somebody close inside.

As she queues with the other beleaguered-looking passengers, as they tick her name off the list, Avril still isn't sure what she's doing here, what she hopes to achieve by this visit. All she can feel is a hot joy inside her, mixed with a sickly fear. The more uncongenial the prison surroundings, the happier Avril feels in this violent schizophrenic place. Vengeance is almost hers. She revels in this novel release of malevolent spite. If she had felt outrage before she had never acknowledged those feelings till now, not even to herself.

And yet, another, softer part of her needs to see Graham once more – the real Graham, not the memory – so she can put him behind her for good. He had cast such a dark cloud on her childhood, hanging over everything: birthday parties, family outings, the most innocent childish games in the garden. He had caused much of the mental distress that had turned Mother melancholy, although whose fault it was to start with was impossible to tell.

He looks like all the others in his faded blue jeans and T-shirt.

'It's good to see you, Graham,' she says.

'Good to see me inside, you mean.' His voice is as ugly as his eyes.

Avril sits down awkwardly, casting her eyes round the room at her fellow visitors looking uncomfortable at their own square, metal tables. Well, she didn't expect a loving reunion but . . .

'You bleeding cow,' growls Graham, one elbow on the table and his fist clenched tight, as if he's about to take part in an arm-wrestling contest. 'All you needed to fucking well do was tell the bleeders I was with you.'

She struggles to conquer her weakness, to say something quickly, to fend off this familiar shock of unexpected, hostile attack. 'I was so surprised I couldn't think. I mean, I didn't even know you were down here.'

'You retard. You've done it for me now. You, Avril, just you. If it wasn't for you I could have got off.' And he flicks open a packet of cigarettes and leaves one hanging at a petulant angle between his sneering lips. Avril remembers him smoking like this when he was in junior school, trying to be big.

She can't help her next question. 'You did it, didn't you, Graham? You killed that old woman.'

'Don't talk shit,' he answers savagely.

'You probably killed Ed Board as well. They're saying you might have done it.' Avril rambles on, aware that she's always done this when face to face with her brother, so afraid that a pause might be the signal for further abuse. 'I was quite friendly with Ed Board; he was teaching me to play golf—'

'What did you come here for, Avril? To gloat? You can go back home like a good girl now and tell Mummy that her darling son has fucked up good and proper this time.'

'I don't think Mother cares any more,' says Avril casually, 'and, by the way, Fluffy has been missing for a whole week now and we're beginning to think she might be dead.'

Graham laughs. A laugh she well remembers. A cruel, mocking laugh. He once put a kitten's eye out with a sparkler. She is pleased to see he's sweating, and his eyes are a little wary, perhaps he is as sorry as she.

'It's funny.' Avril chats on again as if she is at some garden fête or one of Mother's coffee mornings. There are screws in the room and Graham can't hurt her, no, he can't touch her any more. 'You're just the same as I remember, but it's not a disguise, is it? Hiding some frightened child? I'd begun to think it was something like that because people aren't born evil. Oh yes,' Avril laughs gaily while Graham sits opposite in surly silence. There is something disturbing about the sound of her own shrill laughter, but she hasn't the time to ponder on this. 'Silly. I used to make excuses. I used to think it

275

was my fault.' Her expression suddenly changes and she stares at her brother with cold dislike. 'But you were born evil, weren't you, Graham? You were never badly wounded, deprived, lonely or neglected, you are the one they call sinner in church, and I never knew who they meant until now. I always suspected it might be me.'

'You are so full of crap,' says Graham. 'Why don't you sod off, dumping me in the shit then coming here pushing your sick ideas.'

'I think I might just do that,' says Avril, picking up her neat black handbag. 'Is there any message you'd like me to give to Mother or Father?'

'Drop dead, cunt,' says Graham.

'Is there anything you need?'

'Just piss off,' says Graham, lighting his cigarette at last, with a lighter in the shape of a naked woman, the flame spouting out of her fanny.

Avril nods to the screws as she goes, amazed at the lightness of spirit she feels. Strong. Exuberant. Even her step has a swing to it, the swing of a thinner person, and her eyes are bright and seductive. She half expected she might feel depressed, visiting her brother in such a place, seeing him vulnerable and alone. Not so. Hah!

It is half-past four, so she still has time before catching the last bus to the Happy Stay, which only operates during the season. She steps inside the first cop shop she passes and smiles at the sergeant on the desk. 'I would like to make a statement,' she says. 'I know it's something I ought to have done the moment I first suspected, but there's family to consider, and then I wasn't a hundred per cent certain . . .'

'If you'll wait in here, Miss, I will fetch somebody who knows about the case.'

So Avril sits in the stark little room rehearsing her story. It is essential she gets this right. Magdalene was a professional; she never messed up or went off half cock. Revenge was what Magdalene excelled at, and it's high time Avril Stott took her revenge on the devil who killed the little child within her.

Twenty-One

This lid is bound to blow.

The rusty screws are just too tight to hold this build-up of steam. And this is what Bernadette's head feels like as the pace hots up, as contracts fly across the world and the tabloids continue to photograph her and treat her as their own little darling.

Sexy, topical, brilliant, and one in the eye for the literate.

Candice is far from happy with this. 'It is a question of image. That crude picture in the *Mirror*—'

'I know what you're going to say and you're wrong. It was a tasteful picture of me, under the willow in a punt on the water—'

'With your boobs hanging out and a pen behind your ear. You really have got to stop these games or your work won't be taken seriously. You might be the flavour of the month – poor little genius, the phenomenon crap – but this fame is fragile stuff, while the book is enduring, a true work of art. And to see you with your legs round that oar—'

'I got paid, didn't I?' Bernie wheels round. 'How

else am I supposed to live while I hang around waiting for this legal stuff?'

'Bernie, sweetie,' sighs Candice tiredly, 'I do understand, but you must be patient for a little while longer. You just don't have enough experience of this media frenzy to foresee all the consequences. But we're all concerned about the effect your sordid performances might be having on *Magdalene*.'

And worse, Kirsty and Avril, not to be outdone, are trying to cash in on her act. She spent hours trying to explain how quickly money gets gobbled up in London, how high the cost of living is, how clothes and accessories are so essential if they want her to take advantage of this unexpected publicity. And when all's said and done what they're talking about is a couple of tabloid features with pics, one modelling shoot for *Woman's Day*, and she had to give the dress back after, a souped-up life story for *Young and Chic* and a list of her favourite food for *Valentine*.

Dominic keeps nagging her to take financial advice: 'You'll have to sort it out once these advances arrive,' he goes on boringly, 'you can't just put that kind of money into a shopping account. Everything's got to be tied up legally, for tax purposes you need a business with proper accountants and administrators, and this crazy partnership plan has to go out the window.'

Don't say they are holding back with the money because they're worried about Avril and Kirsty. They couldn't do that, could they? Wouldn't it be illegal?

They – Coburn and Watts, her publishers; the

279

American agents and the main film company – think her deranged to even consider sharing her fortune with two nobodies who happened to be around when this prodigy was busy at work. She is too young and inexperienced to handle such huge sums herself; she must be under the influence of two more powerful characters.

Dominic rants on most of all. 'It's absolutely absurd that they should hold you to this promise; you made it in the heat of the moment when nobody had any idea what sort of reception the book would get.' Dominic strides back and forth across the opulent Chinese rug in the drawing room at Arundle Muse after a particularly unpleasant row. Now he stops in front of Bernie, his hands behind his back like Prince Philip. 'Why the hell don't you do what Candice and I advise? Give them a couple of thousand each and call it quits. Nobody could expect any more.'

OK, to them it looks as if this is freakish behaviour, but they don't know the half of it. She needs Avril and Kirsty. One look at the list of 'suggested changes' made by that shrewd old Clementine Davaine, a list she sent, 'because I'm away in the States for a week, but when I come back we must get together and discuss these ideas', made Bernie puke.

Candice Love, normally supportive, had no sympathy when Bernie complained, 'It's my book and I like it exactly how it is. Why must I make these changes?'

'I know, Bernie, I know,' soothed Candice, making Bernie sound like an overindulged child. 'And you don't have to do anything you feel strongly about, but I can assure you that Clementine knows exactly what she's doing, and that these improvements she is suggesting will be well worth following in the end.'

So Bernadette needs Kirsty, Kirsty being the only one who can manage these changes convincingly. And if Kirsty's involved then so is Avril.

'Every single word counts,' said Candice alarmingly.

'But I can't use a computer, I can't even type,' wailed Bernie. 'I relied on Avril; she did all that.'

'Well then, we must find you a secretary,' said Candice Love easily. 'We'll ask her to start on Monday.'

God, oh God.

Most threatening of all, and coming up fast on the calendar, is the tacky quiz show she agreed to take part in, directly contravening Candice's advice.

Bernie's dream is to get on TV.

'But have you ever watched that farce?' Candice was appalled when she heard. 'Have you see the goons they get on it? Celebrities no-one's heard of, has-been and no-hopers making spectacles of themselves in front of an audience of morons.'

'They'll pay me.'

'They'd have to. No-one would appear on that flop for nothing.'

'But I looked it up. It gets high ratings.'

'God, I don't believe this,' said Candice.

The worrying thing about this venture is that Bernie will have to take part. It will no longer be a case of getting by with a flash of her Irish smile and a shake of her curly black hair. More will now be demanded of her – not much, but some.

'Well, you can't just sit there saying nothing.' These days Dominic seems to enjoy making her feel worse. 'You won't get your fee for a start.'

'Don't you believe it.'

'You'll look like an idiot.'

'Oh gee, thanks.'

'It's a quiz show,' he tells her contemptuously, 'there'll be questions and answers. OK, the standard is abysmal, but have you honestly considered how you are going to win one point?'

'If other dickheads can, why can't I?'

'Because, when it comes to general knowledge, or any knowledge for that matter, you are seriously out of the race.'

Bernie seethes with bitterness. 'So how come writers of books need to have knowledge? They use their imaginations, don't they? That's how I did mine anyway. Everyone's different. People might find it intriguing that an author can be thick as shit.'

'But you don't sound thick in *Magdalene*. You sound almost . . . wise.'

Dominic can't get his head round this. He looks at her hard. Suspecting something? Suspecting she can't write a postcard without a dozen spelling mistakes? 'Take Candice's advice and cancel,' he tells her, still staring.

'But it's television, and I need the money. And it's my life,' says Bernie obstinately.

And anyway, Kirsty's all for it. 'Do it! Knock 'em for six.'

Bernie finds this hard to believe, but Dominic has started to irritate her. So precious only one year ago, so elusive she would die for him, and yet now he can't seem to leave her alone, in a patronizing sort of way. Now she is seeing so much of him he comes over as a rather tedious person, preoccupied, like everyone else, with the mechanics of money and the best publicity and saying the right thing to the right person.

Oh she still adores him, of course, and is so grateful for his presence, but not so constantly and not with such cloying ardour. What has happened to the promises he made about not being bored in London, all those friends he was going to call on, all those contacts he wanted to make? He lazes around the flat, takes hours reading the papers, watches afternoon TV and tags along to every meeting, where he bores her silly with his pompous words and says he is looking after her interests.

Bernie fumes when she hears him nattering on the phone to his father, that snooty sod who found against her at the Imperial hotel. Now you'd think she was one of the family as he drones on to Dominic about which building societies she should invest in, which accountants deal best with artists, which tax breaks she should go for, and has Dominic managed to convince her of the foolishness of sharing her fortune with two drop-outs from Cornwall?

Hour after hour they go on together like two old gossips.

And Dominic doesn't half brown-nose the literary folk they sometimes meet. OK, he wants to make his career in this new and exciting world, but to see him creeping and crawling, avidly interested in every morsel that drops from their blessed lips, is almost too much to bear. Twice they have been invited to dinner parties by people eager to meet her. Even the literate are fascinated; they see her as a freak. When these dinners begin to get chatty Bernie falls silent, only alive when first introduced, when her appearance so clearly impresses – she loves showing off her new dresses – and her voice, at first, seems to enthral them. Hallways were her successful places. In large hallways she triumphed. At the dinner table she quietly faded, became subdued, like the lighting, while Dominic took her place, refusing to let her drink too much, remembering the fool she'd made of herself at that fateful dinner with his parents in Chester.

With an extra-smart Candice Love, they dine at the home of Rory Coburn, the devastatingly charming, restless, affluent and black-eyed director of Coburn and Watts. Rory, three marriages on, now lives with his butler, Bentley, in a house with a garden sloping down to the Thames. Candice is besotted by him, Bernie is amused to see.

But who can blame her? Rory is irresistible. Magnificent in every sense, vibrant and supreme, with a magical presence and total confidence. This sort of chic, and the power that comes with it, is a new and fatal aphrodisiac, and Bernie's composure collapses in ruins. This rapturous delight is the result of Rory taking her arm and turning her to face him.

'You are enchanting, Bernadette,' he said.

He has the look of the lecher about him, she has seen seeds of that in Dominic's eyes.

'Don't fall for him, you'll get eaten alive,' warns Candice in the cloakroom. 'He flirts with all his female authors, but I think the bastard might be gay. Well,' she goes on as she powders her nose, 'look at his taste in furnishings.'

Rich oriental carpets are strewn around the floor in a large square room with a fireplace large enough for a bed. And yes, his taste is colourful, purple velvets, chandeliers, jade lamps and carvings and everything luxurious, elegant and swish. There are leather-bound books in the recesses above the fireplace and Bernie feels a twinge of green jealousy because *Magdalene* is not there. No matter how brilliantly *Magdalene* does it will never be bound in scarlet leather.

The unattainable. Throughout an almost silent dinner on her part, Bernie suffers the same yearning pangs she had when she first met the arrogant Dominic, knowing then she was reaching too high, that he would never be hers. Some women seek out the knife that will stab them – she heard that once, probably in a film.

Then she was a humble waitress, skivvying round Liverpool, and he was a university student from a background as different from hers as night from day. He was the prince, she was the beggar girl. He was gold and she was sand. Bernie can blame Mammy's nursery stories for this penchant for impossible romance.

And she shudders as she feels overwhelmed by some unknown but tremendous catastrophe.

She cannot allow this to happen again.

Last time this happened she almost died and Mammy has never forgiven her.

Rory removes his jacket and tie and wears his white shirt unbuttoned at the throat. His head is slightly lowered as he talks to Candice and Dominic, and only the edge of his straight white teeth show when he turns to Bernie and smiles. She rolls a bead of bread into a ball, concentrating wildly on what she is doing, and wishes she could shrivel so small and roll across the table under his fingers.

Purely for survival purposes, for she finds the book so unsettling, Bernie has been re-reading *Magdalene*, going through every chapter as thoroughly. They did *The Van* in English and Bernie understood not a word, but she liked the film of *The Commitments* – well the music anyway. Not a serious thinker by nature, *Magdalene* gives her macabre thoughts, and as she sits, out of place around the literary agent's table, it seems that Magdalene is with her, the faceless spectre at the feast.

Daring her. Seducing her. Blinding her with slippery illusion.

Rory Coburn is a worldly, experienced, influential man who must have had so many affairs he has forgotten most of the women he screwed. He is not particularly tall. He is probably too well preserved. She wonders if he buys men's make-up. There are traces of silver in his dark hair and chiselled lines round a lean jaw; he is erotic perfection. She watches his heavy silver watch, the way his cufflinks spark off the wine, the slight movement of his wrists as he handles his knife and fork. She imagines his long lean fingers turning the pages of her book; she imagines them on her breasts, his mouth closing round them, making them his.

Bernie dreams dangerously on. They are mega-incompatible, Chas and Di, no intellectual companionship would ever be possible between them. He would love Tchaikovsky, she would prefer Oasis; he would read Thackeray while she flicked through *TV Quick*, he would choose the ballet while Bernie went to a rave. And the only reason she is here in his house, in his great presence this evening, is because, as author of *Magdalene*, she must function at his own deeper depth and therefore be spiritually worthy.

Bernie is a woman with no concept of moderation. She cannot love sensibly, it must be obsessively; she cannot grieve gently, it must be preposterously; she cannot accept being merely liked, she has to be special; and she can't smoke five fags a day, it has to be twenty. But Magdalene handles these handicaps and turns them into weapons; she tosses back life's grenades before they explode in her face.

Bernie is drawing perilously close to her warped anti-heroine.

Far too cocky for safety.

Choosing her vegetables from the silver dishes brought round by Bentley, and every choice is equally simple, it's when you make the mistake that you suffer. Mushrooms instead of courgettes, spinach instead of artichokes – at school in Ireland you were made to sit and clean your plate for fear of offending The Lord, or the millions of Ethiopian children who might find out what you'd done. And so the choice is hers, whether to let herself take one step on the slippery slope to disastrous entanglement, or whether to turn away fast and run like hell.

There is much to be said for emotional boredom, and Bernie watches the lesser man, Dominic, as he lays on the charm for the agents and editors sitting round Rory's table. There is much to be said for listening to music and feeling stupidly happy, for walking alone in the twilight without breaking your heart. Dominic, who was once her god, the stars in the sky, the sun and the moon, is a young, attractive, fun-loving guy, but ordinary, *so ordinary*. Jaysus, what a relief to be released from the hellish infatuation that gripped and exhausted her for so long. Never again, please God, *never again*. For the sake of her own survival.

'Don't do it,' says Candice edgily on the doorstep, gesturing towards Rory.

Poor Candice. So jealous.

'Don't worry,' lies Bernie, aflame, 'I won't.'

When the new secretary arrives on Monday and sets herself up the small office at the back of the flat, Bernie is at a loss. She has sent Clementine's notes to Kirsty who has a copy of *Magdalene,* and is waiting for the relevant pages to be returned posthaste.

'I am still working on the manuscript by hand; it's not ready for typing up yet,' Bernie tells Candice in defensive anger. 'Why is everyone hassling me, *why are you all in such a rush?*'

'Calm down, Bernie, calm down. The typescripts we've sent out are your originals, and this is unusual to say the least. We were forced to respond to unheard-of pressure. We must make final copies now. People are clamouring to see them. But take your time, don't worry. How long are you going to need? One more week? Two?'

The thought of Clementine's promised visit

looms large in Bernie's mind – she would like to have something to show her. What the hell is Kirsty playing at? – as does the quiz show already advertised in the *Radio Times*.

'Bernie, don't do it, don't do it.'

She turns on Dominic, enraged. 'I'm not turning down my chance . . . who knows who might spot me. I might be given other work.'

'Sometimes I wonder if you need me at all.'

'And what do you mean by that?'

'You and Rory got on well last night.'

'We hardly spoke.'

'You didn't need to. And Candice tells me you wheedled him into taking you to the studios on Friday.'

'What's this?' laughs Bernie unkindly. 'Are you jealous, Dominic? Of me? Christ, that's a first.' Let him feel some pain for a change. He has probably never been dumped before; it will be a new experience for him, a learning experience that might profit him. They are both undergoing learning experiences. Bernie is now determined to take up the challenge offered by Rory, armed with a clearer understanding. She cannot spend the rest of her life avoiding relationships in case they destroy her, she has to learn to handle her emotions, and if she can take on an expert like Rory she will have good reason to be proud of herself.

'Don't worry, Candice,' she tells her agent, 'I know exactly what I am doing.'

She will not play the snivelling victim again.

She is not addicted to pain, like fat Avril, like the miserable Kirsty.

'You silly fool,' says Candice, when Bernie waits for Rory's car to come and collect her – vintage, of course, one of the first Ford models on the road. And although Bernie knows Candice is jealous – she has set her cap at Rory for years – there is something in her troubled voice that touches a little nerve in Bernie, piercing the fog of the anaesthetic. *Are you really so sure of yourself this time?* At this vulnerable point in your life, are you honestly so certain you can play an expert in his own field and win?

For she knows by now that the destruction of love, even a love as flawed as hers, is a wilderness complete.

How typical and how abjectly pathetic.

And just when Bernie is trembling on the very brink of success.

Twenty-Two

All this nagging about the book. What is Bernie so hysterical about? Let her make a fool of herself on telly, it might take her down a peg or two. As if Kirsty hasn't enough to contend with. And how the hell can she be expected to make the changes to *Magdalene*, either?

Oh, Ellen Kirkwood, where are you?

When, eventually, Kirsty recovered after Trevor's opportune accident, she found enough voice to call from the edge of the void, 'Trev? Trev, can you hear me?'

'You mad cow,' came up the reply on a sludgy sound of stagnation. 'You bleeding well pushed me in here.'

Kirsty paused, thought hard about that, could that be remotely possible? Could she have shoved Trev over the edge during one of her paroxysms of terror, and never realized what she had done? No, she shook her head, trying to clear it of numbing shock, she hadn't known where the hole was, so why would she have pushed Trevor in that direction? She knew there was subsidence near the fridge, but the fact that that subsidence had turned into a mantrap was as much a surprise to her as it must have been for Trevor.

'Look, you sicko,' called Trev's disembodied voice, 'look what's bleeding well down here with me. Come on! Come on, you know very well what's in here, but I want to show you.'

Reluctantly, yet obedient still to her master's voice, Kirsty crept towards the hole. It took time for her eyes to acclimatize to the solid sphere of darkness. 'I'm sorry, Trev,' she stumbled over her frightened words, 'but I can't see anything.'

'There's a fucking dead cat down here,' shouted Trev, 'and we both know about the golf club. When did you put that down here, Kirsty? Did you murder Ed Board? Have you gone right over the edge? You were the one who held the keys to this pigsty, you had to open the door to the law, you put this murder weapon down here and you can't bloody well deny it. Christ Jesus, I think I've broken my bloody arm.'

What cat? What golf club? Not the murder weapon, surely? Had Trev suffered brief loss of consciousness, had he damaged his head in the fall?

'Not Fluffy?' called Kirsty suddenly.

'Fluffy? You raving nutter,' yelled Trev. 'Get me out of here. Go and get help quickly, I can't stand much more of this. Fucking mess, dead cats, slimy muck halfway to my knees.'

She hoped he was wearing his Hush Puppies. His Hush Puppies must be ruined. Kirsty suddenly spotted his car keys hanging on the edge of the cooker. 'Where did you park your car, Trev . . .'

He answered before he had time to think. 'Some

caravan park down the road. Why? What's my car got to do with anything?'

Kirsty swallowed. 'Nothing, nothing. You hang on in there while I go for help.'

'Don't piss about,' called Trevor angrily, 'else you'll be up for a second bleeding murder.'

So she picked up the small bunch of car keys and carefully locked the door behind her.

Mrs Stokes would be missing her at work, Kirsty worried as she made her way along the coast path back towards the Happy Stay, careful to keep a low profile and stick to the rockier path. The registration number of Trev's hired Cavalier was conveniently printed on the plastic key ring and she only had to search for five minutes before discovering the vehicle in the car park beside the shop. Working hard at looking natural Kirsty unlocked the door and got in and, although she'd never taken her test, her only experience being the few bad-tempered lessons Trev gave her when they were engaged, she managed to start it up without revving the engine and drove smoothly out of the gate, under the banner that read, 'Happy Stay'.

She drove for five minutes before arriving at the track that led to the notorious Pengellis Rock. She bumped the car over the first field, opened the gate, relieved to find there were no cows, and carried on over the second until she reached the edge of the cliff. The rock itself stood stark and black, connected to land by a thin strip of crag, like a drawbridge to a fortified castle. Kirsty turned off the engine. How many hundreds of desolate people had sat here in the past, plucking up courage, swigging their whisky, listening to their saddest songs and reliving their hopeless memories before stepping out on that short journey that would lead them to peaceful oblivion?

There was only a paper with a crossword half done beside her in the passenger seat, and two empty fag packets. She got out, wiped the steering wheel clean like a criminal and opened the boot. There was a brown carrier bag inside – she had taken his Adidas bag – and only his wash things were in it. So he hadn't intended to stay long. He must have been very confident that his mission would prove successful: that his wife would end up drugged and incarcerated in some closed unit and his children would be returned. When they let her out, he would bring her home. He knew she would have learned her lesson.

She left the carrier bag alone – he wouldn't need those things any more – and re-locked the boot. She took the car keys with her. On her way back across the cliffs she chose a spot where the water boiled into a black maelstrom of fury that mimicked her own. She threw the keys with all her might and they disappeared in their own small circle before a spurt of vicious spume swirled over the hole for ever.

'I'm so sorry, Mrs Stokes,' she said at teatime, 'only my husband arrived unannounced, somehow he tracked me down and turned up out of the blue demanding to talk to me. I would have come to find you to ask your permission but he's a very determined man and wouldn't let me do that.'

'I must say, it was a thoughtless thing to do, it left poor Marie single-handed.'

'It won't happen again,' said Kirsty sincerely.

'He's gone now. I told him there was no way I would go back to him and in the end he seemed to accept it. He was miserable, probably gone to the nearest pub to drown his sorrows.'

'Men!' huffed Mrs Stokes, rolling her eyes to the heavens. And Kirsty wondered about Mr Stokes and if he was dead, or if they were divorced. She couldn't imagine the grim Mrs Stokes even lying on her back in the missionary position; the thought of her opening her legs was utterly unfeasible. There was talk of the old woman having a relative in America – a child, her child – but it must have been so long ago.

'I believe your children arrive this evening,' said Mrs Stokes in a way that suggested she hoped they wouldn't cause any further disruption to Kirsty's work schedule.

'Yes,' said Kirsty, excited.

'Quite a family day, then, one way and another.'

'I'm glad Trevor's gone anyway,' said Kirsty. 'That takes one big worry off my mind.'

Before she left for the Happy Stay Kirsty called Bernadette in London.

'Thank God it's you at last,' Bernie shouted. 'I'm in a right state here. You must have got the notes last week, when are you going to send it all back?'

'I haven't had a chance to look at them yet.'

'Holy Jaysus, the editor's coming here tomorrow to discuss the changes with me and what am I going to tell her?'

'Surely you can fob her off.'

'She's not that sort of person!'

'Tell her you're in the middle of doing it but you haven't quite finished yet.'

'And I'm on telly on Friday. Kirsty, I'm going to look like a right eejit and Dominic's no help.'

She wanted reassurance. Well, Kirsty was in no mood to bother. 'What about the money?' she said. 'Me and Avril can't wait much longer.'

'I'm doing my best, believe me, but they're fussing around about making you partners; they don't think it's a good idea.'

What is Bernie playing at? 'Well then, just tell them to pay you, forget the partnership, shut up about us, and then we can split it afterwards.'

'Kirsty, there's tax, and VAT and different accounts; it's very involved, it's not that easy. I only get half now, anyway, the rest doesn't come till the thing's published.'

Kirsty gripped the phone. 'I don't believe this, Bernie. You sound as if you're making excuses. What's going on? Are you being straight with me?'

'Listen to me, Kirsty.' It sounded like Bernie was cracking up and yet she seemed so comfortable in her famous role just weeks ago. 'You've dumped me right in it. It's bloody hell here. I'm trying to make out I'm some kind of intellectual, trying to kid everyone around me, there's nobody here on my side, nobody to support me, I'm carrying you all on my own, and now you're accusing me of being a con-artist.'

'It's not so easy back here, either,' Kirsty snapped. 'What with Avril's brother, and I've had an awful visit from Trev . . .'

'No? What happened?'

'I managed to convince him to leave us all alone.'

Did that sound too glib? Bernie knows Trev better than that from everything Kirsty's told her.

'Is that right? That's amazing. Unless he's got some trick up his sleeve.'

Kirsty tried to pass this off. 'That could well be, but there's pressures on all of us, Bernie, and Avril and I badly need money. The kids arrive later today and I've still got no transport.'

'I'll have another go at them, maybe Rory can work something out.'

'Rory?'

'Candice's boss. He's got influence. He knows what he's doing. He ought to be able to get something done.'

'Well hurry up, for God's sake,' said Kirsty.

'And send that manuscript back,' begged Bernie, 'quick. You mess me about again and I'm up shit creek. Pray for me.'

So eager to be reunited with the children she has missed for so long, Kirsty sets off once again for the caravan park. Her few belongings are already there, it didn't take long to empty her room, and Colonel Parker kindly drove her over in the hotel minibus last night.

As far as Kirsty had been able to see, Trev had followed a pile of rubble into the ancient mine shaft and now rested twelve feet down on what was probably solid floor. The shaft must have been a blind one. The jerry-built cottage must have been put up with no knowledge of the old workings at a time before planning permission was required – nobody could have bothered much about foundations, either.

He could call from there as loud as he liked and nobody would hear him; even Kirsty, in the same room, had to strain to hear his muffled words. He'd have no difficulty breathing, and presumably he could sit and rest if he was able to tolerate the uneven floor and the soggy black muck that oozed from it. Kirsty checked her watch. He had been down there eight hours already. He would be frantic by now, hungry and thirsty, cold and uncomfortable, and beside himself with worry over his crazy wife's intentions. He would soon run out of cigarettes if he hadn't already. There was no way he could get out on his own – the walls above and surrounding him were smooth, wet circles of rock, too wide to use as a climbing chimney. And the stench of age-old putrefaction was rank and overpowering.

Jake and Gemma do not run towards her immediately as she'd imagined they would in her dreams. Instead they stand there shyly, clinging to Maddy's hands, while Avril tries to bring them out. 'Here's Mummy! We told you she'd be here soon! Mummy's been at work.'

Kirsty, her heart overflowing, kneels down beside them. She looks up at Maddy, 'At last, at last. I thought this day would never come.' And slowly Jake unwraps himself and drops onto his mother's knee, and the old familiar weight of him, this view of his small head from above, the thinness of his ankle where it disappears into his shoes, warms her through like winter sheepskin, and she wants to fold them both up in these feelings for ever.

'Gemma?' asks Kirsty gently, holding out a spare arm, begging like a mother on a third-world pavement. And the little girl falls silently into the crook

298

of her arm like a conker from an oak tree, round and shiny and perfectly formed. 'Oh, I've missed you both so much.' Kirsty lets her lips lose themselves in her children's clean hair, as if grubbing for some precious food she has been deprived of for too long.

'They're fine,' Maddy booms from above, her wild grey hair in untidy tangles. 'They've been all round the caravan, tried out their beds, put away their things, learned to boil the kettle and put up the front doorstep.'

'Oh, you just don't know . . .' Kirsty murmurs, drawing a sharp gulp of breath as a keen pain bites through her, while Maddy and Avril watch the reunion with soppy smiles on their faces.

'Gemma was sick on the journey, weren't you, poor mite?' says no-nonsense Maddy.

'Oh, Gemma!' Kirsty gives her a special kiss.

'Yes, inside her Wellington boots. And they've brought oodles of things to show you, things they've made, pictures of where they've been this summer. And Jake can swim, just a few strokes, doggy paddle, but next summer he'll be playing with the dolphins.'

'I've made tea.' Avril gloats, with the same beaming smile on her face. 'Pasties and beans and baked potatoes with cheese on top.'

'The dogs are with Maddy's friend, they're having a holiday while Maddy's away,' Jake exclaims excitedly, and his words begin to tumble out and Kirsty can't hear enough of them, words she has been deprived of for five long months and all because of that evil bastard languishing in the empty mine.

She can't stop trembling.

They can just about squeeze round the table. It feels as if they've always done this, Maddy, Avril, Jake, Gemma and Kirsty, such an easy family, so at home with each other, no fear of the man coming home and cutting the happy pink ribbon around them.

'I don't think you need worry about my departure,' Maddy reassures Kirsty heartily, still wearing those terrible worn old tweeds she'd been wearing the last time she'd seen her. 'I'll only be at the hotel and I'll come and see them first thing in the morning. I'm staying over tomorrow night as well in case you have any problems. But they're both such happy kids, Kirsty, in spite of all they have been through, and that must be due to you. You coped so well in such an impossible situation.'

'I think we got out of it just in time. Jake was beginning to show some signs . . .'

Maddy nods fondly. 'But it's all over now, my dear. As long as you can go on coping as well as you have been doing.'

Kirsty looks round the caravan and blesses Avril for what she has accomplished. It's warm, it's bright, and with children's toys scattered around it looks almost homely. 'Hopefully', she sighs, 'we won't be here long.'

'It doesn't matter where you are as long as these two are with you,' smiles the comforting Maddy. 'That's all they want. And it's high time, I think. And as long as that frightful husband of yours stays out of your way, one day soon you might be able to sort it all out legally. Get shot of the blighter once and for all.'

* * *

After the children are asleep – and it didn't take long, they were worn out – Kirsty manages to tear herself away from a silent and marvelling vigil and Avril makes hot chocolate and they both sit down. A single cone of light falls on the table between them, the curtains are drawn and the television flickers with the volume turned down.

In this light Avril's shiny face looks extraordinarily young. Her skin is as smooth as a baby's. Her nervous voice is almost a whisper.

'But you never told me you'd seen Graham.' Kirsty is astounded by Avril's fresh news.

'I never told anyone,' says Avril. 'I suppose I just couldn't face the truth.'

'But now you've made a statement?'

'Yes, I couldn't get it out of my mind. I couldn't sleep. I couldn't eat. But, Kirsty, I feel so disloyal. *He is my brother.*'

'And you saw him on the golf course? Just before Ed died?'

'I'd arranged to meet Ed,' Avril lies. 'I know it seems silly, so early, but it was hard for us to spend any time on our own together, what with work . . . anyway, we both liked getting up early.'

'And you saw Graham? Are you sure?'

Avril nods sadly. Her blue eyes are so solemn. The flowers Maddy kindly brought with her sit between them, arranged in a Nescafé coffee jar. 'I saw Graham in the distance. He was going towards the rough ground where Ed was found dead. I couldn't believe it was him – what was Graham doing down here? I thought I was mistaken, that perhaps it was a hotel guest out for a morning stroll and about to chat to Ed. Anyway,' Avril, very pale, warms her hands

301

round her mug for comfort, 'whoever it was, there wasn't much point in me and Ed meeting if somebody else was about. We might be interrupted, and I hadn't much time and we didn't really want everyone to know our business, so I turned round and went back to the suite and let myself in without disturbing Dom or Bernie.'

Kirsty, dragged into the tale, feels like a conspirator. Avril is lying. She knows. She can tell. 'This is awful, Avril,' she says.

Avril sighs and goes on, tense and earnest. 'Mother, of course, is beside herself. She thinks I should have kept quiet for the sake of the family. "As if one murder isn't enough." She seems to blame me, as if I'd done it, but at the very least she thinks I've joined the rest of the world in clubbing against her.'

'What about your father? He must be finished.'

Avril's lips begin to quiver uncontrollably. 'I can't bear to think about what all this is doing to Father.' She lifts her doleful face and stares at Kirsty beseechingly. 'Kirsty, tell me I've done the right thing.'

Kirsty is forced to move Maddy's flowers in order to see Avril properly. She is carrying these lies off exceptionally well. And so what if she's compromised Graham? It's time she started fighting back. 'Well, Avril, you did what you had to do. If you really believe you saw Graham there, you had to tell somebody. I mean . . .' Kirsty thinks quickly, she mustn't say the wrong thing, Avril is worryingly close to breaking down completely. 'I suppose, as he's already accused of one murder, another can't make that much difference.'

'But it makes him a serial killer,' says Avril. 'They'll put him away for life.'

There is a strange shrillness in Avril's voice. Kirsty looks at her hard and sees a disquieting smugness there.

Twenty-Three

She believes that she convinced Kirsty. She hopes
she convinced them all. The flaw in her story – the
fact that she fell out with Ed the night before his
death and would be unlikely to meet him at dawn
the following day – has luckily slipped Kirsty's
fuddled mind. But Avril is soon sick and tired of
repeating her story over and over, going through
the smallest details and carrying it all, like a film, in
her head.

For a woman who, up until now, has found
lying bewildering, Avril lies like a trooper, and
there's no sign of that give-away blush on her
face. It makes a change from owning up to something she hasn't done – owning up for somebody
else – well, it's using the same well-honed skills. If
she can fool her sharp-eyed mother, Avril can fool
anyone. And the joy that it brings her beggars
belief; it's as good as unscrewing a bolt in her
head, she can almost hear the hiss of hot steam as
years of frustrated rage rush out and finally dis-
perse, she knows not where, like the other poisons
in the stratosphere.

*   *   *

'Your brother denies he went anywhere near the golf course that morning.' The police are relentless with their questions.

'Well, he would, wouldn't he,' says Avril.

'He points out that he had no reason to kill Ed Board, unlike Annie Brenner who he allegedly robbed.'

'But he denies that, too.'

'But we've got evidence against him on that charge. Whereas there's nothing to connect him to Ed Board's death.'

'Except that I saw him.'

'But you haven't seen your brother for over five years.'

'You don't forget what your brother looks like.'

And they write down everything and record every word she is saying.

'He says you fell out when you visited him yesterday. He says this is your way of getting your own back. He used to bully you as a child, can you tell us about that, Avril?'

'I'm sure that happens in lots of families with children of different sexes and with that age gap. It wasn't any worse in ours.'

There is always another question. At first she dreaded the next and the next, but now they have started repeating themselves Avril finds the tension exhilarating. It's like a chess game once you've mastered the rules. 'But Graham was unlike most other lads of his age, I believe. Graham was a hard nut, a screwball, cruel, not the sort of brother it could have been easy to live with. This must have had an effect on you, Avril, and probably a profound one. Your parents' reaction to you must have been coloured by Graham's behaviour. Perhaps you resented that?'

'I didn't like Graham, I didn't like him at all.'

'He used to hurt you?'

'Sometimes.'

'Can you be more explicit?'

'He used to give me Chinese burns. He used to pull my hair and pinch me. He used to tease me when his friends came round, and call me fat and ugly.'

'And when he was put away, how did you feel about that?'

'I was pleased. Naturally. It meant some peace and quiet in my life at last.'

'And you never went to visit him in Liverpool?'

'No, my parents were against it. But I wouldn't have gone anyway.'

'So Graham is right. You do bear a grudge.'

'Of course I bear a grudge. Wouldn't you? He took my favourite doll once, and burnt all the hair off her head with caustic soda. Her scalp came up in plastic blisters. I was so little then I believed she could feel it.'

Avril notices how the policemen glance at each other now and again, as if they've picked up something significant, like the way dentists' eyes, enlarged by the mirror, move around inside your mouth and stop when they find a filling or some vulnerable, soft, pink place.

'Why did you go and visit Graham yesterday?'

'Because I felt guilty, I felt sorry for Graham, I thought I should give him some support.'

'Rather a sudden change of heart?'

'Not really. He had never been charged with murder before.'

306

'Some people might think that fact would harden you against him.'

'From all I've heard, it sounds as if he didn't mean it.'

'But you think he meant to kill Ed Board?'

'I don't know, how could I know? I can't see into Graham's head. All I know is that he was there and I recognized him.'

'But you didn't call out or acknowledge him. The brother you hadn't seen in years? Don't you think that's rather odd?'

'I was very confused. Graham, here in Cornwall? I thought I must have been mistaken.'

'Ah. But now? With hindsight?'

'Now that I know my brother was in the area, seeing him that morning makes perfect sense.'

'I believe you and Ed Board had something going between you?'

'We were friends.'

'No more than friends?'

'We were close friends.'

'Did you ever have sexual intercourse with Edward Board?'

'No. I am a virgin.'

And the men's sharp eyes swivel and snap with significance once again.

'How could you do this to me, Avril?' sobs Mother, sitting, defeated, on the caravan steps. 'Oh, how could you?'

There is elation to be had in this, too. Avril feels no remorse, no sympathy for her grieving mother, no wish to turn back the clock, no shame at the enormity of her lies or the awesome consequences of

307

them. Quite the contrary in fact. She is revelling in her new persona and wonders why it has taken so long for her to discover the thrill of being evil and the acceptance of it as a Godlike state.

And as for her poor father, well, if he'd stood up for himself and not been walked all over by Mother, Graham, his mean employers, the foreman at the garage, the dustbinmen, his next-door neighbour and any Tom, Dick or Harry who happened to bump into him in the street, Avril might have felt a pang of pity at the sight of his anguished face. But there comes a time in everyone's life when one ought to put up a fight – Kirsty's managed it, Avril's done it – and maybe this terrible catastrophe might be a watershed for him.

Magdalene has a theory that the devil and God are one and the same. God invented the eternity of hell and only a demon could think up that.

Magdalene took the veil to hide from the abominations of men.

Magdalene chose a closed and silent order so she could concentrate on her purity of thought.

Magdalene slipped out at night through the vast convent kitchens and changed into the casual clothes she hid in a metal box by the gate.

The understandable media frenzy brings the rat packs of London down to this peaceful Cornish Cove in their droves, to the mortification of Mr Derek, who finds some of them posing as guests, having booked into the Burleston under false pretences.

Thank the Lord Avril has already moved out,

because it's the Stotts who attract these terrible media people. What sort of dysfunctional family could produce the kind of creature who would commit two heinous murders one after the other like that – the first for £1.39 and the second for no obvious reason other than that his sleep must have been disturbed by a probing golf club.

'Let me make you a cucumber sandwich, Mother.'

Mother has turned furtive. She has started darting her way between cars and caravans and taking sanctuary in Kirsty and Avril's large mobile home, leaving Richard to face the consequences of his mutant seed and satisfy the cameras.

The sunbeds and deckchairs have been removed from Mother's caravan garden. The pot plants are now on the windowsill, their leafy profiles hiding the hunted inmates from the press.

Still she cannot acknowledge that this tragedy has affected anyone else but herself and her position in society, which matters so much to her. It wouldn't occur to her that by scuttling over here with the press sniffing at her heels she might be involving two innocent children in the whole ghastly mêlée; it is just a blessing that term has started and Jake and Gemma are at school.

Kirsty, of course, still works at the Burleston, walks there and back every morning and evening, although Avril has tried to persuade her to give it up: 'At any moment now that advance will filter through. We'll be rich! It's all that's keeping me going. We'll be able to buy our own house. Why are you so determined to keep slaving away in that hole?'

309

'Perhaps it's because I can't believe that miracles really happen,' said Kirsty.

'Maybe I will have that cucumber sandwich,' says Mother pitifully. 'I have to eat.'

'I wonder what Graham's eating now,' says Avril deliberately.

'I'd rather not discuss him.'

'Or Father. Did you leave him something cold?'

'I can't be bothered with your father's fussing while all this mayhem is going on. Let him make his own sandwich. There's plenty of ham in the fridge.'

A wave of hatred passes over Avril. It passes over her and drags her out with the undercurrent into a shameless sea of revenge.

Sometimes it seems as if Father and Graham are figments of Mother's imagination, the paper people Avril used to cut out of catalogues when she was small, to be animated or screwed up at whim, named, placed, born, married, buried, but with no real presence of their own.

I wonder what Mother's reaction would be? thinks Avril, fingering the cucumber and sucking wetly on a watery slice.

'I never told you this before,' she says, passing over the sandwich with all the crusts cut off, 'but when I was little Father used to come into my room at night.'

Mother, still in her place on the step, keeps twisting her head this way and that, on the lookout for long-distance lenses.

'It was mostly when you were downstairs in the lounge watching those two-part dramas. Well, Father was never interested in dramas so he used to come upstairs. I think he used to tell you he was having an early bath.'

'What, Avril? I hope your father will keep his word and speak to the reporters this time. If he would just say a few words some of them might go away. But you know how slow he is.'

Avril goes on with grim satisfaction. 'He used to kiss me all over my face and hair and pull my duvet back.'

'Your father used to do that?'

'Yes, and then he would push up my nightie and touch my body with his fingers.'

Mother's neck snaps round. One small triangle of sandwich falls from her lap upon the brown, well-weathered grass.

'Avril! *Stop it!* You don't know what you are saying! Have you lost your mind?'

'Oh, that didn't worry me much,' Avril goes on, swirling a finger in the washing-up water, piling up the liquid froth into weird fantasy shapes. 'In fact, I quite liked it. It was when he got his penis out that I used to feel frightened. It was so big and stiff. I thought it was horrible. And it used to smell of wet skin.'

Mother leaps off the caravan step and hurries inside, closing the small door behind her lest some passer-by might hear. She grabs hold of Avril's arms from behind and pulls her round to face her. When Avril looks into Mother's eyes she sees not sorrow, not pity, but fear, sheer, unadulterated fear. Mother's small eyes are piercing, as if there are arrow heads in them.

'You never told me this.'

'I knew there was no point.'

Mother's fingers squeeze harder on Avril's arms till they reach bruising capacity. '*No point?*'

'You would tell me I was being filthy, like you did that time you came in the bathroom and caught me having a pee in the bath. You smacked me so hard I went under the water, I thought I was going to drown, I couldn't stop choking, but you'd gone. You would think there was something twisted about me, like you did when you thought I'd gone into Graham's room naked.'

'You haven't said this to anyone else?'

'No, Mother. Why would I?'

'Well, you thought nothing of telling the police that you'd seen Graham on the golf course. You seemed to enjoy incriminating him!'

'The two situations are rather different.'

'No, they're not. Avril, you are despicable. You are dishonest and wicked. You seem to want to destroy this family. You seem to be going right out of your way to smash us to smithereens. I wouldn't put it past you to go to the welfare people and tell them these lies about your father.' Tears of anger spurt into her eyes.

But Avril braces her shoulders and sets her face to naught.

'Your father was never interested in sex,' Mother goes on in a high, nervous voice, 'so why would he bother meddling with you, or anyone else for that matter?' She thinks in silence for a moment, her arms falling from Avril's sides. 'And why are you telling me this now, Avril? What are you trying to do, drive me mad?'

'You would rather I'd kept it to myself?' Avril asks, moving over to the table and sitting down, drying her hands on a tea towel which she then uses to twist round her fingers.

'Well, of course I would,' says Mother, joining her, yet carefully making sure no part of her is touching her repellent daughter. 'I mean, why wait until now? What do you expect me to do?'

'But do you believe me, Mother?'

Mother shakes herself stiffly. 'No, Avril. No, I do not. And my conclusions are that you are every bit as wicked as your brother – more sly, underhand, cunning, oh yes, you've always been cunning, all those lies.'

'What lies?'

'What's the point in discussing this now?'

'Tell me, Mother, I need to know, what lies?'

Her skin, robbed of powder, is red and veined, her eyes are hard and unloving. 'Little lies, telling me you'd cleaned your teeth when you hadn't, swearing blind you'd posted my letters and then I'd find them in your duffel-coat pocket, all that bad behaviour at school, and then you'd come home and act as if butter wouldn't melt in your mouth. Well, I knew all the time what you were about.'

Avril can't help being fascinated. 'What was I about?'

'Destruction,' spits mother wildly, like a priest exorcizing a demon. If she'd had a cross she'd be holding it up, warding Avril off her.

'Is that why you tried to hide me away, made me wear unflattering clothes, forced me to have haircuts that never suited my face, refused to let me wear make-up?'

Mother's eyes glare and her voice rises. 'If I had given you your head, my girl, Lord knows what you would have turned into.' And her thin lips curl down, as if she is tasting something bitter. 'Slut. Whore. And now this . . . this . . .' she struggles to find the worst word she can, '. . . this vile accusation, these coarse suggestions against a man who wouldn't harm a fly.' Her fury storms up and takes command of her. 'Your poor father, if he ever found out it would break his heart. I won't have it, I tell you, I won't have it.'

This is the first time Avril has ever heard Mother defending Father.

But Avril feels enlarged, sanguine and grandiose. All her old timorous caution is gone, she can spar with Mother, tease her like a dog at a bear; she wonders how she has ever been at this sad woman's mercy. Mother never loved her – a daughter whose natural instincts frightened her so – she feared her own child might rise up one day and bring her most shameful thoughts to life. Mother, who is so sexually retentive and prudish she poisons everyone she touches; Mother, to whom the word 'urges' brings goose pimples up on her arms. 'Aren't you interested to know if Father ever penetrated me? If we had sex together while you were downstairs watching Ruth Rendell? Or how old I was when he started?'

'I'm not staying to listen to any more of this,' says Mother, standing up stiff as the mop that stands beside the small toilet door. 'I have no daughter,' she says to Avril. 'I have no son. I am childless.'

'You would have been happier childless,' says Avril to the empty space: sweet, timid Avril; chubby, childlike Avril; with skin like a peach and the poem, 'I Remember, I Remember', stuck in the back of her five-year diary.

How could she be so callous?

How could anyone tell such malicious lies?

Especially when you know that 'If' was another of her favourite poems, but she realized early in life that in order to be a man you had to be a boy-child first.

Twenty-Four

'You don't have anything on me,' the sulking Dominic tells Kirsty when she phones him the next day. 'You can't use me any more, I'm out of it now, last week's news. So stuff your threats, I'll be gone from here tomorrow.'

This is worrying news for Kirsty. How will Bernie, that floundering vessel, survive in London on her own? And, without Dominic's nose to the ground, how will Kirsty know what's happening?

But Kirsty isn't the only one thrown into turmoil today. Dominic is going through a painful identity crisis. This young Eros has suffered a fall, he has been chucked for another, a more affluent, cultivated, experienced and debonair fellow than he, Rory Coburn, with the lean and muscled body of one who visits the gym to get fit, and an exclusive gym at that.

'And how the hell do I know what has happened to the money?' Why should he act as informant to Kirsty, the woman who got him into this mess in the first place with her nasty threats of exposure? In fact, the money in question will soon be on its way because the lovely, literary Rory with the silver streaks and the black smoking jacket has taken it upon himself to hassle the publishers over the water and push for an early signing.

'How the hell d'you think I feel?' he answers Kirsty's question petulantly. 'I feel as if I've been used, and not just by you.'

Bernie, too, has used him cruelly. Just when he was about to break into the closed world of publishing she takes up with one of the biggest fish and he, Dominic, who has worked so hard on her behalf, is forced, like a prince turned toad, right out of the pond.

Dammit.

His future now lies in cardboard boxes.

But this is only half of his grievance.

Whilst once Bernie meant nothing to him, just one of the many apertures into which he could dip his wick, since their reunion his emotions have led him into far deeper waters. He soon had reason to thank Kirsty for forcing him to retract; his admiration for Bernie's talents moved some part of him, spiritually and sexually, which had lain dormant before. He enjoyed making love to a prodigy. He adored her status as superstar. He relished the life of comfort and the company of admiring intellectual people, the chattering classes with whom he had previously had no entrée, his father's family having rather more of an industrial bent.

Dominic also loved his status as partner and escort of a *cause célèbre*.

Bernie's added fascination is that she shows no signs of being a phenomenon. Far from it.

Take the TV show last Friday.

Rory accompanied Bernie who was nervous.

Dominic stayed home alone, drank far too much brandy and watched.

It was more than ghastly.

It was diabolical.

'The little lady from Ireland who has stunned the snooty literary world. At the age of nineteen, ladies and gentlemen, no scholarly bluestocking, no stuttering oddball, but our very own scouse, BERNADETTE KAVANAGH.'

And if this wasn't excruciating enough, coming from the poof with the saccharine smile and the hair striped like a badger's, the audience looked like a coachload released from some rest home for the occasion. Why oh why had Bernie insisted? She was beginning to believe her own hype. She thought she was invincible. She even believed the suave Rory Coburn was enamoured by her charms.

But she ought to be able to do better than this.

Quite out of character, Bernie performed with a goggle-eyed stupefaction, which was painful for all to see. Bearing in mind the loud and lack-lustre performances of her three fellow contestants, if she'd been herself she could have survived, shone even. When the host started on the questions Dominic closed his eyes and let his head fall into his hands. The questions were full of smutty innuendo – something that Bernie had never mastered; she never understood the simplest of jokes and detested slapstick. So she took all the jokes at face value and tried to answer the questions seriously, which added to the audience hysteria and made her the jibe of the host's worst taunts.

Everybody but Bernie could see that the out-of-focus picture was an elephant's bum. Yes, this was the level of the quiz: guess the subject of a distorted picture. It became so obvious it was embarrassing. And even when the full picture emerged Bernie couldn't identify it. All she kept saying was two ships' funnels and the audience fell about in their chairs.

Dominic flinched as he watched her performance, as she fiddled with her hair, bit her nails, laughed in the wrong places and failed to get the host's name right.

And as for poor Bernie, she was aware she was doing, not just badly, but catastrophically. How come she handled all that press stuff with such aplomb, it was a cinch, a piece of cake, demanding not much more than smiling and agreeing with everything anyone said. But now . . .

Hell.

Rory would be waiting for her in the hospitality suite, and oh, he would be so disappointed. How was she going to explain this pitiful performance? And just when she reckoned she had snared him. He has already organized a small advance payment into her account, and she and he are off to have dinner after this fiasco is over, at a floating restaurant on the river.

Why should she have to put up with this public mortification while Kirsty and Avril sit back and wait for their fair shares? Her financial advisers might well be right. Why should she share the advance three ways when she was being made a spectacle of, in public, in front of millions?

And here comes the only serious question, one for each of the guests, involving their individual careers.

'What authors have made the greatest impression on me in my life?' Bernie was reduced to repeating this unanswerable question. She couldn't think of one author apart from Shakespeare and that would sound naff. Everyone's eyes were telling her this was a kindergarten question, and yet she sat there silently with her mouth half open, willing a sensible name to come out.

'I'm not a great reader,' she said lamely.

And everyone looked at her askance.

'Well, I haven't had time,' said Bernie. 'I've had to work. You know?'

Where was the power and the presence that she sensed had been guiding her earlier? And she hoped the cameras were being kind and not following her hand as it inched downwards towards her knee to give it a hopeless scratch.

'You were quite dreadful,' Rory tells her unhelpfully as she falls back into the hospitality suite gasping with shame and relief. 'What happened to you in there? Are you feeling unwell?'

'Nerves. I was frightened,' she says childishly, hoping that her vulnerability might redeem her in her agent's eyes.

But it doesn't.

'Any more like that and we're going to have to make out you're a recluse,' says Rory, not laughing. 'And Clementine rang again this evening to ask if you've done any work yet.'

'I can't stand much more of this pressure.' Bernie wipes her brow in a feeble gesture of womanly weakness.

'Perhaps I should take you back to the flat', says

Rory unkindly, 'and let you get on. All these diversions don't seem to be helping.'

'I thought you wanted to take me out! It was your idea,' says Bernie, wondering where the admiration has gone from his hardening eyes. Manipulating Rory is not so straightforward as dealing with Dominic, who has packed his bag and plans to move out of the flat in the morning. He hoped Bernie would beg for forgiveness and plead with him to change his mind, but she has lost interest in her former lover, a young, unworldly student, a drop-out too easily impressed, stale and vastly inferior to someone with the power and charisma of Rory. But perhaps she has read Rory all wrong. Just because he flatters her vanity and uses that publishers' hyperbole, just because he adores *Magdalene*, just because he sees her as the bestselling author he's ever had, does not necessarily mean that he confuses the book with the woman.

Perhaps it's the book he loves, not her.

She remembers the warnings of Candice Love. 'He flirts with all his authors.' And, 'I think he might be gay.'

The rest of the evening does nothing for her battered self-esteem. When they arrive at the restaurant, a haunt for various celebrities, Bernie is chastened to see that his treatment of women is invariably conducted with his own style of effusive elegance. 'Darling, how gorgeous to see you.' So artificial and strained. Will Bernie ever be able to understand all this freakish behaviour? She, who comes from Liverpool, where a spade is called a spade and if you look into anyone's eyes the way Rory looks into hers it's an invitation to jump straight into bed.

How embarrassing that she imagined Rory Coburn fancied her.

How shameful, how simplistic, to honestly believe he was taking her out with her body in mind.

This is the way the man does his job, these are the manners his women enjoy. No-one in this restaurant, except some nerd with her own ill-breeding, would interpret his attentions so wrongly.

It is blow after blow after blow as Bernie is subtly marginalized by these more sophisticated, cleverer women, just as she was back there in the studio. They end up sharing a table with another party of Rory's friends, demonstrating to the indignant Bernie that she is not considered sufficiently qualified to entertain the great man through dinner. For his foie gras to go down smoothly he needs not just the best wine in the house, but the most scintillating and intellectual people, while she is rather unsavoury fare.

And she harbours the horrible suspicion that, after he has taken her home, he goes on somewhere else with his friends without inviting her.

The next morning things get even worse.

'But, my dear, this is quite grotesque.'

Bernie has postponed the meeting with her editor, Clementine Davaine, for too long. Clementine, her brown wig freshly washed and therefore not perfectly settled, insisted on coming today, and now peers down through her thin bifocals in the small office at the back of the flat where the temporary secretary has been working to print out Kirsty's scrappy amendments.

'You haven't understood what I meant at all.' She

sits back and stares at Bernie as if she is an unsettling apparition. 'We can't have this – and what has happened to your style, child? Where has all the eloquence gone?'

'I don't know what you mean.'

'Don't be silly. Of course you know.' Clementine picks up one piece of rewritten A4 type. 'Is this a joke? Look at this! Just look at it! I mean, it hardly makes sense any more.'

'I'll have another go,' says Bernie tiredly. What the hell is Kirsty doing landing her in the shit like this? Is her jealousy making her deliberately spiteful?

Clementine removes her spectacles, disturbing the wig as she does so and moving it slightly out of kilter. Her gnarled old hands rest on her lap, clasped together in what looks like defence. 'No, Bernadette. Let me think for a moment. Unfortunately, you are one of those authors who cannot follow editorial direction. You have tried, I can see that, but all you are likely to do is mess up what was, as it stood, a masterpiece. Perhaps I was wrong to try to make changes, even such minimal ones. But I am going to take this with me and give it to an old friend of mine who might be able to succeed where you failed.'

This sounds too good to be true. 'And I won't have to do any more work on it?'

'No. In future, my dear, I think I can honestly say that I would rather you kept your hands right off this book.' And she stuffs the manuscript in an old leather holdall which contains a pair of manly bedroom slippers and a double pack of ultra-soft, rose-coloured Andrex. 'The sooner we can send

323

edited proofs out to reviewers the better,' says Clementine, slipping an unlikely padlock around the handles of the old shopping bag and locking the thing with a miniature key. 'We've already wasted too much time. We have paid a fortune for this novel and we really must get things cracking.'

These people think they're a breed apart. Clementine rises abruptly and leaves while Bernie's temper flames, fed up of all these insinuations that hers is a stagnant mind. After all, they are parasites every one of them, feeding off authors and artists and bloating themselves like conceited leeches. And the more she frets over the editor's remarks, sitting alone in the office, the more her wrath is fanned into savagery. Bernadette burns to be loved and admired; this is how this venture had started. Everything was so easy then, back at the Burleston with Candice Love, who thought the sun shone out of her arse. Then along came Dominic to complete her exultation, this London flat and the media attention. She paces the room, silent, sullen and testy.

Bernie is quite alone now, apart from Joyce Parfait the housekeeper who keeps herself to herself and cooks an assortment of fish in the converted garage. She regrets chucking Dom out now – he was stale and fawning but at least he was company. It will be different when she can spend her own money; she can leave this dreary flat and go back to Liverpool. She misses Mammy and Daddy and Fran, who treat her differently on the phone now they know she's a literary genius. And all her other abandoned friends. But once she's got money will they accept her?

Her troubles stem from the moment she fooled

herself into believing that Rory Coburn was up for it. He, not little Dom, is the sort of man she wants to be seen with – it is his world she longs to be part of; she yearns to be accepted as one of them. Will there always be 'one of them' for poor Bernie to aspire to? Does the Queen have 'one of them' from whom she is excluded? And every time she achieves an ambition why do the goal posts have to move?

The lonely, dispirited Bernie goes upstairs, showers and throws herself naked on her opulent bed. She picks up her copy of *Magdalene*; she has studied this book, learned paragraphs by heart, memorized the most insignificant characters in case she was ever questioned, what more could she have done? Nobody can come straight out and deny that she is the author of *Magdalene,* not even Clementine, with all her suspicious, witchy looks. But at the end of the day what has it gained her? She will be rich, she will be respected by those who have not met her, but she will never be one of the inner circle.

Throughout her life Bernie has imagined that she is an interesting person.

What is Rory Coburn doing now?

Is he in bed with his butler, Bentley? Or is he, more likely, making love to one of the luvvies he seems to attract with the lift of an eyebrow?

With a reflective smile on her lips Bernie moves her fingers down her perfectly formed naked body, caressing her breasts, her legs, her taut stomach; even her feet are perfect examples of what feet ought to look like. What is the matter with Rory Coburn, and why did he flirt with her in the first place if he finds her so contemptible? He had no right to behave in that manner, assuming she was wise and perceptive. Does he find her ignorance repellent? Is her accent offensive? Are her manners unsatisfactory? Perhaps he considers her vulgar?

How dare he? *How dare he?*

She felt this unhappiness when Dominic hurt her. Dear God, please don't let Rory obsess her. She suspects that she needs him already, that this is the reason for this new desolation. His power to wound would be greater than Dominic's.

Why should she be used and discarded by a slimy little lecher like Coburn? And how can she get even?

She holds back the tears.

The answer comes to Bernie in one easy flash, like a sudden reflection in the mirror, but she turns round and sees no-one.

For one brief moment she feels sick and reaches for the water jug put ready by Joyce Parfait on her bedside table. Gin might have been more thoughtful. But she lights a fag instead, the other hand unconsciously resting on the unpublished novel.

Malice flows through her veins with the blood.

Bernadette is a woman scorned.

The reputation of Coburn and Watts is flying high on the back of their coup to acquire *Magdalene*. After the book has been fully exploited that agency stands to make millions, and the main beneficiary to it all is that tosser Rory Coburn. How easy it would be to tarnish his name, or even better, for the sake of the revenge Bernie feels is due to her, to dump her burdens on somebody who would find it quite impossible to refuse to share an intolerable load.

Still naked, she leans across the bed, looks up his number in her diary, and dials.

In a minute Rory Coburn will hear the worst news of his career.

Twenty-Five

Autumn comes to the country more subtly than to the town, where leaves build up and gutters fill and the starker trees stand out boldly from the sound of muted traffic like russet decorations.

At Burleston Cove distant bonfires of dead leaves fill the air with smoky blues, over-ripe apples mellow in patches of sunlight where rusty leaves replace pink blossoms. The sea rolls into a verdigris green and white lace tacks to the spindrift. At times, white wood smoke from the hotel fires spirals far enough to lie on the water.

When the first payment was made to her bank, distributed fairly by Bernie, Kirsty gave in her notice. It was more money than she would have earned after a lifetime skivvying at the Burleston.

'It's happening now! *It's started*,' Avril screamed with acquisitive joy. 'You must believe in miracles now, you've done it, Kirsty! *You've done it!*'

In a dignified and detached manner, in a nasty mustard-yellow frock which suggested kidney failure, Mrs Stokes enquired about the book's progress. 'Because I don't want you to go and burn all your bridges in some tomfool way, not now you've got your children to consider.'

'They have paid one advance into Bernadette's bank and she has shared it with us already, but pretty soon they'll dole out the rest and me and my kids will be safe for life.'

As she said it Kirsty could scarcely believe it.

'And when is this book due to be published?'

'February the sixth. But the edited proofs will be ready by Christmas. We should have a copy by then.' This is what Kirsty is waiting for: the thought of holding that wonderful work, all heavy and contained in her hands. It feels like a birth, even to her; she did update it, after all, and conceived the whole outrageous idea. And she, so mentally ill, so dull-witted and boring, has not only outwitted Trev, but publishers, agents, journalists and the highest fliers of film and TV.

'I would very much appreciate a copy,' said Mrs Stokes with uncharacteristic interest and no expression at all on her face.

'Oh? Well, I'm sure we'll have one to spare,' said Kirsty on a wave of warm enthusiasm, sympathizing suddenly with this grim-faced old woman who seems to live her life at death's door, whose only relative seems to be a shadowy child across the Atlantic, whose career has amounted to nothing more than a lifetime of counting sheets, kowtowing to Mr Derek and intimidating staff.

Whereas Kirsty intends to start again – basic qualifications followed by university and a decent job, a first-class education for the children, a middle-class neighbourhood, a comfortable lifestyle and no man.

And after handing in her notice the second thing Kirsty did was go with Avril to choose a car. A new one. A neat, bright red little Corsa. Her life is suddenly so very positive, no more beating time to somebody else's drum. No more backward glances.

'Are you thirsty yet, Trevor?'

With pleasure she knows he is not just thirsty but rasping and gasping for water. It is four days since he found her and nothing has passed his lips since then. He has probably tried the rank, oily ooze that laps around his feet, but the cat must be putrid by now, contaminating what moisture there is, along with Trevor's own waste, and causing him extra grief. Has he slept, Kirsty wonders?

'Give me some water.'

'Give me your clothes. This is strip poker, Trevor, remember the rules? We played it in Weston-Super-Mare, you seemed to enjoy it then.' Her eyes are terror-fixed, but Trevor can't see that. She wants him naked. To be naked is to be much more vulnerable.

'I'll give you my clothes.'

No cursing. No threats. No more accusations of madness. Just a hoarse whisper coming from the ground.

'I'm going to lower this rope. Just tie your clothes to the end, your shoes and socks as well, and I'll haul them up. Then I'll tie a bottle of water to the rope and let it down to you.' As she kneels at the side of the hole she warns him casually, 'If you try to pull the rope, Trevor, if you put any needless pressure on it at all, I will let it drop immediately.' Kirsty adds truthfully, 'It's the only rope I have.'

There is a silence while Kirsty watches the slow, awkward movements from the figure down below, his limbs must be aching from the damp and cold, from the sudden lack of exercise. Trevor could well be in quite a bit of pain. Trevor could well be ill.

'That's it,' says Trevor's voice, still muffled.

'Don't forget your crucifix, Trevor.' To her over-wrought mind this broken Christ seems to symbolize so much of her terror.

Kirsty hauls up the rope and is knocked back by the stench that accompanies the untidy bundle. Faeces and mould and putrefaction.

She lowers the bottled spring water and that's followed by scuffling sounds, as if some small animal is trapped down there, but it's only Trev with his stiff, hurting hands struggling to loosen the knot. Then she can hear him drinking it, the gulping of a parched, painful throat which slows as the bottle is drained, and then there's a shocking smash as glass hits the walls and the doleful sobbing of a desperate man.

'Don't kill me, Kirsty,' he pleads, thirst no longer constricting his throat.

Above him, she smiles and refrains from answering.

Let him sweat.

It would be unkind to let him know her plans.

This is strip poker played with no dice and the cards are stacked against him.

'Tomorrow I might bring some Jaffa cakes,' she says as she backs away from the hole. She bundles his clothes on a high shelf before leaving the cottage, careful to lock the door behind her, swinging a barrier into place between her and another world.

Kirsty drives away from the Burleston, all the pleasure of her new car flooding her with satisfaction as she heads, once more, towards Pengellis Rock. This time she leaves her car in the pull-in – she has no intention of muddying the wheels – climbs the gate and jumps down into the field. A solitary sheep lifts its head to watch her go by while she follows the grey stone walls, unwilling to be seen. Somebody has removed Trev's car, so they must be searching for him already. When she reaches the edge of the sheer cliff she cautiously scrambles across the thin bridge of stone that attaches the dark, precipitous rock to the mainland, turning it into a craggy purgatory for souls already dead – only the body left to follow into the void of terror.

It is an eerie spectacle.

The hostile monolith frowns down on her, as old as the world, warning her about dark forces too powerful for man. The wind assaults her face. It is blowing in from the sea and funnelling its way up through twists in the crags. The crumbling edge she stands on, heavy with moss and lichen, drops sheer to a sea of grim desolation. Gulls scream out in turmoil as they rise and dive and swoop over the churning black water.

How easy it would be to hurl oneself down, and how weirdly tempting these places can be, fascinating and frightening. She unclenches her hand and, instead of herself, Kirsty throws down Trevor's cross, that malign crucifix that was present and compliant during every moment of her suffering.

She licks her hand, the thing must have burnt it, and her palm throbs where she gripped it on the short journey. Fighting back like a living pulse? It seems to know that its future lies at the bottom of the world's shifting oceans, that all it is going to be part of now is the ghostly floatings of jelly fish, the flashings of scales, the processions of lobsters. And the heathen thing, corrupt and defiled, flies into the wind and briefly heads for the sky with the gulls before dropping down to the leaden sea.

She cannot weep for Trevor.

The burn on her arm, which is too deep to heal and will leave a permanent scar like the ugly memory of a Nazi hell, is all Kirsty needs to see to keep her nailed to her awful commitment. Trev used to accuse her of hurting herself, cutting herself with broken glass, bruising herself by deliberately falling downstairs, burning herself on the gas ring, and all for some spurious attention. If she moved during these moments of torture Trev would punish her by doubling the pain. So she had to lie still and endure, willing herself not to scream out loud and so prolong her agony. When she first escaped from his clutches she was puzzled by her initial behaviour – some nights she deliberately inflicted pain on her body, like a nun striving to drive out the devils; her identity somehow depended on pain, pain was such a large part of her life. She scrubbed at her hands till they bled, and stayed awake, shivering, by refusing to pull up her blankets. She felt safe with Mrs Stokes's firm method of cold control, feeling that without such discipline, self-inflicted or otherwise, she might be extinguished completely like other useless human wastage.

Since then, to Kirsty's great relief, this disturbing behaviour has stopped. This fog cleared from her mind one slow patch at a time. She never came closer to insanity than when she tormented herself like this, because where did these shameful needs come from? Perhaps Trev had been right. She began thinking along these lines, not able to understand the motives behind her madness. Magdalene, she feels sure, was behind her recovery. Through all her worst, most painful sufferings she heard her heroine's soothing voice. It came like a glorious reprieve. Because that dark and sinister nun with so much revenge in her heart used such simple and obvious devices to cleanse these sicknesses from her spirit. Kirsty could feel the force invade each separate part of her body – she was a cripple but now she could dance.

'*Sin is the deepest and coldest shadow ever to fall on man,*' goes Magdalene's speech to the drunk after she tore out his tongue. '*Sin tracked the Roman in his conquests, the prophet of Mecca in his religion, the apostles of Judea in their teaching of Christ. It pressed its road into the vestal cells of my convent, it throws its chilly mist around the deathbed of the saint and alights upon the baby head of the darling in the nursery.*

'*It is our holy duty to celebrate sin . . .*'

And it isn't only her mental state with which Kirsty feels so much happier, already she looks like a younger, more radiant person, as if this last summer has ordained her with its bounty and left a particular freshness that has been missing from her for too long. Her skin is clearer, her eyes are brighter, even her teeth seem whiter, and her hair has a new and burnished sheen which she last noticed in childhood.

So she did understand how Avril felt when she set forth to spend her first £5,000 on a complete change of image. Avril is almost unrecognizable as the glum, shy, chubby girl who arrived in that minibus at the Burleston Hotel back in early June. These last few weeks have seen the transformation of Avril, since the day Ed showed his true colours when he met her mother at Happy Stay, when he sided with her mother against her, when he showed not a jot of sensitivity to Avril's ongoing filial hell, and since Graham was charged with murder. Avril is totally unperturbed about the double-murder charges. Oddly, she accepts the press, seems to regard them as part of the norm and is happy to give interviews. 'I am the sister of the killer from hell.'

Perhaps it is shock that has jerked Avril out of her old lethargy, that has slimmed her down a good stone in weight, that has energized her and forced her out of her humble, obsequious ways.

She no longer takes any crap from her mother.

She has taken up smoking. She drinks too much for her own good.

Avril's parents, having taken refuge at the Happy Stay – Richard has taken a month off from his gentlemen's outfitters on compassionate grounds – are now talking of returning to Huyton to face the flak on their home ground.

But when Avril returns from her grand shopping spree, she turns to Kirsty for her opinion. Thank God the kids are still at school: children are so painfully honest.

Her short, spiky hair is an unmellow yellow. She twirls round the caravan patting it, peering into the two small mirrors each time she passes. Her eyebrows have been plucked and replaced by fine brown lines of surprise. Her dolly mouth is a vicious red, which fattens her lips and makes her pout.

'Well? D'you like it?'

Her finger nails are painted luminous green.

'Wow, Avril! It'll take a while to get used to. But, yes, it's quite dramatic and arty. Now you could be a drama student.'

'I'd get chucked out of business studies.'

The first item Avril models is a black leather outfit – a jacket with chains and epaulettes, a skirt, black tights and knee-length boots. She must have ventured into an S&M shop by mistake. She looks like a concentration-camp guard, one of those hard-faced, blond-haired dykes, all she needs is a whip in one hand and a couple of Rottweilers on leads in the other.

What can one say?

One doesn't want to be unkind and, anyway, what does it matter?

'It's angry-looking,' says Kirsty, and then, more positively, 'but confident.'

'Well, I am angry, and confident,' says Avril, striding round. 'That's just what I am.'

The tight leopard-skin-patterned trousers, made in some kind of stretchy silk, do nothing to demonstrate Avril's weight loss. Especially when she wears that short, loose chainmail top with the tassels. She looks like she works the pavements of every Union Street in the land. 'That'll turn all eyes,' says Kirsty.

'But it does suit me, doesn't it?' Avril asks.

'It does, in a funny kind of way,' Kirsty lies.

'I'm no longer ashamed of my body,' says Avril, 'and from now on I'm going to flaunt it.'

'Why not?' says Kirsty weakly. 'But don't let your mother see any of these.'

'I don't intend to,' says Avril, 'but if she sees she sees. It's my life, she can burn in hell for all I care.'

From then on things get seriously kinky and Kirsty wonders which shop Avril went in to find some of that underwear.

Nothing about Avril's new wardrobe is plain, good and made to last, in direct flagrance of her mother's teaching. Frankly, Avril looks cheap and common in every single garment she models, and the thought of this ungodly woman buying a house next door to Kirsty does nothing for her peace of mind.

She's got the kids to consider.

Perhaps it's a good thing that her mother kept such strict control over this outrageously overexposed new Avril. Perhaps Mrs Stott suspected something nobody else could guess at.

Good news from London, however, with an extraordinary change in Bernie's humour. No-one expected this new scenario. Bernie is engaged to her agent – *she says*. Her agent will help her with future scripts, Kirsty need worry no further. Clementine is satisfied with *Magdalene* and the final proofs are on their way.

But what is this new wonderman like?

Is Bernie safe? Or, in her silly impetuosity, has she succumbed yet again to another unhealthy obsession?

But Bernie is in jubilant spirits. ' Mother of God, you wait till you see him.'

'He sounds amazing.'

'More than that, he's a dream. And his house, Kirsty, and his vintage car. He has a butler and walk-in fridge . . .'

'Maybe you should give up your share—'

'No way. I want my independence. Don't you?'

What can a man like that want with Bernie? OK, she is ravishing, and rich men go for beautiful birds, but Bernie is an empty vessel, inflammable and skittish – he must be awed by her literary talents – but he sounds like a useful aid for the cause. Bernie must be encouraged to keep him, if only she can behave herself.

'So someone helped out with *Magdalene*?'

'They should have done that at the beginning. What you did was a waste of time. I expected better than that. But the real bugger is they already want more.'

'Well, they'll have to want then, won't they?'

But Bernie goes on, elated. 'There's more dosh on its way. Much more. Only a few weeks to wait and I'll pay it straight into your banks. It's all much easier now I'm with Rory. And there's a world tour planned for the spring, me and Rory are going off together to do signings and talks and promotion interviews.'

What a gullible halfwit she is. She and Avril both watched the quiz show with tears of laughter rolling down their cheeks. She obviously hasn't learnt a thing. They had to turn it off in the end, they were laughing so hard they woke the kids. 'How are you going to cope?'

'Oh, it's all different now. Rory will help me. He can deal with anything.'

'You'd better hang on to him then. It sounds as if we're going to need him.'

For once Bernie sounds truly happy.

'Pray for me.'

Now then.

Down to work.

Which biscuits should Kirsty choose to take to her hostage in the mine?

Chocolate-chip cookies, gingers, digestives? Or perhaps she should stick to plain cream crackers.

Twenty-Six

Avril watches enviously while Kirsty plays with her kids in the evenings. Jake and Gemma have all the best gear – jeans, sweaters, trainers – not for them the excruciating embarrassment of skirts and cardigans and sensible shoes. They are fed their favourite food; they don't have to come home at teatime and face cold meat and sago, boiled fish, prunes and lumpy custard. And Gemma, who wears cheap jewellery, ladybird tattoos on her face and silver spray in her hair, whose favourite sandals are plastic and sparkly, who has her own Walkman and her own selection of Spice Girls tapes, has a short, fluffy hairstyle, stylishly cut, not pulled back from her forehead in two fat plaits.

They watch endless cartoons on TV.

There are no regular punishments, the kids have no respect for their mother.

They take Mars bars with their packed lunches.

Kirsty hides little notes in the sandwiches which say she loves them.

Why was Avril's childhood so grey? Why did she spend her formative years as a fat and lonely lost soul, under constant watchfulness and the subjection of her will?

What was Mother trying to do to her?

And how about Father, who allowed this to happen to his precious little girl?

Oh yes, thinks Avril, with a festering anger, Father abused her all right, but in his own special way.

Mother is letting it be known that she has decided to go back to Huyton. Avril suspects that Mrs Gilcrest, the owner of the site, is fed up to the teeth of the press attention and has kicked the Stotts out, no messing. Since Avril's vile accusations of sexual abuse by Father, Mother has cut her dead, and Father, obedient as ever, has followed her lead. It's highly unlikely that Mother has confided the truth to Father, sexual matters being taboo, and certainly such unmentionable, unsavoury matters as incest. Mother has probably persuaded Father that she can't forgive Avril for denouncing Graham when she could, for the sake of the family, have kept her big mouth shut.

Poor Graham has now been formally charged with the murder of Edward Board, and the police are still searching for that elusive number four wood.

All is quiet on the night that Mr and Mrs Stott sleep their last sleep in the neat little bunks in the Bluebird caravan. The caravan mats are airing on the clothes horse in the garden.

The day was taken up with spring-cleaning. Every shelf and cupboard was polished and disinfected in readiness for the journey home. Boxes were packed

341

and stacked in the boot of the family's green Ford Sierra. The garden furniture, hardly used in the unforeseen circumstances, was strapped up and lodged securely underneath the caravan table. Avril's mother washed her hair and went to bed with her curlers in and Avril's father's last job of the evening was to clean the caravan windows. He polished them till they shone.

The pot plants are lodged on the back seat already, sturdily held upright with bamboo canes.

Fluffy's bed and blankets are sadly laid out beside them, still hairy.

They have not given her up for good, oh no. They informed the police of her disappearance and put adverts in the local papers. She could turn up, who knows? Miracles do happen. Fluffy is very important now they have lost both son and daughter.

On the caravan table beside the bed is the AA route map home, the car keys, the caravan keys, a disposable lighter in case Mrs Stott wakes up and needs to light her Wright's vaporizer, an empty flask ready for filling, turkey sandwiches wrapped in greaseproof, two half-blackened bananas and the final bill from Mrs Gilcrest.

And thus they prepared for their final journey.

Do it now, Avril, do it.

Avril's malevolent urges, as she sits reading ten doors away, grow massive and overwhelming. Her red gingham curtains are drawn, beyond them the darkness is total. She reads *Magdalene* under the small plastic light stuck to the wall above her bed. She has her own room in the mobile home, more like a broom cupboard but sufficient for her immediate needs. Kirsty has a similar room and the children share a double bed in what Mrs Gilcrest so grandly describes as the master bedroom.

A tawny owl hoots from a stand of trees and the whispering of the sea in the distance sounds like the shushing voice of an overanxious mother.

The night air that slips through the gaps in the rivets seems to revive all Avril's grievances and she sits there on the hard foam mattress, unable to concentrate on the book that normally commands all her attention. Her resentments drain her energy and appear to split her head.

'Thou knowest, Lord, the secrets of our hearts,' is the last sentence she reads before she gets up and stares out at the night. A few dim lights peep between the curtains of some of the caravan windows, although most of the holidaymakers have gone and only the few long-term tenants remain. A fierce white glare of exultation begins to fill Avril's head as, suddenly, she knows what she must do. Have courage! Who dares wins.

What now?

Why wait?

Face the future not the past. You are free, you are rich, you are secure, all doubts and anxieties are wiped away. Graham will be imprisoned for life – a just revenge for his evil ways – and when she thinks about this the harmonious pattern that forms in her head brings Avril serenity and calm.

There is no mutiny of emotions. Avril's conscience is as lucid and clear as it was when she visited Graham in gaol. The Bluebird caravan is just over there. With a thumping heart she opens her door and creeps towards the kitchen. She stands on

343

the top step of their van with the door open, staring out in a kind of ghoulish catalepsy. Furtiveness moves inside her as she glances round to make sure no-one's watching. Something devilish drives Avril on.

Whispers surround her.

Do this and your future will be exquisitely lovely.

They have to be punished, as you were punished.

They have to atone for their sins.

If they won't own up she will own up for them.

Avril bends low under the darkness and scuttles across the grass to the Bluebird. Her large body pushes pinkly against the black of her sheer silk nightdress. The grass is icy cold on her feet. Her breath makes patterns on the night. There is a sulphurous taste in her mouth, a foretaste of the cleansing fire. She knows one window will be open. Mother believes if she sleeps with them closed she will suffocate in the night. As the dark clouds scud above her, Avril discovers a window ajar; she stands on the portable step and leans in.

'Yessss. Do it now, Avril, do it now!' A hiss of a whisper splits the night. Avril jumps half out of her skin and presses a finger to her lips. Dear God, Kirsty will wake them up if she does that again.

Avril, still half hypnotized, shoots back to her own caravan where Kirsty waits at the door with a trancelike look on her face. There are beads of sweat on her forehead. Her breath comes in rasps.

'Avril. Go back. Don't stop. This might be your last chance. They have to atone for their sins in the furnaces of hell; there is no comfort like Calvary.'

Avril's bare feet are wet and frozen. Those whispers she heard, they came from Kirsty through the thin partition walls, Kirsty chanting encouragement with the thin rage of a stiletto. But how did she guess Avril's intentions, or is she just finely tuned to the natural processes of nature?

'I can't,' Avril stutters, 'not now.' But her voice is guttural, deep, nothing at all like her own.

'You have to, there can be no going back.' Kirsty's face is bleared and creased, and her voice is calculated and chilling. She quotes from *Magdalene*. '*Be careful or you will die in your sins. How will you escape if you neglect so great a salvation?*'

And Avril feels herself sucked into Kirsty, cell for cell, blood for blood she feels herself going into her, her soul losing its hold on the world, everything unfocused and ill-defined.

But the shocking sight of Kirsty convulsing – foam edging the corners of her mouth, eyes so violently dilated the pupils appear to be black and her clenched fists raw and purpling – is so repellent, so overwhelming, that Avril, waking from the deepest of sleeps, finds reality quite impenetrable. She pitches forward and hangs onto the door frame, tasting horror on her tongue where her teeth grind and join with saliva to clear a gush of green bile. The stench of her own breath is fetid. What hellish compulsion had driven her on to contemplate the murder by fire of her parents?

With a mighty effort of will Avril draws herself upright; still shaking, she finds and lights a cigarette with all the clumsiness of a non-smoker. The acrid smoke is cleansing, she pulls it down deep into her lungs before puffing it into the quiet night air, turning her back on Kirsty. Who is she to condemn or denounce? Was she, too, metamorphosed into a slathering demon when she had gone creeping across the grass? Was her face a mask of perspiring hatred, bared teeth, demented eyes? Something else is asserting itself, coming on the scene to call the tune and pull the strings.

She still dare not look round to face Kirsty. She doesn't want to see, but the sound of Kirsty's breathing gradually calms to a strangled groan and the sound of silence and sanity slowly re-enters the caravan. All Avril wants to do now is get into bed and sleep.

But if Avril hadn't been interrupted she would have turned on the cooker controls by reaching through the half-opened window, she would have turned on the gas, a thousand punishing sentences rehearsed and ready in her head, mind and body craving an opiate, temples beating, limbs shaking. Filled with the passionate anger of a child, Avril would have dropped to the ground and crawled beneath the caravan, obeying specific directions which reverberated in her brain as automatically as school poetry. With the spanner attached to the big gas bottle she would have twisted the valve to open, wiped the spanner on the edge of her night-dress, and with heart racing and body weak she would have gone back to bed.

As if all this had already been written.

But she hadn't done that. Thank God, she hadn't.

The fiery explosion shoots through her, waking her from the deepest slumber with a piercing scream from Kirsty, 'Get the kids out . . . quick. What's happened? There must have been a bomb!'

Figures stumble about in the night, dashing

346

around like cartoon mice chased by cats with choppers. Crazy torchlights span the confusion. Voices call, and over it all flames the funeral pyre of the Stotts. Parts of the Bluebird spit out of the furnace, wrinkled and black and shooting across the grass like faggots at a public burning.

Which is what this undoubtedly is.

Burn the witch! Burn the warlock! The exultation in Kirsty's eyes makes up for the lack of the chant.

So, they had merely to will it.

'My God, is there anyone in there?'

'Has anyone rung the fire brigade?'

'Poor bastards.'

'You can't get near it for the heat.'

People are beating it off with their arms, even though they stand yards away, and everybody turns red with the glow, or black with the mounting embers.

'It's gonna get the car – stand back.'

Kirsty, like any normal mother, gathers up her children and dashes towards the reception building that is joined to the Gilcrests' bungalow. She doesn't pause to find Avril, Avril notices, watching her go. She doesn't stop to think about Avril, and Kirsty's supposed to be her friend.

The flames start licking the green Ford Sierra, the pride of Father's life. All those Sunday mornings spent cleaning his car while Avril wandered back from Sunday school, the only girl in the street made to go, even in summer when beaches and picnics and barbecues in the garden beckoned. He would smile at her over his foamy bucket, stand back and regard his work with pride as trickles of water ran down the road and into the nearest gutter.

Mother would be inside, cooking the all-weather joint. The joint that would do them for the rest of the week, if she eked it out carefully enough.

Father's Sierra goes with a boom and a series of weak splutters. The boot opens and briefly exposes Mother's neat and careful packing. The two back doors crack and fall off, and there is Fluffy's empty bed. Then the proper fire takes over and threatens to spread to the rest of the site.

A sensible cry of 'keep clear' goes up, and nobody has to be told twice.

'They never stood a hope in hell,' says one of the winter residents grimly.

'They wouldn't have known a thing,' says another, as if that makes dying OK, which it does – what more in life can anyone hope for than a quick and painless death?

'I doubt we'll ever know the cause,' the fireman tells Avril afterwards as they sit in the café sipping tea brewed by Mrs Gilcrest's girl. Avril has covered her silk nightdress with an old towelling dressing gown she hasn't yet got round to throwing out. 'Some of these vans are so damn flimsy they burn like paper, leave nothing but ashes. But I've seen this before, the gas going up, someone only has to forget—'

'But my mother never forgot,' says Avril, wanting to take some blame.

The charcoal-faced fireman shakes his noble head. All firemen are noble to Avril, like ambulance drivers, airline pilots and vets. 'Well, someone forgot last night. Perhaps it was your father. Was he sometimes absent-minded?'

'He could be,' Avril muses sadly, 'at times, but

with Mother behind him he never had much chance. Could it be someone who knows Graham? There are people around like that; they were hanging around the court. They send anonymous letters, make abusive phone calls, push filth through people's letter boxes – that's what Mother was dreading happening. Perhaps some lunatic was out for revenge.'

The fireman, doubtful, compresses his lips. 'That's not very likely . . .'

'Yes, but—'

'You've been to hell and back just lately.' The fireman puts a strong arm around her shoulders. 'Mrs Gilcrest told us. What with all that trouble with your brother, and now this. You poor kid. I doubt if you can take much more.'

So Avril collapses completely against his manly chest. She is too confused to do much else.

'They were going home this morning,' she weeps. 'This was their last night at the Happy Stay. If only they'd gone yesterday, or when they were meant to go last month.'

'That's fate for you,' says the fireman grimly.

'I didn't touch that caravan, Kirsty, you know that, you saw me.'

Other than this half admission their talk is innocent, like neighbours commiserating over a fence.

'I know, I know. Was it real? And now I really don't know . . . to lose both your parents like that, and then there was Ed, and all this with Graham.'

'And Fluffy is still missing.'

'I know.' Kirsty shivers. 'It's awful, all this grief, on you.'

There is the strain of careful avoidance. They tiptoe round one another politely.

'Perhaps we should never have come here,' says Avril, 'perhaps there's a curse on the place.'

'Perhaps there is,' says Kirsty, tucking up the children, hoping for a couple of hours of sleep before they get up to face the new day.

Dawn breaks as they sit at the table trying not to notice the steam coming up from the ground and the black, charred gap ten doors along. The remains of the Bluebird have been scraped away. The nearest caravans, though still standing, are streaked with black fire damage, so the whole area, never a picture, now resembles some wartime bomb site, and one can imagine red poppies growing here one day in a happier future. Twisting through the cracks with the brambles.

'I never made my peace with her,' says Avril mournfully.

'She wasn't a peaceful person, Avril,' Kirsty gently reminds her friend.

'And poor Father. So helpless.' Avril brings a hand to cover the gasp in her mouth. 'I wonder if Fluffy knew, if she had some sixth sense?'

'Animals often do.'

'I wonder if we'll ever find her?'

'She's been gone a long time now,' says Kirsty.

It is time to prepare for a change.

It is no longer necessary for Avril or Kirsty to exist in a shabby mobile home. It isn't seemly for Avril to have to be reminded constantly of the tragedy ten doors along, and the children have been badly disturbed by the whole gruesome business.

But Kirsty's children have settled down happily in the small local school, and she is reluctant to move them out of the catchment area. She doubts she will ever want to go to live in London, like Bernie, whatever the success of *Magdalene*, however much money she makes.

'But don't let me influence you, Avril. You must do what you want to do, especially now. You have no family to speak of, no roots, no commitments.'

'I'd never have gone back to Huyton anyway.'

Avril feels ashamed because she has nowhere to go. Neither has she made any admirable plans, unlike Kirsty, who wants to better herself. Perhaps, when the final payment is made and she knows exactly how much she's worth, Avril might decide to run a small business: a boutique, a travel agency, a mobile disco. Something glamorous like that, something that would fit with her new, upmarket image, but until then she dreads being left to live alone.

'You can stay with me till you make up your mind. But I'm going to rent to start with, until I'm sure where I want to be,' says Kirsty. 'They're so cheap at this time of year. I've got it all in my head,' she laughs, 'a lovely big farmhouse with open fires and a stream in the garden.'

'I could help you with the children,' says Avril, hating to seem clingy. 'And if Trevor should come calling again, two of us would be better than one. Together we could outwit him.'

'If only we could find somewhere by Christmas.'

'A proper Christmas,' Avril dreams on. 'A huge tree with needles. Tasteless decorations. No Queen's speech. Stay in bed all day if we like, just eating chocolate.'

'Christmas is going to be hell for you.'

'I know.' Avril remembers all those years – church on Christmas morning and being dragged away from her presents. And then off to Granny's cold house, doing the endless sprouts, and the dragged-out formal mealtimes, silence after lunch for the Queen, Grandpa calling from his bed, Father and Mother at each other's throats, one Babycham allowed, that's all, and everyone watching her drink it in case she has a habit, like Graham's.

Thinking of Graham in his cell, hopefully squeezed in with three or four others. They get turkey and Christmas pudding, she knows, but Avril imagines what it's like – cold, stringy and reheated from frozen. Peas hard and brown and gravy gone sticky. No presents for Graham – Granny and Grandpa won't send him any, they only gave handkerchiefs with AS on the corners, and that was to Avril, who had done nothing wrong.

Hah. No booze for Graham this year.

Hah. No rampages with the lads.

Hah. No raucous football match and home with frost on his scarf, while Avril stayed in watching telly, being told not to be greedy every time she looked at the dates.

But is Kirsty speaking in tongues? Is Kirsty still possessed? Has she forgotten that malignant demonry on the night of the fire? Is she trying to pretend nothing happened, nothing was said? Kirsty is self-sufficient now and puffed up with new self-confidence. Kirsty doesn't want Avril hanging around her new little family. Look how

352

she tore off with the kids when she felt their lives were in danger, never a thought for Avril, who feels hurt and outraged by that, and it was Avril's parents going up in smoke. It was Avril's parents who couldn't be identified because they were so badly charred.

No sooner has Avril's anger burned out when something else comes along to stir it up, some other resentment to corrode her system, as if there is no end to it all. Perhaps she should spend Christmas day in retreat, follow Magdalene's example: eat simply, celebrate calmly, wallow in sorrow and repentance before a couple of plain white candles, and only go out after dark, dressed to kill.

Twenty-Seven

Rory Coburn has worked very hard to get where he is today and he needs to maintain his outstanding success in order to pay off three former wives. He has no intention of marrying again. His bachelor existence, with Bentley to look after him, suits him and his career well. Fraternizing with the great and the good, attending important social events, being seen networking with the powerful – this essential side to his work took its toll on his marriages, but he is happier now than he has been in years.

He has the respect of his colleagues.

He has the love and loyalty of his authors.

He has made enemies along the way, but that is inevitable.

Yes, a contented man with a highly successful business behind him.

That was until the phone call.

That incredible, horrendous phone call, which made him shrivel up on his bed and wrap himself up tight in the sheets like a reluctant chrysalis.

He gets out of bed, eventually, still shaking, and drives his Model T Ford at speed over to the mews flat. Bernie is pacing the drawing room, flounced in a Hollywood-style négligé that frills to the floor in diminishing blues, pulling hard on a cigarette.

'You didn't write it,' says Rory, still trying to take in the enormity of Bernie's confession. 'You couldn't have written it, could you?' He slaps his forehead with his hand. 'Jesus Christ, I knew it, I knew it!'

'Have a drink, Rory,' says Bernie. 'It's not the end of the world.'

'It comes pretty damn near,' says Rory, imagining the publicity, the shame and the scandal, all his credibility down the drain in one little gurgling whirlpool. How many authors would he lose? All of them most probably. Nobody wants to be associated with an agent who is a fool and a prat. And, oh God, how they pushed her, how they exploited this girl, particularly the fact that she's young and Irish and beautiful, the personality thing overtook the book. If she'd been old and covered with warts the book would have had to stand alone, and it would have done, magnificently. *Magdalene* never needed the hype that Coburn and Watts sought to give it in order to make more money, attract more punters, impress the media and the publishers, both UK and foreign. They picked up the baton and ran with it.

The world is more fascinated by this waiflike author than with the blasted novel itself. And it all happened so swiftly and naturally, as if some sorcery was in the air.

With a shaking hand Rory pours a stiff brandy. He is not his old suave self tonight. Bentley is up to his old tricks again and Rory can't take much more.

This 'author' might be startlingly beautiful, fun-loving and childlike, but other than that she is one-dimensional. Spend more than one hour in her company and you yawn and seek diversions. Semi-literate, uncultured and disgracefully educated, Bernie displays an astonishing disinterest in anything that doesn't directly infringe upon her life, and she is an unlikely candidate for change.

'Tell me this is an attention ploy.'

'Why would I want your attention, Rory?'

'If you didn't write *Magdalene*, who did?'

'God knows. All Kirsty did was rewrite it.'

'*Kirsty?*' His face burns. This goes from bad to worse. He will not be conned a second time. He settles down in a large leather armchair and regards Bernadette through narrowed eyes. 'Kirsty? Your friend, the chambermaid at the hotel? You are telling me that this girl rewrote a novel that already existed?'

Bernadette slows down her pacing and stops before the false-flame fire (top of the range): it crackles and burns with a magical reality. She seems to be drinking gin, or water. Energized by whatever it is, her green eyes, which habitually sparkle, are as excited as emeralds tonight, her cheeks have two pink patches in the centre of each and her lips are slightly parted in the way that makes Rory think of orgasm. What the hell is she about? Where is this weirdo coming from?

'Yes. Kirsty Hoskins. She found the old book in the hotel library. She's a battered wife with two kids who came to work in Cornwall the same day as I did. She's still there now, living in squalor in some caravan park.'

'Kirsty and Avril' – the names are familiar – 'your "partners". Those women you split the money with.'

'Well, now you know the reasons for that.'

'So where does Avril come in? What part is she supposed to have played in this ridiculous scam?'

'Avril typed it and corrected the spelling mistakes.'

'Aha, an intellectual obviously. And where does Avril work, might I ask? As a lavatory attendant, a laundry maid?'

'Avril worked in the office.'

Rory lays his empty glass on the shiny arm of his chair. Bentley was missing from the house when he went up to bed earlier tonight. Rory had pressed redial on the phone only to hear the familiar and numbingly painful reply of the Boys' Own Agency hotline. He splays one hand on each arm, spreading his fingers to relax them. But his finely drawn features sharpen. 'And why have you suddenly decided to come out with the truth?'

'Because I couldn't do it.' For the first time Bernadette shows some emotion, her voice shakes slightly. 'The strain, the telly and then this tour. And Clementine thinks something's up, she's not stupid, and with nobody to speak to I felt so helpless and alone.'

'Did you? Did you really?' asks Rory with smooth sarcasm and not a note of the sympathy this wretched creature seems to expect.

'I expected more support from you,' says Bernadette curiously.

'I went with you to the BBC,' he says coldly. 'To my shame. We even had a meal out afterwards.'

And Bernadette suddenly bursts out, 'But you didn't enjoy being with me, did you? And you didn't bother to pretend you did.'

What's this? Hang on? Don't say this is personal. Millions of dollars boiled down to a mishmash of girlish pride. Her face is that of a stupid child who has been refused a toy.

'What did you expect me to do?'

She sits in the chair opposite his and drops her hands in her lap. Her eyes close and remain closed. There are smears of last night's purple make-up on her eyelids. 'You all went on somewhere afterwards – don't try to tell me you didn't – you all went on to somebody's house and you didn't think to ask me. I had to come back here. There's always this door and I can't get through.'

'Bernie, you would have been bored stiff.'

'But I wasn't even asked.'

Rory's last thread of control snaps. His face is as stiff as a death mask. 'So it's this, a sense of vengeance, that has prompted you to confess tonight. To get back at me, personally, and the perceived snub to your own self-importance, otherwise you would have gone on quite happily with this monstrous deception.'

Bernadette's sobs drive him to distraction. She hides her face in her hands. 'I thought you cared about me.'

'Damn you! *Damn you!* Did I ever say or do anything to lead you to think that?'

'You said I was beautiful. You said I had wonderful talent. You said I would be a household name, that *Magdalene* was the most moving book you had ever read.'

'But it's my job to say these things . . .'

'I felt important . . .' she gasps, forcing her voice with immense effort.

'You silly little fool.'

'You made Dominic look simple.'

'Ah, I see, how very ironic, so I am to blame for his departure.' This is getting ridiculous. Rory steadies his voice and breathes in deeply. 'Have you any awareness at all of the consequences of your behaviour? Did it ever occur to you that you might finish us, and our business?'

'*You?*'

'Coburn and Watts. Let alone the effect this is going to have on all those publishers, TV and film companies who have paid you so much money.'

'But they don't have to know.' She is sobbing openly now. 'This can be our secret.'

'Of course they all have to know.' Rory is totally bewildered. This child-woman has no standards, no values, no morality – something Rory finds puzzling. 'We can't go on with this now that I know. Good God, I have my integrity. The truth could come out at any time. Whoever wrote the damn thing is going to come forward one day, believe me.'

'It was Kirsty's idea, not mine, I swear to you.'

'OK. OK.' They can't go forward until she calms down. Rory holds both hands up to act as imaginary buffers. Perhaps Bentley will be back by the time he gets home. Rory imagines the hellish row that is bound to follow and flinches. 'So why did Kirsty get you to act as the author?'

'Because she was terrified of publicity. This violent madman was after her and all she wanted was peace and quiet and a few thousand quid to help her out. Nobody imagined *Magdalene* would cause such a fuss, and I seemed like the obvious choice.'

'Lapping up publicity as you do?'

Bernie sniffs, her sobs becoming quieter due to sheer exhaustion. Her response comes slowly and miserably. 'Yes, I did. But it's different now.'

'You're telling me it's different.' They cannot go ahead with this, it's all over. The writs for plagiarism that they would face would bankrupt not just himself, but everyone who ever touched *Magdalene*. The costs and damages would hit the roof, probably break world records.

And here was he, London's most prestigious agent, thinking he was on to a winner. Extraordinary how Bernie, with her pert provocativeness, fooled them all – Candice, Clementine and himself, never mind the press and the literary establishment. Rory gives her a long, hard look; the kid is quite an actress.

By now it's gone three in the morning and Mrs Parfait, having heard goings-on from below, pops up in her rollers and manly plaid dressing gown to ask if there is anything they want. From her closed expression she suspects she has dropped in on some hanky panky – the young Miss Kavanagh in tears, Mr Coburn drawn and white. From what she has gathered so far from Miss Kavanagh's behaviour – dancing alone in front of the mirror, filling the road outside with her decibels and drinking her fill at the bar – she thinks Mr Coburn might have bitten off more than he can chew this time. She descends to her garage home again and nudges Mr Parfait awake with the gossip.

But Mr Parfait dozes on. What the folks upstairs get up to is none of his damn business.

'So where do we go from here?' Rory asks eventually, too depressed for the energy of anger.

'I suppose I'll have to disappear. Perhaps you can find the original author.'

Oh Jesus Christ. Wouldn't that give the literary world something to split their sides over? He can hear them now, 'What's this then, Rory? A new quiz game? Pick your author?' And Bentley is not renowned for his loyalty to losers. Success is what turns Bentley on – success and power.

'Can this one manage to write a letter without a thesaurus?'

'Wham, bam, thank you, maam.'

'I hear there's a horse down the road swears he's written a book.'

Rory sits with his head right back, easing his taut neck muscles. 'That is out of the question.'

'Of course, I could keep pretending if I was given more help,' lisps Bernie.

Rory manages to lift his head and look his lost prodigy in the eyes, such curious, devious eyes, the eyes of a mischievous faerie.

'Explain,' he says, wearily.

'Well, I might be able to struggle on and carry it off if you helped me. It was a very old book, the author is probably dead . . .'

This is one manipulative woman. Don't say she thinks he will carry on the scam. Don't say she's that ignorant. 'Explain,' he orders again.

'I'd have to be with you,' Bernadette goes on, lowering those smudgy eyelids, and the end of her tongue curls and briefly touches her upper lip. 'You'd have to be near me all the time.'

'Oh yes, yes, of course. I see. Just in case you

dropped a clanger, got caught off balance on the phone, or were suddenly tempted to destroy me.' He rises from his chair in anger and hangs over hers, fists pressing on the arms, and his body threatens her curled-up space. 'You brainless little twat.' His voice rises. 'And how the hell do you imagine I could trust you for one second? One wrong move and I'd be straight in the shit.'

'No, no,' cries Bernie, 'I'd never do that. I would never let you down. I swear.'

'I expect you told that to Dominic, and God knows how many others. What do you want, Bernie? Men chained to your wrist like dogs? And how do you imagine I'd feel? Don't you think I would despise you more than I already do?'

'You don't despise me, Rory.'

But Rory gives a contemptuous laugh. 'You don't despise me, that's the trouble. You're driven by some twisted obsession, some screwball afraid to grow up. Don't try to deny it, because it's there for any cretin to see in your eyes; it's sickening, fawning stuff, the way you gaze up at me like some beaten puppy, and you've not stopped flirting since I came in.'

'Who the sodding hell d'you think you are?' Bernadette pushes him off in humiliation and fury. 'How dare you say that, you pompous bastard! You cocky sod, with your daft airs and graces.'

Rory stands by the fireplace calmly, smiling at the result of his challenge. 'I don't think any arrangement between us would last very long, Bernadette, do you?'

'Have it your way then,' she says, her face still flaming with mortification, her secret so obviously out. She has been exposed, helpless and out of control, swamped by violent emotions, humiliating and weak. 'Go public then. Tell everyone. Let them laugh in your face. It's no skin off my nose. Admit you've been conned by an Irish barmaid with only art and RE GCSEs.'

'Quite frankly,' says Rory, smiling sadly, 'I don't know what to do. But what you're suggesting is ludicrous.'

Extraordinary. She seems to think he's changing his mind. 'I'd never let you down, I swear.' Her stare is rapt and helpless. 'What I feel for you is so strong, Rory. For the first time in my life I'm in love. Don't make fun of me just because you're clever.'

'But, Bernadette, hold on, get real. I don't feel the slightest thing for you, I never have and never will. All I feel right now is disgust.'

'But that might change.'

'For Christ's sake, what books do you read?'

'I don't read books, only magazines.' She tosses the hair from her face, shaking her head so the long swinging mass of it springs and bobs behind her. Still playing games.

'What? You have quite seriously never read one book in your life?'

'Only Roddy Doyle in English.'

He looks at Bernadette with curious speculation. He sighs. 'I'm tired. I've had enough, I'm going home.'

'Can I come with you?'

'I don't think so.'

She gives a gentle sigh and lowers her lashes. She still doesn't get it. 'Will you ring me tomorrow?'

'I expect I'll have to.'

'Will you think about what I've said?'

'I'm going to have to think about everything.'

And she stands gazing wistfully after him.

Why did she do it? Why did she self-destruct like that?

'Follow your dreams and aspirations, never deny your emotions,' Kirsty said when they last spoke. But Kirsty meant her to hang on to Rory. Rory and Bernie together would make a remarkable team, another bonus for *Magdalene*. Nothing else seems to count with Kirsty.

'Who dares wins. Nothing is impossible.' And her old friend, misled by Bernie's romantic misconceptions, sounded so positive. Her words had had a profound effect, but if Kirsty finds out she's blown it . . .

But she can't blame this on Kirsty. Bernadette falls into bed and buries her face in the pillow. How she longs to follow him out, beg him to look at her, touch her and kiss her. She is engulfed by the clean, vigorous male smell of his body, the sheen across his white teeth, even the texture of his skin, which rouses a sudden, unbearable longing to touch it with her fingertips. His domination of her is so complete that she has only one wish, to please Rory in any way she can and gain his forgiveness and approval. Just the tone of his voice seems to stroke her arms, her back, her breasts, making her grow warm and luxurious. Even when she fails to understand what he means, she longs for him to go on speaking. Please him enough, push him enough, and he will give her what she so desperately desires.

But what fatal damage has she done, driven to

this self-abasing confession by her own egotistical needs? She really believed she could blackmail Rory, force him to need her as desperately as she needs him. Tie him to her by deceit if necessary. Magdalene, like Kirsty, would stop at nothing to have her way. But what will happen to the book now if Rory decides to opt out? He can't be allowed to – *he can't!* He must feel something for her, surely it is not possible to love so fiercely without getting some of it back? She will never be able to face Kirsty or Avril. And she lied and told them she was engaged, beguiled into thinking she was jumping the gun by the odd day or two. Had she misread him so completely? What will happen to the money she is already so busily spending, and why couldn't she have thought this through instead of acting on furious impulse?

He said he would ring her tomorrow, didn't he? Well, maybe that is his way of leaving his options open.

He'll be back, she assures herself, and when he's ready she will be waiting.

Bentley is still not back when Rory arrives home, defeated.

It's too late for sleep, and anyway, sleep is out of the question.

He broods on alone in his study, dazed in the silence, well into the dawn.

He faces a life of mockery, pity from some, open gratification from others, a hard slog to win back a reputation that has taken him a lifetime to build. It will probably be impossible for him ever to rise to the heights he is used to, to regain the respect he now takes for granted, to repeat the successes he has achieved. And Bentley will doubtless consider him finished. And all because of some ignorant barmaid who obviously obsesses over every man she meets.

You win some, you lose some.

Why can't he just shrug his shoulders and square them to the burden of life?

Perhaps he could if it wasn't for Bentley and his dark and reckless needs.

But the black mood grabs hold of him and Rory opens his desk drawer and brings out a bottle of barbiturates, which he'd removed from some suicidal author only weeks before. Slowly he crosses the room and picks up a full bottle of brandy. Ironically, the first proper proof of *Magdalene* lies proudly before him on his desk. He sits in the chair in front of it, leaning forward, both arms extended, fingers clasped. He does not sway or moan. Sometimes a shiver runs through him. Soon he will be done for ever with this crazy world.

Twenty-Eight

Candice Love is mortified.

Rory Coburn, a broken man, attempted suicide last week.

He did, however, have the strength of mind to leave her a note before he finished his pills. She would have been happier not to have read it. She will have to go job-seeking soon, and when they hear who she is they will laugh. Perhaps she could be a librarian, or a teacher; change careers, change hairstyles.

Tragic. Because Candice is a good agent and her skills would be wasted.

Still smarting from the ignominious discovery, and keeping her head well down for the moment, most days Candice still sits in a high, plastic, air-conditioned cubicle going through a big, fat slush pile, hanging on at the office till the shit hits the fan. Several of the manuscripts, dog-eared and smeared by their travels, she recognizes as those she has rejected in the past.

But she turns it all off when she gets home; she rarely picks up a book, she would rather watch the soaps on TV, particularly *Brookside*. But what is this? She has just settled down to an evening's viewing when the doorbell jarringly interrupts. A kindly neighbour has taken in her parcel and now rings and deposits it on the step. It looks suspiciously like work to Candice. Some blasted client has had the nerve to post this directly to her home hoping for priority treatment. She will put it at the bottom of the pile, and why must authors use so much parcel tape? She knows these parcels are precious, many of them come recorded, but they don't give a thought to the unfortunate receiver who has to battle with scissors and fingers to wrench the contents from the damn Jiffy bag.

The stale smell of age that seeps from this half-opened parcel is pungent in her modern home, dominated by computers, faxes, shiny new paper and print. Candice delves further and brings out a rust-coloured book with the title stamped simply on the front. '*Magdalene* by Ellen Kirkwood.' The fatal title leaps out at her and her eyes narrow suspiciously. And the date inside – she hardly dares open it with these trembling fingers – is 1913. Published by Bryant, a publishing house she vaguely remembers, which disappeared decades ago.

She grabs the parcel and squints at the postmark. This was posted in Plymouth yesterday, first class, but why here, why her? She has never heard of Ellen Kirkwood and there's nothing here about the author; the fly leaf has been left blank. Tentatively, forgetting to breathe, she opens the first page and reads fast. Is this it? The book that is about to make Coburn and Watts the laughing stock of the literary world? She thinks ruefully of the hyped-up blurb used by the excitable newspapers: 'masterpiece for

368

the new millennium', 'predicted bestseller of all time', 'read it next February and be changed for life'.

But it *is* the same. Shit. In the false manuscript these lovely descriptions had been cut short, but other than that it's mostly the same. Candice flicks to the last few pages and reads them avidly. The characters are the same. The plot is identical. The beautiful style is a replica. My God, she cannot believe her eyes. So Rory's revelations were true and she holds the original in her hands. So weird that nobody's heard of it, a true literary masterpiece, a novel to equal any of the greatest and most revered classics.

1913. An unusual book for that era. Would the public have accepted a book as black and complicated as *Magdalene* back then? Weren't they a protected bunch, cosied by heavy censorship? But no, this was a time, according to the young Bertrand Russell, when, 'the barbaric substratum of human nature was being tapped'. People were in shock, their confidence low. The *Titanic* had sunk one year before, suffragettes were smashing shop windows and dying under the hooves of horses, the kaiser was rattling his bayonet, Kitchener was ready to point his finger; in other words, as usual, the country was in crisis.

Just ripe for a book like *Magdalene*.

Now she knows the name of the author perhaps she can salvage something from the ashes. It must be out of copyright. Maybe she can trace Kirkwood's descendants and find out more about her, mollify the publishers, cash in on the wretched publicity. After all, there's no real need for Candice to go under with Coburn and Watts. She wasn't paid enough anyway. Candice will use her initiative. Anything to fill in time before the hideous truth comes out.

Who is Ellen Kirkwood? What sort of life did this genius lead? And why does nobody know her name?

How can Kirsty leave the area?

She hasn't finished with Trevor yet.

No, not by a long chalk.

The messenger came with the bad news, a police-woman with her hat off, looking doleful.

'I'm sorry to inform you of this, Mrs Hoskins, I can't tell you how upset I am, but your husband's hire car has been found on the cliffs at Pengellis Rock. We have only just traced the driver.'

'Oh no!' Kirsty said. 'Don't tell me!'

'We don't know for certain, of course, but we've been searching for his body and it honestly doesn't look too good, if, as you say, you two had an argument on the day he came to see you.'

'Poor Trevor,' said Kirsty, wiping an eye. 'He wasn't always a good man, but I was used to him. Poor Trevor.'

Today, after she's waved the children to school and dropped Avril at Safeways with a comprehensive list, she pops over to the Burleston with a packet of Jaffa cakes and a large bottle of Highland Spring water. Also in her bag are the ultra-sharp dress-making scissors she removed from Avril's knitting bag.

Glancing to her right and left, although this part of the gardens is rarely used, she lets herself into the cottage that was once to be her home. She and Avril are due to look round a little old three-bedroomed cottage tomorrow; they haven't told the children yet in case they get too excited, but Jake and Gemma seem thrilled to bits with their new caravan home.

They don't mention Trev any more.

Nobody mentions Trevor.

'Trevor,' Kirsty calls, 'it's me.'

There is a small rustle from the hole, nothing more.

'I've brought you more water and something to eat. I expect you could do with something, after all, it's been a long time.'

Four days.

Kirsty kneels where the lino slopes to the edge of nowhere.

'But before I lower these down, Trev, I want you to do something for me.' The smile on her face is a grim one, and her dulled eyes show little emotion. 'Can you hear me, Trev? Are you going to do what I want?'

A throaty grunt is her only answer.

She ties the scissors to the rope and starts lowering them down. 'Remember strip poker, Trev, and the way there was always a forfeit? That was the fun of the game, wasn't it, having to carry out the forfeit? Well, I've got a forfeit for you because we want to make this fun. I'm not a miserable person with no sense of humour, as you used to describe me, and I'm going to prove that to you now.'

There is still no definite response from the semi-darkness of the hole.

'In a minute these scissors will reach you. When

you undo the knot I want you to cut off your left ear lobe, just the little fat bit at the bottom – it's OK it's mostly gristle; there aren't a lot of nerves there – and wrap it in the bit of gauze you will find attached and then send it all back up to me.'

There is a terrible moaning sound. Kirsty edges forward to look. He seems to be squatting down in the sludge, his back against the wall. The golf club is leaning against it, too. He looks like a gnome with a fishing rod, and she is tempted to laugh hysterically. But the stench is overpowering; she has to move back slightly and cover her nose and mouth with a tissue.

'Kirsty.' Trev says her name gingerly, like someone who's just found his memory.

'Don't bother to talk, Trevor, I know how hard that must be for you. Even painful. Just do as I say and I'll send you the water straight after, I promise.'

The rope hangs limp for a while, a good two minutes – but Kirsty's got all the time in the world – before there's a gentle twiddling on the end and she knows Trevor is unwrapping the scissors.

'That's it, Trevor. It's probably easier if you do it quickly, don't think about what you're doing too much. In fact, think about something else completely; it works sometimes, I used to do it. I used to imagine all sorts of things while you were torturing me, you know. I used to pretend I was somebody else: Allis, or Melody out of my book, being wined and dined, or lying beside some lagoon with a cocktail and parrots flying overhead, monkeys gibbering in the trees, a gentle, handsome man at my side with eyes full of love for me.'

Still no reply from the sulking Trevor.

'I don't want to hurry you, that's the last thing I want to do, but I have to get back to Safeways by eleven. I'm having lunch in town with my friend Avril and I daren't be late.'

It sounds as if he's getting up. That must be a good sign. If he has the strength to get up he has the strength to cut off his ear lobe.

'I'll do it with you if it would help,' says Kirsty, 'you know, like you pull a plaster off a child's knee – one, two, three – it works better if you do it together. Come on, Trev, here we go – one, two . . . three.'

Kirsty leans forward again and listens.

'Don't be such a coward. People say they get shot and don't feel the pain until later. And remember, you'll be enjoying your water and your biscuits so much you probably won't have any reaction.'

A muffled scream comes from below, raw with agony. Kirsty closes her eyes until it fades into silence again. Then, very slowly, the thin rope begins to sway and she knows Trevor is attaching something. She won't make it worse by congratulating him, she won't add insult to injury.

She stifles a laugh and bares her teeth. She waits a few minutes before she starts to pull. Good. Trevor has done what she told him. The piece of flesh is wrapped in gauze, but already blood is dripping through because the ear is a tender part and bleeds profusely. Hardly able to look at the gore, let alone touch it, she removes the scissors and proceeds to cut one foot off the rope and the soggy mess comes off with it. She slips it into a small Spar bag and ties up the end with a shudder.

Laughter wells up in her throat again and she has

to swallow it down; it's not decent, not at a time like this. She coils the fresh end of rope round the bottled water and the Jaffa cakes, ties it and slowly lets them down. Let him think she is relenting; how many times has he done that to her – just when she thought the worst was over he would put the mat on the kitchen floor and push her head into a basin of slops. 'Bitch. Know your place. You don't eat with me at the bleeding table.'

And she can't overcome the awful horror that, even now, weak and wounded though he is, Trev might manage to drag himself out.

The hole is a jagged one, three feet across at the widest part, so if Kirsty is going to cover it over she needs a good-sized slab of wood, and the scarred and mouldering kitchen table looks as if it might do the job.

First she throws down his clothes. In a few more minutes he's not going to care whether he is naked or not. He might even think she is going to release him. Then, after covering her face with both hands to protect it from the dust, she kicks down the surrounding rubble, her housewifely heart gladdened by the way this neatens the kitchen. Weak groanings come from below. Kirsty smiles; Magdalene is with her, her hero shadows each move like a haunting. Next, like a woman possessed, Kirsty gathers up every household appliance: pots, pans, an iron, a bucket, ashtrays and two electric fires, the trappings of life, the accumulation of rubbish that kept her Trev's prisoner for eight hideous years. She rips the curtains from the pelmets and drags the blankets from the mouldy beds. She flings all these down the gap in the floor, using the floor mop as a plunger to force them further and tighter, down, down, into the grave.

'DIE. DIE. DIE.'

'God moves in a mysterious way his wonders to perform.'

Her strength is formidable. She is filled with a calm resolve. Nothing seems too heavy, too awkward. When she is satisfied that she can't cram any more in, she drags the table across to the shaft, turns it on to its back and manoeuvres it carefully so it covers up all signs of disturbance.

Kirsty would rather move into the farmhouse before Avril faces the inquest. That experience will be traumatic. Even though she is innocent, much better to have a warm house to come home to, a bath she can relax in, proper hot water, a decent cooker, a comfortable bed instead of a shelf with a hard foam slither of a mattress.

Publication date – 6 February.

When the proofs arrived from the publisher Kirsty had burst with enormous pride as she'd held *Magdalene* to her with all the gentleness of a newborn child. It was like getting your dream at Christmas, the wish you had sent up the chimney with the smoke: the new bike, the pram, the Barbie palace all lit up. So often the toy meant everything because Christmas itself was always sad with Dad trying to do his best and her brother, Ralph, going off to friends. If she'd had a mother it might have been different, but she never blamed her mother for dying. Dad gave her the love he could, but a child is no company for a man; he would rather have gone to the pub to play darts and Kirsty always knew that. They mostly ended up watching sport on the box, he on the lager and she on the Coke.

She drew in the newly printed aura of *Magdalene* with a sigh of ecstatic satisfaction – how much improved this new copy was compared to the musty pages of the original. There were only two copies in the package, one for her and another for Avril, so she couldn't do what she'd promised and give a copy to Mrs Stokes. But she showed her the book all the same, and, for the first time ever, Mrs Stokes looked impressed.

'I never thought this would really happen. I thought it was all a flash in the pan.'

'So did I,' said Kirsty.

At the new and impressive British Library Candice Love does her research.

Wherever she looks, on computer or within reference book, she cannot find a mention of the author Ellen Kirkwood, which is strange and unlikely bearing in mind the novelist's genius. Has someone, for some nefarious reason, deleted all reference to it? Hardly conceivable given the amount of data there is. Is it remotely possible that some joker has had this old copy printed and professionally aged like the Hitler diaries? But forgery seems rather extreme; her imagination is playing tricks.

There must be a mention somewhere.

It's only a simple question of looking in the right place.

But there's no mention of Ellen Kirkwood in any biographical dictionary, nor in the annals of previous authors stretching back through the centuries.

Because the Jiffy bag was posted in Plymouth, Candice moves over to local periodicals. It is remotely possible that the book was limited to local distribution, although why a novel of such giant stature should be treated in this way is a puzzle she cannot solve.

Tired and bewildered, but totally determined to discover the credentials of this missing person for reasons of her own, she is eventually forced to resort to checking births, marriages and deaths. The fact that Kirkwood only wrote one book unfortunately means nothing. Some authors have only one book in them, particularly in those days when it wasn't expected that they should bang out so many. There was silly money around even then; long before Kirkwood's time Dickens was paid £7,500 for *The Mystery of Edwin Drood*, and George Eliot got £10,000 for *Romola*, a fortune in those days.

Candice has one date to go on, and that is 1913, the date when *Magdalene* was supposedly published. She might as well start there, but she is prepared for a daunting task which might take her days, or even weeks. Candice will bide her time hiding in here, waiting for the scandal to break. Her mobile is firmly switched off.

'Ellen Kirkwood . . . died 1913. Plymouth.'

She jumps as the name leaps from the page. Could this be the same Ellen Kirkwood? If so, she died the year the book came out. That is extraordinary and, for the author, presumably most unfortunate.

She has nothing more to go on. So Candice moves back to the local reference sections. She ploughs through them all afternoon only stopping for an apple and a Marmite and cucumber sandwich around three o'clock. On screen she flicks through tomes about local dignitaries till her eyes ache, reformers and performers that drive her silly. Pages and pages of ancient newspapers all harping on about threatened war, politics, crime and punishment – the *Western Morning News*, the *Evening Herald* . . .

An unnatural hush gathers round her.

The bang of a door makes her start.

She suddenly hears clocks ticking where there was silence before.

'Kirkwood apprehended for vile murder.'

'Sensation, more bodies found in Kirkwood case.'

'Kirkwood shows no emotion in court.'

'Kirkwood sentenced to death by hanging.'

The police soon realized they were dealing with, not the ignorant ladies' maid they'd assumed, but a woman of high education and exceptional ingenuity . . .

Ellen Kirkwood was a privileged child brought up by a professional and Christian family. Educated at St Jude's Roman Catholic Academy for Girls until she was expelled for stealing, and disowned by her family at the age of fifteen, Miss Kirkwood then quickly descended through society's ranks until she ended up in the gutter, a fallen woman, where the Salvation Army found her and offered a helping hand. Eventually, being well mannered and well spoken, she found employment as a lady's maid at the home of eminent politician Sir Michael Geary, and it was from this innocent gentleman's house that she started a life of chronic deceit, setting off on nocturnal wanderings, the violent and gruesome consequences of which ended up with cold, premeditated slaughter, the details of which were explained in court for all to hear.

It is still not known how many young men met their deaths at this evil murderess's hand.

Throughout her trial, Miss Kirkwood displayed an iron calm, an astonishing self-control, a power to hide all feelings.

Ellen Kirkwood's just punishment for her ghastly and wicked crimes was delayed for two months to allow for the birth of her illegitimate child. She was buried in the precincts of the prison where she was last confined.

Jesus Christ Almighty.

So – Candice Love runs a hand through uncharacteristically messy hair – *Magdalene*, the masterpiece, was possibly never published. The copy she has in her hand is most likely one of a tiny number – under such sorry circumstances the publisher, Bryant, must have scrapped the print run once they discovered the appalling crimes of their author. Murderers were not in vogue then, just one or two copies must have scraped through. That could be why the novel is not listed anywhere in this vast and comprehensive library.

How different reactions would be today. How they would gather, vultures at a feast, if this killer offered her story today. How the public would clamour for more, how hungry most of us are for our shy little glimpses of evil.

But we no longer hang those who founder, and we don't consign losers to the gutter. Well, not happily anyway.

There are no rights to *Magdalene*?

1913, so it's out of copyright.

The book could still be published and what a story the deception would make.

But what happened to Kirkwood's child? There could be trouble from that quarter.

There is more delving to be done before Candice Love has all the answers. But the place she must start is the Burleston Hotel, the nest from which this masterpiece hatched, the locality of its unhappy conception.

Twenty-Nine

Worn out by a wasted night on the tiles drinking alone in a Plymouth pub, Avril fumes on. Nobody had come to sit beside her no matter what she did with her eyes, nobody seemed to be impressed by the shortness of her skirt, the fishnet tights, the tinted eyelashes, the scarlet lipstick or the come-and-get me look which she had rehearsed to perfection beforehand.

She had caught sight of herself in a mirror and stared stupidly at it. She nearly looked like a man in drag. She was now the sort of woman she would have crossed the pavement to avoid, the very prototype of all mother's warnings: loose, immoral, fallen. Only one man showed any interest and he was over fifty, unshaven, shabby and stank of urine.

She ended up boss-eyed and sick, and went to sleep with her caravan room spiralling around her and Kirsty, of all people, nagging on about bad influences on the children.

And now look, that scheming actress Bernadette has stolen Avril's thunder by resorting to hysterical dramatics over her so-called fiancé's 'accident'. The agent is in intensive care, hovering on the brink of death with tubes up every orifice, according to Bernie, who has decided to return to Cornwall because she can't take the strain any more.

'Just when I was so happy,' sobbed Bernie on the phone, hysterical. 'And I've got something else to tell you. Something worse, oh Jaysus . . .'

Kirsty, who ought to be concentrating on Avril and her coming ordeal – the inquest into the fire is tomorrow – has been taken in by Bernie's charade and is collecting her from the station. They are going to view the cottage together, but why should Bernie be included? Bernie certainly will not be invited to join the select little family. Oh no.

So much for the godlike Rory Coburn and his influence over Bernie's accountants, his assurances of assistance to Bernie throughout her difficult publicity campaigns, so much for a shoulder to lean on. Bernie probably made it all up, she probably got obsessed with the guy and ended up making a fool of herself, just as she did over Dominic Coates. Some women seem doomed to such trauma – loving too much, the experts call it.

And if Kirsty thinks Avril is a bad influence on her precious children, maybe she should look closer at Bernie.

Poor Avril is never at rest these days. The pressure of her pent-up anger has not been assuaged by the tragedy – Avril, who four months ago wouldn't have dared say boo to a goose. It's a complete reversal of character, and sometimes the force of it makes her feel sick and she actually has to vomit – the colour has started to worry her;

could she have some terrible disease. For apart from the contents of her stomach there are unidentifiable patches, like growths, attached to some of the chunks.

She flushes it away in a state of denial, trying not to look. And she sometimes calls out in her dreams and wakes Kirsty.

The children, the children, the bloody children. Everything centres round Jake and Gemma, spoilt little brats who want their heads knocking together. Guilt makes Kirsty overindulgent; she is trying to compensate for their experiences, selfishly making herself feel better but ruining the kids for life. They need a much firmer hand, they ought to be forced to finish their food, stick to a certain bedtime, wash and tidy up after themselves, and there's no need for Kirsty to read them a story every night whatever their behaviour.

Avril watches all this as pulses hammer behind her forehead. Sometimes her fists are so tightly clenched that the veins in her wrists stand out with the pressure of her fury. Let her get her hands on these kids, she'd soon teach them about respect, good manners, gratitude and subservience.

'You look like a Christmas tree, Avril,' Gemma had the nerve to say the last time she got in her evening taxi heading for the bright lights.

'You've got a big fat bum,' said Jake soon after. 'If that bum was mine I'd try to hide it, not show it off in those striped leggings.'

'You mind your own business,' said Avril, fiddling with a large glass earring.

But Kirsty, who should have curbed them with a good slap across their faces, merely gave a sorry shrug and said something silly like, 'Kids, what can you do?'

You can do a great deal, thinks Avril. There's something to be said, after all, for Mother's attitude to children.

Kirsty even suggested allowing the children a day off school to let them look round the cottage – why the hell should they have a say? Avril reminded her that they might get too excited and be disappointed if it fell through. So Kirsty changed her mind. Thank God.

Imagine the shambles those kids would cause. Chatter chattering in the car, dashing about the cottage and embarrassing them in front of the owner, jumping on the beds and rolling around on the sofas and chairs. What makes Kirsty so blind to the unattractiveness of her children?

If they don't get shown some discipline soon they are going to end up off the rails and in real trouble, like Graham.

'Clear up your own toys,' said Avril to Gemma one evening when Kirsty was out. 'Don't think for one moment that I'm going to do it. I'm not as silly as your mother.'

'OK,' said Gemma artfully, wary of falling foul of Avril.

'And you, don't just hang around so slyly trying to get out of doing your share. There's all that washing-up in the sink,' Avril said to Jake.

'I'll make a cup of tea when I've finished,' said the cunning boy, turning on the charm.

I can see through you, sweetheart.

She wanted to slap his leg hard.

*   *   *

The cottage is charming. It smells of woodsmoke. It stands on its own just outside a village. The floors are slate and covered with rugs, the furniture is shabbily comfortable and there is a Rayburn in the kitchen.

The jumped-up Bernie stands out like a sore thumb in the middle of the country, in her pink suede jacket, her long black boots and her fluffy hat. She looks like a Russian ballerina and surely everyone's staring.

She should have stayed where she was in London.

Kirsty and Avril don't want her here.

'What sort of accident was it?' asks Kirsty, all silly concern as they circle their way up the small staircase. 'It must have been bad to put Rory in intensive care.'

'He took something.'

'What? *On purpose?*'

'By accident. He took too many sleeping pills. B–b–but there's worse than that, I have to tell you . . .'

'You mean he tried to top himself?' Avril, certain that Bernie is lying, is determined the truth should come out.

'Why would he want to do that?' Bernie pleads, with that silly little-girl-lost look on her face. 'He adored me. We would have got married and then none of this would have happened.'

'You still can, can't you?' Kirsty is going along with the farce. 'And what d'you mean, none of this?'

But Bernie seems unable to answer. Instead she sobs, 'Bentley found him,' as they go round the three upstairs bedrooms. Avril hopes she realizes there is no spare bedroom for her. 'He was unconscious. They say he was near the end.'

'Some accident,' says Avril tartly, knowing that this larger, sunnier, more airy room will be offered to the children.

'And then there's the attic,' says Mr Pratt, the owner, leading the way.

'Oh what a brilliant playroom,' cries Kirsty. 'Isn't this lovely, Avril? It would be perfect!'

'I would like this room as a study,' says Avril.

'A study? Whatever for?'

How patronizing that they should ask. 'Any work I might decide to take on,' says Avril aggressively. 'And I might like a sitting room of my own where I can entertain friends. I don't want to have to share everything with your family,' she tells Kirsty briskly. 'I need my own space, you know.'

Kirsty hesitates, seemingly surprised that Avril should have strong views of her own. 'Well, yes, of course, if you feel that way, Avril.'

'Well, I do,' says Avril firmly.

Into the tension Bernie blunders, 'I hope you'll be able to afford it.'

Kirsty and Avril turn round, baffled, and Bernie goes on before they can ask her. 'We might have to give it all back.'

'What are you saying?' asks Kirsty, frowning.

'Give what back? The money?' cries Avril.

'No, no, I'm joking, don't take any notice,' wails Bernie distraughtly, her face turning ashen. 'But now Rory's in hospital and I just don't know what's going to happen. You see, I was depending on him.'

'That's your trouble,' says Avril tartly, sounding so like her mother that even she recognizes the echo

386

on the ether. 'You're always dependent on some-body else.'

Bernie, faced with the magnitude of her betrayal but still able to pay for a room at the Burleston, invites the others for an evening meal at which she will break the terrible news, the demise of *Magdalene* and her part in it. The death of their hopes and dreams. The betrayal of her friends. She is terrified of Kirsty's reaction. She feels sick and shaky and blind with panic.

'But surely you don't include Jake and Gemma in the invitation?' says Avril quickly.

'Oh, Avril, they'd love it,' says Kirsty. 'They've never been inside a really posh hotel before.'

'Kirsty,' spits Avril with horror, 'they wouldn't know how to behave! They'd be all over the dining room, shouting, squabbling, showing us up.'

'Of course they wouldn't,' says Kirsty, colouring. 'What sort of kids d'you think they are?'

'If they go I'll stay at home,' says Avril, 'and that's flat.'

'Well, if you really feel so strongly,' but Kirsty seems totally bewildered. 'I had no idea you felt this way. Gemma and Jake love you, Avril, they see you as one of the family, and it's horrible that you don't like them.'

'The Balls will babysit,' says Avril, refusing to be drawn. 'Jake and Gemma can stay with them until we get home.'

'OK,' says Kirsty, cut to the quick, but it's about time someone told her the truth. 'If that's the way you feel, Avril.'

*   *   *

387

'There's something wrong with Bernie.'

'Well, yes, there would be, her fiancé is in intensive care.'

But Kirsty shakes her head. 'No, not that, something else. She's a wreck, she's terrified of something.'

'Well, I hadn't noticed,' says Avril.

Kirsty dresses down, as usual, a dowdy summer dress with a cardigan round it. Avril, on the other hand, makes the most of the occasion; she gets out the black, backless number she hasn't yet had a chance to wear. Her heels are thin and high.

'You can't walk in those,' hoots Jake, 'you look like a duck.'

'Jake, Jake, don't be so rude to Avril,' Kirsty at last responds.

'I can see your knickers,' sings Gemma, rolling around on the caravan floor and looking up Avril's skirt.

Avril kicks out and catches Gemma on the chin and Gemma sets up an infuriating wail. It can't have hurt that much, but the heel has caught her. Her face is bleeding; the wretched child makes a meal of it and Kirsty is fussing all over her, dab, dab, dabbing at the sink as if the kid's been maimed for life.

'That wasn't necessary, Avril,' snaps Kirsty.

'I didn't mean to hurt her,' lies Avril, basking in a pleasing glow; she yearns to follow up her attack, see the brat scream over something worthwhile. 'I was merely trying to protect my modesty.'

'Well, you wouldn't guess that,' retorts Kirsty, 'if you're really intending to go out like that.'

'There's nothing the matter with me,' says Avril,

giving Kirsty a meaningful stare. Cinderella. Miserable cow. 'And anyway, look, it's only a prick, the skin has hardly been broken. It's stopped bleeding now. Give her a plaster and don't fuss.'

Candice Love, back at the Burleston, stops in her tracks when she sees Bernie. 'I never thought I'd find you here.' And her voice is icy.

Bernie averts her guilt-ridden eyes. 'I couldn't stay at the flat, could I?'

'No.' Candice shakes her silken head. 'No, you couldn't.'

'How's Rory?' Bernie seems ashamed to ask.

'The same, as far as I know.' She guesses the reason for Bernie's return. 'Don't tell me. I don't believe it. You really haven't told them yet, have you?'

Bernie hangs her head. 'Don't blame me for all of this. It wasn't my idea. None of this is my fault. They made me carry the whole damn can so it's them to blame more than—'

'God help you,' says Candice, moving on.

After the initial surprise at seeing their agent at the hotel, they sit in the bar sipping cocktails, Kirsty quiet and serious after her quarrel with Avril.

'I had to come.' Candice's expression is hard and cold, nothing like the light-hearted, flamboyant creature of their first encounter. 'If you hadn't all been here tonight I would have had to come and find you.'

'Something's wrong,' says Kirsty. 'What is it? What's happened?'

'I think', says Candice, sitting back in the same

389

old brown chesterfield that once dwarfed Clementine Davaine, 'you ought to tell me that.'

There follows an awkward silence.

'This isn't going to go away,' Candice warns them. 'And neither am I. There has been some deception going on round here, and it's serious and worrying and I intend to get to the bottom of it.'

Nobody likes to answer. Nobody is sure what she means. Everything seemed to be going so well and now they are suddenly faced with this. And why doesn't Bernie look at them? Why does it feel as if she's estranged, all shrivelled up in a corner? Avril and Bernie and Kirsty and Candice know Ellen Kirkwood wrote *Magdalene*. Avril also knows that she almost set fire to the caravan of her parents thus causing their deaths, Bernie knows she drove Rory to suicide, while Kirsty knows that her husband is dead down a mine shaft not 100 yards away from here.

So what should they now confess to?

There is so much – *so much*.

Eventually, after silently eyeing all three women, Candice delves into her Gucci handbag and brings out the copy of *Magdalene* that was sent to her in the post. She lays it on the table beside the olives and the peanuts, alongside Bernie's Blue Ocean Wave, Avril's Tequila Sea Mist and Kirsty's Brandy Alexander.

Kirsty turns deathly pale. Avril whispers, 'Where did you get it?' while Bernie drags defensively on her cigarette.

'It arrived yesterday,' says Candice, 'but we knew about the book by then. It doesn't matter how we

390

knew, but Rory and I found out the truth. The secret is out and now I want some straight answers.'

'But who sent you that? There was only one copy, we thought—'

'I don't know who sent it, but I intend to find out. I spent all yesterday afternoon doing research in the British Library and came up with some pretty interesting facts. I wonder if you are aware of them?' And then Candice turns to Kirsty. 'Where, exactly, did you find your copy?'

Kirsty, dumbfounded, can do nothing but answer honestly. 'I found it in the quiet lounge here at the hotel. It was part of Colonel Parker's collection, a library for the guests.'

'And you saw its merits immediately?'

'I couldn't leave it alone. I was obsessed.'

'So was I when I read it,' admits Avril, trembling.

'I thought we could make some money,' Kirsty goes on quietly; it sounds like she is confessing in church. 'It seemed to me that nobody could read *Magdalene* and not think it brilliant.'

'And, between you, you managed to fool me and all my colleagues. Not only them, but, remarkably, one of the most respected editors in the land.'

'It wasn't that easy.' Bernie sobs, remembering Rory and the wonderful life that has slipped from her desperate grasp. And what if the others find out it was her who went and blew the gaff?

'When I first tried to contact you, Kirsty, that time you gave me your correct name, I rang the hotel to ask for you and a woman answered the phone. We had rather an odd conversation.'

'That was Mrs Stokes.'

'I know it's a while ago now, but can any of you

remember whether Mrs Stokes passed my message on?'

'No, she didn't,' says Avril.

'So she never passed on my private address and telephone number?'

'No.'

'But she had them. She took them down all right. She copied them down, reluctantly, furious to be disturbed, I remember.'

'She's like that,' says Avril, nodding.

'So it must have been her who sent me the book. What did you do with your copy?' Candice asks Kirsty.

'I burnt it,' Kirsty confesses again, 'in the hotel boilers. I watched it burn. It burned to ashes.'

'And you hoped there were no other copies?'

'I wasn't thinking straight. It was done and decided in moments. I never bothered about other copies or author's rights. I was scared someone might remember it, but I didn't even bother to change the title. I was just fanatical about getting the book out whatever it took.'

'And you still are, aren't you?' says Candice quietly.

The next dreadful half-hour is spent listening to Candice Love's biography of Ellen Kirkwood, the author.

'Jaysus, Jaysus, that's why I freaked out when I read it.'

'So it's true life. It's a kind of diary?'

This thought is repellent.

'It would seem that they never discovered how many murders Kirkwood committed, and at that time the whole nation was focused aggressively on the impending war, and it was inappropriate for the authorities to divert the nation's attention to some hideous crime wave in one little corner of the country. The government's War Propaganda Bureau was well oiled and buzzing by the time Kirkwood came to court, the cinemas and newspapers were full of the perfidy of the Germans and it was essential that the whole nation think well of themselves, despite severe economic depression – God is on our side and all that. But the most obvious reason the book was abandoned was because the author was a murderess. In those days it just wasn't done. The very idea would be outrageous.'

'So the publication of her book was dropped.'

'Yes, but only after a handful got through.'

'And Colonel Parker happened to have one in his library?'

'And somebody else near here had another.' Candice offers round French cigarettes.

'But who else might have a copy?' asks Avril.

'God only knows,' says Candice, pausing to order more drinks.

'Family?' asks Kirsty.

'There seems to have been no family, except for the one illegitimate child.'

'It's the sort of thing you might keep and treasure.' The thought is too awful to dwell on. 'If your mother was hanged and you grew up an orphan and were made ashamed of who you were, you might hold on to something like that.' Kirsty's voice trails away, thinking of Gemma and Jake.

'Born in 1913, that baby will be elderly now. Apart from Colonel Parker himself, and that seems very unlikely, is there anyone else you can think of around here in that age group?'

'Hell, eighty-six?'

'She couldn't be, could she?'

'Who?'

'Old Stokes.'

'Seventy-six perhaps, but . . . Ellen Kirkwood's baby?'

They fall into an uncomfortable silence while each one conjures the rigid form of the housekeeper: upright, scrawny, wrinkled, yet still spry and energetic. Her neck is invariably covered by a scarf or a high-buttoned collar. Her hands hide under her cardigans. Hers is not a physical job – she sits in her office most of the time organizing from there – or she creeps round spying on staff, or checking the laundry, or dressing down miscreants.

'Eighty-six, Mother of God.'

'She could be.'

'It's possible.'

'But why would Mrs Stokes leave one copy of her mother's book in Colonel Parker's library?'

'Perhaps she felt it ought to be read,' says Candice. 'Maybe she felt her mother was denied the acclaim that was due to her, the one positive thing she left behind her, apart, of course, from her child.'

'In that case,' Kirsty muses, 'wouldn't she have been pleased to see the novel published at last and recognized by everyone as the masterpiece it is? So why would she throw a spanner in the works by sending you this copy?'

'She wanted the novel published, but perhaps not in your name,' says Candice, seeing a small light at the end of the tunnel. 'She wanted to make certain the truth came out. Once she knew it was in print, even in proof form, she had to act fast to get Bernie's name replaced by her mother's on the cover. But she didn't want herself involved. Even after eighty-six years, Mrs Stokes is still ashamed of her mother.'

I know that feeling, thinks Avril ruefully.

Thirty

Mr Derek deflates like a long, thin, flaccid balloon with all the wind puffing out of it.

'Mrs Stokes,' his hoarse voice begs of his outraged housekeeper, 'don't you think I've enough to contend with this morning? Flagherty has been found dead in his shed.' The second corpse of the summer. Oh my God. His nerve seems to be going. He throws his harassed head back and exposes a shaving nick on his neck. 'At the moment they say it looks like any normal heart attack, but the way things are going round here no doubt we'll be told he was smothered.'

Mrs Stokes, her papery skin flaming scarlet this morning, doesn't take the slightest notice of her manager's dilemma. 'I don't think you have grasped the enormity of what has just happened to me,' she huffs. 'I have been accused not only of being the offspring of some serial murderess, but also of being aged eighty-six.'

Poor old Moira. Her gad-about husband, Alf, never loved her, being star-stuck at an early age by a visiting beauty from the USA. Quite a bit older than she was, he left her and then left the

Burleston only one year after their marriage, never to be heard of again. Moira always fondly insisted there was a child somewhere, the only relative she ever claims, a somewhat tenuous connection by way of her husband's busy loins. Only a few people know this; the hackneyed tale has been handed down discreetly through the ages. But Mr Derek breathes in wildly. 'Well, how old are you, Mrs Stokes?'

'That is nobody's business but mine, but, good heavens, I am certainly not eighty-six.' And she pulls herself up forbiddingly to her full and sprightly height.

'Poor old Flagherty,' sighs Mr Derek, scratching his head so that a section of hair stands up like a child's at the back. 'I can't tell you how long he's been with us.'

'A time-waster and a scoundrel' is the house-keeper's tart reply.

After Flagherty's body has been removed, with the manufacturers' imprint from a sack of bone meal stamped on his face, the police, faced with another sudden death, begin a slack but routine search of the 12 x 10 shed where Flagherty ambled through most of his life. From between the leaves of a faded copy of *Adam the Gardener,* hidden under tins of condensed milk and plastic seed labels, a stained and crumpled note is spotted.

I let the lad take the blame becos he was gilty of one anyway. But I gave Mr Board the biff that kiled him. It was purly accidental! He kindly offerd to teach me to drive and I never got the

*hang of it! I hid the club in the old cottage, down
the hole! Signed Patrick Flagherty head gardener!*

'Hell, this certainly puts a different complexion
on things,' says Sergeant Mallet briskly. He is
dispatched to fetch the key to the bungalow in
the garden, and arrives back at the Burleston with
keyholder, Kirsty Hoskins, and Avril Stott and
Bernie Kavanagh in tow.

'Well, Miss Stott will have to be interviewed in
connection with her damning statement,' he tells his
superior when he expresses surprise. 'It couldn't
have been her brother. She was clearly mistaken
if Mr Flagherty's note is genuine, as it seems. And
Mrs Hoskins and Miss Kavanagh just insisted on
coming with her, sir.' He gives a short, informative
aside, 'Mrs Hoskins seemed quite hysterical. I
thought it best not to leave her out.'

The little party congregate outside the paint-
peeled door. Mallet's superior inserts the key and
they follow him inside. To start with there is nothing exceptional about this miserable place, save for
a repulsive smell.

'Where is this hole Flagherty referred to, I
wonder?' muses the inspector, handkerchief to
his nostrils, eager not to linger long. He takes
some tenuous steps, prodding the ground before
him with a broken curtain rod. He arrives at the
upside-down table and pauses, pulling nervously at
one of the badly splintered legs. 'Could it be here?'
he asks the party. 'There's no sign of a hole anywhere else.'

The inspector makes an impatient gesture. The

two coppers drag the table away and the three of them look down.

'Good God, Mallet, *what a mess*. Come on then, let's get busy, if the weapon's down there we've got to find it. The old guy certainly went to some trouble to cover his tracks.' And he presses his handkerchief harder against his nose. 'There's enough rubbish down here to set up home with.'

Like magicians emptying their pockets, the contents keep coming, never ending. Now there's a pile of household utensils and the policemen, sleeves rolled up and covered with dust, are sweating profusely. One is inside the hole chucking stuff up, while the second shovels it out of the way.

'Hang on,' cries Mallet. 'Hang on.'

'What's up?'

'I dunno, but there's something bloody odd here.'

'Keep delving.'

When Mallet's face next appears it is shocked. His hair is white from brick dust, his eyes are red and rimmed. 'You better take a look, Inspector.' And he holds back the mess with a frying pan handle. 'Further down, under the rubble. He's got to be dead, sir. Got to be.'

The inspector stares down in horror. 'My God. I don't believe it. How long has the poor bastard been stuck here?'

'Who can he be?' asks Bernie, enthralled.

'This is awful,' sobs Avril.

Kirsty stands rigid and silent, her eyes focused on a far-off place.

'Fetch a ladder. We can't reach him from here.' When, five minutes later, Mallet returns with a rope, a ladder and a couple of waiters from the hotel, the inspector ties a large loop on one end and orders Mallet to climb down the ladder. Suddenly he becomes aware of the unofficial presence of the three women. He is not prepared for hysterics. This is work for the experts. 'And clear the room at once.'

Bernie and Avril and Kirsty back out. 'Good grief,' exclaims Bernie, only relieved that her part in the mess around *Magdalene* has so far not been revealed. 'This is unreal. There's a dead man down there.'

Back inside the derelict kitchen the inspector takes a firm stand. 'We might as well be done with it and haul him out, whoever he is,' He turns to the others and lowers his voice, 'Let's hope the poor sod isn't jammed.'

No, fortunately he is not jammed. And, after a hard struggle by Mallet on the ladder to circle the dead man's right arm and neck, the men form a chain which reaches the door and haul hard on the rope to a great and threatening tumbling of rubble.

'Keep heaving,' shouts the desperate inspector, terrified he has made things worse. He should have waited for the fire brigade; he should have waited for the lab boys.

'Heave! *Heave!*'

Slowly and grotesquely the head and shoulders of Trevor Hoskins appear above floor level. Covered in dried blood, his short black hair is matted and white with dust, his face is a yellowed mask of death. 'Jesus!' one of the coppers exclaims.

'Keep heaving,' shouts the inspector. 'Don't let him slip back now.'

His naked torso, once tanned and muscled, is dyed with a hectic pattern in scarlets, purples and blacks. His lower limbs are matted with blood, excrement and slime. He wears no shoes or socks.

'Good grief,' says Sergeant Mallet in shock as he helps to manoeuvre the heavy body over the edge to be laid out flat on firm ground.

'Who is this man?' enquires the inspector. 'And how the hell did he get down there?'

But no-one in the room has an answer.

The inspector leans right over the corpse and suddenly spies the mangled ear. 'Good God, can you believe it, the poor bastard has tried to feed himself by cutting off his own bloody ear.'

'The ambulance will be here soon,' one of the waiters is relieved to report.

'We'll all have to wait for forensics now.'

The inspector pulls back from the stench and the grisly sight of that missing left ear lobe. The poor devil must have fallen in, stripped off his clothes for some unknown reason, shouted for help to no avail and gradually starved to death. He must have been dead when that old fool Flagherty dumped his golf club and filled in the hole. The next object to emerge from the mine is the number four wood. Mallet inserts it in a plastic bag and labels it as evidence.

When the putrefying carcass of Fluffy the cat is thoughtlessly carried out by the legs, Avril, outside, collapses completely and has to be fanned with fresh air. Oh no. Fluffy obviously wandered in there by accident and toppled down the shaft.

But she was nineteen years old, after all.

Nobody ought to be too upset. In a way it's a happy release. She didn't suffer. She was dead when she landed.

*   *   *

The diseased Flagherty's antecedence is given to the police by Colonel Parker. The explanation is quite straightforward.

After young Kirkwood's mother was hanged, her employer, Sir Michael Geary, took him in and found him a home with a respectable family on his estate. The Flaghertys were childless and only too happy to adopt the orphan and bring him up as their own. Colonel Parker blows his multiveined nose on an off-white handkerchief. 'The Flaghertys came to work for me, oh, fifty years ago, and young Flagherty worked in the gardens here where he has been employed ever since. Of course nobody ever let on about his rather unfortunate start. I doubt that Flagherty knew himself.'

'I'm sorry, I'm sorry, I thought I saw him, I could have sworn it was Graham,' lies Avril, blushing, to the cross inspector one hour later. 'I honestly thought I saw him talking to Ed on the golf course that morning.'

Trevor Hoskins is identified by a driving licence in his back trouser pocket.

'Do you know what your husband might have been doing in here?' Kirsty is questioned gently. She makes a pathetic sight, cut to the quick, shocked and terrified.

She peers out through shaking sobs. 'No. We met. We argued. He must have decided to hang around and wait till I came off duty.'

'How would he manage to get inside when you were the holder of the keys?'

'Flagherty had a set of keys, too,' Mallet reminds the inspector.

'This must be a terrible shock,' the inspector sympathizes. 'We thought he'd gone into the sea; it would have been kinder if he had. The mind boggles at the thought of how that man must have suffered.'

And that same day, in the afternoon . . .

'Cause of death: accidental,' announces the coroner at the inquest which Avril has been dreading.

As the forensic evidence slowly emerged, Avril sat at the back in a trance.

'Yes, there's no doubt about it,' said the coroner mournfully. 'Mrs Stott, a rather parsimonious lady, made sure the gas container under the caravan was empty by the time her stay was ended. She was unwilling to pay for gas she might not use. Instead of replacing the large tank, she and her husband rented a smaller, portable bottle from the caravan site shop; this fuelled one gas ring, which is all the Stotts required, and it was this bottle, found to have a serious leak, which caused the fatal accident when Mrs Stott woke up in the night and felt the need to light her Wright's vaporizer.'

BOOM!

'And may I pass on my sincere condolences to the bereaved,' said the coroner in conclusion.

At dinner, over a delicious paella, Candice is left with one straightforward option.

Publication must proceed, copyright being ended, and the real truth of the author's credentials being far more fascinating than ever envisaged.

'You might well have to return some money but that is a matter for the publishers now.' There is no doubt that the real author's grim identity will fill the coffers to overflowing. Nobody's going to back out now. 'But', she tells the three women generously, 'because your re-write was so well done they will very possibly be quite happy to give you the credit and deal with you directly.'

Dollar signs pop into her eyes as she pats the original *Magdalene*, which she keeps by her side at all times.

Candice feels on top of the world while her companions seem pensive tonight. Why this should be eludes her. They are making good money out of this. They ought to be humbly grateful.

'Cheer up!' she encourages them breezily. 'I know, while I go to the loo why don't you order some champagne? It's all on me, don't worry.'

Avril, Bernie and Kirsty avoid one another's eyes.

How can they allow this book to be published?

When Candice leaves they sink into silence, hardly able to carry on eating. They play with their food and stare listlessly out of the window.

It is Avril who gets up and walks determinedly round to Candice Love's chair, her lips pressed together tightly. It is she, with her dyed, spiky hair of banana yellow, who opens the agent's briefcase, retrieves the last copy of *Magdalene* and puts it in her own handbag. The others just watch without comment.

Eventually Bernie looks up gravely. 'What are we going to do with it?'

'Burn it. Does anyone disagree?'

Before Candice Love returns, the three neatly replace their napkins, pick their coats up from reception and head outside into the cold night air. Kirsty leads the way. Kirsty, who knows what she has done and suspects that the others know, too.

What do they imagine they are achieving?

There are plenty of revised copies of Magdalene in circulation. Burning the original will solve nothing now. And it seems that only they have been so grotesquely affected, the three that meddled with the author's work.

But this is something they know they must do. Bernie follows on the path to the cove, a sleepwalker, eyes fixed to the ground. If he had accepted her proposal she would have continued to blackmail Rory until she got her fanatical way. She would have been happy to see him die rather than live life without her. All in the name of love.

And Avril, the timid one, eager to please, who was willing to burn her father and mother, to see her brother imprisoned for life, all in the name of revenge. She can't let her thoughts take her further, she would never have harmed Kirsty's children – would she?

And a cold shiver rends her as she totters down the path in impractical heels.

And as for Kirsty? They have their suspicions. They can hardly look at her.

They have all had such a lucky escape, but only by a whisker.

When they reach the sand they scatter and solemnly gather armfuls of twigs and branches, beachcombings brought in by the tide. The cliffs rising up behind them are a high grey curtain wall, silhouetted against the night sky. They light the fire in the centre of the beach; this is a ritual, a cleansing with pagan symbolism that comes naturally when faced with malevolence such as this. With reverence, as a priest presents a sacrifice to the altar, but with fingers so clumsy they frighten her, Kirsty lowers the book onto the pyre and the sticks crackle around it for a while, white, red and silver, until the book catches and changes the flames to the darker, more sombre colours of evil.

Avril lays a hand on Kirsty's shoulder.

Bernie's eyes are dry and fixed. 'Pray for us all,' she says.

No warmth appears to come from the fire, but a coolness blows off the slate-grey sea and they shiver as they stand round and watch *Magdalene* burn.

And the leaping flames of the fire and the new-found warmth between them are the brightest lights in the harrowing dark.

Epilogue

With Graham Stott's grudging agreement the murder charge has been swapped for manslaughter to which he is pleading guilty. He will probably be out in five years.

Monies already paid in to the personal account of Bernadette Kavanagh are considered fair payment for substantial work already done. A fresh contract has been drawn up and now all those publishers involved are happy to see Kirsty's name on the title as adaptor of the original book.

Candice, true to her nature, half to impress the publishers and half to satisfy her own sense of drama, paints a grim picture of Kirkwood the killer, which is published in the front of the book in the form of a note to the readers.

Perhaps she should not have jumped to conclusions.

Not picked on the first Ellen Kirkwood she found.

In present-day terms, the author of Magdalene *was a vicious psychopath. A killer who stalked the streets of Plymouth with her grisly weapon in her hand, on the lookout for any lone man she could overpower with her apelike strength. She would offer them her body and savagely slit their throats with cheese wire when they were at their most vulnerable. She would then turn her attentions to the still-warm bodies and neatly remove certain parts: fingers, toes, ears, noses, nipples, testicles and penises. These she would wrap up in her shawl and carry home. As these were never found it has been suggested by today's forensic experts that she probably ate them raw in some macabre ritual.*

Throughout the book the discerning reader can detect many examples of Kirkwood's madness. Nobody of a sane mind could write a book like Magdalene *with all its disturbing attitudes, insinuations . . .*

and so on and so forth.

Poor old Mrs Stokes.

She knew she was never loved.

Alfred Stokes broke Moira's heart when he left her after one year of marriage. Thirty years her senior, he had never recovered from the love of his life, an American floozy who visited the Burleston when Alf was an impressionable bootboy of twenty. Got her pregnant, too, with the child that should have been Moira's, leaving her barren in body and mind with a womb like a dried-up fig.

She knew of the child from the start because of the air-mail letters, and anyway, Alf didn't bother to hide it, discretion was not his forte. They kept arriving after Alf left the Burleston – Moira refused to send them on – thin, brittle, drifting letters with all the distance in the world inside them and full of events she knew nothing of.

'Ellen refused to give up her lifestyle for me,' Alf used to moan, expecting Moira to sympathize, 'and who could blame her? She was a beauty. She had style. She was an enchantress and she had a *mind*,' he said, screwing his finger into his forehead and insinuating that Moira had not.

'Huh,' said young Moira in her chambermaid pinny. 'It's high time you got over her. You're married to me now, Alf Stokes.' And she tried to flutter her eyelashes at him.

But all her efforts were useless. Twenty years on and Alfred was still bewitched. She knew how he felt about Ellen, every plea from his heart echoed Moira's own. When he went he left Ellen's books, and Moira put one in the hotel library but kept the other as a painful reminder.

She never bothered to read it.

She doubts whether Alf did, either, for he was not a great reader.

Chuck Stokes Kirkwood Korda was the son she should have had. She felt that he had been ripped from her loins twenty years prematurely.

To allow Chuck's mother's book to be published under false pretences was something Moira could not allow. She didn't hate the American author. Time had tempered those bitter emotions, although she still envied Ellen her son.

So, after much deep thought, Mrs Stokes sent *Magdalene* to Candice Love in an effort to stop this scandalous chicanery. The very idea that that Kavanagh piece and her cronies were claiming ownership of Chuck's mother's work was outrageous and Moira, dumbfounded and infuriated, lost sleep over it, rent by frustrated and righteous anger. What bare-faced deceit. What base skullduggery.

In a vague way Chuck and she are related.

Because of the delicate circumstances Mrs Stokes could not bear to come out with the truth. Proud and upright as she is, she would rather not let the world know that her husband had sired some other woman's child and reveal her shameful, piteable condition.

And then they had the nerve to suggest that she was the child of a murderess, and eighty-six years old.

She could have exposed the fraud quite simply by saying that *Magdalene* was left behind by a guest, but she feared the unpleasant truth might rear its ugly head, someone might do some dirty digging. When she saw the ghastly smear on the name of Ellen Kirkwood, Chuck's mother – psychopath, murderess, what on earth did they mean? – she had no option, she felt it her duty to send a copy straight to the Kirkwood family in South Carolina.

Let them deal with it.

Let the whole mess be sorted out from a decent distance and let herself be kept well out of it.

Judge Homer Kirkwood Korda, nicknamed Rex after tyrannosaurus, examines the book in the parcel before reaching for a copy from a handful of volumes on the top shelf of his study. Granny's big achievement: ten privately printed copies of her novel *Magdalene*, written under her maiden name. (There were twelve before Ellen returned from

410

England and left two with a young admirer she met at the Burleston hotel.)

The judge reads on in his house in South Carolina and his large face purples.

Well, son-of-a-bitch.

No-one had thought Granny's book much cop.

Homer never bothered to read it and he doubts that his daddy did either.

Sweet little old granny – a religious, God-fearing woman with not one mean bone in her body – was greatly loved by all who knew her, departed this life in the early Sixties and has been greatly missed ever since. Granny completed her novel at the age of thirty-eight; she sent it to Bryant for private publication and went to collect the results during a tour of England. She brought ten copies home by steamer in a roomy Gladstone bag. The following year Granny gave birth to her only son, Homer's daddy, Chuck Stokes Kirkwood Korda, and her novel was forgotten as she got on with the job of raising her precious child.

So what the hell has been going on here?

Some goddamn impostor or what?

Some publisher trying to hoodwink the media and hijack Granny's book?

And what's this these folks are saying about the state of mind of the author?

Who the hell is responsible for this? The note in the front says Candice Love. What sort of a goddamn name is that?

Sweet Jesus, these dumb-ass oddballs are going to be sorry for this. Judge Homer Kirkwood Korda is going to take these crazies for everything they've got.

*　　*　　*

Well, surely no-one truly believed that the author of *Magdalene* leapt out and influenced the readers. That's the trouble these days, there's always someone else to blame. That would be very silly. That was never on the cards.

Rory Coburn, of Coburn and Watts, having handed the whole caboodle to Candice and slowly regained his health, was taken on a world tour by his penitent butler, Bentley.

During his tour – in Bali actually – Rory discovered, to his joy, that he had a book in him. It took him six months to complete and it was published last spring under the *nom de plume* of Julia Harper. A hugely successful romantic novel, *Dawn's First Rising*, he hopes it will be the first of many.

THE END

UNHALLOWED GROUND
by Gillian White

Once upon a time, it is said, the devil walked in this valley . . .

On a snowbound February day, when Georgina first saw Furze Pen – a picturesque thatched cottage in a peaceful valley on Dartmoor – she thought it just the place to recover from the recent nightmare of her job in London. True, the cottage was cold and isolated, and the neighbours weird and strangely threatening. But Georgie needed to work out her life, and Furze Pen seemed as good a place as any – until the terrors started.

There was the lone watcher on the hill – at first she thought it was a scarecrow, so stark and still was it standing – and then the unexplained fire, with the remains of a child's doll smouldering in the ashes. But there had never been a child at Furze Pen. And as the seasons turned and snow once again blocked off the remote valley, the frightening began in earnest . . .

In this truly terrifying novel Gillian White has created a world of dark secrets which hide behind the seemingly ordinary lives of her characters. It is a world which is scarier than most people's worst imaginings.

0 552 14563 7

THE SLEEPER
by Gillian White

*'Peace on earth and mercy mild . . .' But there's no mercy
here. There is no telling how long the body has been down
in the cellar, rising as the water level rises . . .*

In a wintry seaside resort an old woman goes missing from
her residential hotel for the elderly, the inappropriately
named Happy Haven. And in a remote farmhouse not
far away, the Moon family gathers for Christmas.
Clover Moon, the farmer's wife, looks forward to the
forthcoming festivities with quiet desperation and dread.

What terrible secrets from the past are coming back to
haunt them? As gales and blizzards cut off the power and
maroon the Christmas gathering, where did the body
come from which is swept into the farmhouse cellar by
the rising flood water? In Gillian White's dark and
disturbing world, where nothing is quite as it seems, a
mystery from the past becomes a terrifying ordeal in the
present, and a traditional family Christmas turns into
nightmare.

'A dark, disturbing tale'
Sunday Telegraph

'A first-rate psychological thriller – perceptive, witty and
full of suspense'
Good Housekeeping

0 552 14561 0

BLIND DATE
by Frances Fyfield

'Her most ambitious book . . . Once you're in its grip, it is irresistible'
John Mortimer, *Mail on Sunday*

How do you make people love you? Emma Davey, who loved gemstones and life, found it easy. Everyone loved her. Until someone put a black bin liner over her head and kicked her to death.

For others, the quest is harder. Elisabeth Kennedy, Emma's older sister and a disgraced ex-police officer, considers herself beyond love or even self-respect. She is haunted by Emma's death and her own humiliating attempts to lure the killer into a confession. Then she is the victim of a senseless attack which adds physical scars to a fractured spirit.

Still convalescent, but wanting to hide from the world, she flees the comfort of her mother's seaside house for her own eccentric home. High in her disused London belltower, she will be safe and anonymous. But the safest places are not sacrosanct, especially the human heart, and the search for love, as well as revenge, goes on and on, like the search for hidden treasure. Elisabeth must find the courage to face a terror which is greater by far than loneliness . . .

'The book delivers. If you like your mysteries complex, *Blind Date* will not disappoint . . . One of the best'
Sarah Dunant, *Daily Express*

'An urgently chilly, stylish thriller . . . An original plot, challenging themes and a nicely peculiar protagonist'
Ruth Padel, *Daily Telegraph*

'A challengingly intricate web . . . The plotting is masterly . . . Seriously unsettling'
Heather O'Donoghue, *The Times Literary Supplement*

0 552 14525 4

A SELECTED LIST OF FINE NOVELS
AVAILABLE FROM CORGI BOOKS

14242 5	THE LEGACY	Evelyn Anthony	£5.99
14497 5	BLACKOUT	Campbell Armstrong	£5.99
14645 5	KINGDOM OF THE BLIND	Alan Blackwood	£5.99
09156 1	THE EXORCIST	William Peter Blatty	£5.99
14586 6	SHADOW DANCER	Tom Bradby	£5.99
13232 2	WYCLIFFE AND THE BEALES	W. J. Burley	£5.99
14116 X	WYCLIFFE AND DEATH IN A SALUBRIOUS PLACE	W. J. Burley	£4.99
14437 1	WYCLIFFE AND THE HOUSE OF FEAR	W. J. Burley	£4.99
14661 7	WYCLIFFE AND THE REDHEAD	W. J. Burley	£4.99
14578 5	THE MIRACLE STRAIN	Michael Cordy	£5.99
14654 4	THE HORSE WHISPERER	Nicholas Evans	£5.99
14043 0	SHADOW PLAY	Frances Fyfield	£5.99
14174 7	PERFECTLY PURE AND GOOD	Frances Fyfield	£5.99
14295 6	A CLEAR CONSCIENCE	Frances Fyfield	£5.99
14512 2	WITHOUT CONSENT	Frances Fyfield	£5.99
14525 4	BLIND DATE	Frances Fyfield	£5.99
14223 9	BORROWED TIME	Robert Goddard	£5.99
13840 1	CLOSED CIRCLE	Robert Goddard	£5.99
14224 7	OUT OF THE SUN	Robert Goddard	£5.99
14225 5	BEYOND RECALL	Robert Goddard	£5.99
14597 1	CAUGHT IN THE LIGHT	Robert Goddard	£5.99
14622 6	A MIND TO KILL	Andrea Hart	£5.99
14391 X	A SIMPLE PAIN	Scott Smith	£4.99
14561 0	THE SLEEPER	Gillian White	£5.99
14563 7	UNHALLOWED GROUND	Gillian White	£5.99
14555 6	A TOUCH OF FROST	R. D. Wingfield	£5.99
13981 5	FROST AT CHRISTMAS	R. D. Wingfield	£5.99
14558 0	NIGHT FROST	R. D. Wingfield	£5.99
14409 6	HARD FROST	R. D. Wingfield	£5.99